# SECOND SON

For Pam Houston,
a brave writer. Good
luck with your travels.

Take care, but not too much.

STEPHEN
STARK

# SECOND SON

*A Novel*

Henry Holt and Company
New York

Copyright © 1992 by Stephen Stark
All rights reserved, including the right to reproduce
this book or portions thereof in any form.
Published by Henry Holt and Company, Inc.,
115 West 18th Street, New York, New York 10011.
Published in Canada by Fitzhenry & Whiteside Limited,
91 Granton Drive, Richmond Hill, Ontario L4B 2N5.

Library of Congress Cataloging-in-Publication Data
Stark, Stephen.
Second son : a novel / Stephen Stark.— 1st ed.
    p.   cm.
I. Title.
PS3569.T33576S43   1992                91-38502
813'.54—dc20                                CIP

ISBN 0-8050-1943-X (acid-free paper)

Henry Holt books are available at special discounts
for bulk purchases for sales promotions, premiums,
fund-raising, or educational use. Special editions
or book excerpts can also be created to specification.
*For details contact:*
Special Sales Director, Henry Holt and Company, Inc.,
115 West 18th Street, New York, New York 10011.

First Edition—1992

*Designed by Lucy Albanese*

Printed in the United States of America
Recognizing the importance of preserving the written
word, Henry Holt and Company, Inc., by policy, prints
all of its first editions on acid-free paper. ∞
10  9  8  7  6  5  4  3  2  1

A portion of this novel appeared in *The New Yorker*
in slightly different form.

The quote from *The Journals of John Cheever* (page 1) is
reprinted by permission of Alfred A. Knopf.

*For my parents, Liz & Ted Stark,*
*and, of course, for my wife, Rachael*

*I would like to extend my grateful thanks to Burton I. Korelitz, M.D., his colleagues (particularly Dr. Audrey Woolrich) and his staff, past and present, for their kindness and generosity. I would also like to thank my editor, Channa Taub, and my agent, Lisa Ross, for their enduring patience and good sense.*

# PART ONE

# APOSTASY

It is possible, I suppose,
that in order to become a
man one has to mutilate
the carapace of one's
father's affections. I pray
this is not so.

—John Cheever

# DIVISION

A dog barks, deep throated and far off—*June, June.* In the distance, where Davis Road veers off toward the left and a field opens away from the canopy of trees, mist hangs in the swales of the gray-green land.

The truck is off now, parked in the darkness at the side of the road where there are no streetlamps. The engine creaks, and Jack has the door open. Damp evening air eddies through the cab. "God am I beat," Addie says. He pulls off his baseball cap, and with the hand that holds it, runs his fingers back through his short-cropped hair. It's just before ten o'clock, and they have been working for more than twelve hours on a job that should have taken less than eight. A flat tire on the way back from the quarry, the truck full of stone for the concrete. A blown gasket on the motor of the rented concrete mixer. Addie loves the exhausted feeling, the tired jangling of every muscle, every nerve, and looks forward to sinking down in front of the television with a gin and tonic on an empty stomach.

Jack starts to get out of the truck but hesitates—one leg out, one leg in, a hand on the dash. He studies the dash with concern.

"I'll be by a little late tomorrow," Addie says hurriedly, to try to make up somehow for today.

"Listen, Dad," Jack says, and the tone of his voice makes the hair on Addie's arms stand up, makes his skin sparkle with apprehension. "I don't want you to think that this has anything to do with you, with us—" But of course it does.

Addie looks at him, at the shadows in the dim light, at the vague movement of branches in the woods beyond the road. He picks up his red-and-white package of Winstons from the dash, then drops it again. Whatever he was thinking a moment ago has completely flown from his mind.

"I was talking to Gary yesterday—"

"Gary Wills?" Jack's college roommate.

"Yeah," he says, and there is silence. The dog barks again. It's a lonesome sound, like deep woods, distance. "He says there's a good chance for a job at Wharton Stokes, the law firm he works for in Richmond. It pays pretty well, and he's going to set me up an interview."

"What do you want to work at a law firm for?" Addie says. He means it as a simple question—Jack has never expressed any interest in law, never shown any desire to become a lawyer. Only when the words are in the air does he realize how niggling, how meddlesome they sound. He starts to say something to take back what he said, to change it, but in the shadows at the other side of the cab, he can see the this-is-exactly-why-I'm-leaving look on Jack's face.

For the last year, since Jack came home from college and went to work for him, he has been expecting this, because nearly everything with his family has had the feel of impermanence to it, the feel of fatality. He had turned off the truck thinking they could just chat, the way it had been so easy to do with Roy, his older son. But now this has come, and he is amazed how it sucks the air thin around him.

"I want you to know," Jack says after a moment of silence, sliding down off the plastic seat of the pickup and standing on the ground, "that this past year or so has been really important to me, working together and all. I mean that. But here my life is on hold. I'm just in a state of inertia." You can see the restlessness in his arms, in the way he stretches his hands, presses them together, and clenches them. "It's not you. I felt this way at school too. I just need to get out. I just need to get out." He says all this not looking at Addie, but into the window of the door. The words have the resonance of glass.

4 |

"It's been important to me too," Addie says. The words, like everything, are slipping away from him. Though it is irrational, it feels as though this is the last time he will ever see his son, but after losing his wife and then losing Roy, this is the thing that springs immediately to mind.

In a moment, the door of the pickup slams, leaving a metallic echo in the cab. Jack is walking across the road and up the driveway to the tiny garage apartment he has lived in since he helped convert it last summer. Addie watches the empty street, watches the garage as the lights come on along the narrow strip of windows. After a time, he starts the truck and pulls into the street. He accelerates, shifts, and the headlights push into the darkness.

I get out of my father's truck and walk across the road—watch the pavement drift beneath me, watch it turn to the darker pavement of the driveway. It's everything I can do not to turn around and look at him as I go; it's everything I can do not to let him know I want to look.

I wait a moment at the side door, stare into the panes of glass and the curtain that hangs between me and the darkness. I want to turn to look at him. I want it, but I don't know why I want it or what it will gain, except to say to him that he's won—that I'm not me but some smaller, less significant version of him. I breathe hard and angry and shove the key into the side door.

He still doesn't go immediately but sits in the truck. I turn on one light, but I go into the other room, still dark, and lean against the sill to watch him. It's damp out, and the air is heavy with moisture, and nothing will focus but focus softly. The pickup is blue, and the shape of him is indistinct.

My arms sing with the hard work we did today. My hands are dry and cracked—concrete work does that to your skin. My whole body feels like it could just dissolve onto the floor, but I don't really think about it. I just watch him.

He doesn't need to bring me home—I could walk the hundred yards through the woods from his house. But he brings me home, and I let him. He doesn't need to pick me up in the mornings, but most of the time he does. After everything that's happened between us—all the unswept broken glass of our relationship—it surprises me that either of us wants to be with the other. And yet we do. It's like a family game of chicken, without knives or cars or trains—love is the weapon, or trust, and we're the two cars that fly toward one another at breakneck speed.

I can see the white of his face in the pickup window: Addie. Daddy. Adolf. Dadolf. I said to Roy once, *"Why is our father named after the most evil man who ever lived?"* and he brushed me off with the same, why-do-you-have-to-be-so-flippant? derision Addie used. I was dead serious.

He's a conundrum, a riddle, a daddle, a diddle. I only wish I could simplify him that much.

But because I am who I am and he is who he is, I can feel the inside of the cab, the cigarette smell of it, and the sweat of our two tired bodies, the stale words I left him with still hanging in the air. I can see the dashboard and the glow of the instrument lights as he goes down Davis Road.

Once when I was seven or eight I filled all of his coat pockets with sawdust. And then I waited and waited and waited, and he never said a word. Every time I saw him wear one of the coats, I wanted him to say something, but he didn't.

A few years after my mother killed herself, he painted in fine white letters on the side of the truck he had then: A. PLEASANCE & SONS. It was one of his keep-the-family-together ideas, and I don't know why but I hated the presumption of it. I know now what he was trying to do, but then I went out and scraped the plural *s* off the side of it with a razor. *It can be you and him*, I wanted to say. *Not me*.

*"You want to be like her?"* my brother said with as much bewilderment as derision in his voice. *"You* really *want to be like her?"* and in his voice I could see what he thought about her, and what he thought about Daddy. *Yes*, I might have said to him. *Yes. As long as I don't have to be like you or him.*

We have a kind of trust between us, my father and me—a working trust. I know which wrench to hand him, and when. But it is not at all like love. Love takes too much of an extension, and I am no more willing to lean out on that limb than he is. It's been broken for too long.

A man's life has so many folds and facets in it, it sometimes feels as though he could be some abstract sculpture that appears different from whatever angle you look at it—you turn only a little bit, and he's completely different. But the way my father is, he only shows me one set of folds—the one that drives the truck away from my house—while the rest of the world sees a completely different set, and when he sees me try to glimpse it, he turns—he is programmed to turn—so I cannot see the Adolf Pleasance everyone else sees.

He's gone, and the street is empty, and the whole of my insides rings with emptiness.

He thinks I don't know, but I know how he sometimes parks the truck down the road and watches the house, how he waits for me to understand what it is he wants, what it is I can say to him.

What he doesn't know is how I do the same thing. How some mornings I'll come up to his house before he has a chance to pick me up, how I'll stand in the woods still as an owl and watch the house where I grew up, stand in the trees and listen for the ghosts I know have to be there—not just Roy and Mother but Addie and me as well, the people we could have been, or once were.

Sometimes it's like a dream, standing there, the woods thick and naked and all of the world echoing and playing our lives, his life, saying *Addie* in the wood shop, *Addie* in the truck. He is the dream I dream, the story I tell myself, the story that tells itself to me. He is always he, him, your father, my father, the only way a father can be. In everyone's mouth, in even my own, he has been the other, the him, the half of my heart that is empty and yet the half of my heart that is full.

I read that in conception after the sperm makes contact with the egg it dissolves, and the two halves of genetic material come together. Dissolves. I could stand in the woods and imagine that:

The smash of the stars of my existence against one another—the half that was my father slamming softly into the half that was my mother and just dissolving, giving way, the two halves making somehow not a whole but another half to ache and ache for completion, the new stars spelling out this slow half-life.

It's astonishing how distant things can be, how he can be right in front of you and still remain a conundrum, how I can remain at the window or in the woods, watching, half him and half not, but still half, completely incapable of penetrating what has always been impenetrable.

Another night, two days later: Addie is sitting in his pickup truck outside Jack's apartment, around the curve from where he was parked the other night. In the back of his mind, he's had the idea that he might find Jack alone, that he might find whatever strong thing it is in himself that could lift him out of the truck and walk him across the gray street to Jack's door.

There are lights on in Jack's apartment, and though the curtain is pulled, the window is open on the warm night air and voices—Jack's, a girl's, another guy's—float to him. He cannot understand what they are saying, but now and then a word or two arrives audible and intact above the others. And then there is laughter, which as it scrapes across the flat of the air only exaggerates his loneliness.

It has been a wet spring so far, and the evening air has the cool of damp. On the lawns, beneath the distant yellow porch lamps, Addie can see the reflectant shine of the lights on the dew of the grass. And beyond this street, on the uneven swell of hills beyond town, the lamps buried in the darkness and foliage glimmer in the irregular movement of air.

The sound of voices and laughter keep him from knocking at the door, and now instead of leaving, he just sits looking, and maybe by looking he will understand what it is his son is looking for in life, if there's any possible way he can help him find it.

Jack always planned to leave, and so his being here has seemed something of a spiritual windfall. Still it doesn't make the separation any easier.

Right now, on the darkened street outside his apartment, it's easy to see that Jack was leading up to this for a long time. Time only has shape when it has passed.

*Sledding with the boys. Deep winter, school closed; the snow still coming furiously:* Roy on his own sled. Addie is holding the sides of the Flexible Flyer with Jack between his wrists, then rushing down the hill, pushing the sled, then easing himself down on top of Jack, the warmth of his younger son palpable beneath him, the snow in their faces. Roy next to them, laughing, Jack beneath him, cheeks red, breath smelling of peanut butter, nose crusted with snot, anger in his eyes for not being allowed to race his brother alone, under his own power—or angry at his father for one of his million other unwitting paternal crimes.

Jack comes out of the apartment with the others, and Addie's heart drives up against the wall of his ribs. He tries to make himself small in the seat. Jack wouldn't understand—would be furious to find him outside his apartment like this.

Jack stands on the blacktop drive with Karen Anderson and a boy that must be Jimmy Dixon. Jack is tallish, wiry, with the same blond hair as his father, but with features more like his mother—patrician, a delicate almost haughty mouth.

They stand on the curve of the driveway, and Jack puts his arms around Karen. Jimmy Dixon turns to walk away but looks back and calls out again before he disappears. And then Jackie and Karen are alone. She hugs him, and he kisses her. Addie can see the silhouettes beneath the yellow light above the fixed-shut garage door. He can see Jack's hands rub up and down the girl's back. His face grows hot, and he looks away.

But Jack never looks his way.

Jack slides through the front door of the Ranchero. He wears jeans and a not-too-carefully pressed white shirt with a necktie. He still has on the name badge from Dunkel's Drug, where he works three nights a week, and through the afternoon on Wednesdays till closing.

But then, as he slips, slim and loose jointed, between tables toward where Addie sits waiting for him, Karen Anderson follows him through the door and trails behind him, hesitant, her eyes going back and forth from the bar to Addie to Jack. She has a windbreaker folded over her arm, and her hair is pulled back from her shoulders. He's amazed and ashamed at himself that hatred mixes so strongly with the fear that climbs his throat and into his sinuses.

Every Wednesday night since Jack moved into the garage at Simpson's and went back to work at Dunkel's, Addie has bought him supper at the Ranchero, and every Wednesday night he has waited at this table with the certain knowledge that Jack would beg off—too much work for a supper break, too little time. Yet he never has, at least not until tonight.

He has watched his son eat, watched him with love so edgy and wild it sometimes feels as though he can climb right out of his own body and into Jack's, to see and taste and hear everything the way his son does. Sometimes it feels that close. His son an extension of himself: when they work together, he hardly has to say a word, Jack knows what he wants at the same time he wants it, can anticipate his needs without a word. But no matter how close it seems, every Wednesday when he stands up stiff legged from the table and watches Jack head back to work, it feels like watching a stranger.

Addie knows Karen only slightly. They've met once or twice when Jack has brought her up to the house, but right now all he can remember about her is that evening by Jack's apartment, the two of them holding one another. Blood rises in his face, and his ears burn.

"If it's okay, Dad," Jack starts, next to the table now, the girl a little behind, looking at neither of them, "Karen's going to eat with us."

"Fine," he says, but the shiver of confusion nearly constricts his words. "Nice to see you Karen," he says hoarsely and stands with both hands hanging onto the worn wooden chair arms.

They order, and when the food comes, it surprises Addie that he talks easily with her—feeling as he does sometimes that his voice has detached from his mind and is just milling along amiably of its own accord. Jack sits in silence. Addie asks her about school—he recalls vaguely that she is a year or two behind Jack, a commuter student. She asks him about their business. Jack looks at his watch, eats sullenly. She pokes him now and again to make him smile, and he does, briefly.

Then she makes a joke, a near-perfect imitation of Jack's cool, haughty way of speaking. Deep voiced, she says: "I gotta stretch my wings a little bit. Get out of this small-town life," and wags her head the way he would.

The laughter hits Addie like a shot in the head—on pins and needles around his son all the time, it is something he would never do. Jack has a mouthful of potatoes, but the laughter hits him the same way, coughs out of him, makes him spit potatoes on his plate. "Oh, damn," he says, "I got potatoes up my nose." He chucks Karen on the shoulder—she flushes. People at other tables turn to see what was so funny.

She comes again the next Wednesday, and he begins to like her more. He finds himself looking forward to the way she follows Jack into the Ranchero, shy to make Addie pay for her meal. The skin of her hands and face is smooth and white, and he likes to watch her hands, the color her knuckles turn when she pulls her arms into herself and squeezes her fists. She astonishes him, and that makes him feel young.

Jack drove to Richmond this past weekend, had his interview first thing Monday morning. As far as Addie knows, he hasn't heard anything yet, and it leaves Addie on edge. He knows Jack will leave anyway, knows that regardless of whether or not he gets the job, there will always be other jobs, other lures. He's glad Karen is around, glad he is at least partially able to see Jack through her eyes. She makes him learn about his son.

He likes the way she talks to him, touching his hand, likes the astounding discovery that her palms are soft and damp. He likes most the clearness of her eyes, the broad, high way her face looks when she speaks to him.

She has the spaghetti special like last week. Addie watches her eat. Jack is silent. It is only later, after dessert, when Addie is paying for the meal that he says, "I heard from Wharton Stokes this afternoon. They're offering me the job and want me to start on Monday. I asked them for another week, just to get things straightened out, with moving and all."

Karen is next to him, and they are crowding the doorway. Addie picks a toothpick out of the little metal dispenser at the edge of the cash register counter—it takes a minute to get it. Everything is slow and thick. He can see the grain of the wood in the toothpicks, can feel the desiccated air around them. He's glad Karen is here. Her being here keeps him rational. *This is Jack, not Alison, not Roy.* This is Jack. He cracks a smile. It feels like his face is out of control. "Goddamnit, congratulations," he says to Jack, and his own voice catches him off guard. The doorway makes him stumble, makes it hard to breathe. Then Jack grins too, extends a dry, hard hand for his father to shake.

"So we'll do this one last time, next week," Addie says.

Then they are outside in the warm late spring evening. Jack and Karen turn away, toward the drugstore.

He says good-bye—it echoes hollowly against the storefronts and the concrete walk—and suddenly the distance between the curb and the pickup feels insurmountable.

The town square—with its swing sets and slides and bandstand that he helped build—is lush with rain, with the coming of summer. You can't even see State Street on the other side. A car slides by, lights on. Jack waves and Karen laughs, and for a moment, as they turn away, he wonders what she thinks. He hasn't thought at all what might be going through her mind with Jack leaving.

# ALONE

The day Jack is to leave, there is nothing but silence in the house. He gave up his apartment days ago and has been staying here. There has been silence. He has spent late nights with Karen—at least Addie assumes that's where he's been. He has never asked. In the morning Addie is up early—in the shop, making work for himself.

It feels to him at this moment that he loves his son with the same reckless abandon he loved his wife, and right now, when his son is nearly ready to leave, Addie is filled with the same wild desire to protect that kept him aloft with purpose the last four or five years of Alison's life. But it is all mingled with the sense of failure. It's not rational, of course, but the failure feels huge and furious.

Jack's old car is parked in front of the house, ahead of the pickup. Addie cleans in the shop, vacuums up sawdust. Listens for Jack to stir. By car it's not a long trip from Hadleysburg to Richmond—maybe two and a half hours. Straight east, almost.

On edge, wishing it would be over, he goes out to the front, takes the pack of Winstons off the dash of his truck, and holds the pack a moment before shaking out a cigarette and lighting it. The match leaves a hint of sulfur in the air. Jack is inside. The house is quiet. Is he up? Addie's been up for hours.

*God this cigarette tastes bad.* He takes another drag off it, then pitches it into the street.

It is nearly summer. Addie can't figure out how he's come this far in his life. Seems like just yesterday it was 1955, and he was just a kid himself—an unbelievable leap of the imagination.

He leans against the pickup and looks off into the hazy distance that is the Blue Ridge, and in a moment the screen door slaps open and Jack comes across the wooden porch with a pair of suitcases. The sense that this has happened before—that there are footsteps and words laid out in front of him that he will walk through almost mindlessly, that there is some integral memory that exists in this yard, on this street—is strong, overwhelming.

Addie waits a moment, then pushes away from the truck and comes toward Jack. "Can I help?" he says.

"No. I got these," Jack says. "There are some boxes by the door."

Addie turns away from him, heads toward the front of the house, legs weak and old. He stops at the edge of the porch, turns, watches a moment as Jack pushes toward the car, holding the two heavy suitcases. Something is pushing, trying to heave toward the surface of his mind. He turns again.

The screen door is closed and, unsteadily, Addie takes hold of the door handle. He has the momentary, unsettling sensation that the solid house is afloat. He is here, but he is also in the backyard, walking around the place where they will build the shop. *Jack has his hand. How old is he? Three? Four? Alison isn't dead yet but gone, having fled to New York. "We're buddies, aren't we, Daddy?" the boy says. "You're my best friend."*

He steps up on the porch, and he can see this clearly and it makes him start to shake. He pulls open the door, bends down, and picks up one of the boxes. It's heavy as stone, dusty: record albums. How in the world did he collect so many?

Jack comes back across the open yard, the suitcases he carried sitting now against the side of the car. "Just put the boxes by the car, and once we get them out, I can decide how to organize them," he says without looking at Addie. His voice has a cold whistle to it.

Addie goes toward the car, and the gravel crackles beneath his feet. He goes toward the car, and he is walking across time, not gravel, walking across ghosts and sorrow, across sunrises and evenings.

"Son," he says, by the car, holding his pack of cigarettes again, pulling one out and straightening it between long careful fingers. Jack is at the back of the car and has the suitcases in his arms. And now Addie puts away the cigarettes and is not leaning on the pickup anymore but floating toward Jack, floating so close that Jack can smell the sawdust, the tobacco. Here is this feeling again, that he can rise out of his own body and become his son. Jack's putting the suitcases into the hatchback, and he turns, and Addie comes toward him, almost falling. He stops, his son's arms are out. All of it is clumsy, patterned, not of either of them but around them, part of the structure of the air, the earth. For a moment, when Addie puts his arms around his son, he has the sensation that he is the only thing that anchors him to the ground, the only thing in the world to keep his son from floating clean off into the morning air. The cloth against them, the earth beneath them, the sky above them. His son's body is rigid and hard, unforgivably separate. Addie releases him and stands there, the morning surrounding him, and Jack turns, bends down to take one of the boxes his father brought out, then hoists it in. And now the car is lurching into the street, and Jack is being pulled back across the void.

Already it's the first edge of July, and in the mornings Addie sits on the front porch, smoking, drinking coffee, staring at the wet lawn, at the Hendersons' house across the street. Alone. The work carries him through the day. Television and gin carry him through the evening until he falls asleep in the chair or in bed, then finds himself here, just after six in the morning, smoking, drinking coffee, ready to go to work again.

It was almost this time of year when his older son, Roy, came home from the service, after boot camp. It never would have occurred to Addie when he drove him back to the bus station with the girl Roy said he was going to marry that it might be the last time he'd see him. It happens that way, and you remember otherwise extraneous details of the day— the smell of the season in the air, the shirt you wore—like the last time he saw Alison, his wife, alive. The mind clings to such things.

And now it is September. Time spins off the now like the tail off a comet, unreal, trailing into infinity. The days are warm, but there is a cool edge to the night and you can see winter in the shape of it. Work is the only thing.

He seldom stays at home this fall except to sleep. He eats at the Ranchero, spends the weekends at Terry's Texaco, talking with Terry or Alf Mueller or Jim Harlan or whoever happens to be there. Goes out to the county Vet's home to play cards with the geezers and cripples. Now and then he writes letters to Jack and tells him what kinds of jobs he's doing, who he's seen. Family is important to him. But it doesn't seem to be important to Jack. Too young. Too busy trying to establish himself in the world.

And now winter has come. It is months after his son left. The mornings sometimes can knock the breath out of you—the vinyl seat of the pickup hard as bullets, the pale steam of breath and the dry taste of cigarette smoke temporary as time itself.

Somehow winter seems like the true, natural state of the world, and everything that comes between is somehow an illusion, a falsehood. Winter now seems always the same as the last one. The children in the playground at the elementary school seem year after year like the same group of children, never aging, never changing. He finds comfort in that sameness. The year ends, summer comes, and now winter has come again. The seasons, like the children, are endlessly the same and give the illusion that life is not finite but constantly renewing, that life is eternal.

He wonders how he ever got through the years that Jack was away at school, or how he got through Alison's and Roy's deaths. And it amazes him that no matter how many times in life you are brokenhearted, it is never instructive for the future.

# WINTER

Richmond in winter. Slush in the flat streets from last night's half-hearted snow, cars going by now and then. It's still early, and the slush sprays onto parked cars, the empty sidewalk.

Barely awake, shivering in my underwear because we can't afford the gas to heat the apartment. I move away from the front window that looks out on bleak Hanover Street, flick on the television, then go back down the long hallway to the kitchen to get a bowl of cereal. When I come back the television has come on—the old black-and-white set my father gave me when he finally decided to get a color set. I pull the kerosene heater close to the disintegrating armchair and light it, then adjust the wick until it glows bright red and the odor of kerosene drifts off in the high-ceilinged room.

This is what loneliness is like: a winter city, one warm corner of a frozen apartment, the blue glow of the happy faces on the "Today Show" as icy as the air on the street. Jean is still in bed; soon she'll get up, get angry at me for not getting her up sooner, then get ready for work. Tomorrow it will be the same again, though tomorrow it will be warmer, or it will be colder.

It is more than a year since I left Hadleysburg, and I am drifting somnambulant through someone else's world. No contact in a year, and still it could be only moments. I try to remember what I have done, and I cannot remember anything but working, picking up my paycheck. Sometimes on the street the pavement turns to water beneath my feet, and a wave of panic hits me: *What am I doing here?*

This is not how I thought it would be—though now I have no idea what I thought. Nothing happens in this small life—neither happiness nor sorrow, only time. Sometimes at night I dream of my mother—I dream that I come up the walk and see her again the way she was the day she died. The momentum of the day hurls me into her legs, and she talks. Her face is frozen, and the language is incomprehensible. Sometimes I dream of falling or drowning, and it is a peculiar comfort to find that death scares me to my bones.

I watch Jean in bed, and I imagine the two of us, halted in time, Jean sleeping, me watching her, the streets outside sibilant with slush, nothing ever changing, all of it reeling over and over into the future.

It's a Saturday, and outside Hanover Street is thick with slush. Jean walks next to me, reaching out to hold my hand, putting her hand in my pocket when I don't reach out to take her hand in response. I push it out, shake it away.

"Don't be so affectionate," she says as she takes a step that puts her half a turn in front of me. She means it to be ironic, funny—sometimes it feels as though irony is the only connection we have. "I don't think I can stand it."

My feet are wet, and I look at her, look beyond her to the winter hazy damp of the street where we are walking, and I can hardly keep down the inexplicable anger that rises and inflates my chest. She doesn't see it; she can't see it. My teeth press together, and I turn away from her, my hands in my pockets and clenched hard, and finally the wave of it passes into something like exhaustion. I take my hand from my pocket and touch the middle of her back with my open palm.

When we met, I mistook her irony for caustic wit—like a broken screen door, I thought it signaled something amiss deeper in the house, but I have found no broken stair, no wheezing attic, no drowning basement. There is neither want nor need in her face, only a frustrating evenness that is too infuriatingly like my father's. Perhaps I had expected someone like my mother.

We moved in together almost instantly—everyone else had someone to sleep with, and I was desperately lonely. The bed is unmade. Her diaphragm is in the bathroom, in its plastic case. Living with her has not changed my loneliness.

Later, in the kitchen, she is making sandwiches. She is working at the counter opposite the sink. A dirty, carbon steel butcher knife lies at the edge of the counter where it could easily be knocked off. I pick it up, and just as I do, she looks at me, and there is a moment when our eyes meet and simultaneously drift to the knife in my hand. I smile at her, drop the knife in the sink. She does not smile back.

On Monday on the bus, on my way home from work, I pull the cord to signal the driver to stop, and then stand up as the bus approaches the corner and find myself caught in the inertial sway and thrust of the bus's movement and, completely unable to move until it stops and the doors open, the recognition hits me: this is what it's like. I say it aloud to make it real. *"This is what it's like."* A woman in a suit and spray-permed hair looks up at me like I'm a staggering drunk who's just pissed his pants. *This is what it's like.*

# INVITATION

At the cluttered kitchen table, halfway through his monthly billing, a cigarette and gin and tonic going, the kitchen lights burning voraciously, he sits only half concentrating on the work he's doing, more often looking outside at the complete darkness of the world and the way the darkness seems to sift back and forth when cars pass in the distance—the lights don't transform the darkness, only move it. *I could daydream myself into oblivion.*

Another bill, and then he is staring out the window again. He's always been the kind of man who took control of situations. He's always been a man of endless patience, who could fix anything in the world given enough time. Even when Alison died it felt that way; even when Roy died—no.

Headlights drench the driveway side of the house: the constant exhalation sound of a car fills the house before it ceases and gives back the silence. Then knocking at the door. "Someone's at the door," he says aloud. When he stands he's glad to be moving.

It's Karen Anderson.

In high heels and white stockings—what must be her work

clothes—she is framed by the doorway, the yellow light of the porch lamp behind her keeping her in silhouette. It's been a year, more, since he's seen her. More. "Hello," he says loudly, roughly. His eyes and hands burn with surprise, and for a moment all he does is stare at her. "Suh—sorry," he says, his eyes moving quickly. Now the shape of her. Now the glimmering porch light. Now the patchy snow on the lawn and the spread of lights down below the hill and on Church Hill in the distance. "Please. Come in."

Seeing her is completely distracting, and after he shows her in—holds the door and catches the fragrance of her passing—he fusses in the cluttered living room to make a place for her to sit. Then he thinks of the cigarette in the ashtray on the kitchen counter, and he backs away from her, apologizing, flustered.

In the living room again, Karen has her coat off and folded over her lap. "Can I hang that up?" he says, nerves jangling.

"All right," she says. But she doesn't give it to him right away. She just looks at him and only slowly, stands up to hand it to him. He offers her coffee. She refuses.

They sit together in the living room, Addie in a chair, Karen opposite him on the couch. He wonders if he should have offered her a drink, but doesn't say anything more. He is embarrassed by his house, by the dust on the tables and chairs, by the old newspapers. He's always been much neater than this, but he's let things slip lately. It seems like years since anyone has visited. He sits forward with his elbows on his knees, uncomfortable, aware of his size, his lack of grace.

"I hope I'm not interrupting anything," she says.

"Naw," he says, not looking at her—thinking if he looks at her he'll wind up staring because she's so easy to look at. "I was just doing my billing."

"For your business."

"For my business."

She's prettier than he remembers. Her hair is thick and leonine, and she doesn't bother to pull it away from her face but lets it fall around her shoulders and back.

"It's been a while since I've been here," she says, "but it looks the same, I mean like when Jack was here. Didja ever hire anybody new?"

"I'm sorry the place is such a mess." Hands together, hands apart. "Oh, um, no. Not permanently. Just couldn't replace old Jack. You know." He gets out another Winston and lights it, careful to blow the smoke away from her. "I've been busy, and I—I don't have too many visitors. Usually I do the visiting. Or it's someone coming to borrow the chain saw or seeder. I haven't really thought of cleaning." The cigarette smoke surrounds him and makes his eyes water. The cigarette itself is big and unwieldy as a tree stump, and he grinds it out in the overflowing ashtray at the edge of the table.

"Looks fine," she says flatly. She folds her hands together, and the muscles around her mouth tighten. She doesn't sit forward or back, but somewhere between, neutral. "So," she says, "does Jack call much? Do you hear from him?"

"Now and again," he says. *This* is her reason for coming—things have dissolved between them. It hurts him to think they are no longer talking.

"He's working hard, I guess. It's more difficult than he thought it would be," he says. "Supporting himself and everything." What he says is entirely made up. It is January now, and he hasn't spoken to Jack since last October. He could have died for all he knows. "But you probably hear more from him than I do. You probably know that."

She says nothing, but smiles and folds and unfolds her hands. His son, he knows suddenly, left her the same way he left him. Sadness and love and sexual confusion well inside him.

It is difficult, suddenly, to think of anything to say. It's difficult even to think how to move. His eyes swing across the room in the silence—the old, threadbare couch, the unused fireplace, the stairs, the stained carpet. So much house for one man.

When she says she has to go, it is a relief.

He helps her on with her coat, then opens the door and watches her go down the walk to her car. "I was thinking," she says, turning in the middle of the walk, "that maybe we should get together for dinner. At the Ranchero. Like we used to do with Jack. I know it would be without him, but I used to look forward to those dinners."

"Me too," he says, cold air punching into his lungs.

"Wednesday, then?" she says.

Something howls from within him. No, it wants to say.

He looks at her face and realizes that he doesn't know her at all, that she is infinitely more complex than he's ever imagined. The thought makes him hungry.

"Wednesday," he says, his voice exploding with happiness, confidence.

She waves as she gets into her car. The possibility occurs to him that a woman could be companionable, pleasurable, a way Alison rarely was. It makes his vision sparkle and his hands wet. When the red taillights descend away from him, the red scars still hang in the air.

# DINNER

Sometimes Addie drives. The sensation of speed, at the very edge of control, is fabulous.

In the dead of winter, when the house shudders with the wind as it comes out of the mountains, it almost makes him mad to stay indoors for hours on end, and so he gets into the pickup and heads out of town. The sun will be out, and the snow drifts at the edge of the roadway like sheared glacier, filling up the dead-wind space between the hills and roads with white blades, hard packed, but precarious for the overhanging weight. He looks forward to the blinding sunlight on the landscape, the way in high winds, blowing snow as fine as steam skates out of the mountains and off the fields onto the tarmac, and just to look is blinding and fascinating and sickening, almost like dream flying.

The ditches fill with snow, grading the road surface and surrounding fields into one constant surface. The stubble of corn stalks stands out over the rolling white between the ragged forest and mountains like whiskers on a man's face.

Where the snow has packed onto the roadway, it melts in the

sunshine, then freezes during the night to leave a dull, white scar tissue of ice on the pavement.

When he hits ice he does nothing, but waits, his breath clenched behind his teeth, his fingers tight on the steering wheel, cold sweat sparking up into the skin of his face and hands. It is foolish to try to do anything. The key is to maintain control over the sudden float of chaos.

Addie stands looking across State Street at the fence of parking meters against the edge of the grassy town square. The sky is so clear tonight you can see stars above the lights of town. The moon is full and raw.

There is still the residue of snow at the place where the sidewalks meet the storefronts, and dark trickles of water where it has finally begun to melt. It's dark, and people come past on the street, in the square. He doesn't see anyone he knows, and is grateful for that. He pitches his cigarette into the street—sparks spin out with ragged hurry—and then reaches for his pack and slides a new cigarette out before slipping it back and putting the pack away. His mouth is dry, and he's certain being here is a mistake.

It didn't occur to him until after her car had sailed down the street and he was left standing alone that her invitation made this a kind of date. Or it did occur to him—that's both why he accepted and why he should have turned her down.

Cars file down Main Street from the traffic light toward the highway, and he watches the long spray of headlights pushing out in front of them. When he closes his eyes, he can see her round bones pressing beneath her skin, drawing it taut and giving it a fine gleam. He can see the shape of her, the dark of her eyes, but then he makes himself stop.

She's late—did he get the time right? The day? Up toward where State Street comes out onto the square, he spots a pair of headlights he's sure are hers. He watches the car turn onto Evans Street and slide out toward the highway. No.

"Addie?" she says, and he whirls around.

"Oh," he says involuntarily, "You startled me."

"Sorry," she says. "Do you mind if I call you Addie? Everyone else does."

He shakes his head, smiles. Despite everything, it makes him grin widely to be standing here with her. If he did not know her age, he might not be able to tell that she wasn't ten or fifteen years older than Jack.

"Sorry I'm late," she says. "I got tied up at the end of work." Her hand drifts out and touches his elbow.

"Where do you work?" he says, still standing stiffly with his hands in his pockets and needing to make chat. "I thought you were in school."

"I am, but I work. At the bank. Three and a half days a week. The other days I commute over to Charlottesville."

He nods. He feels as though he ought to reach out and touch her too, just to reaffirm that he is here, she is here, and they are real. He doesn't, just looks at her.

"You want to go inside?" she says.

"Good idea," he says, blinking, his ears and face burning.

He opens the door for her, and she slides through. The Ranchero isn't crowded, and no one turns to look as they come in. He watches her, the shape of her through her suit and coat—then catches himself. She turns and glances at him, as if to say, "Yes, it's okay," and then says aloud, "How's this?"

He nods, starts to take off his coat, but then comes to her, takes her coat, puts it over his arm, and holds her chair for her. She smiles, almost laughs—her lips are bright and lush, and she looks spectacular.

He hangs their coats together on the rack against the wall, then sits down across from her. He wants to smoke, but he knows she doesn't, and so he ignores the urge.

"This is fun," she says.

"Just like old times," he says.

"Not that old."

"No," he says. He can feel his tension coming and going, and it's a fabulous feeling—like riding a roller coaster for the first time in years and feeling the cars climb up the first huge incline.

"There's something about the food here," she says and laughs a little. Addie lets his eyes wander over to the bar. No one he knows, except old Alf Mueller, the bartender. He looks at the chalkboard where the specials are listed. "Maybe we should get a bottle of wine," she says. For some reason this surprises him, and his eyes jerk back to her.

"Maybe," he says, "Maybe."

"What do you like?" she says.

"Oh, I've never really been much of a wine drinker. I—"

"I could pick something. I'm getting to be a kind of aficionado."

"Are you?" In a moment, the waitress comes.

"Do you have a wine list?" Karen says. The waitress, whom Addie doesn't know, hands Karen a red folder, like a miniature menu. Karen flips through it, laughs, then flips through it again.

"What were you thinking of having?" she says.

"The roast beef special," Addie says.

"So we'll get red wine."

"Let's have a bottle of the Chianti," she says. "And I'll have the spaghetti special."

When the waitress is gone, Addie sits staring a moment, not sure what to say.

The waitress comes back with glasses of ice water and puts them on the table. Addie's looking away from her, across the room, thinking of sitting here with Jack and, long ago, with Roy. Trying to think how the place has changed since Alison died, he hears her say from a considerable distance: "So what do you think about Jack's leaving Richmond?"

"What?" he says, blinking, clicking the word off his tongue.

Darkness crosses her face. "What do you think of Jack's leaving Richmond?"

"Oh," he says, and now he reaches for his cigarettes. His lips are dry, and the cigarette paper is dry, and his eyes focus on the flare of the match. "I think—I mean I hope he finds what he's looking for." He lets a cloud of smoke drift in front of his face so that she will not see how what she has said shocks him.

"Yeah," she says, "me too." When he looks at her again he wonders exactly what the tone of her voice means.

After dinner they sit for a while, nearly in silence, and finish the bottle of wine. He has the feeling that this has all been a mistake, that whatever he built it up to be in his mind has not materialized—the roller coaster car has climbed the hill, but there is no downswing in the track, only a flat plane that goes on into the horizon.

On the street he stands with her in the cold and can't find the proper thing to do with his hands. He smokes again, looks at his pickup.

Finally, it is almost a relief to be away from her, the cold pickup jumping along the highway.

# GRASS

The constant noise becomes its own silence, the inversion of itself. It works a hollow into the center of your mind, a hollow you can sing in. A hollow you can dream in.

The red-and-black mower has this silence as it slips roughly over the canted, uneven ground, all the clank and rattle of its carriage erased by the sheer, perfect noise. After four hours of this there's no sound at all, only persistent silence. At bare spots dust and stones kick up, stinging the bare knives of my shins, while the broken muffler punches out vaporous blue fists of oil-scented smoke.

In the yawn of glue-limbed morning, coffee bitter in your mouth, you can start at this kind of work with relish because of the tangibility of what you will do, because of the clean swaths of cut grass that will come as the day expands, because of the hard green against the sun. The neighborhood lawns become clock hours that rotate into the past, and from the past into the future.

After the "real" job at the law firm in Richmond for nearly two years, this seems like lawlessness, like idleness. Except my body hums with it—hands and shoulders and teeth still vibrate at night with the shudder of the mower. And in the evenings when I ride the motorcycle or drive the car home along the hazy evening highway, then up through the hills to sit on the wooden steps of the trailer, everything feels short, easy, weightless, like being held aloft on an updraft of air.

No one from the real world—the past world, the *world* world—knows where I am. Not the people I used to work with, the men I used to drink with, the women I used to sleep with. Not Gary, not Jean, and most of all not my father. Escape.

I got up one morning and looked at Jean in bed and thought of the conversation we'd had the night before, and just seeing her set me on fire with panic. For the first time it hit me that I had sleepwalked through more than a year of playing house with her, never until now understanding or even seeing the reality of her expectations of me. She saw us getting married. She saw us having children. She saw an eventual suburban life of PTA meetings and report cards and late-night checkbook balancings when the kids were at last asleep, and when she said this to me it made my heart rise up in my throat, made my teeth feel loose in my head. How could I not have seen?

I said nothing because I was filled with terror that the only thing I could feel in the face of her affection was a bizarre sense of abandonment. I had counted on her irony. I had counted on her seeing this the way I did: a game of house, a way of warming the bed. The irony was gone from her eyes. It occurred to me that she might be on the brink of telling me she loved me, and I stopped her before she could say anything more. She looked at me in utter bewilderment, and later we went to sleep in silence.

There are horrors your mind makes you relive—accidents, disasters—seldom in full, though the fullness of them seems to reside in your head in moments of absolute cinematic perfection. And each moment can come out when you're tired or frightened, somehow more real than the actual event. My mother's death and my father's frustrated fury at it is like this for me. Because I was so young I have no way at all of knowing how my memory corresponds to the reality. In bed, anxiously rethinking Jean's bewilderment, a piece of the memory came loose—my father at the back door of the house with a double-bladed ax, bashing at my mother's desk through the opening of the back door so the pieces of it would fit through and he could put them on the fire. Awake, I could see the torn sleeve of his shirt flutter in the light from the flame in the trash barrel. I could see the dirt on his arms and the resolute and abject determination in his eyes, and it scared me sick, scared me in a way that my mother's death, which at that moment was still completely unreal to me, had not.

The next morning, in the quiet, Jean's hair sprawled out across the pillow, her eyes puffed with sleep. She didn't look pretty, she didn't look ugly. She looked like a sleeping woman I didn't quite know. And in the stillness of the rainy mainstreet morning—cars swishing by *mainstreet mainstreet* on the street like fish in shallow water—I woke her, showered, put on my shirt and tie, and put on my slacks, and waited—with the same desperate feeling you get when you've been under water too long—for her to go to work.

She kissed me good-bye and said, "You'd better hurry, you're going to be late," then ran off down Main Street after her bus, her heels clacking and her head bent against the rain. When she was gone, I took off my tie and began pulling things out of drawers and closets, shoving them in grocery bags. I dumped all my books into boxes I had saved in case we moved. As much as I could put into my car, I did, and left. It took two hours to disassemble the life I had put together.

It amazed and frightened me how easy it was to do. I headed west, out of the flat of eastern Virginia and toward the Blue Ridge. Maybe I knew where I was going. Home without going home. South and west of Hadleysburg and Charlottesville, probably no more than a two-hour drive from my father, but in reality as far as the sun.

After I was gone, I wondered what Jean thought—what she did.

I wondered if she called my father. She must've.

I could imagine her rushing around Richmond, to Gary's, to Jake and Marty's, furious, hurt, insulted.

I could imagine her calling my boss, could imagine him saying to her, bewildered, "No, I haven't heard from him, and I'm a little disturbed," because it's not normal just to disappear.

And I could imagine her calling my father, could imagine the tough reedy sound of him answering the phone. It'd be late at night, and he's watching television, and the rest of the house is dark. He's watching something stupid, gobs of sentiment being hurled from the screen, and when the ringing of the phone jars him, makes his insides rattle, he's nearly at the point of tears because someone's dog or daughter has got run over by a truck. He gets up, and it takes a moment for him to loosen up his joints, and by the time he gets to the phone, he's spooked because nobody calls him late except with bad news. On the other end he hears her voice: "Mr. Pleasance? Mr. Pleasance? This is Jean, Jack's—well—

roommate? girlfriend?" and in the moment of silence that comes before his nod of recognition, before she says anything more, I know exactly what would go through his head. He'd know that I'd finally gone and done it—jumped off a bridge or walked in front of a moving car or shot myself—and for that instant, he'd just wait deadlike, wait to see if I really would betray him that way. And if I did, he'd wait to see if his own body would betray him—would he fall down and sob like he wouldn't do when my brother Roy died, or would he blow into a rage the way he did when Mother died, or would he simply hang up and go back to the television program?

And then she says, "You haven't seen Jack, have you? You haven't heard from him?" and it completely confounds him because he's never expected mystery. Life has never given him mystery—always flat-out disappointment. Her phone call has hung him up in the air like old laundry, and he blows with indecision. He goes back to his television program, or he calls my apartment—only to have Jean answer and force him to apologize profusely and hang up. And there is the television program, cold and glowing, a repudiation of his own real emotion.

In the evenings sometimes, sitting on the little square wooden porch of the trailer, I think about the chewed-up mornings where you could already see the sunset at dawn. I think about Jean and am completely baffled that it could go so wrong so easily, so lazily, and without any sort of malign intent. That it could just drift into wrongness from the very beginning. And now all I can feel for Jean is sorry, though I am certain she has taken my leaving as contempt.

I'm sorry that I wasted her valuable—as she put it—biological clock time.

I'm sorry that I never felt anything stronger with her than the sense of having made an irrevocably wrong decision. I know she was hurt—I hope more by embarrassment than anything. Right now she is probably calling me a coward, an irresponsible child, and to think of it twists me up with shame, but I don't know what else I could have done. To go on would have been wrong for both of us. Had I been able to explain it, I would have. But I might have let the softness of her hands, the reasonableness of her voice, talk me out of it, and I would have hated her for that. Now perhaps she hates me, but at least she can go on.

Late in the afternoon, I come to the end of a row, rock the mower back on its wheels, and turn. I start down the next swath and wonder when Harry and Dean will finish up, because I'm ready to drop, to sit down with something cold and let the afternoon flare off into darkness, fireflies swimming in the plasma of night like neurons. I go up the swath, swing around. Suburban houses, lined up; the cushion of haze; vestigial shutters on brick facades, children playing. Swing again; dust comes up; Harry's pickup sits in the shade, the black paint of it gleaming hotly in the single beam of sunlight that bisects the hood.

Finished, I cut off the mower and stand for a minute at the edge of the yard and listen for Harry's and Dean's mowers. I've got my T-shirt off and piled on my shoulder, and my ears ring. Sweat drips down my chest and sides. There's a square concrete slab next to the house that was probably supposed to be a patio but gleams emptily, brilliantly, in the bald afternoon sun.

A column of insects hovers out over the road, more like hollow spots in the air than a place where small creatures exist. They're full of color, shifting—an invisible man juggling a million tiny prisms. An aluminum screen door wheezes shut in the distance, and a woman says something, but it's far off. I push the mower down off the curb and into the street. Clots of cut grass break loose from underneath. The air is strong with the smell of grass and gasoline.

"Young man," the woman in the distance says, and I'm surprised when I turn around and discover that she's standing right behind me. "Should I give this to you?"

She has huge, thick, rose-colored glasses that go from the middle of her cheeks all the way to the center of her forehead. She's wearing black shorts and a sleeveless, low-cut white top. She's probably in her early forties, but it's difficult to tell. She's a trifle buxom, and her hair is jet black but mostly covered by a funny-looking straw hat shaped like one of those fabric hats women wore in the 1920s, close to her head. It hides most of her face and hair—the narrow brim of it rests on the top of her glasses frames in the front, and in the back goes nearly all the way down her neck. She seems so weird, for a moment the idea goes through my head that she's part of my imagination.

She's holding a check in her hand and extending it toward me. She's on the down-slope of her lawn, below me, looking up. She looks at me—at my chest, at my waist, but not discernibly at my eyes—for a long time. I don't move. She's got the check thrust out. Her glasses are so thick and obscuring you can't see what her eyes are doing. A breeze comes along and moves the one strand of inky black hair that hangs out in front of her face.

"You can if you want," I say to her, but I don't reach out to take the check. I just watch her. She takes a step closer to me. Her bosom heaves a little. In the low-cut neck of her top, you can see the soft, mashed-together flesh of her cleavage. Her legs are smooth.

She takes another step, even closer, and I stay where I am. Now I can feel the radiated summer warmth of her.

She's in the midst of the field of insects. They make her skin sparkle and swim. I put my hand out, and she puts the check into it. The soft of her hand catches mine, and I'm aware of how dirty I am, how my clothes are impregnated with the scent of sweat and mown grass, how my hair is stuck with sweat. I'm also aware, suddenly, how female she looks—sometimes you get struck by that, like you've never at all fathomed how absolutely different male and female bodies are. Not beautiful, but healthy, strong. Sexually attractive in an almost elemental way.

"Maybe you'd like some lemonade," she says. Her neutral, almost grudging tone abandons the words in midair.

I fold the check in half and slip it into my back pocket.

She watches my hand, my arm, as I put it away.

"That might be nice."

"Whyn't you come on down?" she says, half turning but at the same time reaching back. Her hand stops partway toward me, and she looks up at me strangely. Electricity prickles up beneath the skin of my butt and my thighs. It's maybe an oncoming migraine that makes it seem so unearthly when my hand slips out into the air and hovers down toward her hand. Fast, artful, her hand touches mine, comes down over the top of it, and squeezes briefly before it locks into the sinew of my fingers and leads me down the sloping yard. I don't know why it doesn't strike me as peculiar she takes my hand. But it has a natural feel to it. All around, the quiet, midday suburban windows range like eyes. There's no sign of Dean or Harry. Her hand is hot.

She drops my hand to push the door open, then stands at the edge of the doorway while I press through, past her. Her house is dim and cool with air-conditioning. The doorway is close. I stand inside the room and wait until she goes past me into the living room—which is dim and leaves a soft impression of deep, grayish green. I follow her toward the kitchen.

Everything is sparkling and neat. The refrigerator pucks open, but I don't look. The cool air of the house feels good. I rearrange the T-shirt on my shoulder but don't put it on.

Ice cubes dink into a glass, then pop under the pouring of liquid.

"So," she says, as she reaches around me to hand me the glass of lemonade. I take the glass and drink from it. I hadn't known how thirsty I was. The sudden cold of the lemonade paralyzes my jaw, sends a wave of paralysis across my forehead. She holds the pitcher in one hand, and her now-free other hand hangs in the air next to me. Even though it hurts, I drink the whole thing down while she stands and watches.

"That's good," I say, more to the glass than her. It's homemade. The flavor of it sings on my tongue, in my throat. A pool of sugar grains shifts at the bottom of the glass.

"There's plenty more," she says and raises the pitcher a little. Her arm extends out away from her body—the back of it, the tricep, has that fleshy sag older women's arms get. It's nice—I'd tell her it was nice if I thought she'd understand. The pitcher is like those you get beer in at restaurants. Lemon pulp and sugar swirl at the bottom of it. I can see the crenulated flesh of her armpit, the dark spines of shaved hair.

"Thank you," I say and thrust out the glass. The air feels soft, like buttery velvet.

Her hand takes hold of mine to hold the glass steady. I can smell her breath, can feel the warmth of it.

"You'll come back next week?" she says, not looking at my eyes but maybe at my chest, my nipples. That feeling of electricity beneath the skin of my butt and thighs comes again, because an image of grabbing her, mashing my mouth against hers flits through my head.

"Maybe I'll come sooner," I say.

She nods. I turn a little bit, don't look at her—only indulge in the sense of her looking at me. Bits of lemon pulp fracture in my mouth and make the flesh of my tongue contract. Another idea comes into my head—she takes off her glasses, opens her blouse—and makes me want to gasp. I turn toward the window again to look at the hot lawn.

Now Dean's at the edge of the yard, looking around for me. In a minute I thank her, put the glass back on the counter.

Her hand takes hold of mine, and we stand looking at one another. I think about taking hold of her. She takes a step toward me. I'm starting to turn. I can feel the soft of her arm in my hand as I grab her, pull her close, and press my mouth to hers.

But I don't grab her. I just take my hand away, rub my hands to get the feeling off.

I turn and start back through the house the way we came in. "Come on back anytime," she says as I go out the door. The heat hits me as soon as I'm outside. I close the door carefully.

"All finished here?" Dean calls, imitating Harry's sweaty, nervous-sounding voice.

Dean is slender, wiry, and has a North Carolina lilt to his talk, and a kind of playfulness I've never seen in anybody without a southern accent. He's the kind of guy who will lean toward you late at night in a bar, after the girls have gone to the ladies' room, and say, "Man, am I *dronk*," and make it sound like the truest, most insightful thing you've ever heard. He is also the only person I would ever have considered walking down a late night street with, drunk, singing earnestly like two sailors in the movies while two of his girlfriends staggered along twenty feet behind us, giggling, pretending not to know us.

He stands at the top of the yard, and I can see already that he knows I've been inside with the lady. He raises his eyebrows—he can do something like that fifty feet away and even at a distance make it seem perfectly lascivious—and gives a pelvic thrust.

I laugh at him. "Y'all gonna get arrested for public indecency."

He laughs, rubs his belly. He doesn't wear a shirt either, and he's brown with the sun. He's a handsome guy, sleepy eyed and loose-jointed—one of those guys whose easy affability ambles along in front of them, always on the lookout for a good time.

I come up the hill to where he stands with my lawnmower. He cocks his head comically and raises his eyebrows as if to say, "Come on, tell me." When I don't say anything, but grab hold of my lawnmower, he snaps toward me and says, "Come on, man, what were you doing in fourteen fifteen's house?"

Harry calls the yards we mow and the people who own them by their house numbers. "Don't hold back on me, man," he says. "If I were in there firin' up the old poodle, I'd let you in on it."

"Drinking lemonade," I say to him.

His eyes light up. "Dinkin' the Lemon Lady?" he says, mocking vast disbelief. He starts to say something disgusting—Dean's got a way of looking at you that makes his dirty mind seem like a conspiracy between the two of you. Girls love it, or some girls anyway. But he cuts himself short and turns to look when an old Ford Torino swings around the corner, pulls up, and stops beside us. Chalky Van Kalkenberg rolls down his window and sticks his ragged redneck head out. You can feel the cool of his air-conditioning. He looks at the lawn and the lawn-mower, and then at Dean. "Still doin' this nigger work?" he says. He doesn't talk to me but to Dean.

"Yeah," Dean laughs, almost sheepish. Why Dean likes him, I don't know, but Dean has the endless capacity to like everything and every-body as long as there's a potential good time in it. "Good time" is Dean's motto, his Grail, and he searches for it endlessly, assiduously.

The sun blazes my shoulders, and I watch Chalky warily.

"Yass," Dean says and folds his hands together, points his face skyward mock-philosophically. "Yass indeed I am still doin' this nigger work. I'm bein' all I can be."

"You're a crazy fuck," Chalky says and looks at him humorlessly, which only eggs Dean on.

"Elvis of the Lawns is what some people call me. This nigger work is fulfilling, and I do get the girls." He leans over the car, his hands on the edge of the roof. "Yes indeed." Chalky looks at him without any hint of humor at all.

Everything has a prismatic aspect to it. The insects are gone, and the field of my vision has begun to graph itself off into segments, and the segments move against one another softly, with colors charging the edges.

Chalky says, "Got some top cue-wall-ee-tay lumbo out at the house, man, you wanna come by and pick some up."

"Might do that," Dean says.

Harry comes up just as Chalky's pulling away. "Who's that?"

"Dean's redneck pimp."

"You make much money doin' that stuff, Dean?"

"I don't exactly make the bundles I do mowing lawns," Dean says, leaning earnestly into Harry's face, "but it can be quite satisfying and fulfilling to help some nice blue-haired lady through her first orgasm since Uncle Orville died in 1926."

Harry starts to scowl. You don't want to say anything to Harry disparaging his lawn-mowing business. He sees himself as a tycoon, a contractor, an entrepreneur, and doesn't have a sense of humor about it. "When he was little," Dean says sometimes behind Harry's back, "they were gonna take out his tonsils, but they missed and got his funny bone. They mighta took his pecker, too, while they were takin'."

I say to Harry, to head off his irritation: "What's next?"

"Two forty-three and two forty-five," he says.

"We should be able to knock those out in a few minutes."

Dean and I lift the mowers into the back of the pickup—my fingers curl under the warm, damp edges of the mower carriage. "So," Dean says, wiping his hands on his pants. "Ya gotta tell me all about fourteen fifteen. D'ja get a bone in?" His eyebrows go up again.

"I told ya, man, we were drinkin' lemonade," I say and try to keep myself from laughing at him, which is what he wants. I reach around behind me and pull out the check she gave me. I flick it open and look at the name at the top of the check. Sylvia Nickerson. 1415 Canaan Lane, Middleridge, Virginia.

"You got her payin' you already?" he says.

"She begged me to take it. What could I do?"

"Would you gentlemen kindly get in the truck?" Harry says sharply.

"I was gonna give you some pointers on how to please a suburban housewife type, but I guess I'll have to save my advice for later." Dean says AD-vice.

We finish the two remaining lawns and then go to Harry's house, an old blue-painted frame house that's cut up into apartments. It's owned by Harry's biggest "account," the guy who also owns the complex Dean's apartment is in. There's a breezeway at the back of the house, and a porch, and there's a washer and dryer on the porch, in the sheltered notch there. Harry goes inside and gets his checkbook, and then comes out and rests it flat on top the chipped white enamel of the washer while he writes out checks for us both.

He doesn't give us the checks right away. He insists on chatting a while, telling us to feel free to come over and do our laundry. He's told us half a dozen times before, but neither of us has ever come. I do mine in town. Dean's building has machines. A girl comes out of one of the ground-floor apartments and asks Harry to move so she can put her laundry in the dryer.

Harry's one of the few people in the world that Dean doesn't get along with. Harry doesn't like Dean's loose way of doing things. Harry has a tight, Protestant way of viewing things. He believes that life is suffering, hard work. That idea makes Dean laugh. "Since when?" he says. "For Harry, maybe."

"Man, I got to get into the shower," I say, to hurry Harry up.

"You going to the bank?" Dean says. "You want to give me a ride?"

When I met him, Dean had an ancient Pontiac Starfire. It was a wild car, big as Wyoming and about as populous, with fins and a walloping old V-8 you could get up to about a hundred and twenty out on the highway. Dean was drunk one night, and out on 12 where the highway forks, he lost control of it. Between the forks there's an old abandoned house surrounded by deep woods. Dazed, Dean hit the intersection at 118 miles per hour, according to his estimation, and traveled through mud and trees nearly a hundred yards before the Starfire stopped. "That fucker took flight, man, and it was somethin' to behold. Yes indeed. Trees whippin' past, birds and bears and stuff lookin' at me like I was from Mars." The car missed the house by six inches on one side and missed a twenty-inch-diameter oak by about a foot on the other side. Dean was so drunk—he said he'd had a bottle of Cuervo; "Just one?" I said—he didn't even get scratched. The car went deep enough into the woods you couldn't see it from the road. It's still there, up to the chassis in mud. You can't get a tow truck in to get it, but even if you could, it wouldn't be worth it. Dean was too drunk to walk back to town, so he just lay down and went to sleep in the car and hitchhiked into town the next day.

Harry reluctantly gives us the checks, and you can see his disappointment when we take them and head out across the lawn toward where my Chevy is parked on the street. He stands there waiting, looking at us, hoping we'll turn around and come back, have a beer. When we go off by ourselves, it confirms his notion that we think he's a dick. I feel sorry for him, but he is a dick.

I unlock the car, put up the hatchback to let out the superheated air, then arrange the towel I drape over the plastic seat during the summer to keep the plastic from sticking to my legs. I don't turn around, but I know Harry's watching. Dean gets in the passenger side when I reach across and open the door. Neither of us looks back at the house while I start the car and pull away. The car falters a moment, stops, then gets going.

"You know that fucker's got twenty-three power drills?" Dean says as we pull into the street and head toward the center of town. "I mean I can see the point of havin' two or three—maybe a heavy-duty one and a rechargeable or something, but twenty-three? You ever seen his apartment? He's got power tools everywhere. Like you got books, he's got power tools. Sometimes I think one night he's gonna roll over in bed, hit a switch, and saw a leg off."

I laugh. Dean always talks about Harry with something approaching contempt, but there's always a tone of respect, too. "One thing you got to say about Harry," I say, "is he isn't anybody but Harry."

# SUPERSTITION

When Addie wakes up, it is dark in the house, and his waking comes suddenly—as if he has not been asleep at all, but fallen out of the sky, fallen from some long, continuous state of waking, like limbo, or purgatory. Incredible stretch of time, incredible loneliness. The heat is up too high, and the bedroom is arid and stifling. He sits up and listens to the empty house breathe.

He listens for something in the house—mice, ghosts, anything—but there is nothing. When he presses his eyes closed, shapes smear across inside his eyelids, like aurora borealis across the night sky. That's the way the silence is, the brain filling up like madness at the emptiness of the house, the emptiness of the road outside, and the emptiness of the world beyond.

He gets out of bed and smokes, then in his underwear paces around the dark bedroom, his chest as tight as if the silence were a mile of water above him. Now and then he stares out the window at the moonlit street, the cigarette smoke as dry as the air.

He thinks of his wife and then of Karen. His wife when she was

Karen's age—some summer when her legs were the perfect brown of new oats.

Now, on occasion, he wonders if maybe like music, death might be a gift. Sometimes it could be right. It seems to him that beauty is tragic, and in proportion, tragedy is beautiful. And then he is asleep again, almost consciously trying not to dream. Prayer, tears.

Home early from work one afternoon: the telephone rings, and it's a young woman's voice. At first Addie thinks it's Karen, but the idea dissolves. "Is Jack there by any chance?"

"No, I'm sorry," he says, the age-old worry finding his veins and nerves, making him think of the two men in the government car who came to give him the news about Roy. "Can I help?" he says, meaning to say, "Can I help *you*?" but the line is dead before the string of words gets out.

# ·45

Chalky's dog Bitch lies on a bare space of polished dirt, her ass tucked beneath the wooden porch at the front of Chalky's house. The muggy evening sun has come out from behind the low clouds and makes everything oppressive. My sneakers are stained green with cut grass. I mull the idea of taking a shower: the heat of the water, then sitting on the porch and drinking a bottle of beer.

The migraine's begun to return—now there are some bright sparkles and a small hole in my vision—and I know if I don't get home before another hour and a half passes, I'm going to be blind with it and have to try to drive with half my vision gone.

I sit on the outside edge of the group, my feet in the dirt and my elbows on my knees. I close my eyes to see if I can rest them, but it doesn't have any effect. The sparkles and the hole are still there.

Chalky sits in a metal-and-vinyl chair that came from an old dinette set. Dean sits below him, between Chalky and me, on the gray, unpainted wood of the porch. Chalky's wife, Sandy, sits on the broken porch swing—she's tiny as a sparrow: anyone else sat on it it'd come crashing down. Beyond her the screen peels off the screen door.

Chalky's fiddling with a .45 pistol, spinning it on his finger Old West style, now and then leveling it and sighting down the barrel at some point off across the field ahead of him. The empty high grass of the field is motionless in the still air.

Bitch lies propped on her elbows, tongue lolling just above the dry dirt. Every time a breath comes out of her mouth, little bits of dust wing up and spin—though it could be just the migraine.

Chalky looks like a cut-rate country musician: tall and gangly and narrow faced, with longish, ratty hair, sometimes cowboy hats. Somebody you maybe ran into late one night, when you were coming back from throwing up outside a redneck bar. Or maybe he was the guy who, drunk, walked by your table, tripped on something, and to keep from looking stupid to anyone who might have seen, glowered at you, invited you outside to get some idea just what kind of men you both were.

He cradles the gun in his hand and slips the clip out, then punches it back in again, like a cop on television. I'd just as soon go—guns make me nervous, and Chalky makes me nervous—but here we sit, everybody but Sandy with a can of Schlitz, and Chalky fiddling with his gun. "Guy I know," Chalky says, his lips peeling back from his twisted, wolf-teeth as he talks, "says he's asleep on his couch one night in front of the television, and he wakes up when he hears a crash, right? So he looks up, and right in front of him is some nigger walking off with his stereo." Sandy has a book open on her lap, and she looks up from it at Chalky, silent, eyes focussed stonily on him, but he ignores her. Chalky jerks his body to imitate his friend waking up, then opens his eyes wide. " 'Hey, muthafucka,' he says, and the nigger drops the stereo and takes off running. This guy, he just sits there and listens while his front door slams, because he hasn't got a gun. If it'd been me, that would have been one dead nigger." He lifts the gun up again, like he's done half a dozen times over the last five minutes. I'm watching as he does it, somehow knowing, this time, that he's going to fire it, and I see the tendons in his hand and forearm move, and there's a knife of flame from the barrel. The sound of it slams down the field and off the hill that borders the field. It jars my teeth and makes waves of sparkles bash out into the hole the concussion of the shot has left in the air. The dog jumps but falls because her hind legs are beneath the porch. Chalky and Dean laugh as she struggles to her feet and then stands panting in the yard, aimless now and staring back at Chalky. The slow cloud of blue smoke drifts away from Chalky's face, like it came from his laughing. The sparkles blow and hang in the air like colored veils. Chalky points the gun at the dog.

The house where Chalky lives is outside Salem, Virginia, twin city to Roanoke, half an hour's drive from Middleridge. The house is beat up and small—paint peels on the outside, leaving bare, silvery spots of wood. Three cars rust in the front yard, one half on blocks, half on wheelless hubs. Most of the time, Sandy drives the Torino. Chalky drives the old gunmetal GTO when it runs.

The house is on several acres of land and distant from any of the neighboring houses. It used to be part of a farm, with pastures in back of the house, but it's all overgrown now. From where we sit, the land slopes down and away for maybe a hundred and fifty yards. There's a pond, and then there's a hill that juts straight up away from the pond, sheer as a cliff and maybe fifty feet high. The grass is tall in the field, and there are little pines and locusts growing—the first step toward it becoming woods.

When I shift my eyes, Sandy is watching me watch Chalky. I've got sunglasses on, and I don't move my head, so maybe she doesn't know I'm looking at her. I can't decipher the expression in her eyes. She's pretty as hell, and it always surprises me to see her with Chalky. She's no more than five feet tall, skinny so you can see the veins in her arms, but at the same time full breasted and ripe looking.

The two of them have been married since she was sixteen. Now she's twenty-two or twenty-three, and I can't imagine what they have in common. From the look of them, I'd say nothing, but I don't know either of them.

I stare out across the sweltering, summer-dry grass and close my eyes against the flares and sparkles of the migraine. The air is colored; the humidity is colored. I try to imagine Sandy climbing out a window in the middle of the night to sneak off with him. Easy to see how a certain kind of fifteen- or sixteen-year-old girl could fall for someone like him. I open my eyes again and shift them toward her. I don't know why I even think about it, but it hits me that she's dying to get out of this relationship. It's like I can see it in the way she sits on the swing, in the way she looks at me now, eyes sharp and clear.

"It's a fast gun," Chalky is saying to Dean, "or used to be. There are foreign ones—" he says FAR-in "—that are ten times faster now."

"Yeah, man," Dean says, nodding, his shoulders hunched, his arms propped on his knees, and a can of Schlitz between his hands. "Technology catches up with everything, man, even guns."

"Especially guns, man," Chalky says. "Especially guns. They lead technology, man."

The etiquette to dope buying dictates that you have to socialize for a while and not let on that you've come only for the dope. So you sit around places where you don't want to be, waiting for someone to get you the dope.

I watch Chalky shift the gun, click the safety on and off—then slip my eyes back to Sandy. She has her legs pulled up beneath her, and her knees gleam with the pressure of the rounded bones beneath them. She wears cut-off jeans and a cream-colored sleeveless tunic top that buttons up to her neck.

Her hair is brown and straight, and she keeps it short, just above her shoulders. The book on her lap is a paperback with the covers torn off.

In a minute, Chalky and Dean get up and go inside to make the transaction. Chalky wears those kind of jeans with no pockets in the back, the kind a girl wears to show off her butt. The wooden screen door with peeling, rusted screen slaps shut, and Sandy and I and the dog are left here alone in the silent pressure of the sun.

I sip from the beer, and it tastes lousy, warm, and does nothing at all to help the migraine.

Chalky and Dean are in the house a long time. The silence is continuous, broken only by the panting of the dog, the shrill of crickets in the field. I hate the silence. I don't know why, but it draws attention to the migraine.

"What are you reading?" I say finally.

"Oh," Sandy says, and holds up the book. "I don't even know." She laughs, turns the book over in her hand. "My girlfriend at work loaned it to me." She smiles, looks at it. The swing trembles with her movement. "She reads a lot and has all these paperbacks. She rates them, puts a number one to ten on the cover, and a letter to say whether the book is romantic or not, and loans them around. She's a regular library."

It's the longest continuous string of words I've ever heard Sandy say, but then my question is probably the longest string of words I've ever said to her. Now I don't know what to say. I sit and look at my hands. A blind spot is starting, and I test it to see how much vision I'm losing. Right now if I was driving and a dog ran out in front of the car, there's a pretty good chance I wouldn't see it.

"I don't usually read romantic books."

"I don't know too many men that read."

The air is practically on fire with the migraine, and half my vision is gone. "I read a lot. Got a lot of books."

"Like what do you like?"

"Faulkner, Hemingway, you know."

"No. What are some of the books they wrote?"

"*The Sun Also Rises*, you heard of that? *To Have and Have Not?*"

"That was Humphrey Bogart and Lauren Bacall."

"It was Hemingway first. *The Sun Also Rises*. And *The Sound and the Fury. Absalom Absalom.* Those are Faulkner. He also wrote the script for the movie *The Maltese Falcon.*"

"That's Humphrey Bogart too."

I nod.

"You should loan me some sometime."

I look at her. She's even more attractive than before. "None of them are romantic. Well, they're all romantic in the sense that—" I stop myself. "*The Sun Also Rises* is romantic in a nice way. Sad. You should read that."

"I didn't say they had to be romantic books. I said my girlfriend rates her books on how romantic they are, then loans them around."

"You did, that's right."

The porch swing creaks. Dean and Chalky laugh inside, the dog trots out in the yard, into the deep grass. "Who's your favorite author?" she says.

"I don't know—how could you pick out one?" I mean it to sound glossy, educated, but in the air it sounds arrogant, and I try to soften it. "I have favorite books, though. You know."

"Yeah," she says and pulls at her lower lip. I can't figure if I've insulted her.

Chalky and Dean come back out onto the porch, Chalky in the lead, his cowboy boots knocking on the wood of the porch. Dean sits down next to me, and Sandy looks down at her book. Chalky has the gun in his hand. "Where'd that goddamned dog go?" he says. "Bitch!" He looks out over the hazy field for the dog. I look away.

Dean gets out a pack of Club rolling papers. Thinner than cellophane and without adhesive, they're a little like rolling cigarettes out of butterfly wings, but Dean folds the single sheet out between the fingers of his left hand, and with his right, sprinkles weed from an open baggie into the fold, then works it expertly back and forth between the thumbs and second fingers of both hands, forefingers hanging over the top to guide the trailing edge.

There's an explosion, waves of sparkles fly out away from the corona of my vision and hover out over the field. Chalky holds the gun out in front of him, aimed somewhere in the weeds.

"If you shoot that dog, Chalky, I'm going to shoot you," she says with flat, angry annoyance. Chalky stares at her, his jaw set and hard. Sandy glares back at him. The gun is in his hand, and she doesn't move. Her legs are out from beneath her, her feet dangle without touching the porch. She has the book closed in her hand, and she leans forward, ready to stand.

And then Bitch comes loping out of the high grass, tongue out and panting, and if it weren't that she told him not to, he probably wouldn't. But the thing about a gun is it asks you to shoot something. It's made to be fired. The dog starts across the bare of the yard. Chalky turns; the dog is maybe fifteen yards out, coming toward him. He pulls the trigger, and again there is the flat whack of the pistol's report, and a blue jet of smoke.

Bitch stops dead in her tracks like some giant invisible thing has slapped her down. In the hollow the gunshot has left in the air there is a very long moment of silence. Then a sodden noise comes out her throat, and her legs push at the bare earth as if she's willing to expend every last ounce of energy just to stand. Now she's still, a heap. There's a shitty smell when the gunpowder smell goes. One of her forelegs twitches again and stops. My belly knots with the stink and the sight. Now Sandy screams, and I can see the waves of it in the air: red to orange, rippling. Chalky laughs sheepishly. Sandy jumps up. She screams, but as she does, she chokes, coughs, and then vomits on the porch. She leans away from the porch reflexively and retches into the dirt. A sound like a groan comes out of the dog, and it makes Chalky turn, look at the dog, then at the gun. Sandy chokes and spits. Her book is on the ground, in the dust and vomit. Her hands are fisted.

"You hated that dog," he says slowly, almost accusingly. She turns, kicks the swing—it falls as she slams through the screen door, and when she's gone it creaks back and forth on the single remaining chain.

"Shithead," Chalky mutters. He shoves the gun into his back pocket and goes to where the dog is. He sighs—I can't tell if it's regret or annoyance. He picks the dog up by the hind legs and drags her deep into the weeds.

I look at Dean. His face is pale and tired, and suddenly, without the shine of his grin, he looks older than I've ever seen him look. "Check ya later, Chalk," he says and starts toward me.

We're in the car, and gravel spits underneath the floorboards as I pop the clutch and swing out onto the main road. The car is hot, and the heat seems to go with the migraine. Dean says, "That poor fuckin' dog." I suck deeply at the air. It's hard to get the look of the dog out of my head. The searing road disappears beneath us, purple flamed, nearly invisible.

Dean has the joint he rolled in his hand and looks at it. "You want to smoke this thing?"

I shake my head. "Me neither," he says.

When we are on the highway, he says, "I saw a guy shoot a dog like that in the service," and adjusts himself in the seat. It surprises me that this information pricks my ears, makes me turn to look at him. My brother was in the service when he died, and he would've been about Dean's age. "That kind of shit——" He pulls out a cigarette and lights it.

"I didn't know you were in the service." The wind gusts through the open windows and blows at my hair.

He rolls up the window and then rolls it down again. Drags on his cigarette. "I kinda got booted." He blows smoke, and the smoke is whipped away. He studies the tip of his cigarette. Right now I see something in his face I never knew was there, and it makes me feel as though I've underestimated him.

"My brother was killed in the service," I say. I stare out the windshield ahead of me, concentrate on the road. I can feel him look at me.

"Good a place to die as any, I guess."

"When my brother left," I say, "I hated him for leaving me alone with my father. I remember my father sitting at the kitchen table reading his letters, and I used to come in and interrupt him, make him look at me." Dean and I don't talk about much more than girls and drinking, and I don't finish what I was going to say. I hated Roy for dying, and since he did I've done everything I could to push him out of my mind. But here is Dean, gray eyed and smoking, and it occurs to me now at this moment, in this haze of migraine, that Dean is *like* my brother, that he has a connection to my brother that I do not have, and that I now, desperately, need for my own.

"What branch were you in?" I say. There is fire at the edge of my field of vision. Blue as flaming gas jets.

"Air Force," he says.

"So was my brother." A wave of nausea comes up in me. I have to get home soon, or I'm going to wreck the car. I try to concentrate. "What happened—I mean, you know, if you don't mind."

"I don't know how to read, and I lied on the applications. Service was mostly fuckups in them days. Guys didn't care what you were like. They just wanted bodies. That was the way it was then. Guy at the recruiting station filled out the forms for me—*he's* the one really did the lyin'. Anyways, I fucked up a lot because I couldn't read, and when they found out, they gimme a dishonorable discharge for lyin'."

I take my eyes from the road to look at him. He pinches the corked end of his cigarette between his fingers as though he's going to pitch it away but then drags from it.

"I thought they'd teach me how, you know, so I could get my GED or somethin'." His face turns dark; it hurts him to talk about it. "Those fuckers," he says. "I was in fuckin' Georgia when they booted me, and I hadda hitchhike outta that fuckin' place. It took me five fuckin' hours at the side of 95 to get a single fuckin' ride." Now he pitches the cigarette and rubs his hands together. "That's where I saw that fucker shoot the dog. Georgia. This guy, his name was Sam and he was always talking about killin', and one night I pulled a guard detail with him out in the woods on this Huey that'd gone down." I look at him and then look back at the road. Questions swarm. "It was a nasty fucking woods, man, full a cottonmouths and shit, and I'm standing at the edge of this clearing and on the other side I hear shootin', and this fucker's just massacred this dog. Some sweet, mangy lookin' stray, and he just smashed it. I couldn't get over the stink of it. All fuckin' night long there's this stink. I could have bashed his head in for doin' that." I turn off in town and head toward his apartment building.

"My brother—" I start, but Dean cuts me off.

"Some guys, man, get a good fuckin' deal from the service. Some guys leave feelin' like they owe their lives to it." He shakes his head. I start again to ask, but he says, "Do me a favor, man. Don't tell Harry."

"Don't worry." I watch him in silence for a moment. Georgia. I am whirling out of my head into the swamp where my brother's helicopter went down. *"Roy's gone,"* my father says. *The kitchen of his house is cold when the winter wind blows.* I drive and stare hard at the road—let the vibrations of it tell me I am still connected to it. After what seems too long a time, I say, "I never woulda guessed you didn't know how to read."

He laughs. "You learn—you know. Pretend you lost your glasses, that kinda shit."

"I could teach you how," I say as we pull into the parking lot of his building.

"Man," he starts but doesn't go on. The car is stopped, and he has one hand on the door latch, but he doesn't get out yet, just looks at me. "You'd want to do something like that?"

I look at him and shrug. "Why not?" In a minute, he gets out of the car, and I watch him walk across the lot for a moment before I knock the shift back into reverse and head back out of the parking lot.

The thing about a migraine is you can't really do anything about it except sleep. It's one of the few things I remember about my mother, that she would have headaches that made her come in from the outside, and then disappear for hours while my father made us be quiet. She'd say she couldn't see, and I always thought it was figurative—I couldn't understand, until the first time I had one, how pieces of your vision could simply disappear and leave huge gaps in your vision. You think you're going blind. But I was proud when I first got one. Proud there was something so specific and idiosyncratic, something so apocalyptic, that had been passed along to me from my mother. I didn't care that it could be so debilitating—I was proud that it was.

Right now, I have to turn my head sideways and catch everything out of the corners of my eyes, because most of the vision is just a gray hole. The highway is mostly empty, and by the time I get to my turnoff I can barely see, in the shade of the trees, the white siding of the trailer down the hill.

I slam the door and walk down the hill in my own darkness. The shade is cool. With only peripheral vision, the scent of the woods, the earth around the trailer, the sound of the squirrels in the brush, birds above—all of it becomes more important than the vision.

I get out the keys, unlock the door from memory, then lie down on the floor inside.

# THE FIRST SON

Addie keeps the television on constantly, watching in particular the shows about love. He hopes somehow they will teach him something. They never do. He'll sit on the floor with popcorn and gin and watch. He'll often find himself repulsed by the things he sees, or ashamed at the way people act, but there is nothing else to do in the long evenings when his other friends are with their families. Stupid as they are, the shows make him cry.

Finally he'll make a last drink, take his cigarettes upstairs, and crawl into bed with the bedroom television on.

Sometimes at night, having fallen asleep during Johnny Carson or some late movie, he awakens, and it will be nearly dawn, the room will be flooded with the irradiating glow of the television, and all the channels will be off. Nothing but snow, endless snow. He'll light a cigarette and stand up, the TV glow making him a ghost, making the smoke ghostly.

The air tastes like nausea, and he turns, goes for a light, then turns off the television.

Tonight he goes out the front door, onto the step, and sits on the edge of the porch in the dark. Spring. The air smelling like honeysuckle, ready to slide toward summer.

He lights another cigarette, and when his eyes have grown accustomed to the dark, given up the searing glow of the match, there is someone walking up Hamilton Street. White T-shirt, blond hair—all the same color as the TV glow. He comes up the walk slowly, like a sailboat drifting in a vague summer breeze. Roy.

Of course it can't be Roy. "Daddy it gets colder in Georgia in the winter than you'd think," comes the sound of the voice that floats in the darkness. "Damp." Of course it's a dream. He closes his eyes and opens them again, and the young man comes up the walk. It is Roy.

"Son, I'm sorry."

He flicks ashes and says, "I was in the kitchen that afternoon. It was late. I was peeling potatoes in a T-shirt, running water in the sink, thinking about when you were little, and how just to be funny you'd call it Walter, the water, like 'Can I have a drink of Walter?' And I heard a car—car doors slam, and it's one of those things you understand, you *know* at the center of your soul. I had a paring knife and a potato in my hands when I opened the door. It was whistling cold outdoors, and two men were getting out of a car, and you know that feeling you get when you've done something painful and your mind tries to back up, to negate it—well that's the feeling I had, like maybe I could back up, backtrack my steps, and it would change. *It can't be, it can't be*, is what I was saying to myself. And they came up and said, 'Mr. Pleasance? Mr. Adolf Pleasance?' and just then in the distance I saw Jack coming up the hill, where you came just a minute ago, and I thought My God if I have to lose every member of my family and have only one left, why on earth should the living one be Jack? and then hated myself for thinking it, and they said, 'We have some bad news for you, sir. Maybe you'd like to go inside and sit down.' 'It's Roy, isn't it?' I said, and they said, 'Michael,' not knowing I guess that you'd always gone by your middle name, not your first name. 'That's Roy,' I said."

"I've seen mother—"

"Roy—"

"There were so many things I never knew about the two of you. I'm the one who's sorry, Daddy."

And in the darkness Roy puts out his hands and touches Addie on the shoulders, holds him—and it occurs to Addie that this is not Roy, not Roy but Satan himself. If there were such a thing as the devil, and if ever he were going to come for Addie, this would certainly be the time, and the way, to do it.

"It was faulty equipment," Roy says. "Government lies and says it's pilot error when the only error the pilot made was thinking the Apache would be safe."

His son looks older now, like some earlier version of himself. Dead, he would not have expected him to age. "You'd be what? twenty-eight? twenty-nine now?" he thinks he says.

"There's a moment between the time you realize you're going to die and the time you actually do. I thought I'd think of you. I thought you'd be the thing that popped into my head, but it was Mother. Sitting in that place where Jack and I visited her in New York. Reaching out to me because she knew Jack loved her. I had the feeling it was her fault, but I don't know why. I always had the feeling when anybody died it was her fault. Death was her friend."

He turns away from his son. The horizon is lit, the cigarette has burned out at the filter. He pitches it away, and when he looks back, his son is gone. "Roy," he says weakly.

In the morning, when he is on his way to the day's job, he passes a blond young man hitchhiking on the other side of Route 28, and when he slows, turns, and comes back to pick him up, he's gone. There has been no other traffic, and the closest place to where he was is a pasture—a hundred yards at least to the treeline.

# SYLVIA

When I get up again in the early evening, I take a shower, then sit on the porch. There's a breeze in the trees, and the heat has abated somewhat. I'm hungry, but there's nothing to eat in the house. Things feel peculiar, restless.

I go up the hill to the shed and open the flat, clanging door, pull the motorcycle out, walk it up to the road, and stomp the starter. The hollow throating of the pistons in the cylinders. The bike's an old Kawasaki, and the guy who rented the trailer to me left it as part of the deal. "Go ahead and ride it," he said, " 'cause otherwise it ain't gonna be worth a shit when I get out." He was on his way to jail for evading alimony and child support when he rented the trailer to me. It's his wife who gets the rent.

I stomp the starter again, and the engine catches a little—a spurt of wet, smoky vapor; I nurse it to life. The bike warms, and I let out the clutch slowly. Gravel pops beneath the tires, the bike swims a little.

I go slowly down the hill, past Swanson's house, and there's a light on in a room, and the yellow color of it there somehow makes Sylvia

Nickerson come into my head, her cleavage and soft manner, the sweet bitterness of her lemonade.

Now I go up the other hill, the gravel-dust gray in the evening light. When I get to the paved road, I swing the bike out, shift up, pull back on the throttle, and feel the pavement start to recede beneath me.

The sky is still blue, but the sun is gone behind the trees, behind the hills; there's no more than half an hour left until sunset. The road here is barely wide enough for two compact cars to pass one another, and it goes down the slow side of the mountain where my trailer sits, down by a rotted split rail fence that's falling into the creek, through ragged fields where animal-shaped stones stick out through long grass. Then back up again through other hills as you head out to the highway. You can open up the bike a little, drop it down one side of a hill, then hard up another so you get that downslung thank-you-ma'am sensation of leaving your insides in another county.

The wind is hard in my face, and I can feel the deadwind tunnels it makes above my eyebrows, behind my ears, at the back of my head where the hair stands out and tendrils randomly.

The road goes up now, and there are fields, the edges eroded; in the coming sunset, cattle stand wide-eyed and motionless by ancient barbed wire fences. An old school bus someone has turned into an Appalachian chicken coop rusts at a fork in the road.

The hill crests, and it's a long, straight downhill slope toward the highway. High grass spreads away in the fields on either side, and I close my eyes, tug back on the throttle a little, and try to dream out into the wind. I do this all the time, close my eyes while the motorcycle's on the flat road, count to ten, maybe to fifteen or twenty, then open them to see how well I've kept the road. Most of the time it's easy, the road has a shape—a crown in the center and a downslope on either side—and if you concentrate you can feel the shape of it in the frame of the bike, in the spinning tires. Sometimes when I open my eyes, I'm right where I started, on the slope of the road; others I'm heading toward the ditch, or right at an oncoming pickup truck: it all has to do with balance, memory, touch.

These fields, the summer feel of the air, remind me of my father and my brother: how we would go out fishing early on summer mornings, or summer evenings, after or before the heat of the sun's day. My father would be too busy helping us to catch anything himself—maybe bringing in one or two, while Roy would catch seven or eight, I three or four: Daddy standing at the edge of a lake, wearing shorts and now and again slapping at the backs of his legs when the mosquitoes bit him, or adjusting the floppy straw hat he liked to wear (which Roy and I threw out in secret because it embarrassed us), and then whooping with childish joy when he caught his single fish, while Roy methodically, silently, reeled them in and put them in his bucket.

The western sky is purple when I get to the turnoff for the highway. I don't know where I'm going, I'm just here.

Except I do know where I'm going. Even thinking about other things, Sylvia has been walking around at the edge of my thoughts, her legs bare, her shoulders bare, her hair thick and wavy over her heavy glasses.

I start heading toward town, going slowly now, trying to think of what, if anything, I'll say to her. I have it in my mind that she knows I'm coming, expects it the same way I do.

But still I somehow don't even realize what I'm doing when I pull the bike off the road and down into her driveway. I park it next to a maroon Buick that wasn't there this afternoon. Light spills through the blinds and onto the lawn. Someone's walking a cocker spaniel in the street when I click off the bike, turn off the headlight. It's dusk now, and the neighborhood with its soft scent and soft sounds—TVs growling, cars passing, children shouting, all muffled by distance—makes my heart hurt with desire. Not sexual desire but another, less easily defined kind. I stand for a moment where I am, and there are two of me: one with a child's heart, heartbroken by the quiet of the town evening; the other just emptiness, a sexual will and short vision that shows me the sidewalk, the grass, the square shape of the door, and the textured glass that borders it in long rectangular strips.

I knock on the door, and it surprises me to hear the sound, to find myself where I am. And in the seconds after knocking and before the door opens, it hits me how fundamentally lonely it is to be a human being, how it is impossible ever to know what people are like, what they are feeling, and how it aches sometimes to have the truth about others. It feels like the earth is wobbling a little bit, and I turn around with the idea of running—but of course what I'd want to run from is not something that's escapable.

She opens the door incautiously, like a woman who has no reason to be afraid of anything, or wants her life at this moment to be interrupted. Her appearance, her form, are more robust than I remember them, and yet she's smaller too, more slight. She's wearing another low-cut top, one that ties off about three inches from the top of the black skirt she's wearing and leaves her midriff bare. The skin is as taut and toned as a girl's. The hat from earlier is gone; her hair falls over her bare shoulders.

She's surprised to see me, and at first there's a glimmer of recognition, then a look of total bewilderment. "Can I help you?" she says loudly.

"Who is it, Syl?" comes a man's voice from inside the living room. The inside of her house is still air-conditioned, and now it has that interior smell of recirculated cigarette smoke like you get in motel rooms.

She looks at me, hesitates, then turns toward the voice. It feels like she's making a decision—there's the flavor of hidden calculation to the way she moves. "It's," she says slowly, "the gardener. I couldn't find my checkbook when he was here before."

"I'll pay him for you if you can't find it," the man says. He says *cain't*.

"Won't you come in?" she says, the way women used to say it when as a kid I was collecting on my newspaper route. Then, to him, "That's all right, Lee, I found it."

I come in, past her like I did before, and her hand comes out and touches me on the lower back, just at the base of my spine, and I can feel the heat of it through my clothing. Before we get to the living room, she lets it fall away.

I didn't see the living room before. Now, with the lights on, it has a suburban, catalog look to it, like you could have walked into some weird Sears or Montgomery Ward showroom, and here we'd be, Sylvia in front of me now, the surface of her body hot and radiating, heavyset Lee in a sunken, immobile position on the couch, an open can of Budweiser in front of him, and me at the edge of it all.

"Lee, this is . . . ," she starts, and I'm ready to fill in for her when she stops, because I'm certain she doesn't know my name, but she goes on, "Jack, Jack, this is Lee."

"Pleasure," he says. The old family joke goes through my head: *No, Pleasance*, but I keep it to myself.

"Nice to see you, Lee," I say.

"Now, let me get you that check," she says and turns. I turn as she comes past me, close, and follow her into the kitchen.

"Did a right nice job on the yard out there," she says loudly as she opens her checkbook. It's on the kitchen table, which is between us, and she has to stoop over to write in it; I know she knows I can see down the front of her blouse, where the freckles and tan end in white.

When she's finished writing, she tears the check out—it makes a loud, satisfying sound—and hands it to me. "Thanks, Ms. Nickerson," I say loudly and then look at the check. Where the signature goes is the word "void" written in sharp little block letters, and on the pay-to-the-order-of line, continuing down to the dollars-and-cents line, it says, "Go outside but don't leave. Give me a half hour."

There's a moment of silence as I look at the check and then look at her. She's closer to me now, leaning up against one of the chairs parked beneath her kitchen table. She has soft-looking, heavy lips, and the bottom one has a plumpness to it that makes me want to grab her and kiss her hard. Lee laughs at something in the other room—I didn't realize the television was on. I come forward a little, reach out, and with my fingers lift the front of her skirt, and just leave it lifted up for a moment. She wears black underpanties. I look in her eyes. Then I push my other hand up between her legs and press it hard there a moment while I stare at her. And then I break away and head for the door.

Outside the warm evening is completely dark now, and when she closes the door and snaps the locks shut behind me, I look at the Buick, then at the house, and I know she's going to get rid of Lee. And I know I will go back inside and peel her like a grapefruit.

I swing a leg over the bike, kick the starter until it catches. I have no phone, I don't get mail except for bills, and I see almost no one but Harry and Dean. I've seen a couple of girls—friends of Dean's—but I've consistently tried to cut myself off. Yet Sylvia hit me at a moment when I wasn't expecting anything like her. I could taste her in my mouth, feel her on my hands, on my skin. Instantly she cut loose the wild need in me to be pressed against someone, to be protected from the solitude that has begun to erect itself around me. I squeeze the clutch and kick the bike into gear, then let it out and throttle up the drive and swing down the street in the dark, the headlight needling out in front of me, a very, very microscopic star in this vast galaxy.

Herbie's is nearly empty, and I go up to the counter and order two fried eggs light, on toast, with potatoes and sausage, and a bottle of Pabst, the only beer Herbie's sells. The waitress wears a patch on the breast of her white uniform dress that says Louise. The vinyl-covered swivel stool creaks when I turn toward the door and back again. The diner stands alone on the highway—a mile away you can see the lights, and when you get closer, you can see the patrons, framed in near-daylight from the inside and the odd blush of mercury vapor from the outside, and it makes you think of the food you'll eat, or the woman who's sitting at the counter with the chunks of her butt flattened out on a red vinyl-covered stool. It makes you think that somewhere in the distance is real night, more lucid and whole and more profound.

There's a blackboard on the wall behind the counter and scrawled in a sloppy hand, Meat loaf $4.25, Sallsberry Steak $4.10, Chiken Soup $.75¢. The wall used to be white, and then it was yellow, and now it's brown; you'd never be able to tell except there are old Gainsborough-style prints of British wildlife—dogs, horses with riders—and you can barely see the animals, the age is so thick.

I'm so hungry I'm trembling.

When the eggs come, I cut the soft yolks open and spread the yellow as far as it will go over the toast and sausage and potatoes. "Hungry?" Louise says when she sees me finish the eggs and toast, then go through the potatoes.

"Eating's my hobby," I say, mouth full. "I do it when I can afford it."

"I gotta eat, or I get headaches."

"I get headaches no matter what I do."

"In *Redbook* they say you can avoid a lot of headaches if you just have a little bit of food. My problem is, when I start eating, I keep eating."

I pull the check Sylvia gave me out of my shirt pocket, look at it while Louise talks, then put it back again. I try to smile politely. I put the bottle of beer to my mouth and drink hard from it. God, it feels good to have the carbonation scrape at my mouth.

I finish and ask for a glass of water, and she gives it to me with the bill. I pay it, give her a dollar tip, and she stares at me a moment, and I wipe my mouth to make sure I don't have egg on my face. Then she smiles like, no, that isn't why I was looking. I drink the water down.

When I turn around and head for the door, there's another car pulling into the lot, and the doors are opening as I push through the glass door. It has the sharklike grille of Chalky's '73 Ford Torino and I don't especially want to see him, so as soon as I go through the door, I turn toward the bike without looking at the car. The concrete walk is greasy, old, dark; the curb edge is crumbling onto the blacktop parking lot.

Then behind me there's the word "Jack," in a female voice, and it turns me around slowly.

There are three women lit up from the parking lot lights and in the spill of the lights inside the diner. One's tiny and wears a black miniskirt, the other two are taller by a couple of inches and stand on either side of the tiny one. All three of them are young—as young as me or younger. "Jack," the tiny one says again—it's the same voice. "How are you?"

"Sandy, hey," I say. "I didn't recognize you." They drift toward me without walking. "I'm okay." I point to the restaurant in a way that strikes me as furtive—"I just had a little supper."

I know why I didn't recognize her, despite the car. Out of the plain light of Chalky's porch and with makeup on she looks like a single kid, early twenties, out looking for excitement. She looks pragmatic around Chalky, pragmatic and never fun. I look at her hard, at her eyes. "How are you? You okay?" I can still see the dog in the dirt, can smell the heavy scent of her fur.

She smiles, looks away. Shrugs. "You come here a lot?" she says.

"Didn't have anything in the house to eat," I say.

She smiles, breathes through her nose. She wants to say something else, and so do I, but it doesn't seem like there's anything to say. I rock back on my heels.

"My God, my manners. Jack, these are my friends Karen and DeeDee." She takes hold of the sleeves of her friends and nods in the direction of either when she says her name.

"Hi," I say and reach out to shake hands with them. DeeDee giggles when I take her hand first—it's damp and dazingly soft. Karen's is damp too. "I used to have a girlfriend named Karen," I say. This makes Karen blush.

There's silence again, and I nod. "Well, see you."

"Yeah, Jack," Sandy says loudly, "see you."

The parabola of light bobs out in front, and the wind peels the hair hard back from my scalp. A two-lane highway at night is based mostly on trust or hope—you take it for granted that the road will remain beneath you even as you are blinded by the oncoming lights of traffic. If there's a pothole or an opossum scurrying across the road, you won't see it until the moment before you either hit it or don't, and so you trust the blackness, or you let it worry you.

It's a long time since I left Sylvia's house, and I have the check in my shirt pocket. When I stop the bike in front of her house, I don't even know that I'm going to go in, except the thing about being a male and a human being is that once the idea of sex gets planted in your mind, it pursues you until you manage somehow to prosecute it.

The grass is damp with dew, and the sky is getting cloudy. The Buick is gone, and there is only the kitchen light on. My shoes scrape on the walk. I knock on the door, and the knock echoes in the neighborhood. The street and houses are different from when I was here before. Everything's dark, there is no sound of children. The air is full of pine scent, the scent of weeds and nightly damp. I knock again, and the knock echoes. I used to walk through town neighborhoods like this delivering papers when I was a kid, enthralled with the spellbound look of night and its emptiness.

Light splines out onto the step, then spreads to the shrubs and lawn; Sylvia's head peeks from behind the door, and her shadow makes a dark spot over the rectangular pane of glass beside the door. The look of her shadow, the way she peeks, sends the thought through me that she's buck naked, and that's why she took so long to open the door. It hits me hard in the chest, makes my hands tremble. I step into the doorway, into the air-conditioning—which now she doesn't need but which also seems an integral part of her house, her being—and she closes the door behind me. She's wearing a kind of robe I've only seen in old movies, silky and with a fluffy collar of some kind of feathers.

She closes the door, and I can see the good shape of her through the cloth of her robe. "You finally came back," she says into the door. The locks snap.

"I was hungry, I went to get something to eat."

"What'd you have?"

"Eggs."

"I was thinkin' about eggs all day. We must think alike, you and me."

She's in front of me, turned toward me now, her arms folded across her front but now unfolding. There's no sash on the robe—it's her arms that hold it together. Behind her there's a wall, and on it a flimsy knickknack shelf where there are porcelain figures, a salt-and-pepper-grinder set. Now her arms have come all the way down, and I look at the edge fold of her robe, which still overlaps, and now I watch my hand extending and taking hold of it. The soft of the fabric slides between my thumb and forefinger. In my chest and head the veins constrict, and things get warmer; the air gets thinner when I can see beneath the fold.

What is her name?

Her name is Sylvia, and Sylvia is against me now, all heat and softness; her mouth is against mine, hot and pressing me back toward the door. You never dream the heat of another person: it's the thing that most surprises.

"I want some lemonade," I say. She pulls back from me now and looks straight at me. I watch her in return and at the same time push the robe off her shoulders. Now I let her go, and I can see all of her. I reach out and take off her glasses. I'm surprised she doesn't stop me. Her eyes are dark, indistinct. She blinks. Her face is prettier than I'd thought, and I look at her a moment. I put the glasses in my shirt pocket, then I come toward her, put one arm around her back, crouch, put one behind her legs and pick her up. She has a good feel to her, solid, light; her breasts move as I carry her into the kitchen.

In a minute we're standing where we were when I was here before. I reach past her and push aside the glasses and beer cans on the counter next to the refrigerator, then I put my arms around her, grab hold of her butt, and lift her—she hops—up onto the edge of the counter.

The robe's in the hallway, and I'm standing between her legs. She's at the very edge of the counter, her heels on my hips, her knees turned outward, her head against the cabinets. She opens my jeans and pushes them down with her heels and hands: I'm looking in her eyes, and she's looking in mine when her hand closes around me and she guides me against her. "Here," she says, and there's resistance, and then suddenly the resistance is gone and I'm engulfed. The warmth is everywhere. "Aw, Jesus," she says, soft as a bird. I put my hands on the cheeks of her butt and push at her. "Harder," she says, and I move faster, slap against her. It's smooth like this, the near kind of dreamstate you get, coupled with someone else, enclosed in her warmth like this.

She says: "Hit me."

I stop. I'm almost all the way out of her, and I look at her. Her eyes are wide, and her teeth are clenched together. "Don't stop," she says. "*Hit* me."

"I ain't gonna hit you," I say.

"Don't stop, damn it," she says and reaches around to push at my butt. "I don't mean hit me, I mean *hit* me."

"I don't know what you're talking about, but I'm not going to hit you." Now I can't stand being outside of her like this any longer, and I push slowly back inside her.

I can't go any farther and have to let it go out of me. She whispers, "You didn't really have to hit me. You could just slap me."

"Why?"

"I like it."

I'm still inside her, against her, looking over the curve of her shoulder at the yellow-and-white porcelain canisters that stand side by side next to her stove and say SUGAR and FLOUR and TEA on the front. There's a Hamilton Beach mixer with a clear plastic cover over it. The stove is spotless.

"You like the idea. I can tell you do. I can feel you liking it."

"It's you that turns me on, not hitting you. I don't want to hit you."

"Don't be stupid. You do too. All men want to hit women."

"That's dumb."

"Don't call me dumb."

"I wasn't calling you dumb," I say. The compressor in the refrigerator comes on, and it makes the counter vibrate a little, like Magic Fingers. For a moment she doesn't say anything but licks my shoulder, and I just hold onto her, glad the subject of hitting her has passed and beginning to enjoy again being here with her. An image of Sandy in the ugly spill of lights from Herbie's goes through my head—her skirt and high heels, her friends Karen and DeeDee and—

Pain snaps me backward, but she holds me tightly. She's biting me. *Biting* me. I smack my head against hers, but it's just hair against hair, and then I grab hold of her hair and yank. Still she won't let go. She's got her teeth latched onto my left shoulder, biting hard.

"Goddamn it, let go." I spit the words, take hold of her hair at the front of her scalp, and pull. I pull harder, then bring my left hand up sharp and grab her around the throat. Her teeth let go, and there's a flush of relief all along my shoulder and arm. I've got hold of her hair, and I jerk her head back, look at her, then crane to look at my shoulder. There's a round red mark, indentations of her teeth, but she hasn't broken the skin.

She's smiling. She likes the hand around her throat. For a long time there's silence. I have an erection, a feeling of disgust. "You like it," she says. I don't say anything, just stare at her unfocussed eyes, aware that I am *in* her body, that I am next to her, and that I do not know her at all. "If it's all softness, it's boring," she says. "If it's all softness then it's all softness, and what's the fun of that? It's got to hurt a little."

My hips start moving again.

"You liked it," she says, a look of triumph on her face. I let go of her neck.

"I didn't," I say. "Maybe something in my body liked it, but I didn't."

"You could bite me. Surprise me. Out of the blue just bite me. It changes the softness."

I drag the bike down off the kickstand and push it up the hill and into the street. The neighborhood is dark, and the sky is all milky with stars. I can smell her on me. I can see her eyes when I took off her glasses, I can see her eyes when I took hold of her throat, and for a minute, something—I don't even know what it is, loneliness maybe—hits me and I nearly feel like crying. I jump down on the starter and then do it again when the motor doesn't catch. The wind claws at my throat. There is wetness at the edges of my eyes—for sadness or for something else. I jiggle the throttle, jump the starter again, and now it starts to catch.

What hits me is that I'm twenty-six and while the world is chugging mechanically onward, I'm standing absolutely still—standing on some desolate night street in Middleridge, Virginia, outside the house of a fortyish woman I have just finished fucking, and all I can feel in the world is emptiness and a lingering taste of how easy it is to fuck and be fucked, and how it can be the sorriest, saddest thing on earth.

# THE
# PERFECT FATHER

The night is cloudy and utterly dark. I have no idea what time it is, but I can hardly see the forest and fields that surround the roadway for the completeness of the dark. The only light is the horseshoe shape of the motorcycle lamp; it shudders and shakes up the road and dissolves into the mist. The wind rushes past, and my shirt on my shoulder where Sylvia bit me presses hard in the wind.

I go up past the school bus chicken coop and then down the hill. The sky is gray. Down past the driveway at the hairpin turn, over the creek. I could swear I hear a car behind me, but there are no lights, and when I look into the mirror I don't see anything. A glint, maybe—no. Tiredness, probably, even a new headache. I don't know what to make of Sylvia and don't know what to make of my reaction to her—I'm hoping the ride and the wind will shudder it into sense.

A police siren slaps a wall of noise up behind me: the shock wave of the sound convulses the air. And then white light smashes through the darkness and drowns me in its blaze. Red and blue floatbeams roll over me, wash into the woods. The bike wobbles when I jump and turn to look into the searing white of the headlights. The road's narrow, and I nearly run into the ditch at the right side of the road. My body shudders, and my heartbeat is in my ears. The skin of my ears is hot. The skin on the backs of my arms and fists burns. *Goddamn you, Darrell*, I say to myself because I know the crazy fucker cop behind me.

I slow the bike down, come to a stop in the narrowest part of the road. The land is canted: there's a bank rising up from the road on the left, and a barbed wire fence beside the road on the right where the land falls off and goes toward the creek. I start to get off the bike and at the same time look behind me, behind the wall of light, and I can see when the door of Darrell's car opens and his leg comes out. The bike's still running, and I let the clutch out, swing around, and zip past his opened door.

I can see the look on his face when I go past, but I don't do what he thinks I'm going to do—which is take off—I just pull the bike up behind his car and leave the light on. I climb off—he's back in the car now, doesn't know what to do. He knows as well as I do that I could have left him sitting here by himself.

I swagger up as he starts to get out again. "I see your driver's license, son?" I say, using the cop-sound he gives his voice when he's doing this crap.

"Goddamn it, Jack," Darrell says as he climbs out of his car, "One of these days you're going to kill yourself, and I for one sure as hell ain't going to feel sorry for you." He's out of the car now, and he's finishing off his sentence right about when I square off in front of him. He's getting out his cigarettes, only half paying attention to me, and there's something about the whole situation—me riding along, him scaring the pants off me with that lights-and-siren trick, and then him moralizing at me like scaring the pants off me was something he was doing for my own good—that shoots a jet of white hot anger through me. He's got a cigarette in his mouth and he's got his hands cupped around a match he's going to light, and I reach out and grab him—hard—by the loose fabric of his shirt inside the arms. I grab him and slam him backward fast, and he hits the car, his head snaps backward and cracks against the light rack. He drops the matches, but he's still got the cigarette in his mouth. It stuns the hell out of him that I've done this. His hands still hover around his face, still ready to light a match they no longer hold. And for a moment we're reduced to who we are, not what we are. For a moment, I'm Jackie Pleasance, an older kid who lived down the block from him when he was nine years old, and he's just Darrell Planey, a kid who sometimes got to play in the backfield in the neighborhood football games when there weren't enough bigger kids around. I knew how it felt to be one of the little kids, because it was my older brother and his friends who organized most of those football games, and I always tried to get Darrell in the game.

"Thanks, Darrell?" I say. "I nearly ran off the road—I almost ended up in that barbed wire fence." I say *bob*wire, because that's how you say it around here.

"Jack, you know it's illegal to ride a motorcycle in the Commonwealth of Virginia without a helmet. I've warned you before, and I'm not going to let you go again." He pushes me backward. I push him back. "Don't you touch me, Jack Pleasance," he says. "That's assaulting an officer of the law."

"That's assaulting a fuckhead of the law. The whole idea of law, Darrell—the whole great philosophical wonderment of the social agreement of law—is the protection of the citizenry. Period. I have no desire to be protected that way. I'll take my chances."

"You're violating the law, Jack," he says. He bends down—keeps his eyes on me—and pulls his nightstick out of his car. "I'm going to arrest you for obstruction if you don't shut up."

"You're not going to arrest me for anything, Darrell, because I'm not going to let you."

For a moment he just stands and looks at me, bewildered, full of the anger of frustration. Now he brings his hands up in front of his chest and clenches his whole body and spits through clenched teeth: "Goddamn it, Jack, just shut up."

"Fuck you, Darrell," I say. "You almost killed me back there. If I want to die, I'll do it by myself, I won't have any fucking problem. I don't need your help."

"Yeah? And who's going to clean up after you? Huh?" He's shaking now with anger. "It's goddamned well going to be me, and I don't want the job. Who the fuck cleaned up after your mother?" he says.

I take a step toward him. I'm going to hit him. I don't care what happens. I'm going to knock his teeth in. "Don't you ever . . . ," I start. I see the nightstick coming.

He fumbles with it a moment—it's one of those sort of hammer-shaped nightsticks with two handles, one to use it as a weapon and one to use it as a shield, and I don't really believe that he'll use it. There are

words in my mouth, and his body is framed in the lights from the car—
red and blue and white—and I don't see his face. The radio in his car
crackles something inaudible. I can see the nightstick. Now he's got it
right, and I can see the polish of it, the places where grip grooves have
been lathe-cut into it on the side handle, and I can see it as it comes
around, but I know he's just doing it to make a point—that he *could*—
and won't really hit me.

There's a flash of pure white light, and then the top of my left ear and
the outside part of my left eye socket explode. My knees wobble, and my
arms are out, and things are spinning as the white subsides and the
mottled darkness returns. There's a pinging sound in the air now and the
rush of wind, and I'm back on the motorcycle, heading for the ground.

My right hand catches at the edge of the pavement: the grit scrapes
the palm; and the other sinks into the loamy, leafy dirt at the bank. Now
my face is in the dirt, and I can smell the rot.

My head is on fire. There are lights in the dirt, and I want to vomit.

I start to get up, but I can't. Sylvia. Herbie's. *Sandy says, "My God,
my manners. Jack, these are my friends Karen and DeeDee." She takes hold
of the sleeves of her friends and nods in the direction of either when she says
her name.*

Now there's real darkness, and it's started to drizzle. I don't know
how much time has passed, but the motorcycle chugs patiently. Darrell's patrol car hisses. He's turned all the lights out except for the
headlights.

I turn over, roll onto my back in the soft earth. Fog is falling.

I can see Darrell moving. Can see the underside of the patrol car, can
see the open door and the underside of the dash. The Motorola FM two-
way radio. It seems very light out. But it can't be dawn.

Now Darrell kneels down beside me. He has his regulation flashlight, and now he's got on his wide-brimmed Stetson with the back
strap, like the state troopers wear. In high school we used to joke that
the back straps were supposed to catch in the burrs of their hair.

The flashlight comes on, and it comes into my eyes. "Stop it,
damnit," I say and bring up my arm to shield my eyes, but a jet of pain
snaps through my head and I have to put my arm down again.

"I'm trying to see if you have a concussion," he says.

"You're a real fuckhead, you know that, Darrell?" I say, but I'm
ashamed by the weak way it comes out.

"I always thought you were going to turn out different, but you're going to wind up just like old Junior Harlan—in jail, worthless. I always thought because of your father and everything," he says but doesn't go on.

I laugh. I mean it to sound derisive, but it comes out weakly, and that hurts too.

"Your pupils are the same size," he says. He turns off the flashlight and sits down next to me.

"It's been a long day," I say, because it seems like eons since I walked through Sylvia's door.

"I used to think your father was the perfect father, I mean looking the way he did, helpful the way he was to everyone." He's on his butt on the side of the road, and he's got his arms around his legs. "The way folks said he'd tried so hard with your mother. I mean people used to say—" He stops, purses his lips. "I don't know—I got no way a knowin', but I used to wish my father was like your father. Even after we moved away I sometimes used to think about him. How hard he did for everybody else."

"I don't talk to him."

"You got a hard head, Jack."

Darrell gets up, and I can hear him sigh—I can hear the keys and whatnot jangle in his pockets. The radio in the patrol car crackles, and then a woman's voice comes on. The woman's voice says what sounds like, "Nero gone crazy," and then I can hear that the woman is black, and I get a view inside a tiny, brightly lit room where the woman is sitting, chunky, middle-aged, a cup of coffee gone cold next to the radio console with its white-and-gray stand-up, push-button microphone.

The leather of Darrell's holster creaks. From down here he looks tall as a mountain. His feet scuff across the pavement. He cuts off my bike, then drags it off its kickstand and brings it to the side of the road where I am. I don't hear the kickstand go down again, but he leaves the bike standing next to my legs. In a minute he's in the patrol car. I can see his feet lift inside and the door close. The car clunks into gear, and the rushing of the engine pushes it away. For a while the roadway is empty. There are birds singing. It's getting close to morning.

Off in the distance, Darrell's car turns around, and in a few minutes it whisks past, leaves bits of twig and leaf whirling in its wake. I don't want to get up. The leaves whirl. Fall comes when I'm lying here. The leaves turn—the maples first, like fire in the hills, and then the others. The oaks are last, and the leaves drift across the road and into the ditch. When cars pass, the leaves whirl and whirl and grind to fine dust. When it rains, they stick to the road, nearly make it disappear. I don't want to go to sleep, so I just lie here and feel the leaves gather round me, feel the rain on my face. My father says, "Let's get to work, boys," but he says it in a dream because Roy is dead. *"Roy is dead, Daddy. I'm the living one."*

"Let's get crackin', Son," he says.

*I'm just gonna sleep a little while longer* is what I think but can't say to him. *"You work by yourself today."*

Y̲ou still steamed about this job?" my father says as he comes around the side of the house, a black-painted wooden toolbox he made in one hand and an orange extension cord slung over the opposite shoulder. He doesn't look at me, but even if he did it'd be hard to know, because most of the time he's inscrutable and won't let you know if he's thinking or feeling anything.

I'm leaning against his pickup truck, waiting for him. I've got a cup of hot black coffee from the percolator in his kitchen, and I'm watching the steam rise and dissipate in the air.

The two of us are doing a countertop job today for Jim Harlan, who is a drunk—or at least a part-time drunk—and it's just like my father's goddamned notion of a man's humility to take a job from someone he knows is never going to pay him. The new countertop is already in the back of the truck. It surprises me that he says anything, because he's usually not the kind to meet anything but work head on.

I don't say anything to him. There's really not much to say. It's almost July and the morning air is cool in the shadows, but in the direct sunlight it is already deadly hot.

"So what do you think?" he says. "It'd be better to get stiffed by a rich man than a workingman?"

I look at him, and I can't see his eyes at all now for his baseball cap and the glare on his glasses. "No," I tell him, "I don't think it'd be better. I'd rather not get stiffed by anyone." I wait a minute, then I add, "I just think it's a lousy idea to take a job from someone you *know* isn't going to pay you."

"I don't know that," he says. "I *don't* know that. I got to give Jim Harlan the same consideration I'd give anyone else."

I shake my head, close my eyes.

"It bothers your pride, doesn't it? You just don't like the idea of maybe working for somebody you think is beneath you."

"I didn't say that." But he knows what I think—that I hate this whole business, not just Harlan, and that like my mother, I cherish the thought of escaping it—but I don't give him the satisfaction of airing it.

"Didn't have to," he says as he turns away. I look at his T-shirt, at his brown arms when he gets out another Winston and lights it. I could hit him now, I really could. It makes my knuckles itch to think of it.

"You want to get the skilsaw?" he says, and for a moment I don't move, only watch the smoke he leaves in the air when he goes around the truck to open the door. I look at the colorless mountains in the distance and the bright blue of the sky.

Wordlessly, I push off the truck and go into the shop. I can hear my father close the tailgate. The saw is at the door, cord wrapped neatly around the handle. I pick it up, come back to the truck, and wedge it up between the toolbox and the side of the truck. When my father starts the truck, there's a fast blue cloud of smoke. He sits inside, waiting, smoking with the window closed, filling up the truck with smoke. I wonder how he can stand it.

We go across town in silence; the tools rattle quietly in the back. My father stares fixedly out the windshield.

When we get to Harlan's trailer on State Street, we haven't spoken since leaving home. We get out, slam the doors. All over the street there are dead garter snakes—"garden snakes" most of the people in town stupidly call them—glassy and rotting in the sun, flies snapping in the rot-smelling air.

"Old Jimbo must have been out with his shovel last night," my father says acridly. He pulls down the tailgate and gets the toolbox. Town is full of garter snakes, so many of them sometimes they make the grass writhe. They mate in balls, a dozen or more sometimes, turning and boiling masses of them. They're harmless, though sometimes they'll chase your heart up into your throat if you step on one. They're good for the land, but it's easy to kill them, and nearly everyone but my father does. My father doesn't approve of killing them, and you can see the disapproval in his eyes as he picks his way through them with his things.

My father lights another cigarette, and we go up the hill, up the broken walk, up to Harlan's wooden porch.

When Harlan opens the door, the scent that comes out is like the Ranchero Grill on Sunday morning. He rubs his messed-up hair with one hand, then picks his Pall Malls from his T-shirt pocket and shakes one from his pack. Since it's morning, he's not drunk. He carries a white, styrofoam cup of coffee in his other hand, and his eyes are bloodshot, startled.

"Morning, Addie," Harlan says. "Morning, Jack."

I nod and listen; no evidence of Junior. Harlan's son, Junior, was a friend of mine a long time ago. He's a big, burly, bear-sized guy who dropped out of school, and spends his time doing I don't know what— drinking or sitting in his old pickup with Sam Ryzinski, sometimes spending the night in jail. The last time I saw him was to get into a fight with him, which I lost.

"Morning, Jimbo," my father says.

We go inside, along the narrow hallway, through the living room, and into the shabby little kitchen. Harlan shows my father where the valve is, and my father turns off the water to the sink.

A trailer like this is not made like a house; all the parts are prefabricated and fastened together with staples. It's not made to be repaired, so you have to be careful tearing it apart because you can do real damage without intending to. My father hardly speaks when he works, and we've worked together for so long we really don't need to say much to one another.

First we disconnect all the plumbing, then set to work tearing out the old counter. The work space is very tight, and as soon as we've been working for half an hour, it starts getting hot, too. It's not rational the way everything my father does irritates me. I keep looking around, expecting to see Junior come into the room.

Harlan watches from the dining room. It's when we actually start taking out the counter, sawing and hammering, that Junior wakes up. He comes to the kitchen, his hair wild and his eyes shot with blood. He lights one of his father's cigarettes and says "Shit" and shakes his head. "How'm I supposed to eat breakfast—," he starts, but his father stops him.

I don't look at him but pay attention to my work, busting up the old countertop and pulling it out.

In a few minutes, after he has come back from the bathroom, Junior says, "How you doing, Jackie boy? How's old Sugarpants?"

"All right," I say. I don't say any more. It is Karen Anderson that he is talking about, and it was about Karen Anderson that we got into the fight.

"Hear you're headin' on back to college soon," he says.

I crouch away from him to pull out staples with a pig's foot. My father doesn't say anything. Neither does his daddy. I have no idea whether either of them know what's gone on between us, but I don't care.

"When you go," Junior says, "why don't you leave old Karen to me?"

I start to say something, start to let the heat in my face move me, but I don't. My father cuts it off. "Why don't you clean up here? I'll go out and get the top and we'll fit it in. Jimbo, you got a garbage can I can use?"

"Jimmy?" the older Harlan says to Junior. "Go get a garbage can."

Junior stands for a moment looking, then crushes the Pall Mall in the ashtray and says, "All right, Daddy" and leaves the room.

When I'm alone in the trailer with Harlan, I don't say anything, I just work, and when I'm finished, I pretend I've still got things to do. That way I don't have to think of anything to say, don't have to look at him. When Junior comes back, I don't say anything to him, I just dump all of the stuff into the garbage can, then sweep up. I guess he's bored with taunting me, or it's not as easy to taunt me when I'm standing up and can look him in the eye. He doesn't say any more. When my father comes back, I help him carry the countertop into the kitchen, and we set to work making it fit.

It takes most of the day to get the job finished, and we work long after I think we ought to have called it finished, but my father's a perfectionist, and we can't do anything half-assed, even for Jim Harlan. Harlan helps us carry the tools to the truck. I take out the garbage, then wait in the hot cab of the pickup. I watch my father on the doorstep, talking with Harlan. I know the conversation has gotten away from the job by now, away from money. They are probably talking about baseball now, or maybe the Redskins. I hate my father suddenly—for being weak, for letting someone like Harlan dick around with him.

They talk for a long time, and finally—the cab is unbearably hot, and I've got to go to the bathroom like crazy—Harlan slaps my father on the back, they laugh, and my father comes down the steps and through the ratty yard. I look away. At the snakes in the road. At the metallic glisten of the flies.

My father gets in the truck. The door slams. He pushes in the cigarette lighter. *Don't light another one of those goddamned things*, I want to say. But I don't.

Halfway home, I break into the silence. "He pay you?" I say. I've thought over asking for a long time, but it comes out wrong. I haven't spoken for too long, and my voice cracks.

"Don't worry," he says, "you'll get paid."

"I don't want to be paid out of your pocket," I say sharply, surprising myself. "I want him to pay."

My father says nothing. In a few moments, he pulls up in the drive and lets me out. He hands me fifty dollars. I say nothing, and at first I don't want to take it. But I take it anyway.

"How much does he owe you?" I say quietly.

"Hundred and twenty-eight dollars," he says. I don't know why he tells me this time. Maybe to goad me.

"He's going to send it?"

"Don't worry about it, Jack. He'll pay me."

When I awaken, I cannot breathe. The air in my room is too hot, too thick. I have been asleep forever. The clock says 11:10. It must be wrong.

I can't get back to sleep, and I keep staring at the ceiling.

After a while, I get up, get dressed without turning on the lights, then go downstairs in the darkness. Outside the night is cool and damp.

I get into my father's pickup—I have a key—roll it down the driveway without turning on the lights, then roll it down the hill away from the house, start it only at the end of the block where I'm certain no one will hear.

I drive across town to Harlan's and sit outside in the dark, looking at the trailer. Inside, the lights are on—in the living room and where I know the kitchen is. I wait, looking to see if Junior is home. I'm almost certain he isn't, his truck's nowhere in sight, but I want to make sure before I go in and do what I know I have to do.

Finally I get out of the truck and walk up the broken walk. It seems spongy, like it's stuck on top of wet peat. I look out for snakes, but I know there are none in the dark. When I go up the wooden steps, I know Harlan can hear me creaking on the boards. Maybe he's ready for me and knows what I am after.

But I knock anyway, and in a moment, Harlan, a Budweiser can in his hand, comes to the door. He looks awake now, but drunk nonetheless. He sways a little, focussing his eyes. "Jack," he says, and I have the impression that he is surprised, wary.

"Come on in, son," he says, ushering me into the trailer and closing the door. "I get you a beer or something?"

I shake my head and stand close to the door. "I just wanted, I just wanted to know if you—if you liked your new countertop," I say, my lungs turning to birds. I'm looking, my eyes going across the tight, cluttered space, ready for Junior. Things don't seem real. The trailer is hot.

"Hell," Harlan says, his body like a sponge for the odor of beer, "it's the best goddamned countertop I've ever seen. Your father—you all do the best work I've ever seen." It's the talk of a drunk. For a moment I'd swear he was going to cry with joy for the beauty of the countertop.

I say, "You like it enough to pay for it?" I wait, let the question soak into the air.

"What are you talking about, boy?" Harlan says, his face turning to red, red rising up through his neck.

"I'm talking about paying my father for the work he's done. The work *we've* done."

"What ever gave you the idea I w-wouldn't?" he says, and from the look on his face I know he's never intended to pay my father. *I'm right.*

"I never said," I say. I look at Harlan, press his eyes. "I just want to make sure."

Harlan laughs, his broad, red-lipped, elastic face moving sadly, like death. "You're all right, Jack," he says when he's finished laughing and his slack, old expressionlessness returns. "I wish my boy'd go around sticking up for me."

His words make my fists clench, and I step close to him. "If that's what you think I'm doing," I say, "You're wrong. I'm not sticking up for my father. I'm worried about getting paid myself." I move closer to him, look him hard in the eyes, make him back up. His trailer is very quiet. So is the world outside. You can hear trucks miles out on the highway, tires whining, climbing the mountains out in the distance.

He turns away from me, but I grab him and pull him around. His breath is almost intoxicating, his eyes slosh like oysters. "I want a check by Wednesday," I say.

"No need to threaten," Harlan says, pulling away. For the first time, it feels like his trailer has come into focus—even after today, after spending all day here, I didn't see it, didn't pay attention—but now I can see how filthy it is, how old and tiny and sad, and how pathetic Harlan really is, old and beaten, the skin of his face turned red with broken blood vessels, nothing to do in his life but sit in this empty, silent trailer all night, drinking and waiting for his obscene son to come home. I'm disgusted with myself because it feels like I've just threatened an old woman or an invalid. A moment ago this was the right thing. Right now I don't know what it is.

He looks at me, as though waiting for something, and I turn away, slap him on the shoulder.

I'm going down the wooden steps in front of the trailer when a truck cuts through the silence. I can see it way down the road, the lights scarring the darkness, catching the moisture in the air. I can hear the clank and bang of it, and it sails around the corner and onto the weedy yard, throwing color into the grass, the road, the blue fields beyond. It's Junior, and for some crazy reason I'm glad it's him. I've got this idea in my head that he'll be ripped drunk, that he'll try to pick a fight with me and I'll blow him away.

It seems like a long time between when his truck shuts off and when he gets out. He sort of falls heavily, so the grassy dirt beneath him gives a hollow thump. He takes two steps toward me. "Jack?" he says. I can't tell whether he's drunk, but then he has to be. "What'cho doin' here?" he says.

I shrug, but I don't know if he can see this in the dark. He walks slowly up toward me, and when he comes into focus I can see that he's already been beat up. Bad, too. His face is swollen and blackened with blood and dirt. There's blood in his hair, and it sticks up wildly. "Shit," he says and rocks a moment, his eyes going out of focus, then he just falls right over in front of me. He goes so fast I can hear the air sweep out of him, can hear his jaw clack shut with the impact.

I don't know whether to leave him there or go back inside and get his daddy. For a moment, I just look at him. Then I turn and go up the rattling wooden stairs again and knock.

"Junior's out here, on the lawn," I say. "Looks beat up and just fell over."

Harlan sighs. It's a tremendous note of weariness, full of sorrow and a million other things I don't understand. For a long time he just looks at me wet eyed and old.

"You just leave him there," Harlan says finally. "You just leave him there." Then he turns and closes the door, and the lawn is quiet again.

"Where'd you go last night with the pickup?" my father says in the morning. His question takes me off guard, takes me out of the cool early sunshine, out of the damp of the grass and air, and for a moment I can see the dark, broken-veined skin of Harlan's face.

"Nowhere," I say, hoping my father will drop it.

But he doesn't drop it. "I saw you roll it out of the drive. I saw you go. You go to Harlan's?" He does not look at me but cocks his head sideways and rubs his fingertips together. His voice is almost jovial. He looks at Croutys' house next door and down the gray, winter-cracked street to where it falls off into timber.

"No," I say, watching my father's fingertips move, watching them stop.

My father looks at me, his eyes gone clear and hard. "I got a check this morning," he says. "I told Harlan he could wait till the end of the month, until his pension check comes." He purses his mouth. "You know anything about that check? It was taped to the windshield." He squeezes the words dry as he speaks, and they come out even, and hard.

"I don't know anything about it," I say.

My father squints, takes a step forward. "I think you do," he says, his lips white, the check appearing suddenly in his hand like a scarf pulled from a magician's fingertips.

"All right, I went to Harlan's," I say. "I was going to bust his head if he didn't pay me."

My father stops, purses his mouth, then turns to the side and starts to laugh at me, like I'm just a stupid goddamned hotheaded kid who doesn't know his place.

We are standing at the edge of the drive, out in the dew-damp grass. Without really knowing I'm doing it, I wind up to hit him as hard as I can muster. It's completely out of the blue, how it happens. It takes years to happen, my arm straining, pulling through the summer air— every pore open, the wind coming against my knuckles—and he is completely off guard. I catch him in the soft of his cheek, and when the flesh of his mouth flattens against his teeth and skull, I can feel the *bam* sharp sting of it in my knuckles. He's off balance, and he reels backward. In a moment he's on the grass, sprawled out, his eyes blinking, his baseball cap off, his glasses askew. I guess it's surprised hell out of him that his son would pop him, because he starts to laugh. In two seconds he's laughing hysterically. I don't know what to do, and I just stand there wringing my hands. He stops laughing. He looks at me, and his eyes are soaked. He gets up off the ground, straightens his hat and glasses, and, suddenly embarrassed, he walks briskly around the side of the house to his shop.

I follow him, to apologize. The wet grass and the white side of the house swim by. A dog barks somewhere in the distance. He's standing by the door of his shop, staring into the back of the house. He's got his hat and his glasses on, and I have no idea what the expression on his face means.

He purses his mouth. Looks away from me. Inscrutable is what he is, and what he's always been. "I'm going in to get a cup of coffee," he says. "You want one?"

# CROWS

Some days in summer, his work done, Addie drives out into the fields with his rifle and shoots at crows. It's hard to hit a crow with the .30-.06, and he makes it impossible by leading them too much or aiming at them directly in flight. It is enough to be in the field, the sun and air on his face, the blades of corn sawing at his bare arms.

Other times when he goes into the fields, he puts his rifle down and takes off his clothes. He doesn't do anything but stand there, surrounded by the dense, coarse green, some crazy thrill going through him like a million years ago skinny-dipping with friends. Standing there he hopes for some kind of spiritual release, but most often, after dressing and going back to his truck, he feels foolish, and worried that someone might have seen him.

He begins to find work pleasant again, begins to lose himself in it again the way he hasn't done since even before Alison—working for great stretches of time on projects of his own. He tears apart the basement of his house, then hangs sheetrock, puts up shelves, and paints. He thinks of building himself a new house, outside of town somewhere, and even draws up some rough plans.

He thinks of taking a trip—to Bermuda or Europe. The idea awakens in him a sense of possibility that he hasn't known in some time. He visits a travel agent. Later, at home, poring over the travel brochures with a cup of coffee and a series of Winstons, he begins to realize—as if he has never realized it before now—that simply by putting down money and driving to the airport, he can be anywhere in the world in a matter of hours.

For weeks he spends his time in his head, imagining the places in the brochures, imagining the time he could have there. He thinks of his son. He thinks of the South Seas. He thinks of the Anderson girl, and somehow, foolishly, he imagines them together on a beach somewhere, or in a French hotel with an ancient elevator and a bed that is bathed in soft morning sunshine.

In this season it is as though something is falling away from him, not like sanity or stability, but something useless, like old skin. He writes to his son at Jack's Richmond address, jotting a PLEASE FORWARD on the front of the envelope. He tells him of his life alone, but there is no answer, no offer to visit.

# SANDY

We've been painting all day because of the rain—some shitass little job Harry cooked up at the last minute to save the day—and since then Dean and I've been drinking at Cotton's, a sorry little rundown cinderblock bar on a sidestreet in Middleridge that opens at six in the morning and caters mainly to devout alcoholics. I've got paint flecks all over my arms and face, and my face aches where Darrell hit me, and my shoulder aches where Sylvia bit me.

I leave Dean alone in the bar to finish his beer, and the afternoon feels heavy, like it will only grow heavier as the evening comes. It rained all morning and most of the early afternoon, and now it's begun to clear.

The breeze is going, and water stands on the hoods and roofs of cars in trembling drops. With the taste of beer in my mouth, I go toward my car, which is parked nearby at a meter that has run down.

I'm reaching down to unlock the door when I look up and there's Sandy Van Kalkenberg. She's standing on the busted concrete sidewalk on the other side of the street, like maybe she saw me a block away and followed me to where she is and just stopped. A shadow drapes over me and the car, and where the sun strikes on the other side of the street, a long, angular patch where Sandy stands, the wet has dried up. The sky is rough with clouds. I stop what I'm doing, stare at her, jingle the keys, then grab them tightly in my hand. She's wearing a T-shirt, jeans, heavy Western-style boots that because she's so small make her feet seem disproportionately large. She looks good, a little redneck. Determined. There's a hard look in her eyes.

"I thought it was you," she says. "I seem to be running into you everywhere." Her voice is softer than I expect it to be.

"Hi," I say and involuntarily look around to see if Chalky's with her.

"I was just getting my hair trimmed down at Sally's—you know, Sally Rogers has a place on Quimble."

"I didn't know."

"Well," she laughs. She starts across the street toward me. "You wouldn't know. It's a ladies' place, so how would you know?"

"I was sorta worried about you."

"About me?" She laughs, but the laugh is wooden, and the smile drifts off. "Don't," she says. For a moment she looks old and wise and impervious, but then the look softens. "You don't need to worry 'bout me."

She's close to the front of the car, in the shade now. I don't see any difference in her hair from when I saw her in Herbie's parking lot. She brings her arms up and hugs herself. There's gooseflesh on her arms. "It's cold in the shade," she says. I look at her eyes, but at the same time, the word "boobs" goes through my head because of how her arms frame her chest, and I can't help thinking how perfect a word it is.

"It's nice to run into you—," she starts, then, now that her eyes are accustomed to the shade, she sees the side of my head. "Jesus," she says. She's next to me now, and her hand floats up, and very gingerly she touches a cool finger to my skull. "What the—"

"You know Darrell Planey?" I say.

"Sure," she says, withdrawing her hand and folding her arms together again.

"I sort of ran into his nightstick last night."

"Good idea," she says and breaks a wry grin. It's something I might have said. "Maybe I should worry about you."

"We go back a long way," I say. "We grew up together, but it was a stupid thing to do. He nailed me pretty good."

This makes her reach out and touch my face again. "I'd say so." I can see her bare arm, can see the texture of her skin and the place where it goes inside the sleeve of her T-shirt: the softer skin, the shaved under-arm. I can see the shape of her mouth and the single, fine red vein in the white of her right eye. The cool of the air has made her nipples pucker, and I can see them through her bra and T-shirt. I try to hold my breath because she smells so good it makes me light-headed. There's something about women that just paralyzes the hell out of me—I don't mean in a fearful way. It's an amazing thing about women: sex could be the farthest thing from your mind, and then you see a beautiful woman and suddenly to look at her becomes nearly an obsession; you feel irremedia-bly cheated if you cannot look at her—the swell of her hips, the curve of her butt and breast—and keep looking.

In a moment she puts her hand down, and we just stand here, damp pavement, damp sidewalk. Kids playing at the elementary school two blocks over, cars shushing past, a long way away the sound of semi tires whining against the highway.

I look at her and in her eyes I see something I haven't seen in a woman's eyes before, but as soon as I think I have figured out what it is, I can't find it anymore. The world should have been assembled differently—men and women shouldn't have been put at such odds.

"You're going to loan me some books," she says. I'm staring at her, not meaning to but stuck on her face.

"Anytime," I say, thinking as I say it that she's not serious.

"How about right now?" she says, and the words make my heart jump up in the back of my throat. I try to think, but my mind is blank—all I can think of is Sylvia Nickerson last night and the same thing happening with Sandy. No.

I wait, and suddenly my arms are cold. "Sure, okay."

"I'll meet you at your house."

"You want to follow me?"

She nods. "My car is around the corner. Open up and you can drop me off, then I'll follow." It goes through my head what one of my professors in school said about *Lolita*: "It's a tradition of literature that the woman always seduces the man—what we have to decide is whether there is some fundamental truth to that condition, or if it's nothing more than the product of the male imagination."

It feels like it's been years since I've had a woman in my car. There's trash on the floor—old newspapers, Dean's cigarette cellophanes—I won't let him throw them out the window. The ashtray overflows with his butts. "Just kick it out of the way," I say. "There's nothing important."

My hands tingle with the light of nerves. Everything feels lighter when there's a woman around. In the old days, during college, when I went out with Karen. In Richmond, with Jean. It always seemed to me like the simple presence of a woman would change everything, but then never having a woman around when I was growing up made them seem rare as aliens.

The car feels empty when she climbs out and gets into her Torino. I watch her, the narrow shape of her jeans, the piece of T-shirt tail starting to come out at the hip. She starts the car, then waves. I let the clutch out slowly, drift through the cloud of rich blue smoke her car leaves in the air, and head out of town. I watch her in the mirror as she backs out of her parking space and pulls behind me, the tiny woman in the huge car. She looks good in the car, confident, redneck—an arm propped on the open window and hair flying.

My trailer looks shabby and old to me when I get out of the car and wait for her to follow me. Her boots pop gravel as she comes around her car and follows me down past the aluminum shed.

"God, it's quiet here," she says. The silence hits you when you first come out here, cut off your car, and get out into the absolute absence of sound. It makes your normal voice seem overwhelming.

I unlock the door, then search around inside for the light switch.

"It's kind of spare," I say, meaning it to be wry. "I don't really have a lot of stuff anymore." We go into the narrow living room, and there are boxes piled around. Books, mainly. Some of the boxes are open where I've gone looking for particular things, but most are closed. I keep them against the walls and use them as chairs.

"Why don't you have any stuff?" she says.

"I left it all behind," I say, not looking at her but going for the kitchen to get a glass of water—mainly for something to do.

"Where?"

"Richmond—you want something to drink?"

"No thanks. You like country music?"

I look at her a moment for the out-of-the-blueness of the question. "No," I say. "Not really."

"Me either," she says. "Chalky does."

The kitchen of the trailer is about seven feet wide and is next to the rear bedroom. There's a counter and a rack of cabinets that separate the kitchen from the dining area, and I can't see her for the cabinets as I pour a glass of water and gulp it.

"But you brought books?" she says when I don't say anything for a while.

"I don't know why, really. I don't even know why I left, really." I brush the dust off an empty kitchen shelf with the side of my hand, then rub my hands together. "It wasn't very sensible, I guess, but they were the only things I felt very attached to."

"Yeah." She laughs through her nose. "When I left home I took a teddy bear with me. How's that for corny?" She rubs her nose with the back of her hand. "Chalky thought it was real cute. But I was only sixteen. Or not quite sixteen. Just a baby. God, when I think of what a baby I was."

I'm standing now at the side of the cabinets, in front of the door to the rear bedroom, and my hands are cold and my head and shoulder are sore. I'm stuck here, knowing I could probably sleep with her but also knowing that I nearly desperately don't want to for all sorts of complicated reasons, not the least of which is that I like her, suddenly, chemically, instinctively, more than I've liked anyone in a long time.

"Why'd you leave home?" I say because it's easy to imagine her with a teddy bear, and I like the picture.

"Why'd you? Lot of time reasons are just reasons and not much else."

Because she wants to be evasive, I stand here and stare at her to make her say more.

She laughs at my silence. "No particular reason. Just boredom. Restlessness. Fucked-up family, you know." She has her hands stuffed into the pockets of her jeans and shrugs.

"Fucked-up family?"

"You ain't gonna let me change the subject, are you?"

"No."

"I'd goddamned well like to, though, because I ain't too proud of my past anymore."

Sometimes it makes the skin on your neck crawl to hear just a word of truth from someone. These particular words, *because I ain't too proud*, and the way she says them, half-regretful, half-resigned, blow a hole in the tissue of what I've assumed about her until now. Suddenly, I can see a million things about her as a woman—but mostly I can see how at this stage of her life she's backpedaling on the track of regret.

It makes me want to leap out and grab hold of her to keep her from blowing away, but I don't. It's maybe a man's notion that a woman will blow away because she's more insubstantial than he is. Maybe we want them to blow away without us.

She stands in silence and smacks her hands together, and then we just stand here for a while looking at one another. A bloom of sheer panic floats up in my chest. For a second, looking at her is like looking over a cliff, and the rush of it jams through me, congealing the saliva in my throat, paralyzing my hands and arms. I just want to stare at her. Keep staring. For a minute, I do, but the panic makes me choke a little. She turns—boots, jeans, hair—and looks out the window. What a weird place the world is sometimes.

"What do you feel like reading?" I say, finally, voice thin from lack of use.

"You decide." Her voice is quiet now, and the softness of it changes the trailer. Makes the inside of it soft, secret.

*The Sun Also Rises* is a good place to start," I say. "But the question is whether I can find it."

I'm going by her across the hollow wood-linoleum of the floor toward the other room where most of the boxes are, and she says, "Jack?" Just the simple single syllable of my name, soft, damp. I stop dead and look at her. The linoleum is dull from age, and in places it's puckered. She's got her bare arms up on the windowsill, and I look at the shape of her, at the fall of her hair on her shoulders, at her worn blue jeans and her boots. "Do you want to sleep with me?" She's not looking at me but out the window. I can see in my mind what it would be like stripping her: on her skin the lines from her underpants and jeans, the hair matted, the flesh around her breasts creased from her bra. I don't say anything, because I don't want to say no. Except this feels like something I have to say no to, something I have to do everything possible to avoid ruining.

I force myself into the other room and kneel down on the floor and start rooting around in the closest box, just shucking books and stacking them up on the floor, too flustered to pay attention to them. From the other room, her voice echoing a little, she says: "It's okay. I understand. A lot of guys are afraid of Chalky."

"Fuck you, Sandy," I say. The sharpness of the words surprises me, and I'd like to gulp them back too as soon as they're out. I take a deep breath and look at the books I've just pulled out of the box. *Bury My Heart at Wounded Knee, Bullfinch's Mythology, Luis Bunuel.* But then I just sit down in the corner, collapsed by the weight of things. She doesn't say anything, but she doesn't stalk out either.

"It really isn't Chalky," I say and then watch her for a long time. "It's you I'm scared of." When I hear my words it only feels as if I've dug myself in deeper, because I can't explain what I would explain if I could. She starts to laugh but stops when she sees the look on my face.

There are probably hours of daylight left, but the sun is deep in the trees now and the trailer is getting dark. I'm in the shadows when she comes through the doorway from the other room. "I never met anybody like you," she says. "And I ain't sure I mean that as a compliment."

I pick up a box and put it on my lap. It's still sealed shut with clear cellophane tape, and I tear at it. At first it won't come, and I yank more until it rips down the side and books fly out. Among the books is the paperback copy of *The Sun Also Rises* I bought in college. I push the books off my lap and get up. It takes a lot of effort. A wave of dizziness hits me as soon as I'm upright, and I have to bend over a moment to get the blood back into my head. Now the bruise on the side of my head starts to throb. I take a step toward her and hand her the book. When she reaches out to take it, I don't let go, and she looks at me. She says, "Why did you get into a fight with Planey?"

"He said something about my mother. He knows the right buttons to push—like I say, we go way back."

As soon as she hears me say "mother," she cracks a smile. "That's kinda sweet," she says.

"It's not sweet. Sweet is one of the two or three things it wasn't."

She squints but doesn't stop looking at me. For a little while we just stand here. I'm only average height, but it feels as if I tower over her. "I can see how maybe you'd make somebody feel like shit just talking to them," she says. I can't tell if there's anger in her voice.

I lean toward her. Maybe there's a moment when she thinks I'm going to grab hold of her—a moment when I think how easy it would be and how good it would feel—but I reach past her and push the door open.

The air outside seems much richer than the thin air in the trailer. "Let's go outside," I say, but I don't need to say it. Her boots knock across the porch and down the stairs.

"I better go," she says and starts up the path.

"You don't have to." I sit down on the porch and hope she'll come back across the bare black path and sit down too. "I don't want you to."

"It'd probably make more sense," she says. And then I get up and come across the space between us and take hold of her face and kiss her softly on her cheek. Her cheek is so soft you want to eat it. "I do want to sleep with you," I say. "It just isn't right right now." She stares at me, mouth pressed closed, eyes steady, and suddenly she looks like a little girl who's about to cry. She reminds me of my father for a moment—the eternally tough and impassive exterior suddenly appearing to give way. And then, like his face, hers snaps back to its impassivity. Except this glimpse of her vulnerability leaves me hung out and ringing.

"Jack," she says.

"Yeah?"

"There's something I've been wondering since we talked the other day. I don't mean to be nosy, but I look around at Dean and Chalky, and I just wonder why the hell you're here."

"Gotta be somewhere," I say and smile, but it makes the ground beneath me feel less steady. She still looks at me with the same expression, as if to say, *Now it's my turn to pursue you.* "I don't know. I wish I knew. I'm here because I want to be alone."

"What do you do alone?"

"Read. Think. Walk. Try to figure things out."

She waits for me to explain, and I don't. I want to touch her again, but I know if I did it would set us on the completely wrong path. Up the hill there's a cluster of young spruce, and forty or more doves flutter from tree to tree in what looks like almost a game of tag or musical chairs. The birds are gray-white, and they burst from tree to tree, cooing and hovering. I look at them and shake my head in bewilderment.

She looks, then looks back at me. "So that's why you don't have a phone?" she says, allowing herself for now to be satisfied with an incomplete, evasive answer.

"Part of it."

She looks at me for a long time. It's an appraising look, a look Karen Anderson might have given me, and it makes me step sideways, shove my hands in my pockets.

"Thanks for the book," she says. "I'll let you know how it is." Now she turns and heads up the path.

"My pleasure. And I want to know what you think." Wooden, constricted by my own heart.

She doesn't say another word, doesn't turn around, so I go back inside the trailer and shut the door. Up the hill, I can hear her car blast to life, then take off. She hits the accelerator, and gravel sprays over the side of my car and back into the woods.

I lie down on the dining room floor and look at the dirty ceiling. I want to scream. I know I've fucked this up. It sings out shrill and strong that I've fucked it up. And I didn't even know there was something to be fucked up. But there was the finest thread hanging between us, and all I did was talk wooden circles. And the thing that surprises me is how angry I am. I don't even know at what. Chalky. Myself. Now, when the most I want to do is get up and smash my fist against the wall, I keep myself still, breathing evenly, just to show myself that I can.

# THE HADLEYS

My grandparents' house was at the edge of town, on the eastern end. The town, Hadleysburg, was named for them, for their family, but they seem to have no relationship at all to it. I never saw them in a store, never saw either of them anywhere but at the house or in a car. Since my mother died, my father had nothing to do with them, except when we were still little to take my brother and me for annual visits, during which he would sit in the car and wait while Roy and I sat inside, stifled in our suits, waiting for our grandparents to say something. "How was it?" he would say afterward, but it was inexplicable.

The furniture was pristine, overwhelming, gave the impression it would swallow you if you did anything but sit stiffly on your hands.

There was hardly more evidence of Mother there than at home. She was nothing at all to anyone except a trail of genes that ended abruptly with us.

Before I left town for college I went to visit on my own. Though I knew how it had always been—the silences, the utter discomfort of their lives—I had some idea that it would be somehow completely different. Maybe I thought they would hand me a check, but I had imagined them, had convinced myself they were warm, caring, a way they never had been.

Up the long driveway, wearing the shirt and tie I wore to the prom, my shirt still wrinkled and smelling vaguely of perfume.

The sky is blue, and the fences trail down the green hillsides like bursts of electric current. It's hot, but the air is dry and birds sing in the distance. It takes a long time for anyone to answer the door, and when someone does, I am led inside. I have the same sense that I have always had—that coming to their house is as unreal as coming to Oz. My grandfather is slender, tall, bluish in appearance. He folds his hands over his knee and stares. His breath has the scent of age. My grandmother comes through the room and looks at me, then continues along, her suit rustling, her back hunched with age. I want from them, and they do not give. I have always wanted from them. They do not understand what want is.

"I'm afraid she doesn't recognize anything but W&L," he says. "Virginia is a hotbed of left-wing sentiment." It could be a joke in another man's mouth. He smiles vaguely.

Washington and Lee is where he and his father and his father's father went—where my mother would have gone had she not drawn the second X chromosome. Instead, my mother went to UVA. I have never thought of it before, but the vague smile he gives leads me to believe that her going there might have been an affront to my grandmother. "For Hadley men," he says. He brushes imaginary lint off his knee, and I imagine this to be his judgement of me, of my brother and my father, and I want to hit him.

*But I'm not a Hadley*, I am surprised to find myself thinking—I've always fiercely prized the idea of my being part Hadley as my own singular heritage. My brother was not Hadley at all. Never liked to come here and sit out their petrification, never found a way to accept it as part of him. No matter how stultifying my visits were, I always thought of myself as one of them, an intellectual. Never a workingman.

For a moment, I have a wild sense of panic and then anger. My mother left me nothing—a nothing my father won't even let me have. I can tell by looking at my grandfather that her marriage to my father and subsequent suicide is and was their great shame in the world. *Roy sits across from me and scowls. Daddy says, go, and so we have come. Our grandfather turns his head, and Roy makes a face where he can't see. I sit properly, refuse to let him make me laugh.*

My relationship to them edges toward understanding, then slips away again.

"Oh," he says, and it sounds entirely of another conversation.

In a moment, he gets up and wanders away. I sit stiffly where I am for a long time, wondering if one of them will return. The house is huge and hollow as a lung. Sunlight sears the sparkling windows.

Finally I get up and slip out silently into the spring afternoon.

# THE
# FUNDAMENTALS

We lean on the hood of my car, and I give my newspaper to Dean. He laughs—he's embarrassed to be doing this—but he lights a cigarette and takes the paper from me, folds it out comically like a TV dad at the dinner table, and squints back the cigarette smoke.

"Where do we start?" he says.

"Where do you want to start?"

He shakes his head in bewilderment.

"How about the comics?" I say.

He laughs. "All right." He sheafs through the paper, but I stop him.

"Just have a look at the index," I say. "That'll tell you what page."

He searches the front page and finds the index in the corner. "All right," he says. "Comics. I don't see it."

"Maybe it's under something different. Like—" I lean over and scan the index "—there. Entertainment Page." I point at it, hope he can read it. I repeat the words. He turns the page.

He stops at "Peanuts." "Lucy says, 'Linus, I want to have desperate, incestuous love with you on your little blanket.' "

"Lucy ain't even on the page, Buzz."

We go through "The Phantom," "Dick Tracy." He sounds out the words, and I help him. His face freezes in frustration. He can read a little, but I guess he's functionally illiterate. It hurts to see the frustration in his face; it's the frustration of a seven-year-old, preserved in a thirty-year-old's body. As he reads, I think about the other night—I've been thinking about it a lot: if he knew my brother. It's a silly idea. The Air Force is a big place.

People come and go from their apartments. Two little girls in plastic diapers wander up to stare at us, then wander away, back to a bare dirt patch in the front of the building.

He stumbles, mispronounces the words. I help him along, prompt him. The words are some kind of taffy he's pulling off the page— flavorless, all peculiar mass—and once he gets them off the page they start to take shape, begin to acquire flavor.

By the time we get all the way through the comics, it's dark out. I'm getting restless. He stands looking at me, blue eyes incandescent, hands in his back pockets, the newspaper tucked under his arm. There are lights on in the apartments in his building. In the apartment next to his, a fat lady in curlers hovers over a sink, rinsing dishes behind tendrils of hanging ivy.

"Thanks, man," he says.

"Get the paper tomorrow, and we'll do the same thing." I slap him on the shoulder. "Tonight, man, go back over the comics."

"Homework!" He grins.

"Seriously. Remember the words and what they look like. It's all practice. The next time you see the words you won't have any problem."

"You're crazy, man, doing this with a fuckup like me."

"You're no more of a fuckup than I am. And what else have I got to do?"

# AFTER
# AND AGAIN

Sometimes in the evenings when Addie drives—out to the Vet's home to play cards or just to get out on the road and unwind—he drives by her house, just to look, just to see if he can see her. He always goes in the dark so she won't see his truck, but he never sees her.

For a while, it is almost as if she has disappeared. There is no sign of her, not at the bank, not in the grocery, not anywhere. Sometimes he's certain he sees her car in the bank lot, but when he goes in, he doesn't see her. Maybe she's left town. Then again, maybe it's just coincidence.

# BLACK IDEAS

All day it's the same: lawns rotating into the past, mowing, leaf raking, mulching. The elemental fragrance of commingled gas and oil and smoke and shredding leaves and grass. My arms are hard, and my shoulders shake, and my legs are dogged. Endless. The shadows are longer, and the light is softer. No longer the hard white wash of summer sun but the softer, bluer light of fall.

I eat lunch with Dean on the tailgate of Harry's truck while Harry's off collecting checks from customers. My sandwich is soft with the warmth of the pickup, potato chips are smashed from sitting on them. Dean drinks iced tea from a thermos and reads the comics to me. He gets better, but he seems bored with it already. I can sense his restlessness. He keeps looking up, expecting Harry's stumpy figure to appear and embarrass him.

"Hey man," he says, eyes like blue neon, "I saw that lady, fourteen fifteen, with one of her friends. Fourteen fifteen, man, she looks like she could lock and rock, but her friend looked run hard and put away wet." Dean laughs.

I've never met any of Sylvia's friends—I always wanted to avoid the complications of a "real" relationship. I watch Dean look over the comics. He starts in on the comics again but folds up the newspaper when Harry starts up the street.

"I don't know why you keep worrying about him so much," I say.

"The fucker, I don't know. I just don't wanna give him any leg up on me."

"He's just some Joe, Dean. He's forty-five and mowing lawns for a living. If he was really some goddamned tycoon, he'd be on Wall Street with all the other high rollers."

After lunch I do Sylvia's lawn, and she invites me inside. Today she looks older, plainer. It's late in the afternoon and I'm tired from working, and when I come through the door into the air-conditioning it makes me sleepy. I look at her, and she feels the way reading must feel for Dean—slightly distant, a concept impossible to grasp firmly. It's bizarre how you can be so intimate with someone and know so little about them at the same time.

At the corner of the kitchen there is a knickknack shelf I've passed many times before but never really noticed. There are dozens of turtles on it—porcelain, jade, glass, plastic. Turtles and more turtles. I look at the shelf and then at her.

"I'm an absolute turtle fanatic," she says, by the refrigerator. It pucks open, and she gets out a pitcher of lemonade. Already this seems so worn—refrigerator, lemonade, desolate fucking. Already this seems as worn as Richmond seemed after nearly two years there—two years that have condensed in my mind into three or four moments—the rest of it I can no longer account for.

I look at Sylvia again, now blankly. She puts the pitcher on the counter and comes back to where I'm standing. "Needs dustin'," she says and picks up the nearest turtle and wipes it on her sleeve. "Each one of them has a story. Each one of them." She looks up at me and smiles, then pushes a wisp of hair off her forehead. "I got this one in Daytona Beach, Florida, at a little shop called Mystic Terrapin. A terrapin's a turtle, in case you didn't know."

I look at her blankly, in disbelief.

"I had fun the other night," she says. I try to think. I can't remember which night she is talking about. None of them stand out.

"Come on back tonight," she says.

I raise my eyebrows but say nothing.

When I go out the door, she says, "I ain't gonna let you go, no sirree. I ain't gonna let you go." It seems apropos of nothing at all, and for a moment I just stare at her in her doorway. For a moment, I see the look that Jean used to give me, and I look away, hurry the mower up the hill. I first came here that evening because it felt edgy, unreal, as though there were things to be discovered, and then because her friend was here and it felt like I was taking something from him. Now it all seems pathetic and shameful. I look down at her from the edge of her yard and wonder at the emptiness and stupidity of it—and wonder if she can see the regret in my face.

On the porch in the evening, sitting with a can of beer; a pair of headlights needles up through the woods. It's one of those warm fall evenings where the dark is earlier but the weather has yet to go off to the damp and cold of winter. The color of the light, the feel of the air, and the smell of the leaves remind me of the years when I was in school, and how after supper Roy and I and the others in the neighborhood whose parents would let them out after supper would play until we shivered in our T-shirts and could no longer see anything but the stripes on the ends of the football.

There are only four houses near here, and the headlights have passed all but mine and the other trailer that's farther up the lake. The sound carries—the gravel beneath the tires, the rush of the engine. When the car comes over the hill, you can see the beams of the two headlights clearly defined in the darkness; on the hill, blacking out everything around them, they look like tubes of light, the search-lights of a spaceship. You'd never guess the geometric precision of them when you sit behind the wheel on a highway and push along at the darkness.

Darrell Planey makes a pass up here every few nights. It could be someone lost. And it also could be someone looking for me. Sometimes I dream my father will show up one evening, that maybe we'll have a beer together and he'll tell me how he found me, tell me how his life has changed since we last talked. Sometimes I dream that someone from the Post Office (I don't know why it's the Post Office, but it always is) comes up from town to tell me that my father had died and been buried a week ago. God.

The car stops at the nock in the trees where I park my car. It looks like Sandy's car, and a wire of adrenaline pricks up in my arms and legs.

All the time I'm hungry for her. All the time I think about leaning forward and kissing the soft soft skin of her cheek.

The headlights cut off and then the motor, and there's complete silence in the woods. A door creaks open. Then the other. "This is it?" says Chalky. The sound of his voice immediately puts me on edge.

"Yeah," comes Dean's voice.

"I thought my place was in the middle of fucking nowhere, but this fucker beats the band," Chalky says. People talk loudly like that when they come out here—they have no idea how easily their voices carry. Dean's been out here before, so he knows and talks more softly. Then there's another voice, one I don't recognize. "You sure there's a fuckin' house here, Deanyman? I don't see a fuckin' house."

"It's a trailer, man."

They're in the woods now, past the shed. "That it?" says the third voice.

"That's a shed, Buck," Dean says. Dean's the only one of the three who doesn't have a cigarette going. The orange cones bob and disappear and bob again in the darkness. The sky is clear enough that when you're used to the darkness you can see everything. If you had a rifle and the volition, you could pick them off like a sniper at the trenches.

"Hey, bro," I say to Dean when he gets close enough that he should be able to make me out in the darkness.

"Hey bro," he says. "Chalky was around, and I thought we'd come out and see how your head was healin'."

"Don't you have any fuckin' lights?" Buck says.

"It's healin' okay," I say. Then I stand up. Buck is a friend of Chalky's and Dean's, and I've met him once or twice before. His real name is Berke McClanahan, but they call him Buck. Like Chalky's real name is Vaughan Van Kalkenberg, and they call him Chalky.

"You got something against the dark?" I say to Buck, but I don't give him a chance to answer. "Seems pretty damned nice to me, the dark."

I don't intend to be prickly, but where Chalky's concerned, I can't help myself.

"No wonder Planey leveled this guy," Buck says. "This guy's got a smart-as-hell mouth. You got a smart-as-hell mouth, man."

"Thank you," I say.

"You should shut up and have a beer," he says. Dean's holding a six-pack in either hand, and Buck yanks a can from the six that's closest to him and hands it to me. It's slightly warm—bought on the highway at the 7-Eleven and sitting in the car for half an hour. I can't see the label, but I pop it open and drink from it.

"Should we go inside, or should we sit out here?" Chalky says. I can see the flash of their faces in the darkness as he lights another cigarette with a disposable butane.

"Considering Jack ain't got no furniture inside," Dean says, "I'd say we stay out here."

"You got no furniture?" Buck says.

"Left it all with my old girlfriend," I say. Even with Dean here, I keep thinking there's a reason Chalky's here, and the only reason I can think of is Sandy.

"She musta been something," Buck says.

I sit back down, now against the wall, with one leg pulled up against me and the other pointed out to the side, away from where Chalky and Buck are sitting. Buck's butane fires and lights his face. He's got a joint pressed between his lips, and now I can smell the sharp scent of reefer.

Buck's at least ten years older than the rest of us. Been in the service, been in prison—the way he talks about it, prison is a run-of-the-mill thing a guy goes through, just like the service—lot of guys go to prison for assault, assault and battery, maybe possession. He has big, soft-looking ears that look prosthetic, maybe made of pale glove leather. His whole face has that soft, baggy glove leather look. And he has a wide, low-set nose, the septum of which extends beyond the nostrils and descends halfway down his upper lip.

He sucks deeply on the reefer—the fire zips down the side of it, and he licks his finger, touches the wet tip to the paper before he hands it to Chalky. Chalky takes a big hit off it too, and now the one-sided coal extends halfway down the side. He hands it to me. It's damp and hot and smells of burned paper. I take a hit off it; it has the rich, densely textured smoke of exceptionally strong dope. I hold the smoke down, pass it to Dean. Ready to cough, I look at Dean, then at Chalky. There has to be a reason.

By the time the reefer comes around for another hit, I'm already beginning to float off, and I know the buzz has barely started. The second hit has a distance to it, and I make it a small one, pass it, then drink from the beer.

"Ain't there fishin' around here?" Buck says.

"Fuck yeah," Dean says, like a hostess desperate for all the guests to get along well. "Good fishin' too. There's a lake right over your shoulder. I caught a seven-pound blue cat in here."

"Seven pound? That s'posed to be a big fish?" Buck says.

"It is when you catch it with your dick. Anyway, I'm talkin' manmade lakes, dude." Chalky takes the jay from Buck when he passes it, and I watch his nose and mouth in the glow from the coal.

"Man, in the old days," Buck says slowly, dreamily, "we used to go night fishing all the time. Once in this pasture—used to hop fences and fish farm ponds 'cause you can really do some exceptional bass in farm ponds . . ." He stops, makes a sort of groan, and then cranes around and looks between the three of us with a bewildered expression on his face. "What the hell was I saying?"

"A pasture," I say. "A farm pond." I have just these words—the rest of what he was saying has floated off into the night.

"Right, right," he says. "So I'm sittin' here, fishin', drunk as a coon, and I hear this sound. I look over my shoulder, and here's this motherfucker of a bull, man. I mean I seen four-wheel Chevys that were smaller'an'is motherfucker. And right then, I got a hit on my line, the biggest bass I ever had on—fucker nearly pulled me into the water, was how big it was." He motions with his hands. Beyond him, Chalky drags from his cigarette, then pitches the still-burning butt out onto the path, in the leaves. "And the bull starts snortin', smackin' the ground under him with his front hooves. Thunder, man, real thunder."

Now he stops. I have to stay plastered against the wall and not move, because I am so high from the reefer that movement would send the various parts of my being eddying out into the darkness. "Jesus," I say, and the word feels remote, "this reefer is somethin'."

"Red bud," Chalky says, deep throated. Buck starts up again. "So I start reelin'. I'm thinkin' if I don't move too much, if I stay calm, he'll stay calm."

"I'm the one who's reelin'. How the fuck can you talk, man?" Dean says to Buck. The words muck out of Dean's mouth.

"No faze, man, no faze." He lights a cigarette and keeps going. "Slowly I'm reeling, thinking this is the best fight of my fishing life and I'm not enjoying it because of this motherfucker bull, and then as I'm thinkin' this and reelin', the bull starts lopin' on toward me. I jerk the line and the bass takes off in the other direction and my line snaps, and I go 'shit,' and the bull starts comin', and I grab my tackle box and take the hell off runnin'. I never ran so fast in my life. The bull was right behind me, and I dove over that fence. You know what?" He leans forward and pushes a hand out toward me. "You know what? That bull pricked me in the ass with a horn as I dove over the fence."

"You talk so fuckin' much," Chalky says. "What you really mean is that bull stuck his prick up your ass, and that's how you got to be Dean's mommy."

Buck laughs, then sighs, "You just wait, and if you're nice, I'll show you how I can blow smoke through my ears and out around my eyeballs."

Chalky snorts, then we all sit in silence, breathing. I get a picture in my head of Bitch going down. The dust around her, the legs just splaying out, stopping. It makes me want to ask why he's come. Because of the dope, the image is bright as a feature film, and I can't shake it. There are crickets. Out on the lake now and then there is the lowing of a bull frog. I sit up straighter and try to maintain. *Maintain.*

"So what the hell'd you do to Darrell Planey to make him fuck you up?" It's Chalky talking, but it comes from faraway, a tiny blink of light that swells as it gets toward me. My mouth is dry.

"I was riding my bike without a helmet, and he pulled one of those sneaky cop tricks—comin' up behind me with the lights off in the dark and then hitting me with the floods and the siren and everything. I almost fell off the bike, and it pissed me off so much I tried to start a fight with him. He nailed me with his nightstick." The words come out disembodied, rattling.

Buck rubs the whiskers on his chin. "Tryin' to pick a fight with a cop is just plain stupit. How come you ain't in jail?"

I blink, then blink again to try to make the dark come into focus, but it's out of reach. I want to get up and walk away. I want to disappear into the dark. "We sort of go back, Planey and me. Used to live near each other growing up." The words come from me slashed, hard, uneven. "Used to chuck a football around when we were little."

"I'd shoot the fucker," Chalky says, and it seems to me he's holding a .45 in his hand—I can only see it because it's darker than the night. It flashes and disappears. The backs of my hands prickle with moisture.

I take a swallow from my beer, and it tastes bitter as bile. "Like I say, we go back, and even though I wanted to kick his fuckin' ass, he's still sort of a bro of mine."

"I'd still shoot the fucker. I'd like to shoot the fucker anyway,"

Chalky says. It seems like the gun is there again, and I stare at it, stare at Dean and Chalky and Buck.

"I wouldn't like to shoot the fucker," I hear myself saying almost in disbelief. "I can't think of too many things that'd be more foolish." The words are there, and they wait in front of me for repudiation. Dean is quiet, the way he gets when he's stoned, and I wish for the drunk Dean, the voluble fool. Buck stares at me.

"You ever go frog giggin' out here?" Buck asks, and I'm glad he's spoken.

"I ain't so crazy about frog legs." Still, I watch Chalky.

"Aw, man, you do 'em right, and they're better than sex."

"You spent too much time in prison to think anything's better than sex," Chalky says.

"Whadda you know about sex? Your old lady ain't let you have it for two years," Buck says and slaps Chalky on the shoulder.

There's a bustle between the two of them, and Chalky has the gun out, has hold of Buck's hair, and presses the .45 to his temple.

"Come on, man, you don't need to pull shit like that. You don't let me go, I won't show you how I can blow smoke out my ears."

"You're gonna be blowin' more than smoke out your ears, fucker," Chalky spits through his busted teeth but slowly releases Buck. I hate guns, but I'm beginning to wish I had one.

Chalky turns toward me, and the gun is gone and suddenly in his fingertips is the copy of the book I loaned Sandy.

This is it—my fogginess has fled, and everything is on alert. "You lended this to my wife?" He says it formally, respectfully, suppressing the last moment's anger. He turns it in his fingers.

I nod, raise my eyebrows, though I don't know if he can see me in the darkness. I can see him. His mouth is open, and I can see the fucked-up whites of his teeth and out of nowhere something Dean said about him once jumps into my head—*You think Chalky uses a weed whacker to floss his teeth?*—and it takes every ounce of self-control I have to keep from bursting into irrational laughter.

"Listen," he says, "I don't mean nothin' disrespectful or nothin', but I don't exactly take too kindly to other guys lendin' my wife stuff. See, I'm—," he says and props himself more squarely on his other arm, "I'm the jealous type, and my wife is always fuckin' around in one way or another—I mean I know that's how she is." He stops, and suddenly I almost feel sorry for him. His face seems slack and sad. "I just get ideas, man," he says, and he holds the book up, shakes it in a clenched hand. "And the thing is, I like you, man, and I gotta tell you I don't want to be havin' black ideas about you, man."

I don't say anything for a long time, but in my head, I can see Sandy in the trailer, leaning against the window a few days ago, asking me if I'd sleep with her, and I can see the sunlight and taste the air and the image I had in my mind of her after she'd peeled off her clothing, and I'm glad it's dark, glad there's no way to detect the heat inside a person. It's such a full and brilliant picture, it seems as though her words ought to be as audible as anybody else's.

I lean forward, worried a little because I have no idea what I'm going to say. "Listen, man, I respect what you're saying, and I got no designs on Sandy, but you maybe don't know how I feel about books. A good book is like *the* good book, man. People have got to read it. If Sandy asks me about a good book, I got to tell her." If it was anybody else, I'd feel embarrassed by what I've said.

"It's true," Dean says, mustering words out of the darkness. "He's funny about books. That's all he's got in his fuckin' house." He pulls out a cigarette.

Chalky looks at Dean, then back at me, then flicks his butane and lights Dean's cigarette. Dean's eyes are narrow, red. I'm sitting up perfectly straight now, and I've got no idea what he's going to do.

I say, "She asked me, and I loaned it to her. That's all, man." I watch him hold the book. He doesn't know what to do with it.

"I can respect that," he says but says it so I can't see what's beneath the surface of it. "Just do both of us a favor and don't lend her nothin'. Let her go out and buy it."

I don't say anything.

"See, I caught this fucker dancin' with her at Charades, man," he says, and he waves the gun, "and so I took him for a ride in the car, man, and—" he brings the gun up and aims it at a blank space in the air "—I gave him the choice—" now he brings the gun down fast and points it at Buck's crotch before Buck pushes it away and smacks him "—of havin' his dick shot off or jumpin' out the car." Chalky grins. "Guess what. He jumped out the car."

I look over at Dean, and he's just gelled out, leaning over, staring at his cigarette. Chalky sees me looking and nudges Dean on the shoulder with the gun, and Dean looks up, startled, then slaps the gun away. "Cut it out." The only thing I can think of is Bitch.

"Why don't you put the gun away, Chalk," I say and try to say it wearily so I don't insult him. "If you want to shoot Dean, do it someplace where I won't have to talk to Darrell Planey again." Chalky laughs—tentatively at first—then puts it away.

I know exactly what's going to happen, his coming here and saying what he's said makes it inevitable that I will sleep with her and do it sooner than later. It's easy to see what will happen after that.

There's a long silence. Dean drags off his cigarette and blows smoke into the darkness. An owl hoots somewhere off overhead. Leaves crackle out in the woods underfoot of some animal.

"We ought to do a 7-Eleven," Buck says.

"You been in fuckin' prison too long," Chalky says, "they got safes and never have more than fifty bucks at any one time. Nobody does 7s."

"But I could use some cash, man," Buck says. "We could do a gas station, do some voodoo economics, man."

"Not in my car," Chalky says. "Steal a car first."

"Jesus, I am stoned," Dean says. I look at him. I almost want to run inside and get him some liquor, to pull him out of this stupor and back into the silly way he usually is.

Chalky runs his thumb across the edge of the book, fans the pages, then puts it down on the step with a slap. "Sorry, man," he says in a perfunctory way, like a kid you've gotten into a fight with on the playground and the teachers have made you shake hands with. The backs of my hands burn.

When they finally get up to leave, I watch them go up to Chalky's car, Dean at the rear. Chalky opens the door and the interior light comes on dimly, then he screams one of those "Yeeee-haaaah," rebel-yell screams, and there's repeated muzzleflash followed fast and hard by the repeated *bash bash bash* of the gun as he fires the clip into the air. When there's silence, there's giggling and the slamming of the Torino's doors.

You can shoot all you want around here. Nearly everybody who lives out here has some kind of weaponry and uses it indiscriminately.

I look down, and *The Sun Also Rises* is sitting on the step where he left it, and know I'm going to have to have a gun of my own.

# PAPERING

It's fall when Addie sees her again, afternoon, the day after Thanksgiving. The air smells of woodsmoke, and the sky is overcast and cold. He's coming out of the Ben Franklin, and she's coming out of Worldwide Hardware. She turns in the same direction as he does, toward the Post Office, and walks along the square. Before he even sees her hair, he knows it's her, and follows her. Past the Ranchero, past the bank, past the new Pizza Hut and the Lamont Women's Clothier. It's cold out, and she wears a light brown overcoat with a scarf that trails over the back. She has a lovely walk. Still on the square, she turns the corner and goes into Dunkel's Drug. He walks up the sidewalk to the drugstore, then stops and pretends to look at something in the window. Men on one corner are putting up the first of the holiday decorations. He looks for her but can't find her. He can see his reflection on the glass, and he is pleased with the way he looks. And then suddenly she's standing next to him on the walk, a young man next to her.

"Hey, Mr. Pleasance—Addie," she says, smiling, her nose and lips red in the winter air. "How are you?"

The young man stands in back of her, alternately looking at Addie and then at the store window. He is handsome, clean-shaven, and has an Adam's apple that stands out just above his scarf. His hair is dark and short, and his eyes are dark too. He has the smooth, characterless face that youth allows. His hands are shoved deeply into the pockets of his overcoat. He smiles when Addie looks at him.

"Hello, Karen, how are you?" His voice has a booming, false, holiday sound to it. But when he notices the emptiness of his own voice, he thinks he notices a certain falsity in what she has said too.

"I'm fine," she says. "Just fine. You remember Jimmy Dixon?"

"Oh, yes." He says it haltingly and looks at the young man as if for the first time. It is Jimmy Dixon, but his thoughts of Karen have all but obscured everything else around him. "How are you, Jimmy?" he says and extends his hand to shake.

"Nice to see you, Mr. Pleasance. Jack home for Thanksgiving?"

Addie laughs as though the question were a joke. "No, not this year," he says. "Not very sentimental, that way, old Jack," he says. "Talked to him on the phone yesterday, but that's about it."

"Well, say hello when you talk to him again."

For a moment they all stand looking at one another in silence. Jimmy seems ready to go, but Addie and Karen look at one another.

"I haven't seen you around in a while," he says, wanting to say something to her, to break up the silence.

"I've been around," she says.

"Well," he says.

"Nice to see you," she says. She begins to turn. The young man takes her arm. "Happy Thanksgiving."

"Yes. Happy Thanksgiving."


A few days later, when he's working in his shop, a woman who says her name is Trudy Anderson calls. "We've been trying to get this room wallpapered in time for our Christmas party, and well, my husband is just not the most talented wallpaper hanger in the world, if you know what I mean. My younger daughter says you do that sort of work."

Karen's mother. The thought makes him see her on the street with the young man. He can see her mouth in the cold air.

"She says in fact you're the best in town."

"I don't know about that," he says, "but I do hang wallpaper."

"If you're not too busy in the next couple of days, I was wondering if you would—if you can come over and give us an estimate."

It is dark as he goes down Rogers Road and turns on South toward the Andersons'.

He parks the truck and then sits a moment in the creeping cold. Her car isn't there. He has shaved, and his chin still burns from the razor. He has put on aftershave and a tie, then combed his hair with Vitalis that has been in the medicine cabinet for years. When he gets out of the truck and heads for the house, he smooths down his overcoat and holds his notebook tightly beneath his arm. It has been a long time since he's worn a tie and aftershave. Roy's funeral, maybe. It's only after he is on the step that he begins to feel ridiculous for dressing this way.

Despite the chill, despite the trembling of his hands, his underarms are wet, and the moisture drips down his sides.

Charley Anderson opens the door when he knocks, then shows him in. He's a round, blond-haired man with soft-looking skin and a soft handshake. He's a schoolteacher, that much Addie remembers. Trudy Anderson comes into the hallway as Charley takes Addie's coat. "I'm Trudy Anderson," she says, putting out her hand to shake.

There is a moment of awkward silence. Their faces are similar— Trudy's and Charley's—moonlike and smiling and feminine. Trudy has thick, dark hair, like Karen's. Addie scans the hallway, the kitchen, the Andersons' faces. "Well," he says, suddenly wanting nothing more than to leave, "where's the room in question?" He is in love with their daughter, and the absurdity of the fact hits him in the chest. *Love.*

As a group, they show him the living room, half of which has been papered sloppily. The rest is cluttered with covered furniture. Mrs. Anderson, heavy as her husband and slightly taller, floats around the room and tells what she wants done. It's a simple job and will only take a few hours. He gives them a price, and they agree.

"How's that old Jack?" Charley says.

Addie sweats at the collar and tugs at his tie involuntarily. "Real well," he says jovially. "He's in New York now. Really likes it." He makes it up as he goes. Jack isn't in New York, but he could as easily be there as anywhere and it's the only thing that pops into his mind. He stands nodding his head. They have drifted back to the hallway. There is music now on the radio that Addie didn't notice before. Trudy and Charley stand close to him. On the wall there are baby pictures of Karen and her sister—the kind of pictures you get taken at Sears, on special. Suddenly Addie gets hit with a tremendous wave of loneliness and even envy for the sweet banality of their family.

Finally Charley gets him his coat, and he backs toward the front door, the two of them still following him; then he turns, and the door is open, and the cold air hits his face and seeps up beneath his coat. It makes his lungs shudder. *Love.*

He starts the truck, guns it, then turns on the lights and heads up South Street back to Rogers Road. He waits at the intersection while another car, moving faster than is safe, swings around the corner and barrels past. The car is red, a Maverick. His headlights catch the driver and freeze her fast in his mind like a frame lifted from a movie—all brown hair and white skin and brown overcoat.

# GAME

"Want to play a game?" Sylvia says. We're in her dining room, and she's starting to make us drinks but stops. She's wearing a towel, I'm wearing my undershorts.

"What's the game?" I'm listening as cars pass for the sound of one slowing down and pulling into her drive.

She comes over and stands next to me—puts a thumb down the front of her towel and adjusts it. "I been meanin' to ask," she says, eyeing me. "What'd you do to make the deputy wanna whap you so?"

I tell her about the trick Darrell pulled and the argument.

"What'd he say about your mama—?"

"It wasn't exactly like that." The television is on in the living room, and it's the only light in the house. Somewhere in the back of my memory is an image of a woman, naked, getting up off a couch in a television-lighted room and leaving me—suddenly cold—for the bathroom. "She died when I was about five, and my brother and I found her." My voice sounds sleepy, detached, a television voice—I don't even know if she can hear me over the laughter from her television.

"Oh, shit. I'm sorry." There's curiosity in her voice, but I'm not tempted to say more. She just stands there a moment next to her liquor cabinet—undoes her towel, looks inside but doesn't open it, then does it up again. "What—what do you think about it?"

"Death is death."

"Death sort of makes me horny." She rubs the front of her towel.

"What's the name of the game?"

"Oh. Don't have a name. What it has is a principle. I take this here shot glass and fill it up with something, and I get to feed it to you, and you have to drink it. Then you get to do the same. To me. I got all kinds of liquor. The thing is, you say you want to play, then you got to play if the other person plays. And you got to be blindfolded when you drink."

"Blindfolded?"

"Blindfolded, yeah. You don't have to be tied up or nothin', only you can't see what it is you're drinkin'. You'd be surprised what happens to your sense of taste when you don't know what you're drinking."

"Awright," I say, my voice hoarse from the dryness of the house.

"Good," she says. She opens up the cabinet and starts pulling out all kinds of liquor. 158-proof rum, crème de cacao, crème de menthe, Jim Beam, Rebel Yell, Wild Turkey. "How many kindsa southern whiskey you got?" I say. Gin, vodka, amaretto, Kahlua. She keeps pulling them out and setting them up on the cabinet.

"Here's your shot glass," she says and hands me a thick bullet of glass.

"Who's goin' first?" I say.

"Ladies first," she says. "But first we gotta be nekkid."

She pulls off her towel, and I push off my shorts. She goes in the other room, and I can hear her rooting around a little bit. She comes back with a red bandanna, rolls it up, and ties it around the back of my head. I reach out, grab the soft of her. There's blackness and the pressure of the blindfold against my eyes. The top comes off a bottle—air bugs in. Now her hand holds my chin, and the hard rim of the shot glass arrives at my mouth. The liquor smells sweet, undefinable. It's hot in my mouth and scores my throat, but I chuck it back and swallow.

"Your turn," she says and gently takes the blindfold off me.

I get out of the chair, and she sits down. Close to her, pressing against her, I put the blindfold around her eyes. I fill my shot glass to the rim with the high-powered rum. She sits patiently, naked, her arms squeezed in to her sides, and there's something about the vulnerability of it—the blindfold—that makes me sad for a moment. It's maybe because suddenly she looks older than I first thought, older than I had looked for. There's something about it too that seems dreadfully empty—both of us utterly naked, but strangers too. I know and have known that she is no one I will ever love. It's a stupid thought, but I think if the world ended right now, if a neutron bomb burst right over us, this is not what I'd want to be doing.

Maybe it's just the drink, which has gone straight to my head. Despite the blindfold and the vulnerability, I don't trust her—but worse, I don't know if I trust me.

I put one hand on her face, then gently bring the shot glass to her mouth. She opens, and I tip it back; some dribbles on her cheek, splashes on her leg. She gulps.

We change places again. I can feel whatever it was she's feeding me starting to pull apart the strands of my sensibility. In the darkness of the blindfold everything else is magnified while I wait for her to pour something and feed it to me: the movement of the air on the surface of my skin, the sound of her feet, her hands, the screw top of the bottle, the compressor in the refrigerator, and in the background, the constant sound of the outside world's respiration.

"Here," she says, and then there is the warmth of her hand on my chin, the shot glass warm with the temperature of her skin. It's bourbon. I can tell by the taste and texture. I can feel the brown of it, the light wavering in its layers. "It sharpens the hell out of your taste," I say as I pull off the blindfold and stand up.

"You want to keep playing?"

"Yeah," I say and grab hold of her. And even though I don't love her, maybe don't even like her, I love the fucky bounce of her, the soft squeeze of her.

She ties the blindfold around her head, and I feed her another round of the high-test rum. She knows it. When she stands up again, you can see the wobble in her legs. She laughs, hits me in the chest. "You got to stop feeding me that rum," she says.

"No I don't," I say. "It ain't in the rules that there's anything I can't feed you."

She can hold a lot of liquor. After four or five shots, I'm starting to wobble, but except for some giggling and punchiness, she seems completely in control.

I put the blindfold on, and the room is drifting away in the darkness. There's a subdued dribbling sound—she's far away. The warm glass against my mouth. Taste is salty, hot. I can't smell right. "You know what that was?" she says to my darkness. I shake my head; the darkness sparkles.

"It was my pee. I peed in the glass."

I know she didn't. I pull off the blindfold and get out of the chair and come to where she is in the kitchen. I turn on the light. I know she could have. I know she even might have, and then suddenly I know it was. Maybe. The only aftertaste in my mouth is liquor. So what I do is grab her by the hair and pull her toward me, smash my mouth against hers, force my tongue into her mouth.

"So what if you did?" I say. As I'm asking her the question, I'm also asking myself the question. So what if you did? So what if she did?

"It don't bother you?"

"You didn't do it, and even if you did, why should it?"

"God, you're a weird son of a bitch. Even kinky fuckers have some kind of reaction to it."

"I ain't a kinky fucker."

"So what are you?"

We're sort of doing a dance, the two of us. We're standing close together, but only barely touching if at all, and she's going around to her left, and I'm following; we're turning slowly. Kitchen clock, stove, refrigerator, counter. "Why should I tell you anything?"

"Because you want to."

"There's nothing to tell."

"There must be. There's always some kind of weird shit to tell."

I reach out and put my hand between her legs. We're still moving, and she doesn't act at all as if she notices.

"Hit me," she says.

"No."

"You're really somethin', Jack," she says. She stops. For the first time, she seems shy. "I never quite met anybody like you before. I tell you one thing, I ain't gonna let you go." She kisses my chest. "I ain't gonna let you go, no sir," she says. I put one arm around her shoulders and then reach down and scoop her up and carry her into the living room. I put her down on the couch and kneel down between her legs.

# LEAVES

Dean's got his bamboo rake turned upward and is tugging the dried grass and punctured leaves from the tines. All morning he's been jumpy, more giggly than usual, hooting even at Harry's limited jokes. He looks as though somebody's pumped him full of air and he's ready to burst. I laugh at him because he was so subdued the other night.

The leaves have a scent halfway between tea and malt. I like raking the same way I like mowing grass—I learned a long time ago from my father that working is something you can drop into, drop away in. It's a clean space, and it spreads around you.

"Man, I don't want you to be pissed off at me," he says as soon as Harry works his way around the other side of the house with his gas-powered blower.

"What?" I say. "Why?"

"You gotta promise me you won't get mad at me."

I laugh at him. "Okay, I promise."

"Cross your heart, man."

"What are you, ten years old?"

The neighborhood we're working in is older than the one where

Sylvia lives. The streets are tree lined, and at this season, the roads swirl with fallen leaves. We've got four houses in a row here, and Harry's working his way away from us. The shriek of the blower gets softer.

Dean looks around, then digs into his pocket and pulls out a wad of bills, then grins wildly, eyes bright as sunrise. Now he shoves the wad back in his pocket.

"Oh, shit," I say involuntarily.

"You promised, man."

I just stop raking and look at him. "Tell me you didn't do it." He's got his shirt off and he's tan, and he has this look on his face as though I'm supposed to laugh the same way I did when he wrecked his car, the same way I did when I came to pick him up one morning for work and some naked girl answered the door and Dean was still so drunk from the night before that he couldn't come to work. Some guys—athletes, people who can knock you out with their looks or how funny they are— can go through life and get away with almost anything. People will trip over themselves to forgive them because just being around them re- deems their transgressions. Until a minute ago, I was ready to forgive Dean for almost anything he could do. But right now I just look at him in disbelief. "How could you be so fuckin' stupid?"

"Come on, man." He looks hurt that I can't get involved in the wonder of this. "It was just like the fuckin' movies, man. It was such a fuckin' rush, man. I'm sittin' in the car while Buck pumps the gas and Chalky goes to the can. I got the engine runnin', and the guy comes out of the station to get the money for the gas, and Chalk comes up behind him, like a fuckin' cat, man."

I'm paralyzed with disbelief.

He gets closer to me as he talks, speaks more quietly. "He puts the gun up to the guy's head and makes him lie down. Says if he's nice and polite, everything's gonna be fine, and the guy lies down. He was just a little fucker. Some old gray-haired guy. That was the only part I felt bad about. Chalk must've give him the scare of his fuckin' life, 'cause he pulled back the hammer and the guy pissed his pants. Didn't look at no one. Just lay there. Chalk reached into his pocket and took the bills. He was lucky they didn't get peed on. This fucker must've been collectin' cash all day long, man. They got in the car, and I took off like lightnin', man, like lightnin'." By the time he's finished, he's right next to me, and his voice is a hushed, excited whisper.

We both look up as Harry scurries toward us across the yard. I hadn't noticed the sound of the blower quit. "Gentlemen, gentlemen," he says, the blower banging against him as he comes. "You got to leave some leaves on the ground, gentlemen. A yard's got to hold in moisture." He lifts both hands into the air to demonstrate the dynamics of it: one hand covers the upturned palm and straining fingers of the other.

"You leave shit on the lawn, and customers will think you did a lousy job."

"Your job ain't to think," Harry says, breathless. "I'll think about the fuckin' customers." It occurs to me for the first time that Harry hates Dean, and hates him because of what he looks like, what he is. Harry just stands there for a moment, poised for something that doesn't materialize. Then he sighs deeply, turns, and heads back across the yard and around the house.

"Got 750 in cash and split it three ways. I got 210. We went out and had some serious drinks, man, and got some blow too." He sniffles as if to punctuate it. "But easy money is greasy money, man, it just slides out your palm." He slides the palm of one hand off the flattened, upturned palm of the other.

"Whose fucking aphorism is that? Buck's?"

He looks at me dumbly for a moment and then a look of hurt comes across his face. Leaves fall in the yard where we've just raked; a walnut, bright green and heavy as a baseball, falls with a thud on a pickup in the drive beyond the yard and its wire border fence.

Back at Harry's, Harry finishes putting the rakes and his blower in his aluminum shed, but he stays in the shed, moving oil cans, adjusting the rakes. All of it compact and nervous. I wonder what's coming, except I know. He comes out finally, clapping his hands together and still pacing. Work always winds down at this time of year.

"Either of you gentlemen want a beer?" he says. I say yes, because I want to let him get to the heart of the matter and get it over with, but I don't want to pressure him, either. Dean says okay too.

"Awright," he says as if it's the best thing that's happened all day, then disappears inside his house, head bent forward.

"What's goin' on with him?" Dean says.

"I think he's going to fire us," I say. Dean seems surprised, then the look fades and he shrugs his shoulders.

Harry comes back out with three cans of Coors and hands one to each of us and keeps one. It's typical of Harry that he's opened all three

of them in the house. "You know Coors is a right-wing-nut beer?"
I say.

"Whaddaya mean?" Harry says, holding up the can and looking at it
queerly.

"I mean Joseph Coors is one of those right-wing nuts who gives guns
and money to the Contras in Nicaragua, contributes money to that crazy
general who goes around the world selling Amway products and anti-
communism."

"Where do you get all this crazy information?" he says, momentarily
derailed.

"I read the papers," I say.

Harry turns away a little, shakes a Tareyton from his pack, and lights
it one-handed with a disposable butane. "Listen, guys," he says, not
looking at either of us, but staring down at the lighter, making like the
flint wheel has jammed, his words coming out in little puffs of smoke.
"The work is going to start to tighten up here in the next couple of
weeks. I mean it's fuckin' winter, man. It's fuckin' winter. And my
business is a seasonable business, man. There's maybe gonna be a few
weeks where I'm going to need some help shoveling some driveways and
the like, but I'm just not gonna need two people." He frowns, looks
down. Then after a while, shoots a quick glance at either of us searching
for approval. Dean isn't looking at him, but turned away, one hand in
his pocket, the beer dangled at his side. Since Dean's turned away,
Harry looks at his back earnestly. "I'm sorry to say that I'm gonna have
to lay you off, Dean."

"It's okay, man, I'll just hold up some gas stations," Dean says as he
turns around. Harry laughs, but it's a painful laugh, like from a guy
who's got lung cancer and can't laugh anymore.

"I still want to use you for the next couple of weeks, but I just wanted
to give you some warning," Harry says.

"Yeah, okay, we'll see how things go," Dean says, imitating Harry
with the tone of his voice. *We'll see how things go.* I don't look at him and
then finally I do. It surprises me the look of hurt on his face.

I look at Dean, and I sort of want to grab him and mess up his hair
the way you do with little kids. I don't know why. And then I hear
myself start talking: "Listen, Harry, before you go doing anything rash
here, I think you should know that I got another job."

Harry is nervously stepping up and down off the porch, and he stops,
turns around, and looks at me. Dean is staring at me too, but I don't

look at him. "I was gonna tell you about it, but since, you know, this. It won't be for another few weeks yet, but I'm gonna sort of be going into business for myself."

What I've said echoes in the air around us. It's not true at all—it just popped into my head this second. Beyond Harry's breezeway, in the front yard, leaves are falling in sunlight. I want Dean to have the job. I can do something else easily—or more easily than Dean. At least I can read.

"Shit, Jack," Harry says. He holds his beer lamely in his hand, then touches it, looks down at it like it's become glued to his palm and can't get rid of it. I can tell by the look on his face that he doesn't want to keep Dean on, not really. He looks away from me, at Dean, then back again. Dean looks at me too. "Well, Dean," he says after a few uncomfortable moments of silence have gone by, "if you want to stay on, then we'll see how things go."

Dean nods in silence, sips from his beer. On the way home he says: "You really going into business for yourself?"

"Yeah," I say. "I got some possibilities. Don't forget I'm the son of a fix-it man." At this moment, I don't know why I said what I did. Right now I don't know if it was for Dean or if it was completely selfish.

"I don't need that fuckin' job, man."

"Bullshit you don't. You can't go robbing gas stations for a living, man."

"Shit," he says. The fingers of his left hand are curled inward, and he looks at the nails. "Shit," he says again. "Why you so mad at me? We was just havin' a little bit of fun, thass all." I look at him, and for some wild reason he reminds me of my brother. I wish none of the business with the gas station had happened, because now it feels like everything has shifted.


Sam Huff and Sonny Jurgenson are on WMAL in Washington with the Redskins game, which comes in here distantly, scratchily, on my AM radio. The air is brisk, but I'm sitting on the porch in a sweater and listening to the game. Leaves fall now and then. A car rattles onto the distant gravel at the turnoff. I take a bite of the hotdog I'm eating, lean away fast so the dollop of ketchup drips off into the leaves beside the porch.

It's late November, warmish. Sometimes it would be so warm at Christmas I can remember walking through the woods with my brother in light jackets—can remember in February once lying half-naked with Jean in the sun in Richmond in the park at the end of Boulevard, baffled by the warmth, then taking her up into the woods and making love there in the leaves, both of us looking hotly over our shoulders as children played nearby, dogs barked. Winter in Virginia. One day it could be seventy, and the next it could be ten below.

The car is easily visible through the winter-stripped trees, and it's one I've never seen before—a boxy Chrysler convertible. It comes slow as hell, stopping and starting like the driver's lost. Finally it stops in front of my place.

Sylvia gets out.

Harry must've told her where I live, because I never did.

"Hey, you," she calls out musically when she catches sight of me. "You waitin' for me, sugar?" Her voice carries out clearly in the quiet air.

"Listening to the football game," I say quietly.

"Oh, God, not you too," she says as she descends down off the road onto the path. "Don't tell me I'm gonna be a football widow."

I look at her—she wears tight designer jeans, a tight, low-cut blouse, and a pink, fluffy sweater; her makeup and high heels make her look like a whore who's taken a wrong turn. There's a brittle sound to her cheerful voice that sets me on edge.

"Why the hell you live all the way out here?" she says when she's got close enough to make eye contact. She looks ill at ease, but maybe that's because I've never seen her out of her house—I've always seen her as part of the house.

She's looking down, sort of walking on tiptoes to keep her heels from sinking into the soft dirt of the path. "Cuts down on the number of Jehovah's Witnesses who come bicycling to your door," I say.

She looks at me a moment, evidently trying to adjust her mental picture of me. Then she just looks down again and keeps walking until she's at the step.

"Isn't it cold to be sitting outside?" she says. I look at her blankly: I don't get up, don't say a word. Now her hands find her hips, and she frowns.

Joe Theismann connects with Charley Brown at the Eagles' thirty-eight. He dodges one tackler, two. He could be going all the way. Sonny's and Sam's voices rise in pitch the farther "downtown" Charley Brown gets down the field.

"Do you always screw women and then just buzz off, pretty as you please, like I was a pinball machine or something?" Her voice is loud; she hasn't got used to the quiet out here. "I think I have a right to know what I did."

"What you did?" I say, and I look up at her. "I don't know that you did anything. I just—"

"Well, what's a girl supposed to do, exactly? If you had a goddamned phone, I could have called you."

She looks on the brink of tears, and I'm completely baffled. I've missed something crucial again, and for a moment, all I want to do is cover my head.

"I've been sitting for three and a half goddamned weeks tearing my hair out and drinking and not doing anything but wondering where you were. If it's over, then be a gentleman and tell me, but don't leave me lovesick like a goddamned teenager." She stamps a little, wobbles because her heel gets stuck in the ground. I've seen the look she wears before, and it amazes me.

"I thought the whole thing was about sex. Sylvia, I don't want to be obligated to anyone."

She doesn't really seem to be listening to what I'm saying. "I was getting to like you a lot. You got a nice way about you." A chill blows across my arms.

I cut off the radio, but the silence makes me uncomfortable. "You want to go for a walk?" I say. She says nothing, and it irritates me. Then: "I gotta put my lunch stuff away."

She shrugs. I pick up the bag of potato chips and my plate and pull the door open, let her go in first. The house is stuffy and closed-up smelling after the jet-clean fall air. She wanders into the main room and looks around at the boxes. I go past her into the kitchen and roll up the open, crackling end of the potato chip bag, put my plate in the sink.

"I'm a piece a shit, ain't I?" she says. She comes up behind me while I'm at the sink and puts her arms around me. "You think I'm a piece of shit."

"Let's go for a walk," I say. I dry my hands and shove them into my pockets and look at her. She backs away from me, out of the kitchen. Her eyes are almost colorless, and you can see every particulate grain of makeup on her old face. You can see, in the light, the drawn lines around her eyes, the blue on her eyelids. There's an overwhelming aura of emptiness about her, and it makes me afraid, makes me feel like I could fall into it and keep falling. Before, the sex disguised it, but the polish of sex has worn off and now all I have in me is weariness and a bizarre commingling of contempt and need. But I only need her the way when you stand at the edge of a high place something in you needs to leap.

"It's real pretty around the lake this time of year," I say, because if I don't get us out of the house I will explode.

It's a relief to be outside. The breeze has stopped for the moment, and I lead the way down the hill and through the trees. Everything's changed or changing with the season, and the ground is thick with newly fallen leaves. She picks her way behind me. I lift up the branch of a beech tree for her to pass beneath, and now I'm behind her. "Which way?" she says.

"Anyway you like," I say.

"It's so quiet," she says, getting used to it.

"It's hard to be in a place so quiet once you're used to noise all the time," I say. "You sort of have to learn to listen all over again."

There is mountain laurel, and it is dense. She picks her way through it, and I am behind her, close. "Summers you have to watch out for spiderwebs," I say. "You walk into them strung between the branches of the laurel. In the spring and summers there are hundreds of them."

Now the lake is in front of us, and she stops. It does that to people.

"The flatness of it," I say, "always amazes me. It's absolutely level. And the levelness of it makes it look from a distance as though it's rising in the air, because your perspective is used to land."

She turns around. "I am a piece of shit, ain't I? You can go ahead and say it."

"Stop it," I say. She wants her weakness to arouse me the way it arouses her.

She looks down. Her arms pull tight around her and she hugs herself. The earth beneath her is mossy, green. Slowly, she releases herself. Her hands touch her breasts, then her face, then her hips—some mysterious genuflection.

I reach out and put my hands on her shoulders. I don't know what it is I want from her—if it's only sex or if I'm searching in her for some kind of self-immolation or -revelation.

"It is pretty," she says. I drop my hands to my sides. Now she turns and presses up against me and wriggles so her backside rubs up against my groin. I want to say, *This really ought to stop. I don't want to do this anymore.*

"Don't you get lonely out here?" she says after a while.

"No."

I'm scared. Of her, myself. I've always felt in control, and now I am not. Capsized in the James River once, I felt this way. My face is in her hair.

"Hit me," she says and presses up harder against my crotch.

"Shut up," I say. She does, but she presses harder against me and it makes me angrier.

She is flypaper, and I'm the poor bastard fly who flew into the scent of her, got his wings stuck, and now the more he struggles, the more tightly pressed into her stickum he gets.

Suddenly all I have for her is hatred, and I want to be rid of her—more, I want to be rid of the thing in me that causes me to make such foolish choices.

She starts away from me, and I am a bundle of anger, of erotic desire. I watch my hand reach out and grab at the waist of her pants, pull her back toward me, the single word of my name coming out of her mouth as she stumbles against me in her shoes.

I've got her against me roughly. I reach around her and take hold of the waist of her jeans, tear open the snap, half picking her up as I do it, then rip open the zipper and jam the pants to her knees.

My body *smack* jutters with adrenaline, with the tremble and warm of her naked backside. I keep hold of her like she's going to get away. *I'm just a piece of shit.* I keep one arm around her hips and with the other, I undo my own trousers and shove them down. Then I push her forward. "Bend over," I snap, and I pull her legs apart. Her pants catch at her legs, and she stumbles a little. Her breath chucks. I pull her close. My throat closes shut, and I stop breathing. I want to split her in two. I push my head down hard between her shoulders, reach beneath her. Hair then flesh and wet, and I shove as hard as I can. I want to tear her apart.

"That's my baby," she says with dreamlike impossibility, and I look at the lake, my hands locked on her hips. *This is not what I want.* My hips smack against her butt, and the flesh recoils with the impact and she says, "That's my baby." The lake gleams, and there are no boats only the vague ripples from the breeze. *This is not who I am or ever was.* Trees hook at the sky. I look at the branches above us and the jays that squawk hard in the air, and I dig my fingertips into the flesh of her hips and shove at her like I could break her apart, but she says, "That's my baby. Harder, baby," and the anger grows inside me. I pound at her and pound at her.

The swelling grows until finally it bursts, and it burns and burns and burns as it floods out of me, but I don't stop shoving until I am utterly empty and staggered, like the bones have been pulled out of me.

Now I am against her, empty, nausea dragging at my throat. One hand comes up and covers my mouth. A crow calls out across the lake, and the lonely sound of the caw echoes.

My penis dribbles out of her. She straightens up and turns around, her pants still at her knees. It hits me right now how foolish, how *pathetic* we look—bare white asses, my penis dangling and cold in the moving air, the insides of her legs wet and shining, the pink of her vulva visible in the matted hair.

Two animals rutting in the woods.

She smiles—she likes this picture of us. I pull up my pants. She waits a moment before she does hers.

"Sylvia, I don't want a relationship." If anybody was near enough to hear they'd hoot at me in hysterics at the lunacy of it.

"Honey, I think we done *got* a relationship," she says and laughs.

"That isn't what I mean. I don't want to see you anymore."

She gazes at me as though there is thick and filthy glass between us and she is trying to make out my features. "Do you always have to wreck things by saying something hurtful?"

"I haven't wrecked anything. There's nothing to wreck."

"Nobody can give you what I can give you." I look at her eyes hard, and there's a storm in the distance.

"I don't want what you have to give." The words suck at my throat. The desperation surprises me.

"You just took it. You must've wanted it."

I turn away from her. Leaves fall. If we stood here long enough we could rot and be covered with them. I turn back to her.

We walk up the incline of the land, back toward the trailer, back toward her car. She is slightly ahead of me. She is talking, how sometimes she feels close to me, how others she feels as though I am completely unknown. What she says sounds as though it came from a women's magazine. My body is raw; I have nothing but shame. I have the drowning sensation I had in Richmond—everything seems hopeless, dead-ended—and I think about fleeing, but I don't know where I would go.

There's the sound of a boot on the porch, the gunshot of knuckles on the door.

"You expectin' someone?" Sylvia says.

"I wasn't even expecting you."

I slide past her and start around the trailer. On the road behind Sylvia's car is Chalky's Torino, and a charge of adrenaline zips through me. I come around the end of the trailer, and Sandy is on the porch.

The breeze has picked up, and it licks into me, sends a ripple of gooseflesh across my arms and chest.

Sandy is standing at the far edge of the porch wearing a short denim skirt, boots, a cowboy hat, and a too-big denim jacket. She's turned away, and when I come around, she wheels at the sound of my feet in the leaves.

"Jack, oh, hi. I'm sorry." She stumbles. "Did I—," she starts, but then Sylvia comes around the trailer. I look at her at the same time Sandy does—her blouse is open, her hair is a mess. She looks like a middle-aged housewife who has just spent the afternoon with a gigolo.

A hopeful thing in Sandy's eyes changes.

"Jeez," she says, shakes her head, and turns away. There's something painful about the way she moves—the way her mouth tightens and her hair flips.

"I'm sorry to interrupt," she says, "I just wanted to let you know that Chalky took the book." She shoves her hands into the pockets of her jacket and doesn't look at me directly. Her legs are bare and reddened from the cold, but the shape of them is fabulous. I've always hated cowboy hats, but this one seems nearly unbearably erotic on her.

"He gave it back to me," I say.

"Oh, shit," she says.

"No big deal," I say.

I haven't any idea how much time has passed, but Sylvia comes up and stands next to me. Reflexively, I take a step away from her.

"God, I am so embarrassed," Sandy says.

"You want the book back?" I say.

"No. I bought one. I read it, and I wanted to talk about it."

"You gonna introduce me?" Sylvia says, all breath and sex.

"Sylvia, this is my friend Sandy. I loaned her a book, but her husband didn't like the idea."

"Keep a woman stupid, and she'll never know why she's leavin'," says Sylvia, "she'll just leave."

Sandy looks at her a moment, surprised, and then jerks her gaze away. I almost look at Sylvia with surprise myself, but I don't want to think about her. Not now. I don't want to think.

"Maybe you should get a phone," Sandy says, and it's either anger or disappointment I can hear in her voice. She turns and shruggingly says good-bye. There's a finality to the way she says it that I want to reach out and make her take away. But I can't do anything. I watch her walk up the path. The Torino starts and heads up the road. In a moment the only evidence it was ever here is the cloud of blue smoke hanging in the trees.

I look at Sylvia. "You're cute when you're angry," she says and runs her hand over my shoulder.

I slap her hand away. "Go away. Please, just get the fuck away from me."

# THE EDGE OF
# THE ROAD

In the evening when Addie finishes the Andersons' living room, he piles
his tools into the pickup and heads out of town. It is dark early, and
when the buses rumble through town after five, the bright, greenish
light from the windows smears and leaves a trail against the town's own
pristine darkness. All day long he has worked with a nervous edge to
everything he's done—sure that since she set this up, she will appear.
All day long he has expected the door to open and Karen to appear. All
day long he's been flushed with anticipation at seeing her, and now in
the backwash of it he's exhausted, frustrated, starved. He doesn't want
to go home but to think, clear his mind, so he drives out of town. Maybe
he'll go to the Vet's home. Maybe he'll just drive.

He drives up the county road and out of town, past Church Hill and
the Baptist church, past the cemetery, and out into the broken fields.
All of the corn has come in by now, and the gray-brown stubble,
bisected here and there by a stream or a drainage ditch or ragged forest,
rolls away from the roadside to blend into the forest or mountains.

He goes along dreamily, thinking of his son as he drives, thinking of
Karen, watching the smooth, lovely road rise and fall beneath him. And

then suddenly at the intersection of F-909 to Henryton, there is a car in the middle of the road.

He has registered the lights coming up on the rise of the hill, and he has turned down his brights, and he thinks the other driver has seen him. But the head and taillights slowly creep across the pavement, accelerating only slightly, the light burning into the flat plane of the darkness the way light burns into photographic film. It's unreal. The car just pulls into the intersection without stopping.

The steering wheel is in his hands, hard; his fingers are tight, now tighter on the knurled underside of the wheel. He hits the brakes, then hits them again and again, trying to sap the momentum of the floating pickup. Adrenaline shoots into his heart, into his lungs, and makes the skin scald. Then his headlights hit the car, and he can see the red paint, and through the driver's window, the black interior, the striking brown hair. Skidding, now on sand and gravel, pulling the steering wheel toward the right, the noise of the tires against the road filling the truck, there is a sudden flash of white and then silence as the truck jumps across the intersection. He can see the mountains, the vaguely red-tinted sky, the beautiful distance, then a sudden flash of brown as the corn stubble comes up in clear focus and the truck drops headfirst into the ditch. The momentum—slight now compared to what it was—jolts him against the steering wheel and throws him on his side. The engine stalls, and there is silence, except the radio keeps playing, loud now because of the silence. The headlights burn into the black soil and stubble. He rights himself, swears, bangs his hand against the steering wheel in anger, then turns everything off.

Rattled, bruised, he makes his way out of the truck and stands in the ditch a moment, trying to collect himself. He hears her car door slam, then turns and watches her run across the pavement. Her high heels strike the pavement sharply as she runs. She wears a short dress and the same overcoat he saw her in a few days ago. Her hair is different from the last time—tied up and pulled back from her face.

She stops at the edge of the ditch, brings her hand up to her mouth, then turns, steps away, and swings back again. "Oh God," she says, through her hand. "Oh God. I'm, I didn't—"

The ditch is six or seven feet deep, and knee deep in brown dry grass, at the edge of a cornfield. The truck is pitched downward, the nose and front bumper in the ground, having knocked down the short, barbed wire cattle fence that borders the field. The tail end of the truck is hung up on the edge of the ditch, and though he can't see, he knows the muffler and tailpipe are smashed.

"Are you all right?" she says.

He stands below her, angry, his face at the level of her feet. Her overcoat is open, and he can see her legs—glowing whitish in the dark—and beneath her dress. "I'm fine," he says. "I think I bruised my chest." He takes hold of the pickup door and hurls it shut. The noise seems to startle the girl. He looks at her briefly, then leans up against the truck and tries to think. Suddenly he is confused. The anger that welled up in him initially has subsided now, and it leaves a sick feeling of hunger, of nerves and frustration.

"Are you all right?" she says again, coming closer, coming to the edge of the brown grass now and crouching down.

"Don't come down here," he says sharply. He almost says more but stops himself. He makes his way out of the ditch and walks past her, then stands behind the truck. A pair of headlights comes out of the distance and speeds past—a sports car. He looks at her as she turns in the sudden splash of light, then he watches the lights descend into the distance.

Seeing the truck like this—half of his goddamned livelihood— makes him so angry that he wants to take hold of her and shake her, howl at her for the stupidity of it. But then the sick feeling creeps up in him. He has no idea how fast he was going. It may have been entirely his fault.

"I'm really sorry," she says, staying a specific distance from him, as though under a force of gravity. "Is it wrecked awfully?"

He looks at her and pulls his lips tight. It makes him want to laugh. "Not totally. There may be nothing but a couple of scratches."

"It's the first time I've ever been involved in something like this," she says. "Look, my hands are trembling."

He looks up the highway, but there is no sign at all of traffic.

"What do we do?" she says.

"I've got to get my truck out of the ditch," he says sharply, staring at her.

"Can I, can I give you a ride or something? Into town?" In the darkness her teeth and eyes have a blue glow. He has begun to grow cold.

"I don't suppose I've got any choice," he says. The thought of leaving the pickup like this, where people can see it, embarrasses him.

He follows her across the intersection, then waits while she gets in and unlocks the door. The interior of the car is black and clean, and there is an ugly-smelling strawberry deodorant wafer hung from the mirror. He tries not to look at her—at the movement of her legs and hands—as she turns the car around and heads toward town. Soon the rush of the engine fills the car's silence, and the highway rises and falls beneath them. "Heat doesn't work too well," she says, and doesn't say anymore until they reach the edge of town.

It makes him strange, hugely abstract, to be riding with her, in the passenger side of her car. As they come into town, he expects people to turn and look, but there is no one there in the cold and dark.

They go along Main Street, then turn up State. He tells her to go to the Standard. He doesn't want anyone at Terry's to see his truck like this.

She pulls into the brightly lit parking lot of the Standard, and he starts to get out but hesitates. He doesn't want her to follow him back out to where the truck is—but is it presumptuous to think that she might? He looks at her. She is not a child. There are the beginnings of lines around her eyes, and she hardly seems like the girl who came to dinner with his son. Her skin makes him want to reach out and touch her. Oddly, it occurs to him that she is older now than Alison was when he married her.

When he gets out into the cold and tells her to leave, he is stiff and sore, and it is almost difficult to walk. He goes inside, and the young lanky kid there with hands black from grease gets the keys to the tow truck and drives him back out of town to the pickup. He tries to explain, as they drive, what has happened. The kid doesn't seem interested, just laughs and stares over his hands at the road.

He stands in the dark with his hands in his coat pockets while the boy hooks the winch up beneath the truck. It seems to take a long time, and once in a while a car comes whistling up out of the darkness, its headlights visible for miles on the hills, between the slow, silent farmhouses and skeletal trees. The lights make him feel empty.

When he's got the truck hooked up, the service station kid tells him—as if he might be a woman or a child or a feeble old man—to get into the truck and steer. He wants to say, "I know what to do," but instead scowls—it is lost in the darkness—and does as the boy says.

It is as he suspected—not much more than a scratch. That's some relief, though the cold wind still blows and the truck makes a heck of a racket with the busted muffler.

He follows the kid back into town in the truck. The truck is as loud as a machine gun. The tow costs fifty-five dollars.

At home finally, nothing more in his belly than bourbon and potato chips, he goes to bed. It takes him a long time to get to sleep. He can see the roadway in his mind, the Maverick in the intersection in the hollow space the headlights cut. Can see the sudden jumble of sharp images of field and highway and sunset, and taste the regret in his mouth as the pickup skids toward the ditch.

And then Karen at the side of the road, the high heels and the short skirt, and the angle of it, where her strong legs go up beneath the hem of the dress, and the muted dark image of her panty hose and underthings.

Rising out of the blackness is climbing a long way toward a distant understanding; rattling in the hallway, the lights in the drive, but no lights, no sound, silence again. Knuckles, the sharp rap in the sleeping town like gunshots. Stumbling across the carpet, legs weak and old and stiff, a flavor in his mouth like nausea. Bruise on his chest sharp and painful. Down the stairs. Pins in his heels, in his knees.

Before opening the door, he looks through the side window, and it is Karen, still dressed the way she was earlier. When he turns on the front light, it is sudden and bright and burns on the porch and walk. She seems to wobble a bit on her heels as he opens the door and lets her in. "Hello, Addie," she says, touching him, laughing at his bathrobe. She is drunk.

He closes the door, turns off the porch light, and turns on the living room lamp.

"Did I wake you up?" she says. "Your hair looks funny." She laughs. She holds onto his arm and stands so close he can feel the points of her heels in the floor. "I'm sorry I woke you." And then her face hardens and becomes regretful. She says, "I really wanted to say that I'm sorry." She is looking at him, her eyes wide and lovely and wet. "And I've been thinking about it all night, and I'm just so sorry."

If he is not weak already, the way she looks at him makes him weak. "You're drunk," he says.

"I may be drunk, but I'm not a fool, you fool," she says, and then the stoniness is gone from her face and the laughter returns. She punches his arm gently. "Don't you see that I've been trying to say this to you for a long time?"

"Say?" he says and looks away, embarrassed.

"When—" She stops. "Shhh." She turns away from him, then makes a complete circle and faces him again. "Oh, God," she says, putting a hand to her chest, "That's dangerous." She shakes her head. "This is coming out all wrong."

He looks at her. His head is too thick with sleep. It is difficult to think. Things tear loose and float in his mind. She is so pretty it almost hurts to look at her. "Are you all right?" he says.

"I think I might be sick, actually," she says and laughs again. "Just kidding."

"Do you want me to drive you home?" he says.

"No, I do not want you to drive me home. What I want you to do is kiss me." She steps toward him, and he looks at her in disbelief.

"See," she says, swaying, "the thing is, I used to think you'd always be here, you know. I mean you always were, and then tonight I saw you at the side of the road and I got to thinking that life is short, you know. Life is goddamned short—"

Then she is kissing him. Her hands are on his chest. "The thing is—" He can taste vodka in her mouth and can feel her breath and the whole rising warmth of her rushing through him, coming into his head with a concussive brilliance that stops him, that wants to blind him with love, with youth, with a million things he has not felt in years. "I think I'm a little in love with you."

It is like molting, like giving up something that wants to be given up. She kisses his eyes and his cheeks and his face and his ears and she holds him, and he cannot believe but knows that his whole life, after so much, has begun again.

# PRETTY

I go through the boxes and dig out my running shorts and shoes, an old sweatshirt and sweatpants, then change. It's Saturday and it's chilly outside, and when I go out on the porch to stretch, it surprises me how stiff everything is, how stiff everything can get when you haven't exercised in a while. Still, doing the work with Harry—all that mowing and raking should have been good for something.

I start out slowly, and as soon as I get out on the gravel road and pass Swanson's I start dropping into the old rhythms. I'm not in good shape, but not in as bad shape as I thought.

I warm up quickly. My hands are damp by the time I reach the gate and turn off, and I head down the hill, watching the pastures, the split rail fence, but thinking too—about Jean and Richmond. When I put on my shoes this afternoon, there was still dried mud between the treads where it stayed since I last ran one slushy day two or three days before I picked up and left. If I closed my eyes I could be on the street in Richmond, the winter darkness all around, Jean in the distance just coming in from work, on the step at our house, unlocking the door and not seeing me, unaware of me.

I'm going down the hill now, listening to the silence, watching the cows in the pasture, listening to the sound of squirrels as they snap into the brush at the side of the road, watching the blur of the trees, and split rail fences as they jog past. What I'm trying to remember is what if anything I felt watching Jean without me, watching her the way when I was little I can remember sometimes watching my mother—amazed by the distance of her, that she could exist separate from me. Watching Jean I think I hated the distance between us—hated it even though I didn't love her. Something about the natural and unbridgeable distance between even living people terrified me, still terrifies me. With Jean, it made me want to run and keep running.

I go down the hill and my breathing is surprisingly strong, being out of shape, but I know it's not going to be so strong going back up. A creek scraggles beneath the roadway. The water's high, and there is driftwood wedged against the concrete drainage pipes that run beneath the road. I like the sound of the water. I like the way it covers my breathing and heartbeat for a moment.

Up the hill on the other side. It's now starting to get to be like work. I can feel the strain in the fronts of my thighs, the muscles that do the pushing. I start bargaining with myself how far I'm going to go—up to the school bus chicken coop, then back again. It's okay to walk.

At the top of the hill, at the "Y" in the road where the chicken coop is, I have to stop. The breath heaves in my chest, and the breeze catches my sweat, makes me shiver. I'm not in bad shape, not at all, but I've bitten off more than I can swallow for the moment. I can hear a car in the distance—it comes up fast, then whistles past on the other side of the "Y" in the road. I can feel the turbulent air it leaves in its wake long after it's gone. Then there's another car, and I'm jogging now, heading down the hill, trying to keep up a faster-than-walking pace. This time it's Darrell Planey in his cruiser.

He pulls up next to me, slows down. "Hey Jack," he says. "How's the head?"

I don't look at him. "Okay," I say, "only wish I'd been wearing a helmet." I say it half sarcastically.

"Anything weird going on out here I should know about?"

I look at him and laugh, his round face hangs moonlike in the open window of his cruiser. "Like what? Orgies or something?"

"You know what I mean, Jack. Suspicious." I'd like to knock him one for the officious look on his face—that and other things.

I shake my head. "Sorry, Darrell. Things are pretty boring out here."

"Know anybody's who's into robbing gas stations?" he says.

I stop. I'm too tired to run anymore. I wish I could tell him what I know. It pisses me off that Dean got himself involved in this nonsense, because if it were just Chalky and Buck, I'd tell Darrell right now. Instead, because I'm tired, and I'd still like to get even with him for whacking me, I say sarcastically, "Why? You get involved in that shit, Darrell, and it could screw up your job." Once it's out, I wish I'd just kept my mouth shut. I don't envy Darrell his job.

"Ha, ha." He flicks his sunglasses unconsciously. "You don't ever change, do you?"

"Do any of us?" I look at him hard.

"I don't know, Jack. I hope so."


I'm walking down the hill toward where my car is parked, my running shoes crunching in the gravel, when the Torino comes over the hill. My sweat has dried by now. It's getting dark. When the car goes past, I get over on the edge of the road and watch the car rattle to a stop in front of my place. She gets out and starts back toward me—a skirt again, no cowboy boots. She's wearing a white blouse and a fleece-lined denim jacket that's too big for her.

"I'm glad I didn't miss you," she says.

"Me too," I say. In a moment she's right in front of me. I can smell her perfume—except the night outside the diner, I've never smelled her wearing perfume, not like now. I'm aware of being covered in dried sweat. The night is dark around us. There is light on the lake—the glow of the sky through the trees, the glimmer of one or two dock lamps. I can taste the texture of her breath on the back of my tongue.

"I was out running," I say.

"I didn't know you were into exercise."

"Used to be. This is the first time I've run since I left Richmond. Sorry if I smell a little sweaty."

She doesn't say anything but looks at me. The whites of her eyes glow in the darkness, the whites of her teeth.

"So Jake is in love with Brett, but he can't do anything about it."

I nod. I want to reach out and touch her, but I keep myself from it.

"It's a beautiful book. I mean. I've never been. I've never known, I mean—. When I came to your house the other day I wanted to tell you. I had a bottle of wine in the car. I was happy as hell. You know, like—"

| 133

She bites at the inside of her mouth, and her hair hangs just at her shoulders, and there's a long silence when we are standing here on the gravel road, looking at one another. "But you were with that woman."

"I don't—I wish you hadn't seen that. I wish you hadn't seen me like that. I hadn't even intended—" I am floating "—I really hadn't intended to start anything with her except she keeps appearing at my house."

"Jack," she says. Behind her, around her, the woods sough with evening. I can smell the pine and the oak and the salt on my face, I can hear the falling leaves as they auger down through the slow-moving air.

It happens. The gravel slides beneath my feet. It happens roughly, clumsily, my hands on the soft fabric of her jacket, one lip hitting her teeth and stinging with the impact as I push forward to kiss her. We're at the side of the road, and I don't have a very good footing, so I'm stumbling into the ditch as I hold her, and I'm grabbing her, one hand on her butt, the other still on her jacket. Her mouth is soft, is melting my mouth. Everything is trembling because I'm worn out from my run, worn out, and there's nothing left but adrenaline. Still I've got my mouth on hers.

"It made me so fuckin' hungry, that book," she says, gasping, taking her mouth from mine but then putting it back again, gasping still, the air of her aspiration sliding across my face. My hand moves beneath her skirt. Her legs are bare. I grab her underthings and go for the bare of her butt. "I just thought, there's so much world. So much world out there." We're against a tree now, steadier. I grab both hands beneath her skirt, and I'm gasping, shaking. "It made my life hurt. I mean I know things, but it made my life hurt to be the way it is." I have my hands on her butt, and the tree bark grabs a wisp of her hair and holds it up, and I look at her, and it almost tears up my heart to look at the wideness of her eyes. It tears up my heart to think of things. Now I put my hand between her legs, and she's soaking. I'm swollen, exhausted. I don't know what to do, but I lift her up, her back against the tree, bark coming off, and push down my sweatpants. She groans and I'm afraid I'm hurting her, afraid I'm crushing her, but her eyes say no. I don't have any idea how much noise we're making. I don't have any sense at all for the level of silence around us—cars, people in the distance. She bucks up, strains her legs around me. We're in the trees, and I'm buried inside her.

"I brought the wine," she says. "I went to the grocery and got French wine. I didn't—I didn't know what to get, so I got something French."

"It doesn't matter," I say, pressing, pressing, pressing, not wanting to allow myself to move but the fractal movement of her butt starting the chain reaction in my hips and groin.

And then we're in the trailer. Her skirt spreads around her on the floor. I haven't had enough of her. The wine she got is a good Bordeaux, and I can tell she doesn't know whether to like it. I've poured it in a tumbler, and she sips it hurriedly, as if she's missed too much wine in her life and has to make up for it now.

"It's a blend of two different grapes usually," I say, "merlot and cabernet sauvignon. If you saw them on the vine, they'd look small, black. They'd taste bitter and have little seeds in them."

"Have you been to Paris?"

I shake my head. "I've never been anywhere. Paris is different now, though. Everything's different."

She rubs her face with her hands, a child trying to wake up. Now she's crying, and I just watch her, amazed, happy. "You know in seven years of marriage to Chalky I never screwed anyone else. I think he thinks I did, but I didn't. You're the first. He was the first person I ever did in the first place, though, so you're only my second. I feel like. Jesus. I feel like something has been ripped out of my head or my heart or something."

She laughs at the way I'm staring at her. "I don't mean I'm in love or something, Jack. I mean maybe I am in love. With something." She drinks from the glass, and it stops her for a moment. "I just feel like such an ass, like I've been such an ass all my life."

I drink from my own wine, then put the glass on the floor, to the side, and crawl toward her. I take her by the back of the neck and pull her toward me, kiss her hard. I unbutton her blouse. I keep my face pressed against her face because the wine, the lack of food, has me so unsteady I will fall over. Her hair is in my mouth, and I am breathing in the fine fine filaments. I'm almost tearing at the blouse. When it's open, I stop and look at her. She's breathing hard. "Chalky was gone. I started reading the book on the couch, in the living room. It was at night, and I started reading it. I was bored at first. I have to tell you that. But I kept reading, because he had taken it away from me." I push the fabric from her shoulders and then hold her narrow shoulders in my hands. I like the feel of the bones beneath the soft skin. I like the way she looks at me straight on, wide-eyed. "And then I kept going, and I felt like I was lost. I mean Chalky was out with Buck, and I thought *I hope you just disappear off the face of the earth*, because I didn't want anything to interfere with what I was doing."

She's prettier than I thought she was—I mean she's prettier than I would have allowed myself to believe. I hook my thumbs clumsily in the shoulder straps of her bra and pull them down her arms. She smiles, gulps air. She picks up her wine glass to drink from it. She slides her arms out of the straps, and I peel back one of the cups of her bra. When she puts her wine down, I peel the other one. "You know which one you reminded me of? Or which one reminded me of you? The characters, I mean. In the book." She's tipsy from the wine. She laughs. I can't stop looking at her, can't stop touching her. "Not Jake. But I can tell you wanted me to say Jake. You're not like Jake. The one who reminded me of you was Bill, the one Jake goes fishing with. Where they're drunk and always telling jokes together."

"He's kind of a funny character, if I remember right. He's funny, but he's got a kind of emptiness to him. But they all do."

"He's sad," she says. Her mouth is open and moving toward me. Her tongue is in my mouth, and she's going backward, against the wall, now on the floor.

"Why did you say before you wouldn't sleep with me and now you're doing it?" she says when I'm on top of her, inside her again.

"Because I didn't want it to happen so fast, not right after—"

"Right after what?"

"God, you look so beautiful."

"Right after what?"

"Right after sleeping with Sylvia."

The expression on her face changes, as if she's completely forgot about Sylvia, about coming by here the other day. "Who is she?"

"Just a woman whose lawn I used to mow with Dean and Harry."

She stops moving, and so do I. I have a sick feeling in the pit of my stomach from the wine, from being convinced I've done something to ruin this again.

I prop myself up on my elbows, run my hands through her hair. The house smells musty, used up. "It was a weird thing, what happened with her. I hadn't been with anyone at all in months, and that night you saw me in Herbie's, I was on my way to her place."

"I wished I hadn't been with Karen and DeeDee."

"I didn't even recognize you. That was the first time I ever saw you without Chalky." I move a little, try to take my weight off her leg. "I said no, too, because I liked you. I liked talking to you, and I didn't want to ruin it."

She puts her hands on my shoulders and rubs softly. "How do you think they can be—the people in that book—how do you think they can be such happy people and such sad people at the same time?"

"I don't know. Maybe they're not happy at all—only occupied, you know. Doing things. Is it possible? Do you know people like that?"

"Sure," she says. "Sure. Like you go into Charades sometimes and you dance with somebody and you find yourself laughing, and then in a few minutes your mouth hurts and you don't know why you were laughing. Sometimes everything seems so old and worn away in this world. Maybe Paris would be different."

"Maybe Paris would be different, but I don't think so. Maybe if you were in a place that was different your mouth wouldn't hurt. If you could just hop in a car and go see the bullfights in Pamplona, you would be there instead of here, and I don't think it would be different." I'm moving against her again, the sick feeling gone and something else replacing it. She closes her eyes. I don't know whether to keep talking.

"For those characters it was just after a war, and maybe they thought they knew why life was sad." I know what it is—a kind of resigned melancholy, as though in the last five minutes of making love to her, talking to her, she has gotten closer to defining the thing that has remained out of reach for me for as long as I can remember.

"Maybe," she says. "Maybe. But God, anything would be more interesting than this life. How much would it cost to go to Pamplona?"

"I don't know. You could probably get there for five hundred dollars. You get a good deal, and it could be a lot less—half of that."

"Really?" she says. "Is that all?"

I smile. "What'd you think?"

"I don't know. I never thought. I always just figured it was out of reach because no one I knew did it."

I laugh, and she laughs. "Don't make me feel like an ass," she says.

When it's over I lie with her pulled against me, against the corner of the trailer. The night is utterly silent around us. I can't imagine her going back to Chalky now. I can't imagine letting her. I try to picture it in my mind: her walking into that house in the darkness, him stoned or coked up on the couch, fiddling with one of his guns, the television on, the bleached sunless light of the blue machine leaping around the room. It wants to seem like a long way from here to there but it isn't, and it makes me sad to think so.

"What's going to happen now?" she says. Her face is next to mine and I'm looking at her eyes, but she's looking at the ceiling. Her tone has an open quality to it, as if hoping anything could happen but knowing nothing will happen.

I want to find the right thing to say. There are a million choices, but there are only three or four that will happen.

"Why don't you stay here with me?"

"I somehow wished you'd say that," she says. She sits up, pushes her hair back from her face. She looks for her wine glass, reaches out for the bottle of wine to fill it again. I like the coincidence of her breast in the shadows, her outstretched arm. "But we both know I can't. I wish I could. Maybe sometime I can."

"Let's go to the city and drive around in taxis late at night."

"Any city?" She drinks from the wine, offers me some. I take the glass and drink from it. The room wants to spin, but I blink it off.

"Will Chalky be home when you get home?"

She shakes her head. "He and Buck have been out late every night for weeks. Comes home late and coked up, and if I'm not asleep I pretend to be."

"Have they been out with Dean?"

"I don't know. Sometimes, I guess." She takes the glass back.

"Shit." I sit up, prop myself against the wall, and look at her. The light is dim. Everything suddenly feels tentative, rushing forward. I reach out and touch her breast, then let my hand drop down to her thigh.

"What?" she says, not because of my touch.

I shake my head. "I think they held up a gas station. Dean said something."

"What?"

"I don't know. Maybe they're not. Dean said something about it— Buck one night, the night Chalky brought me the book back, was talking about it."

"So that's where he's getting the coke."

"Chalky?"

"Yeah. Suddenly he's got coke all the time."

We're sitting facing one another. There's a long time of silence, and I feel as though I've awoken to find myself adrift in a completely different ocean. I wish I knew what time it was, but right now I can't even think what day it is. I'm hungry, but more hungry for her.

"I hate what that shit does to people. Him up all night and roaming the house like a coyote, then watching television and drinking to try to take the edge off so he can sleep. I hate that shit. It makes me hate him more, but at least he loses interest in sex." She laughs and shakes her head as if to clear away the thought. She picks up her wine glass and drinks hard from it.

"You could get used to this stuff," she says.

She reaches down between my legs and touches me. "How much energy do you have left?" she says.

"Some," I say.

"Then make love to me again," she says.

I've broken into a sweat by the time she cringes against me—her body hardens, her legs lock around me, and she starts to sob. The sobbing takes me completely by surprise.

The sun is on the other side of the planet, and I can feel the moon burning in the cold fall air above the trailer. I tell her I want to know everything there is to know about her. I don't know what time it is. Midevening. The season makes it difficult to tell.

"What do you want to know?" she says, half-coy, like a girl getting ready to play doctor, asking, "*What do you want me to take off first?*"

I look at her more seriously than I intend to. *Everything is what you should take off.* "Everything," I say.

"My, um," she says, "well, shit. Everything's a lot of nonsense. I first lived in North Carolina. My father used to own a hardware store there. How's that?"

"That's great."

"Do you want me to tell this?"

"Absolutely."

"Don't grin or giggle."

"I won't."

"My daddy, as I was gonna tell you, was the nicest guy in town, and you know, when he had the store people would sort of come around and ask his advice about things, what they were doin'."

"Kinda like my dad."

"Your dad have a hardware store?"

"Fix-it man." My voice is hoarse. "Friendly. Help everyone out except his family."

She nods. "My mother's always been very religious. She went to the New Life Gospel Promise Church. My father wasn't religious—he called it crutch instead of church—and my mother wanted me and my brothers to be, like if you didn't go to church you couldn't be a Christian. She used to donate money like mad, like you had to do that to be a Christian too. 'You got to accept Jesus Christ as your savior,' she'd say. I remember that shiny collection plate coming down the row and my mother's hand dropping a twenty in it, that old woman-looking guy on the bill—"

"Jackson—"

"—staring up at the ceiling and then floating away on a sea of hands all the way down the pew. It felt like a crime to me, I don't know why. Like that's where all the souls were goin'. Those dollars'd just float away on that sea of hands, and it made me hurt inside."

I don't say anything but look at her, then look away. The wall of the trailer is paneling—thin particleboard with a cheap vinyl veneer.

She turns toward me, then away again. "You're really interested in this shit?"

I nod.

"My old man'd stay at home when the rest of us was at church. Sit alone happy and have his—'Sunday Beers' is what he called them, drank four cans of Schlitz every Sunday, no more, no less—while he watched the football games or mowed the yard or whatever, and when we'd come home he'd laugh and grab us and maybe play around outside. He'd get you in the sweet air of his breath."

She sighs deeply, and it makes me hurt to think it's hurting her to continue. "You don't have to say any more," I say.

"No," she says, "now I want to."

"I'll tell you, too," I say. She puts her hand against my face, as if to put her fingers over my mouth, but she doesn't, and the hand just drops away.

"I got my period around the time I was ten, and after that I couldn't be no tomboy and get pregnant by the time I was twelve. I had to stay in the house to try to learn how to become a woman, which all was a failure, as you can tell. I had to learn to cook, that kind of crap. And I'd watch her and watch her and look for the thing you can sometimes see that makes things right—like that sparkle or that little bell in the movies. And I'd ask her if she was happy. She said to me once, word for word, 'What in the world has happiness got to do with anything, child? Jesus died on the cross for our sins and that's happiness.' She used to say stuff like that—still does."

I can see her eyes in the darkness. I can see the pale of her skin.

"And when I was in high school, one night my father was working late, and a couple of guys who probably weren't a lot older than my brothers came banging on the store door. He was closed, and they shouted through the glass that their car was stuck in a ditch and they just needed a come-along or something to get it out. My father could never say no."

"Mine neither."

"He opened the door and they burst in, and one of them pulls a sawed-off shotgun, and they start knocking him around, you know, for fun. They forced him to open the till. Thing you've got to remember about my father is he had a kind of soft, teddy bear look to him, friendly, like I say, so these guys didn't take him serious. He had an old .38 he kept in the store, right next to the till, and he was behind the counter—he's told this story a million times, he sometimes even tells it in the dark when he's drunk, like it will change things—and he brought the gun up and pointed it at the one with the sawed-off. His voice was soft and he said to drop it, and the kid just looked at him and smiled. He says even now he wonders what went through the kid's mind, whether he woulda used the gun. The kid smiled and brought up the shotgun, and my father shot him twice in the chest. It knocked him back into the window. He died. The other one took off running. My father's small, but he was a sharpshooter in the Air Force."

"Jesus," I say. The trailer smells old and sad and somehow safe. Really safe.

"They turned out to be well-off kids. Brothers. Their daddy owned a moving company, and they only did this stuff for kicks. My father got to thinking later on that for the kid it was like a game of cops and robbers. His dyin' just wasn't in the story. But of course my father had no way of knowing that when the gun came up and pointed at him. Chalky always says a man had better mean it when he points a gun at someone else because it might well be the last thing he does.

"The funniest thing of it was that my father got arrested. Because their daddy was a prominent man and because as a prominent man he was dead sure his boys wouldn't've done something like that, my father was arrested for involuntary manslaughter. He was finally let off. But it messed him up like a motherfucker. Even if he hadn't been arrested, it had already messed him up good. He started drinking more and more, then he'd sit there in the dark and try to sort things out. You know that sorta idea gets into your head and say, 'Maybe I can just back this up; maybe I can just change it if I think about it enough'?" She shrugs. "He sold the store because he couldn't bear to be in it, and my parents moved north to Virginia, and now he maybe does some work around the house in the morning, watches television, and then just sits in a room and drinks Rebel Yell or Gilbeys until he passes out. My mother's even more religious, last time I saw her. She was and is dead sure he'd be okay today if he just let God in on it. I swear, though, in that house it was like havin' someone sittin' on your chest and keepin' you from breathin'. I was fifteen and ready for some action, you know, and not with the acne-faced boys at the Church Circle, either.

"Then Chalky rode up on some big motorcycle one day, and he might as well have had a billboard on his chest that said 'This way out,' because that's what I saw in him."

She laughs, and I don't have any trouble imagining it.

"Like I told you before, I brought my teddy bear. I got my father when he was drunk to give his permission to get married. But drunk he was like a bar of soap—I coulda squeezed him and made him go any which way. It was a lot of fun for a while, Jack. I got to tell you that. Like spending years at a funeral and then going to a party.

"But the other day when I saw him shoot that dog." She stops. Rests her forehead against her hand. "You know things change." She stops again. "Change and then you get to a place and there you are, not how you planned it all. Somebody else's movie."

When she gets up to go it's only 10:30, but it feels like it could be days later. It feels like the whole world has happened since she came here.

"I want another book," she says, and I give her *As I Lay Dying*. "Don't tell Chalky where you got it—tell him you bought it."

"It has your name written on it."

"Go out and buy a new one, then."

We're standing next to the gravel road, by my shed. "I love that last line, 'Isn't it pretty to think so?' in *The Sun Also Rises*."

She takes a step away from me, takes a step up the hill, and opens the car door. I hate the thought of her leaving. I hate the thought of her at home with Chalky. But mostly I hate the thought of what has just happened being in the past. "You were right about it being romantic," she says. She opens the door.

She holds up *As I Lay Dying* and says, "I'll read this soon, and then we can talk about it." She grins.

I laugh. I'm shaking. I start toward her, to kiss her good-bye, but she's turning and closing the door. I stop where I am. In a moment the car is gone.

There's no food in the house, so after I shower, I get the bike out of the shed and head out toward the highway to Herbie's. It's cold, and I'm wearing a helmet because of the cold, but it feels good to have the air slice up beneath my jacket, freeze my bare hands. My whole head is filled with Sandy, and I don't have any idea what I'm going to do. Things feel precarious, but for the first time in the months since I've been in Middleridge, for the first time since I left college or even home, I feel alive. Maybe the way the world works is that it has to feel as though it's going to fall apart before it feels as if it were ever right in the first place.

At Herbie's I order eggs and corned beef hash and potatoes, smash the soft yolks, and spread them all together. An old man comes walking in with a shoebox under his arm, and he sits down at the counter, puts the shoebox on his lap, and orders a sandwich. He has a strong smell of tobacco to him—burnt tobacco—and I remember seeing him before, late at night, wandering in the parking lot of the Food Lion or the Kroger in Middleridge with his shoebox, collecting cigarette butts. The first time I saw him I had no idea what he was doing, the second or third time I started to figure it out. He couldn't afford cigarettes and so scavenged butts and rolled his own.

When his sandwich comes, I'm nearly finished with my eggs—wolfing them because of my hunger. There's a slice of dill pickle with his sandwich, and he picks it up with reverence. I'm standing now, putting money on the counter to pay for my food, and he's putting the pickle into his mouth. It's his reverence for the food he's about to eat, the almost prayerful attitude he has toward it, that makes me taste the pickle in my own mouth.

Outside, I still have the flavor of it on my tongue when I kick-start the bike and head out onto the highway.

The cone of the headlight bobs out in front, and I head out 15, in the rough direction of Charlottesville—I go 15 because I need to ride, and it's two lanes most of the way, full of curves and hills. I squeeze the throttle, smack it down into fourth gear, and pretty soon I'm going eighty miles an hour, up and down the narrow highway. It's a spectacular feeling when you hit a snake turn in a valley in the dark—how the downward momentum of the bike carries you into the turn, then thrusts you to the side and upward again.

I slow down when I come through the little towns, the shops and gas stations closed and dark, the houses mostly dark. Porch swings. Now and then the late glow of a television set in a window. And then outside the towns I throttle up again until my hands are frozen and my face feels like stone.

When I hit the turnoff at 76, I take the main highway back toward Middleridge. I'm tired now, shivering a little, the exhilaration and the food and wine saying *sleep, sleep*. I keep it at seventy, pass the all-night gas stations, the 7-Elevens, and fast food places.

I'm going past the brightly lit Texaco lot at the corner of Route 34, near Placidburg—the lights are mercury and bathe the whole area, which is asphalt and broken off from cornfield and highway and bare grassland—when the lights suddenly go out. I've watched the lights approach from the distance, bright as daylight, and then suddenly to see them go out is eerie, as though something has gone wrong with the world. I zip past, and what's left in my head is a nearly photographic image of the parking lot, the station, the gas pumps, the empty little glass booth between the rows of pumps where the cashier usually sits like a ticket taker at a movie theater. There was a car, a gray Buick or Chrysler, and there was someone in it. But the rest of the station was empty. I close my eyes, and I can see the image brightly. All I can think of is Dean in the car.

# THE NEWSPAPER

Square-faced and handsome and clear-eyed, Dean is carrying the paper when I pick him up in the morning. It's sunny, and he slaps the newspaper against his leg. The door opens, and he climbs in. He laughs without saying anything.

"What's so funny?"

"Nothing, man, nothing," he says. His voice has a tight twist to it. "You want to read the funnies, man?" he says.

"Go ahead," I say, and he folds open the paper. I pull out into the street, head toward the job Harry's got for us today, which is cutting up and taking out an old walnut tree in someone's yard. In the street, halfway through "Dick Tracy," Dean stops. "Let's read some news, man. Let's read some news."

"What's with you today?" I say. We're at a stoplight. He's wound up tight as a top. I turn to look at him.

"Nothing, man. I just wanted to read some news."

"So read some news."

He reads the headlines, slowly. "The town council," he gets out.

Then, animated: "Why the hell ain't it kounkil or sounsil—how come there's two ways of saying exactly the same letter?"

"Arbitrary. I don't know. How the fuck am I supposed to know?" I say.

"Don't shout at me. They ought to change it," he says. "It'd make reading easier."

I laugh. Of course they should.

He reads more headlines. "There was one story I was looking for," he says. He laughs nervously. Then laughs again a moment later. It has a weird sound in the car, lonely, metallic.

We're in the neighborhood now where we're supposed to meet Harry. I'm looking for the turnoff, looking for Harry's truck.

"What's that?" The newspaper rustles. His hands are shaking.

"Gas attendant wounded," he reads. He sounds out the words slowly, stumbling.

Involuntarily I take my foot off the accelerator and look at him. In my head I can see last night, flying down the highway, the dim green lights from the instruments of the motorcycle in front of me, the solitary nut of light from the headlight on the street—then the gas station lights, and the sudden disappearance of the mercury-blanched parking lot, the single figure sitting behind the wheel of a car, the pale steam of exhaust bleating from the tailpipe before the lights went out.

He's fixed on the page. He reads slowly, painfully. "A nineteen-year-old man was shot," he reads. "And—and sear, sear-ee-ous-lee wow, wown-ded during a holdup," he says. I glance in the mirror, then just shove on the brakes.

"That's pretty good," I say, the anger rising in my throat. "You're reading that really well."

"Oh, shit," he says. "The man, I-dent, dentified as Day, David Ferris, of Mechanics—"

I grab the newspaper away from him, search the page for the story. "Was the lone attendant at a gas station during a midnight holdup. Shot once in the chest, he remains in serious but stable condition at Albemarle County Hospital. He was discovered unconscious by passersby in the rear of the Texaco station, at the corner of Route 76 and Route 34 in Middleridge County." I crumple the newspaper and thrust it at him.

"You stupid fuck. You stupid, stupid fuck. How could you get into this?" I say and bang on the steering wheel.

He laughs when I say this—a kid in school, caught doing something he shouldn't. He puts his hand on top of his head. "I didn't do it, man.

They did it. They told me they didn't do it. They were all coked up and I heard the fucking shot, but they said it was just to scare the guy. Fuck," he says, "serious condition" and bangs his head against the window. "What if the guy dies?"

Harry's truck is parked up the street. I hit the accelerator again and jerk the car forward. "Even if the guy doesn't die it's still attempted murder, and you're still part of it."

"Shit," he says.

I pull the Chevy up behind Harry's truck. Dean gets out a little brown bottle with a tiny spoon attached to the cap of it, screws the cap off, and spoons white powder out. Bent over, he sniffs—right nostril, left nostril. I get out of the car. Harry's sitting in his pickup. It's cold out. Harry's holding a cup of 7-Eleven coffee. I nod toward the huge, scraggly-looking tree in the front yard. The green and brown, baseball-sized walnuts are everywhere. "That the guy?" I say. I'm floating on a cloud of anger, a tight, wide capsule of white energy.

"That's the guy," Harry says and nods toward the tree.

I reach into the back of Harry's pickup and grab his chain saw before he has a chance to do it himself. "Let me at the fucker," I say.

Dean comes up behind me, runny nose, cigarette going. "Morning," he says to Harry.

"Mornin'," Harry says but doesn't look at either of us, just leans over the bed of his pickup and sips coffee through the torn plastic lid of his coffee cup.

I flip the switch and pump the throttle on the chain saw, then yank the starter. The starter handle is cracked and soft in my hand, and I hold it tighter, let the cord cut into my fingers. I pull the starter cord twice, three times. It gives a hollow throating but won't start.

"It don't have any gas in it," Harry says, and he and Dean both laugh.

"Well, let's put some fucking gas in it," I say.

"What's with him this morning?" Harry says.

"I think he needs to get laid," Dean says. It's a sure thing that Harry'll laugh at this, and he does. I carry the chain saw around to the back of the truck and drop the tailgate. I crack open one of the little cans of two-cycle engine oil that Harry's got in his tool kit and pour it into the tank. I do it without a funnel and some of it spills on the chain saw, on the tailgate of Harry's truck.

"Hey, man, be careful with that shit," he says and rushes around to where I am. He has a funnel wrapped in a rag, and he whips it out and wipes the spill with the rag and shoves the funnel into the mouth of the tank. I fill the rest of the tank with gasoline, then put the cap on. Harry shakes his head and wipes off the funnel with the rag, wipes again at the place I spilled oil on his truck.

I flip the switch and pump the throttle again, then yank the starter cord, yank it again. The chain saw comes to sputtering life. I nurse the throttle; bright blue smoke puffs out until the motor catches good and hard and it really starts to sing. I wave it at Dean, glare, then go into the yard and toward the walnut tree. The weight of the saw feels good in my arms, and when I get down on one knee next to the tree and sink the spinning chain into the wood of the tree, I do it with relish.

The three of us are sitting in the 7-Eleven parking lot. I'm covered with wet, sticky chainsawdust; it's in my hair, on my clothing, in my shoes, and in my pockets, and there's nothing I can do short of showering and changing that will get rid of it. Right now the tree lays in the yard, waiting to be hauled off, which we will do after lunch. Right now, I'm eating my damp sandwich and smashed potato chips and drinking chocolate milk, and my arms sing with the strain of the saw's constant weight. Dean eats a beef-and-bean microwave burrito, and Harry drinks coffee. Harry's telling a leftover joke from the 1980 presidential campaign that I've heard before; I'm eating the last of my sandwich, trying to ignore him. Dean freezes up hard as rigor mortis next to me, and it makes me look up. Two cars down from us is Chalky's Torino. The door opens, and Dean's still frozen, but he begins to relax when Sandy, in sunglasses, with a scarf pulled up around her neck and her cowboy hat on, gets out, steps up on the curb, and heads inside.

Both of us watch silently as she comes out again with a bag. I look at Dean and then at her. The sunglasses and hat barely cover the bruises on her face. The half-chewed food in my mouth turns hard and dry. I put my sandwich down on its piece of folded waxed paper and stare.

"Shit, look at her," Dean whispers. She doesn't recognize Harry's truck, and she doesn't look anywhere but straight ahead of her, the entirety of her being focussed on getting into the car. She's wearing makeup—you can tell by looking—but it doesn't cover everything.

I start to get out of the truck. I reach for the latch handle, but then I stop myself. I look at Dean and then at the Torino as it backs out of the lot and roars into the street. I swallow, but the food doesn't want to go down.

# WORK

The motorcycle kicks up a trail of dust on the gravel road. It's cold, and the cold shifts through my jacket and shirt. My hands sweat in my gloves despite the cold, because I have no idea what's going to happen, or what I'm going to do. It's foolish even to go, but I have to talk to her.

A little way down the road from their house—the Torino is in the dirt driveway—I cut off the bike and put it in the bushes, then walk the rest of the way up the road, listening to the sudden quiet, listening for any sign that he's home. The dark feels naked, vulnerable.

I go across the bare yard, between the ragged bushes. There are two lights on in the house, one upstairs and one downstairs, at the back of the house. I try to remember if I've ever been inside, but I can't. The downstairs light is probably the kitchen.

Now I'm on the path that leads to the front door, and it goes past beneath me, frozen, bare. There's no sound from inside. I step up onto the porch, turn around, look at the road, at the place I left my bike. I don't know what I'll do if Chalky answers the door—but I don't know for sure that he beat her up because of me, or that he knows anything about what happened between us.

Every follicle of hair on my body arcs in its socket when I reach out, pull back on the wooden screen door, and knock softly on the red-painted front door. The skin of my butt crawls. There's nothing but silence, and I knock again, harder. The gloves muffle the knock. Everything in the world feels like the knock—as though there's distance and padding between all solids.

In a moment, there's a sound inside—feet on the stairs. Then Sandy's voice: "Who is it?"

"It's Jack," I call softly.

The door opens with a sucking sound—only opens a foot or so—and she leans her shoulder against the edge of it and presses her face out into the darkness. "What are you doing here?" Her voice is tight, anxious. She looks worse than I thought. Both eyes black, the left one nearly swollen shut. Her cheek swollen and purple.

He wanted people to see that he'd beat her up.

"Oh, Jesus," I say, almost involuntarily, "You look awful. That motherfucker."

"Jack—"

"I saw you today at the 7-Eleven. I wanted to know what happened."

Angry, pulling back to look over her shoulder. "What do you *think* happened?" she says, then: "You'd better get out of here. I mean really. If Chalky sees you—"

"Does he know?"

"He doesn't know exactly, but he—oh, shit, Jack, just get out of here, please. He could be back any minute."

"Come with me."

"Where?"

"I don't know where. To my house. To Richmond. Just get the fuck out of *here*." The door's more open now, I'm nearer to her. I can feel the warmth of her breath in the cold air.

"He'd come after me. He would. I'm gonna close the door now. I'm gonna go back upstairs and go back to the book."

In the distance there's the sound of a car on gravel, and the volition leaves me—just completely leaves me—and suddenly my arms and legs are heavy as stone. She starts to push the door closed. "Oh, Sandy," I say, but the door is closed and I turn, step down off the porch, and start across the yard, toward the road.

. . .

It's not Sylvia who opens her door but another woman, about her age, slightly heavier, slightly more matronly looking. I look at her and think about turning away and leaving—I had intended to come to say *I don't want to see you anymore,* but it's impossible now. But here I am.

The woman at the door has permed hair and the heavy, almost ageless preserved look some middle-aged suburban women get. "Oh, hello," I say. "Is Sylvia around?"

"You must be Jack," she says, smiling, her form not exactly filling the doorway but moving, undulating, telling more than I want to know.

"I must be," I say, but she giggles at the hard edge of my voice. She stands aside and motions me to come in. I shouldn't be here—black and blue, Sandy's face hangs in my head. Everything is loose and frayed and coming undone.

"Syl?" she calls as she closes the door. "Your friend Jack's here."

In the distance—false distance—a toilet flushes. "I'll be right on out," Sylvia's muffled voice says.

"So Sylvia says you do odd jobs," the woman says.

"I work for a guy who does odd jobs. But I'm not going to be working for him much longer."

"On to bigger and better things?" she says. She hasn't stopped moving since I laid eyes on her. One of those ants-in-her-pants girls you meet in school who puts holes in her underwear and climbs the jungle gym in the playground so the boys can stand beneath her dress.

In the house everything feels like glue.

Sylvia comes down the hall, wiping her hands together. "This is a nice surprise," she says, partly sarcastic. "I take your coat?"

Restlessness creeps my bones. I really want to say that I never want to see her again. I really want it to be over.

"I was just in the area," I say and shrug off my coat. I don't know why I take off my coat—I don't know why I don't just turn around and walk out. "We're both adults," I said aloud in the car, "and it was fun. But I can't keep up with it anymore." But I can't say it; I can hardly even think it.

She takes my coat and folds it over her arm, and when she goes past me toward the closet she pinches me on the back of the arm. It's a gesture that spills hatred in my chest.

"Jack was just telling me he's going on to bigger and better things."

"What's that supposed to mean?" Sylvia says, turning, halfway to the closet, stopped cold by her friend's words.

"I'm quitting working with Harry," I say. "No big deal."

She turns, hangs up my coat.

"Did'j'all ever get introduced?" Sylvia says. We are all in the kitchen now. I do not know the steps to this: I was at Sandy's; now I am here.

"Not properly," her friend says, swishing her butt from side to side in her chair like a cat trying to get comfortable.

"Delia, this is Jack. Jack, this is Delia. Delia lives up the street. We been pals ever since her divorce these many years ago."

I nod. "So what'cho gonna do now?" Delia says.

"Odd jobs. Painting, wallpapering. Same thing, except I won't be mowing lawns." I don't really know what I'm going to do. I have money I saved in Richmond, and I don't *have* to do anything at the moment. Maybe I'll take Sandy to Paris.

"Painting and wallpapering," Delia says. "Well you know that's funny because I was just telling Sylvia here that I am so sick of the way my kitchen looks I could just scream, and it's all because of the paint. It hasn't been painted since Ron left, well, even before Ron left. It just looks so dingy."

I look at Sylvia as she's pouring water into her coffeemaker, and her mouth is shut tightly in annoyance. There are pits of flicker in my vision; soon there will be a dead spot.

"What do you do? Do you give an estimate, like?"

"I could look at your kitchen."

Sylvia puts the carafe beneath the filter housing on her coffeemaker and sails back to the table where we are sitting. "After coffee," she says, excess cheer in her voice, "we could walk over and all three of us have a look. And I might even have some work for you to do over here."

A migraine is beginning, and the air warbles with irregular waves of light, and the light edges off its own spectrum, the waves breaking up, rebounding, skittering. Mercury on glass. The smash of particles. I do not want this, and I try to will it away.

The three of us walk up the street in the darkness. There's no sidewalk on this street so we are in the middle of the road, me in the middle, Sylvia and Delia on either side of me. The coffee makes me more restless than I already am and doesn't help the way the air has begun to come apart at the seams. I can't get out of my head Sandy's bashed-up face. For the first time I wish I had a telephone. I don't like being here, being away from the trailer. If Chalky goes out, or if she decides she has to leave, she would come by and I wouldn't be there. I hate the thought of her standing alone in the dark woods, waiting for me. I wonder what I would do—what I could do if a full-blown migraine hit now.

Sylvia tries to take my hand, but I slip it from her grasp. She looks at me, a mix of hurt and something else I haven't the patience to analyze. When a car slips by, it swings wide of us and the headlights leave a trail of afterimage in my head. The air remains parted, roiled. I feel like hitting something. I feel like running hard and fast. I feel like exhausting myself.

I'm almost jumping with caffeine and hallucination when we get into Delia's house. She's messier than Sylvia is—dishes in the sink, old newspapers piled by the back door. The kitchen used to be yellow, but the walls are stained by inadequate ventilation, lack of paint. I point to the stains. "The walls need to be cleaned because the paint won't stick to that. It's just old steam, grease—you know, you make a hamburger and grease escapes. Whole thing would take one day, maybe two, depending on how hard the walls are to clean." It feels like they should see the holes that are opening up in the fabric of reality around us, but they don't. No one ever does.

I tell her I'll do it for two hundred and fifty, and I'll start on Monday, but she has to get the paint. "Pick out three gallons of semigloss in a color you like."

She looks at Sylvia, and Sylvia shrugs. Sylvia likes it that I'm not responding to her friend's sexual signals, but she doesn't know what to make of the rest of things.

"Sounds fine to me," she says. "Syl, you go with me out to Sherwin-Williams and pick out a color?"

Sylvia shrugs.

"Listen," I say. "I forgot I've got someplace I've got to be, so—" I turn, head toward the door. I have to get to sleep before my head explodes. "I'll be here eight o'clock Monday morning. You get a roller kit, a one-inch brush, and a three-inch brush, and get good ones. Make sure you got a mop and an ammonia detergent."

She flutters a little bit, then writes this down on a pad on her kitchen table. When I get out the door and onto the street again, things feel desperate. I know where I can get a gun and tomorrow I'll go there.

# GUN

The heat in the car is on, and the highway slips by. The sun is setting, and the horizon to the west, at the mountains, goes from rose to orange, but you have to keep looking, because the colors change and keep changing.

As I get closer to Hadleysburg the side roads get more familiar, and it's everything I can do to keep my mind on what I'm doing and not just turn off and head back into the twisting roads of my childhood.

Once I'm in town, I take the roads I know are hardly traveled. I don't want my father or any of his friends—or any of my old friends—to see my car. I don't know if anyone but him would recognize it, but I don't want to take the chance. Karen would. Karen Anderson would recognize it.

It feels strange to be here, like it must feel breaking into someone's house while they are home, asleep.

It's cold when I get out of the car, about fifteen degrees colder than when I left Middleridge.

I leave the Chevy parked in the woods off Davis Road near the apartment where I lived briefly, after college, then pull tight my coat collar and start through the woods, up the hill toward my father's house. It's early evening—it was light when I left Middleridge, but since it's nearly December, it's dark as midnight. I know these woods, and if they've changed it's only to grow thicker. When I was first living on Davis Road I would walk up this way in the mornings to go to work with my father, one hand held in front of me for spiderwebs left during the night. That was before he started picking me up every day. I walked up through here so much there is still, now, the impression of a path through the trees. Now I shove one hand in my pocket and with the other, hold up the flashlight in front of me to catch the spiderwebs if there are any in the winter. I keep the flashlight off.

My father's house is one of three on his side of this part of the street—Croutys' and Jansens' are the others. His house is white, obscured partly by his shop in the back where he does his work. There's no light on; the house looks empty and desolate in the cloudy almost-December absence of light. For a moment the notion that he could have done exactly what I did—up and fled—slides through my midsection like a slice of cold air.

I'm in the yard now, out of the woods, the place where the garden ends and the grass begins. The sky is low with clouds, and the grass is frozen so splines of ice break off beneath my feet. He could be traveling, he could've up and gone to China.

An owl hoots somewhere off in the woods, and the sound is cold. I wish I'd called, if only to find out if his number had been disconnected. When people return to the place they grew up they always talk about how small the house looks, but what hits me about my father's house is how insignificant it looks. What was once center of the universe is now a smallish house in the midst of other smallish houses. Beyond Jansen's house and down the hill I can see the very edge of the house where Darrell Planey used to live. I turn around and look at the woods, and then at the house again. The sky is low and I feel dizzy, but I continue across the grass anyway.

I slip up around the side of the house, between the shop and the house, and the smell of it hits me—sawdust, the particulate odor of my father, my own blood reflected back at me. I know now for certain he didn't move, that he hasn't died; it surprises me that this is a relief.

I slip around the side of the house, toward the front, and I can see Jansen's house: someone walks by a yellow-lighted window—old Mr. Jansen with his oblong-shaped head. Roy used to call him BP, short for ballpeen hammerhead. The window is a long way away.

The driveway is empty: my father's out to the Ranchero or some-thing—one place or another.

*He's out.*

I still have a key, but my father almost never locks the house—it's too much of an inconvenience, and always has been, even after we were broken into once when I was in high school. I go to the back door, and it is locked.

Quiet as I can, I get out the key, slip it in the lock—on the off chance someone is here, I don't want to startle them.

And then it hits me that I don't have to think like a thief. I'm only thinking this way because it's what I'm doing. If someone surprised me, it'd be easy to say, "Hey, it's only me, Jack, no problem." Except I don't want to see anybody. All I want is my father's Winchester .30-.30.

The door comes open softly, and in a moment I'm in my father's kitchen, someplace I haven't been in so long. The whole effect of it hits me like having a stumbling drunk grab hold of me—intoxicating, momentarily panicking, and I want to fight off the sudden intimacy of it.

I move, stunned, a million things going through my head: the air feels full of ghosts, thick and hooting. *Stop.* I'm in the living room now. He's remodeled—or not so much remodeled as updated. Or no. Maybe not. Just rearranged. I stop by the couch, my hand uncon-sciously on the back of it, the worn fabric. I wonder what I would do if he suddenly appeared, whether I would shake or run or just stare. I look at the stairs, at the front door. I turn toward the stairs, trying to think where the gun would be. His closet. The attic. He used to have two or three, an over-under .410-gauge shotgun that was Roy's, the Winchester, and a .30-.06.

I go for the stairs.

It takes forever to get there.

I go down the hallway, poke into my old bedroom. It's exactly the way it was when I left it. Empty. My old bed, a few boxes, an old rocking armchair I didn't take to Richmond.

Then into his room. The same old bed. *"How can you sleep in that thing?"* I said to him once, angry, trying to hurt him. Because my mother had slept in it. "A bed is all it is," he said in his weary tone. "An inanimate object."

The closet door slides open with the pressure of my fingers. I poke the flashlight in. The sudden light hurts my eyes. There, in the back, is a gun case. Dusty, perhaps even forgotten. I reach in slowly and draw it out. I put off the flashlight, but it's ruined my night-sight. I find the zipper and draw it partly open and reach inside. It's the .410. I'll take it if it's the only gun I can find, but it's small caliber and only two shots. I zip the zipper back up and slip it back where it leaned a moment ago, turn on the flashlight again. Outside a dog howls—then I could swear I hear voices. I cut off the light again, freeze. Strain. No. My ears fill in the silence with the sound of ghosts.

I stick my arm inside and feel against the wall. No sign of the Winchester.

I close the closet slowly, quietly, turn off the flashlight. Now into the hallway, I check the hall closet. No sign of it there. I go to the attic. There's a folding ladder built into the ceiling outside what used to be my bedroom, down the hall from his bedroom, which is at the edge of the stairs. I reach up and pull the cord that will bring it down. Like everything in his house, it's well oiled, refuses to creak. It unfolds silently. Down with it comes the scent of the attic—old clothing, must, insulation, the brisk cold of the outdoors. At the top of the stairs I flick on the flashlight, let the narrow beam of it slide among the jumble of boxes, central air-conditioning ducts, and roof support beams.

There are things I don't remember. There's old furniture at the very end of the house, down the long, narrow regular framing of the roof. Boxes. Bags—clothing perhaps. I turn the other way. And then I freeze.

The sound his pickup makes in the driveway washes over the house. The lights sweep across the front of the house, spray into the guest bedroom next to his. And when they've swept through the house, they go out. Darkness now, the hiss of the truck and then silence.

I scramble halfway down the folding ladder and pull the bottom section up behind me, then jump onto the narrow walkway, lie down. His footsteps rasp on the walk. I reach down, pull at the ladder mechanism—it's loaded with countersprings and it resists coming. His key in the door. The attic closes slowly, there's a tiny last whoosh of warm air, then the cold of November takes over and I lie frozen, trying to think of what to do.

# PARANOIA

Addie swings the pickup off Hamilton Street and into the drive. The headlights splash up against the red-trimmed white house, throw color into the grass, the drive. The air is cold when he hops out of the truck with the bag of groceries and goes up the walk. The air is still. There is no sound anywhere around him—the whole world has been sucked dry of sound. The yellow lights that glimmer in the dark accentuate the distance. Like flying alone in deep space.

Shivering with the cold, he stops in the front hallway, just inside the front door. He has just put down the bag of groceries, just begun to take off his coat and turn on the hall light, but he stops. The hot shape of panic comes loose in the air and forms in his mouth.

Someone has been in the house since he left. He isn't sure how he knows, but he's sure of it. And he's just as certain that whoever it is is still in the house. He stands fast where he is and listens. Nothing. He strains.

He can see the dark living room, the dining room, and the edge of the kitchen. In the kitchen, the refrigerator comes on, and he can feel the shudder and hum of it through the floor, through the static air. His head rocks with the beating of his heart.

They were broken into once before, back after Roy died, when Jack still lived with him. A couple of high school kids, out for a lark. The boys who'd done it were arrested, but he hadn't pressed charges. You can't send boys to jail.

He tries to think, but he's paralyzed with indecision. He thinks of circling the house, of finding the broken window or forced door. Then he'd go over to Croutys' and call the police. But he thinks of the .30-.06 in the hall closet, not three feet from where he stands.

Slowly, sliding across the carpet and taking hold of the door handle, he holds his breath and pulls the door. It feels like waiting for something to explode.

The door opens soundlessly, and he moves closer to it. The darkness moves, trembles. The shape of the things in his house seems strange to him. The familiar scent of the closet—wool, age, mothballs—breathes on him softly. He reaches in, behind the overcoats and raincoats, and runs his hand along the wall. The rifle is gone.

His mouth turns solid, and he can't swallow. He moves his hand along the wall, desperate now, and scared, hoping for the feel of the leather case against his trembling fingers.

And then it is there, where it wasn't before.

Silently, he draws it out, then pulls the zipper enough to slide the rifle out. He pulls back the bolt. The rifle isn't loaded, but there's a box of cartridges on the closet shelf, and he takes a handful—the *dink* sound travels into the hall and hangs in the air—and loads the rifle.

There is no sound in the house, no movement, but he knows there is someone here. He can smell it. He takes the safety off.

He goes along the short hall and turns back toward the bathroom, toward Roy's old room. The gun out in front of him, he pokes into the bedroom, then turns on the light. Nothing. He checks the closet and then beneath the bed. The gun feels heavy, as though it might stretch his arms.

He leaves the light on and goes into the bathroom. Again, nothing. He checks in the shower, pushes the plastic curtain to the side with the barrel of the gun. Nothing. Then he goes back out along the hall and into the kitchen. Still nothing. Leaving all the lights on, he goes upstairs, more relaxed now. He checks his bedroom, his closet, the upstairs bathroom, then the empty bedroom—Jack's old room—and checks that closet too, then, the lights on, goes downstairs again and to the basement.

Finally, almost satisfied that he is alone, he unloads the rifle, puts the safety on, and puts it back where it belongs. Still there is uneasiness in the air.

He checks everything—the silver, the televisions, his tools—and nothing is gone. Everything is precisely as he left it. He looks at all of the windows, even goes out to the shop and looks, and nothing shows any sign of entry.

Then it occurs to him that it is his wife who has been here. The scent is hers.

He will never allow himself to believe in ghosts, only dreams, but just this moment, crazy with nerves and the shapes that dash across in the darkness, he believes that she has been here. "Adolf Pleasance," he says aloud, "you been watching too much television," and then he listens to the ringing of his voice in the empty house and wishes it would dissolve. His skin has the hard, tight texture of gooseflesh, and he can't make it go away.

Then he says, quietly, "Go away, Alison. Please." It doesn't hurt to say it—not as long as there's no one else around to hear.

For a long time, he keeps all of the lights on and sits in the kitchen smoking, trying to make the trembling in his hands go away. Finally he gets up and makes himself a drink. He takes a couple of sips. Suddenly his legs feel heavy, and he thinks he will vomit. He looks at his drink and then at his bottle of tonic water. Frightened, he gets up. He can feel his chest contract. He holds up the bottle, and he is certain he can see a vague discoloration in it. He opens the cap and smells it, and it is all wrong. He's dizzy now and can't breathe. He is almost certain that he's been poisoned. He thinks of calling an ambulance. But what if he's wrong? What if it isn't poisoned? People will think he's crazy. He goes to the bathroom and makes himself vomit.

"You paranoid old sonofabitch," he says, sitting down on the bathroom rug. "You paranoid old sonofabitch."

When he feels better, he pours out everything in the refrigerator that isn't sealed. It feels crazy to do it, but he can't help himself. Then he goes and gets the bag of groceries he left at the door and puts them away.

In the living room he turns on the television. The cool blue light bathes the room; it's the only thing that makes him relax.

# THE PICTURES

I can hear him walking through the house. He knows I've been here—knows someone's been here—because he walks slowly through the whole house, room by room, and I can hear him close below me—when he comes up the stairs I can hear him breathing—and to be this close to him yet be so far away makes me want to explode. I don't want to see him; I don't want him to see me.

The lights blaze for a long time. The light snakes through the cracks at the seam of the folding ladder. I prop myself up on my elbows and look around. There's nowhere to escape to up here. Not now. Either I wait until he goes to bed, or I wait until he leaves again, which probably wouldn't be until morning.

I wish I'd dressed more warmly.

Then I can hear him in the kitchen, doing dishes, making a drink. And then I can hear the television go on, the volume up loud. The sound of it strained out by the emptiness—if you had never known such a thing existed and heard it, it would sound like madness. The crackle of laughter, the heightened bent of pitchmen's voices, all of it jamming back and forth against itself, back and forth, like walking through an asylum. It's hypnotic, like the cold. I pull my coat around me, lie flat.

*My mother bends down over my face and kisses me on the cheek. I'm not asleep and when she does so I turn to kiss her cheek, but I don't kiss it. I bite it. This makes her start, then it makes her smile, and she stays bent over me, looking at me. "I love you," she says.*

*"I bit you because I love you."*

*"People do different things for love," she says with the same impenetrable smile. There's the sound of water behind her—a running stream, a waterfall. There is whiteness around her. I am lying on whiteness. We are in the sewing room. I'd forgotten it was the "sewing room," or that they called it that. The guest bedroom later, after her death. She works in here. It's her own room. There's a sofa and that's where I am, and the wall that separates the room from the hallway is gone, and beyond us the forest has grown up to the house. How could I have forgotten. I sit up, and she has her hands on my shoulders. "Where's Roy?"*

*Still at school.*

*"Where's Daddy?"*

*Still at work.*

*"What are you doing?"*

*Preparing some things.*

*"What things?"*

*A story about a woman who is not.*

*"Not what?"*

*Not. Not. Simply not.*

*"What's the story about?"*

*About the end. About how the end became the end and how it was the beginning.*

*Her hands lift from my shoulders, and she lifts up into the air, white and huge as a bird. She moves to the desk. There are pictures, but I can't see who's in the pictures. Next to the desk there is a smaller piece of furniture, a nightstand except not used as a nightstand.*

*My father drags the desk partway out the door and when it won't come any farther, raises up his ax and smashes the part of it that protrudes. You can see the red of his face. You can see the muscles straining in his arms when the ax comes down in the twilight and splinters against the old, burnished wood. Halfway out the doorway of the kitchen, stuck on the stairs like a moaning cow, he smashes it with his ax and it splinters, then splinters again. Pieces of it fall off, and he drags them out, throws them by the trash barrel, then goes back, drags it out farther, and smashes it again, smashes it until it's all in pieces and falls on the grass.*

I awaken with a start. I've drifted off in the cold, and I'm shivering. I've forgotten where I am, what I was doing, and waking comes hard. I have no idea if I've made any noise, but I'm not lying in the same position I was before. The house seems to be dark and silent. I strain to see my watch, but I can't tell what time it is without any light. It's still dark, or there would be light through the vents at either end of the eaves. Slowly, stiff with the cold and inactivity, I pull myself into a sitting position.

A wave of shuddering goes through me like fever. It starts on my head and neck, and my whole body is shaking with the cold, and for a moment I'm completely out of control, unable to stop it. But it's not just the cold, it's the dark and where I am. It's like claustrophobia, like if I don't get out I'll drop into hysterical shaking. My heart begins to race. I turn on the flashlight and point it out in the direction I know to be away from my father's bedroom. The light softens things, anchors them. I lay the flashlight on the walkway and pull my jacket up close around me, adjust my scarf. Then I pick up the light again and look around to see if there is anything—clothing, blankets—close by I might use to keep warm. But there's nothing I can get to without making noise.

I turn off the flashlight and sit here in the darkness trying to calm myself, trying to figure out what to do. It takes a minute or two, but I get the panic of my breathing under control. If I have to, I'll wait until he gets up to go to work to leave. In the distance, I think I can hear him snoring. I lie back down—maybe if I go back to sleep.

When I wake up again there is sunlight through the louvered vents at either side of the house, and the house beneath me is silent. I am amazed that I have slept at all.

I have no idea what time it is—my watch says ten o'clock, but it doesn't feel right—and I have no idea if my father is still here or if he's gone. I pull myself up into a sitting position, try to stretch a little. It's fractionally warmer than it was last night, so it may well be later in the morning.

I look around the attic for the rifle, flick on the flashlight. Over in the corner, opposite the central air-conditioning ducts and behind some bags of what are probably old clothes, there is what looks like another rifle case. Slowly, as silently as I can manage, I crawl toward it. My father built the narrow walkway I'm crawling on, and it has his trademark perfection—smooth-sanded planks tight as barrel staves, countersunk finishing nails puttied in with plastic wood. Implacable.

I pull the case out from behind an old nightstand, then open the zipper. The case is old and brittle with dry rot. I reach inside, and as soon as I touch it, I know it's the Winchester. I pull it out slowly—the narrow beams of the roof supports hover in close—roofing nails protrude through the plywood roof. Once I have it in my hands, cold, smelling of oil, I turn it over, examine the cocking mechanism. Still well oiled, in good shape. I start to cock it, just to see, but then think better of it. I don't want to make noise if he's still around. I slide it back into the cloth and leather case.

What I need now is ammunition.

Next to the rifle case there is an old nightstand, a piece of furniture that registers in the back of my mind, wants to pull something loose.

Slowly, aching still with the cold and the strain of the quiet, I slide open the drawer at the top, thinking maybe there's a box of shells he put away and forgot about. The wood of the cabinet is dry with the cold and slides smoothly. There are no shells, not in this drawer, but what appears when the drawer is open and the beam of the flashlight splashes inside presses my heart up into the back of my throat, and I can hardly breathe.

I have always believed that my father destroyed every bit of evidence of my mother's life that existed. With my brother, I saw him do it. I don't remember it precisely, but it became sort of a myth between my brother and me, how it happened. We had been taken away from the house and were next door. He disappeared for a while after they took her away, and when he came back, he was a different man than we'd ever seen before—and a man we never saw after. He raged through the house and took everything out to the back to the barrel where we burned trash, and he set it on fire. His rage resides in my head with an almost cartoonlike quality—I was five years old when it happened—and in my mind I can see the walls of the house swell and relax, swell and relax with his rage.

Letters, pictures, clothing, furniture. He destroyed everything. I remember the fire. Roy and I talked about him that night while we slept at Croutys', and to both of us it felt like he had gone away with mother. While she had not been replaced, he had been replaced by some twin that came and replaced his evenness of temper, his reasonableness, with angry madness. But then the next day the twin was gone and our father was back again, pale and gray and exhausted and doing everything he could to make life normal again for us. Almost like nothing had happened. Like he had been rehearsing for this for years, and now he was playing the part he had memorized. But he had not written parts for us.

During the time I was growing up, only rarely did I see photographs of her—she was like some ancestor who existed before the advent of photography. She was always "her" or "she" or "Mother" or "your mother" or "Mrs. Pleasance," and she was never referred to with love or humor but with a drawn seriousness. Never Mom or Mommy. Some people in the neighborhood had pictures of her—coincidental photographs from picnics or holidays. You could see her standing in the background, holding a plate of food, or chatting with someone else, out of focus, some other beaming face in the foreground. Sometimes spectacularly normal looking, spectacularly average. Or more often, standing by herself, not looking at the camera but holding a drink and staring into it, or looking at the ground. One where she stood in a schoolyard in winter with my kindergarten teacher, steam around their faces, waiting for me and some of my friends. My mother mysterious: a woman who had ended her existence and then had her existence denied by my father.

At the top of this drawer, beneath a layer of dust, is an astonishingly clear photograph of her. She is sitting on a long row of benches that curves around out of focus to ascend out of the picture. She is alone, the sole subject of the photograph. It is early winter, perhaps early spring, because the trees nearby are bare, but she wears no overcoat. Her hair is jet black, and her hands are folded tightly together, and there are pigeons on the incidental pavement in front of her. Beyond her, out of focus, is what looks like the Arc de Triomphe but isn't. She looks clear-eyed, brittle.

*My mother stands at the doorway, her hand on my shoulder. We are side by side. My shirt is thin, and her dress impresses its fabric on my shoulder. Her hand is in the back of my hair; her hand is on my skull. It is spring. "Do you remember me?" she says, and I look up at her and wonder what it is she wants from me. I tell her I remember her better than anything. "Do you remember New York?" she says. I nod my head. Not long ago at all. I remember it. I loved her and sat at a table that Roy refused to sit at. We ate cherries. I remember. Daddy sent us to visit her and then came to get us. "Do you remember the silver dollars?" she says. I shake my head.*

*"I have a silver dollar for the years you and Roy were born."*

*I nod. The darkness seethes. There will or will not be a storm. It is spring. The trees will scrape the house, and I will dream my mother in the lightning.*

I take the photograph out of the drawer and blow off the dust. My hands are trembling. My lungs have been squeezed shut.

I have never had a very good recollection of what she looked like— every time I try to picture her all I get is a blur of dark hair, pale skin. But of course your mind blocks things out until sometime when you are unaware and something, a dream, a scent, peels a clear image out of the depth of your memory. But suddenly here she is, in sharp, close focus. This one photograph seems to explain so much—the structure of her face, what you can see in her eyes. And yet it creates other mysteries. She looks like I remember my brother looking—she has the same nose, the same reticent mouth. I always thought I was the one who looked like her. Now suddenly a great vacuum I never even knew existed has opened up and it sucks things and they begin to rise out in my own internal blackness.

It is to the best of my recollection the only photograph I've ever seen of her in this house since she died. And here it is, a window open across a twenty-year chasm. Nearly terrified, I lift out the one beneath it—this one, in color, of both my parents on a beach somewhere, his hair blonder than I can ever remember seeing it, the natural blond still in it without silver. His swimming trunks are wet, and he looks slimmer and harder and handsomer than I remember him; her swimming suit is completely dry, and she wears in her eyes the conviction she will dissolve if the water touches her.

I just stare at them. My mother as a young woman. Not as a cipher but as a woman. Maybe it's just the photography, but her eyes have a rattled look to them. My father looks happy but desperate—the look of a man in a foreign country trying to make the best of a language he doesn't understand.

In the other part of the nightstand there is an old UVA library copy of *For the Union Dead* by Robert Lowell.

I am shaking with disbelief. Everything else recedes temporarily. There are maybe a dozen photographs.

*I am walking up the May sidewalk, school having been closed early because of a burst water pipe.*

Some color, most black and white.

My breath is shallow, getting shallower.

# BOSSA NOVA

My older brother, Roy, stands next to the diner window, his hands shoved deeply into his jeans pockets, his blond, slightly too long hair drifting in the mid-September breeze. We're waiting outside while our father is next door, in Dunkel's Drug, buying cigarettes.

I stand next to Roy and put my hands in my pockets too. Inside the diner it's bright with fluorescent light. The windows along the brick and cinderblock front of the diner are only waist-high, but there are yellow-white curtains that run along the broad windows about chin-high. It's early evening, so it's still light outside, and I look at the side of my brother's face—the sharp jaw and the faint blond moustache on his lip—and then follow the focus of his gaze. There are two waitresses: one of them older, maybe fifty. Her name is Rose and she's worked at the diner for years. Never takes your order with a pen and pad like the other, younger one, but always remembers exactly what you ordered even if you change your mind five times while you're telling her.

The other one is about twenty-five—or somewhere in the indecipherable world of women's ages between twenty and thirty-five. I say twenty-five because she seems at least ten years older than me. She wears exactly the uniform that Rose does, but the way she wears it—the way the waist cuts inward with the shape of her, the way her breast juts beneath her name tag, the way when she turns and the skirt end of it moves and fills your head with the hard shape of her butt—makes her look like an entirely different kind of being. It makes me glad I have my hands in my pockets—because at fourteen nearly everything female makes you want to sit down or keep your hands in your pockets.

"What are you looking at?" Daddy says, electric-voiced, from behind us. Neither of us expected him to take more than a minute in Dunkel's, but the both of us jump when he speaks. I turn toward him first. He has a cigarette punched in between his lips. He needs a shave and squints behind his glasses through the cigarette smoke.

Roy, more comfortable somehow, turns slowly and edges toward the door—maybe he wasn't thinking about the waitress the way I was—and folds his arms together. My father glances at him, then back at me. I look at my feet, then beyond his shoulder.

Across State Street is the town square, and there are kids on the swing sets, a little girl in diapers running by the slide. Two women with strollers stand near the gazebo, which my father recently painted; it glows white in the low evening light.

A pickup truck goes past on the street between my father and the square, and the air feels empty once it's gone. Emptiness makes me nervous. "I was trying to see the Specials Board," I say, because the emptiness wants something to be said.

"Anything good?" he says around the cigarette and steps toward us. Sometimes it's impossible to tell how he means things, and right now it feels like he can read my mind.

"I don't know. I couldn't read it."

"Maybe we ought to have your eyes checked," he says. The cigarette is out of his mouth now, and he turns as he speaks—his posture confirms that he was reading my mind. He pitches his cigarette into the street and pushes toward the diner door.

We come here usually once a week, and tonight we sit in one of the two booths in the corner where we always sit. The diner is on the corner of State and Post streets. The State Street side is where the town square is, and where Roy and I were looking in the window. Roy sits in the corner, opposite Daddy, facing toward the door. I sit on the other side, next to our father, where I can't see what's going on in the diner, except for in the reflection in the window opposite us. The windows on the Post

Street side are higher up than those in front, and you can see the loading bays of the Post Office. It's too light outside yet for the lights inside the diner to cast a good reflection.

Someone Roy knows must come in, because he gives a little lift of his chin in recognition.

My father takes his Winstons out of his pocket and puts them on the table, and I'm glad he doesn't light one. At the edge of the table, against the wall, there are sugar and salt and pepper shakers, a bottle of Heinz ketchup, and a cubical napkin dispenser. Behind them there are four menus. They have a sticky, dog-eared look to them, like there have been hoards of high school kids sitting in this booth, fingering them.

My father lifts one out and offers it to Roy. Roy doesn't accept the menu, doesn't even look at it. "I already know what I'm going to have," he says. I look to where he's watching the younger waitress setting down plates of meat loaf and steaming mashed potatoes in front of two old men in the middle of the room. When she puts the food down, she smiles— we're all three of us suddenly watching her—and turns toward us. There's an image of us that goes through my head, barely decipherable—three guys, alone. It wants to tell me something but it's too fast, and now she's right in front of us. The stiff white fabric of her uniform rustles against the edge of the table.

"Hello, Mr. Pleasance, how are you?" He's on the inside of the booth, and he has to crane around to look at her. He smiles, shows the yellow, tobacco-stained fronts of his teeth. The name tag on her uniform says Diane.

"Have you made up your minds yet?" she says, "or would you like a little more time?" She doesn't look at Roy or me.

"What do you recommend?" my father says. He always says this and always orders what she recommends.

"The meat loaf," she says. "The meat loaf looks really good tonight. And the chicken." She has one of those bright voices like on television, never anything but shiny, perky, absolutely convincing.

"I'll have the meat loaf," Daddy says and smiles again—the same craning, whiskery, yellow-toothed smile.

"Me too," says Roy, "and a Coke."

"I'll have the chicken with french fries and a Coke," I say.

When the waitress is out of earshot, my brother says, "Have you ever noticed that she never looks at either one of us, only at Daddy? And have you ever noticed that she knows him by name?"

When Roy first starts talking, my father doesn't say anything. He just wears the weary, annoyed look he always wears. But then the look turns harder, and as Roy's finishing, Diane comes back with two amber plastic tumblers full of Coke, and from the same uniform pocket where she keeps her order book, she takes two paper-wrapped straws and puts them on the table next to the Cokes. She could—would—have heard the tail end of what Roy is saying, but it would have been senseless to her. Still, blood rises up into my father's face. "I'll bring your coffee in a moment, Mr. Pleasance," she says. He never orders it but always gets it. She stops a minute and gives her smile a chance to hang in the air before she turns to go back toward the counter.

"What I think," Roy says, sort of leaning up on the table and pressing himself toward Daddy, "is that she's kind of sweet on you."

If it were another tone of voice, or another subject, I'd guess he's trying to be funny. But his voice is deadly serious, challenging, and women are not the thing to be funny about where our father is concerned. If our father has had a real date since Mother died, I don't know about it. In the old days, we talked about what it would be like if we had a new mom. We liked the shows on TV or the movies where the kids would try to get the adults together—and we'd watch them for hope, advice, a way that we could help. But you'd say something, and it'd be like suddenly winter had come.

His face as red as the cellophaned Winston package, he looks out the window, picks up the cigarettes, and then drops them again. Now he looks hard at Roy—the two of them look a lot alike, the same chin, the same blond hair, the same blade-sharp nose—and when it seems like he's about to say something, or do something, like smack Roy across the table, Diane comes back again, his cup of coffee in one hand, and someone else's meat loaf rested in the crook of her other arm.

She leaves again, and Roy looks at her, then back at our father. Roy is seventeen and just starting his last year in school. He's as tall as Daddy now, but skinnier. He'll probably be taller when he finishes growing, but he'll never be as solid. He's got wire-rimmed, pilot-style glasses just like our father's. He's not going to college next year but is going to go to work for Daddy full-time in the fix-it business, which has been the plan since Mother died, or even before.

It's always been the plan, the way, even though I'm only fourteen, my going off to college and doing something completely different has always been the plan.

"Maybe you should ask her out or something," Roy says. His voice still has that sound to it. Like suddenly tonight Roy is sick and tired of our father being the way he is, and he's going to change it all, right now, tonight. "Go to a movie or something."

I look at him, then turn away quickly. The look of my brother turns the tongue in my mouth cold. For something to do with my eyes, I stare at the two old men eating meat loaf. The silence waits for the explosion. Forks move against plates. Cups set back down into saucers.

Daddy says, "How was school today?" to me like Roy never spoke.

"Two girls got in a fight," I say quickly, making it up. "It was amazing. They started pulling each other's hair and stuff. It's crazy to see two girls fight." I look at my father, and he's not looking at me, not paying attention. "Isn't it, Daddy?"

Roy says, "You could. I think she'd probably say yes."

Daddy's hand shoots across the table and takes hold of Roy's arm just below the shoulder. It's fast, decisive, the way you'd grab a snake you've just pinned behind the head. You can tell from the look on Roy's face that he is in pain. "Don't you ever make such presumptions," Daddy says. His face is like stone.

You'd never guess from looking at our father, or from knowing him, that he's capable of this kind of thing. Everybody says what a kind man he is. But there are certain topics.

There are tears in Roy's eyes, but his face is stony too. He says, "Yes sir," between pressed teeth.

My father is no longer red in the face when he releases Roy. Veins still stand out on his neck, but the red is gone from everywhere but his ears. The air in the diner feels loose and rubbery to me, like the tension kept everything in place and now there's nothing to hold things from floating off.

I look at my brother, and I'm glad he's wearing glasses, because maybe no one else can see the tears. I look at him again, and he picks up a menu and starts looking at it. He knows I can see the tears, and I look away.

When the waitress comes with the food, we are all sitting in silence. Some kids Roy probably knows come in and sit at a booth by the front. It's dark enough out now that I can see their reflection. A girl with wheat-colored hair stands next to the booth a moment while she takes off her jacket, and I have to watch the movement of her sweater as she sits down. They all laugh and make a lot of noise.

Out on the street after dinner, Daddy heads for the pickup. It's nice out, warm and dark, and you can see stars. Roy says, "Maybe we'll walk home." He pushes my shoulder. "Yeah, Dad, we'll walk," I say.

He shrugs. His lighter clinks, and in a moment the air is rich with the scent of naphtha and cigarette smoke. He climbs into the pickup without us, without looking at us or saying anything. In a moment the lights are on, and he's backing it out of the angle-parking spot. He pulls up right next to us, and the truck feels huge. The rush of the engine fills the air around us. Roy's eye-to-eye with our father, and I'm eye-to-eye with the place on the side of the truck that says A. PLEASANCE & SONS. "Come straight home," he says.

Roy nods, and in a moment the truck is out of sight and the night is silent. We go along the square in the darkness, next to Dunkel's and the Lamont Women's Clothier. Except the drugstore, all the stores are dark, and I like the lonely way the evening feels, my brother and me the only two in the universe. Across the way you can see the Ranchero with the neon Pabst sign in the window. Someone opens the broken screen door and pushes the inside wooden door open, and you can hear the jukebox droning.

We turn off State Street and start up the hill. Porch lamps are on in the darkness, and trees loom over the road. We don't walk on the sidewalk but on the dew-wet grass next to it. "Sometimes I hate him," Roy says after a while. I feel the same way, but it surprises me he says it—the two of them have always gotten along with nearly telepathic ease, like they were two parts of the same man.

"When he grabbed you," I say, "did it hurt?"

"Naw," he says, but the words make him rub his arm. I try to imagine another world than the one where Roy finishes high school and goes to work in the fix-it business and the two of them work together, day in, day out, endlessly. I try to imagine it for myself, and even though I work with the two of them all the time, the thought of myself alone in my father's pickup, with no end to it ever in sight, makes me want to explode.

After a while, he says, "Maybe we should go by her house once and talk to her and see if she'll ask *him* out."

"He's so much older than she is."

"I know," he says, slightly ahead of me now, his voice as dark and weary as his face.

"Why do you even think she'd want to go out with him?"

We are walking by a dark house, and there are scraggly fruit trees at the edge of the yard. He pulls a dry branch off one of them and breaks it to bits in his hands. I can smell the sap. "I don't know," he says.

Then, after a while: "It's just not natural," he says. The words extend far out into the air, and I don't know what he means exactly. It's been the same way for years, and I don't know why it should suddenly make a difference to him now.

Finally I say, "Do you know where she lives?"

"No, but we could look her up in the phone book or something."

I float along in the darkness next to him. My shoes and socks are wet with dew. We're nearly halfway home, but I don't want to get there. I just want to stay in the darkness. A car comes past. Before it comes into sight over the hill, you can see the lights reflected on the telephone wires.

After that night, we don't go to the diner again. Daddy doesn't say anything, he just doesn't take us back there. When we eat out again, it's at one of the places outside town—the Midway Truck Stop, the Hardees on the highway.

Winter comes, and he stops working outdoors and starts working indoors, painting, remodeling. Life with him always has the same feeling of predictability to it. Every morning when I get up, he will be in the kitchen, smoking, drinking a cup of coffee. Then Roy will get up, and the two of us will eat the same kind of cereal for breakfast. It is like a tunnel. I know when Roy finishes school things will change—some-how—but it has been this way so long it is impossible to imagine anything different.

It is toward March that a woman named Mrs. Stannard, who lives alone in a big old white-with-red-trim house at the corner of Marlin Court and Davis Road, hires my father to paint the interior of her house.

She's about Daddy's age or maybe a few years younger. She has a husky, loud voice, a squarish face that's pretty when she smiles, and while she's not fat exactly she has hips that are too big for her—when she stands up from a chair, you expect something different.

When Roy and I come to help out the first Saturday—Daddy says it will be a two-week job—she has the evangelical station on the radio, but she turns it to jazz music once we're in the house. She brings the three of us Cokes and sandwiches for lunch. She jokes with Roy and me but doesn't say much to our father. It strikes me as funny how different the lives of men and women alone are.

When we're finished for the day—Roy and I are in the back of the house, running icy water from the outside spigot into the paint trays and shaking out the brushes on the winter-dead grass—Daddy comes outside and says he's going to have dinner with Mrs. Stannard. He says it without looking at us but while inspecting one of the roller trays. He says it in a dead-voiced kind of way that makes you want to stare at him hard and know what's going on.

He gives us money and tells us to get ourselves something to eat in town, then get on home. Roy looks at me when he goes back inside. All day long I haven't seen him say a word to her, except for "yes ma'am" and "thank you ma'am."

"What do you think?" Roy says when we get away from the house and are walking down the road toward town. I can't make out the tone of Roy's voice.

I rub my paint-speckled hands together. Latex paint peels right off your hands like the rubber it is. "What do you think they're going to do?" I say, though I regret asking as soon as the words are out.

"How the hell would I know? Have dinner probably." He kicks gravel at the edge of the road, and I look at him. For a moment, in the dark, he could be Daddy.

The two of us have dinner at the diner together. It's different with just us. I like it that we're covered with paint, I like the image I have of the two of us together, alone, working men.

Diane and Rose are there, and Diane waits on us. "Haven't seen you boys around in a long time," she says. First, I like the way she recognizes us, and second, I like the way she says "boys," not like children but good old boys. I rub the paint on my hands. She bites the inside corner of her mouth when she looks at Roy, and I look at him. There are flecks of paint on his glasses, but I envy the clear-eyed look he gives her. I'd have to look away. In a moment, he pulls off his glasses and wipes at the paint flecks.

"D'yall know what you're going to have?"

"What do you recommend?" I say before Roy can say it.

"I'd personally go for the Salisbury steak special," she says. "Gravy and mashed potatoes."

I nod. "And a Coke."

Roy puts back on his glasses and looks at her for a moment. It's a little like he's trying to translate something she's saying with her eyes. "I'll have the same thing," he says.

We're in the kitchen, doing the morning's dishes when he comes home. It's not late, but he's had maybe a couple of drinks, and he comes into the kitchen and rubs our heads like we're five-year-olds. He smells like gin, and he's smiling a gin smile, not the late evening gin scowl. His nicotine-stained teeth show when he says it's mighty good of us to have cleaned up the kitchen.

It seems to make Roy angry that he's smiling. I ignore it because I'm glad to see him happy. He turns on the radio and fiddles with the dial until he finds the jazz station from Charlottesville that Mrs. Stannard had on while we were at her house.

"Know what that is?" he says, referring to the music, sort of dance-floating back from the living room into the kitchen. His grin is embarrassing, it's so strange. I shake my head. "That's bossa nova music," he says. "It's from Brazil, and it's mighty good to dance to." He puts one hand to his hip and the other in the air and swings around a little, like Ricky Ricardo in "I Love Lucy." I have to look away from him.

In the morning he's in the kitchen when I get up, smoking and sipping coffee. I have the idea that his exuberance from last night is going to carry over into this morning, but he doesn't say anything, just stares at the tip of his Winston, which he rolls to a sharp cone in the ashtray. Just like any Sunday.

Roy's gone most of the day. He comes back after Daddy and I have eaten supper. He comes into the yellow light of the kitchen looking pale and queasy. Daddy says, "Where the hell have you been, young man?" but Roy just stands there teetering like he's fixing to fall over, then turns and runs for the bathroom. Daddy starts laughing. He takes off his glasses and laughs harder.

Worried, I get out of my chair and follow Roy down the hall. He's vomiting. "You okay?" I say.

"Leave him alone, Son," my father calls.

It's the middle of the night when I run into Roy in the hallway, on the way to the bathroom. I've been asleep, and I'm in my underwear. I look at him a minute, and he seems different than he did yesterday. "Where'd you go?" I whisper. "Today."

"I went to Diane's house," he says.

"What happened?"

"She fucked me. We got drunk, and she fucked me. Never happened to me before. I was sitting in her living room, and she came out of the bedroom buck naked."

The only light is from the streetlamp outside, and it comes bluish from the window at the end of the hall. I can't see him very well, and I don't know whether he's kidding or lying or what. If I had my eyes closed, I'd swear it wasn't his voice at all. He has a smell to him like walking past the Ranchero on Sunday morning. I wait for him to say more, but he doesn't, just slides around me, down the hall.

As school is winding down, Roy disappears a lot. Maybe this is a kind of preparation for him for the end of school. Things are the same between my father and me, but the balance of the house is different now. If Roy gives any explanations for his disappearances to Daddy, I don't know. He does his work, and that's all I know.

Now and then, Daddy sees Mrs. Stannard, in the evenings for dinner, even though the job is long since finished. Sometimes I eat at friends' houses, and sometimes I eat alone—fry hamburgers in the skillet and cook tater tots in the oven. I watch TV in the evenings, hang around with my friends, drive out into the country, and drink beer in empty fields. I'm always the first one home.

When my father and I eat together, we don't say much—he reads the paper, and I pretend to do homework.

I like the evenings when he goes over to Mrs. Stannard's. The couple of drinks he has over there aren't like the ones he has at home—they put him in a good mood, and he listens to bossa nova at night on the radio station from UVA, sometimes dances around the living room.

At the beginning of June, Roy graduates from school and goes to work for Daddy. He just slips right into the working routine after he comes back from his graduation night trip to the beach.

Since Roy's eighteen now and a "working man," he can do what he wants. He keeps his own beer in the refrigerator and goes out nearly every night. I see him now and again with his friends in the parking lot behind Audie's Ford dealership out on the highway. A lot of the older kids hang around there at night, drinking beer and showing off their cars. Guys have Torinos and GTOs and Firebirds and Camaros, and they'll get in and stomp the accelerator and lay down thick patches of smoking rubber as the cars fishtail out onto the highway. Then they'll come back and do it again.

One night toward the end of June, I go out there with some of my friends, and Roy is there with Diane—I've never seen them together before. He's never brought her around the house, but there they are, him leaning up against the side of someone's Buick, his arms around her, and his hands on her backside. She's wearing tight jeans, and she looks younger than she does with her uniform on. She could be eighteen.

In a little while I see them walking, and he's smoking a Winston and she's got one of her hands stuck down inside the back of his pants. "Look at that," my friend Jason says.

"So what?" I say.

Roy comes in much later than me, and I can hear him throwing up in the bathroom again.

We used to do a lot of things together, and tonight he didn't even say hello. He used to bring me along for stuff—like, "Hey, Jack, want to go to the movies?" or "Hey Jack, want to chuck the football around?"

I watch him in the morning at the breakfast table, and he doesn't look at me. He just gets up to go to work with Daddy, a pack of Winstons in his shirt pocket.

During the summer, I'm a counselor at the YMCA. I spend all afternoon at the day camp, teaching kids how to swim, and when I finally leave, my head feels waterlogged from being in the pool all day, and I can't get out of my mind the millions of images of the girl counselors in their bathing suits. It always seems so remarkable to me that they can be at ease at all with who they are, what they are—the shapes of them in their suits and the way the wet makes the nylon cling. Everything about them seems so completely and ineradicably memorable to me—I walk along the street and I do not see the cracked pavement or the sidewalk but Judy Myerson in her white-white nylon suit, dry now, one pointed toe stabbed into the crystal water, and I know what will happen as soon as the suit hits the water. Or Lori Daniels in her yellow suit, sitting in the lifeguard chair, her nose covered with zinc oxide, her arms and legs as brown as coffee.

This afternoon, when I go home, I just wander, my towel wet in my bag, my bag shifted in front of me to hide the constant evidence of my unavoidable dreaming.

Instead of going up State Street like I usually do, I turn off on Davis Road. It's stiflingly hot, like the air's a person who won't quit following you. There's more shade on Davis Road, and I walk in and out of it, shirtless, feeling the sunlight and the shade on my shoulders, but not thinking about anything at all but the bright blue water of the pool, the sudden translucence of Judy Myerson's suit, the instantaneous coffee-colored pucker of her nipples.

Davis Road goes by Mrs. Stannard's house, but I'm not thinking about that. The street goes the width of town, then keeps on going indefinitely out by the fields and farms outside of town. Where it crosses Marlin Court, where Mrs. Stannard's house is, the street is flat and shaded. I don't even know that this is where I am until I hear the music. Bossa nova.

And then I look, and there's my father's pickup in front of her house. The house is set back from the road, and there are bushes and trees at the edge of the yard, by the road. There is a wide, rectangular patch of yard that has turned brown from the midsummer sun, and then the wide porch with the swing on one side, and an old, busted-looking Toro mower at the side of the house with tall grass growing around it.

There's shade on the near side of the street, where my father's truck is, and I float toward it. I stand here for a minute, next to his truck, smelling the shade and the lawn, listening to the music. The music is faint but strong in the air, the way perfume can be. Now, with the heat of the afternoon and the stillness of the air in the shade, I can hear something in the music I never heard before—something that has to do with my father at Mrs. Stannard's house and my brother in the parking lot with the waitress.

The drive is blacktop but cracked and soft as moss at the edges. I take a few steps and then stop. The music is clearer. I think I can hear laughing. In a minute I'm almost at the end of the driveway, in angled sunlight where anyone who wanted to look could see me. My heart is high up in my chest, pressing at the back of my throat.

The walk between the drive and the porch is slate set in concrete, and it drifts past distantly beneath me. My hands are shaking. I don't know what it is I'm doing, but I'm drawn by the fact of my father's pickup on the street, by the sound of bossa nova, by the possibility of my father's happiness, and by the barely tangible notion that there are a million things happening around me that I cannot see.

The porch is painted gray—my father probably did it for free. I try not to make any noise. The music is louder now. Through the screen door I can see the shadows of the interior now, can hear laughing clearly. I can smell the dust of the porch, the human smell of the house breathing.

I slip up the steps, then go across the porch toward the window on the side of the swing. There's a black WELCOME mat by the door. The window is open, and when my eyes get used to the interior light, I can see my father and Mrs. Stannard, their arms around one another, dancing in the living room. The room looks different from how it did when we painted it, and it takes a moment to remember that when we were working it was covered with drop cloths. I get close to the screen, crouch down. I can smell the metal of the screen. They're whirling and swaying and laughing. My father has one hand on the small of her back, and with his other hand he holds her hand high in the air. Their faces are close together, staring at one another and not looking anywhere else. A world is concentrated between them. It amazes me to see my father like this. Completely amazes me. I don't want to stop looking.

The music changes, not so bright now, slower—it's a saxophone now, slow and husky, so soft and full you could go adrift on it. They slow down, and the hands that were in the air descend; they hold tight against one another. I can feel the music in my chest, and in a minute I've got tears in my eyes, and the porch beneath me blurs. Quiet, reaching out in front of me to keep from stumbling off the porch, I crouch in the dry grass of the yard and run like hell.

In the morning we are all together for breakfast, and I look at my father and there is nothing of the man I saw yesterday in the man who drinks coffee and smokes while Roy and I eat cereal. I want to ask him why, but there aren't adequate words.

I look at Roy and he doesn't say anything, and I wonder what has happened. Ever since our mother died the three of us have been close in a particular way, maybe too close, and now it feels like it's all breaking apart.

Another morning a few days later: my father has already had breakfast by the time I get up. It's hot already, and I'm in the kitchen in nothing but cut-off Levis, sitting at the table eating a bowl of Cheerios when he comes through with a cigarette going. "Morning," I say to him, but he says nothing, just goes out the back door. The screen door slaps shut behind him. I like the smell of cigarettes against the fragrance of morning. It's the only time I like the smell of cigarettes.

He's usually gone by this time of the morning, but I think about it a moment, and I don't recall having heard Roy come in last night. For a moment I sit listening. The refrigerator hums. I can hear tools clanking in the shop. I get up and leave my half-eaten bowl of cereal on the table and go to Roy's room. The door is open, and it doesn't look like he's been home at all. When I go back to the kitchen, my father is standing there, and he looks old suddenly. He has his glasses off, and he's rubbing his eyes.

"You don't know where your brother is," he says. It is not a question.

"No sir," I say.

"Get dressed. I'm going to need your help."

"Daddy, I've got—" I start and then I look at him. He's got his glasses back on, and he's just looking at me. "Yes sir," I say. They'll do without me for a day at the YMCA.

It's a paint job we're doing, painting the exterior of a house across town. I spend most of the day on a ladder with a putty knife scraping paint flakes off the second story of the house. When we get home in the evening, I go in the house first, and there's no sign of Roy. My father doesn't say anything, but when I'm in the shower, through the open window I can hear tools slamming around in the shop.

Roy's still not back in the morning, and I have to go with my father again. That evening, when we come home, there's still no sign of him.

Two mornings later, there he is at the breakfast table, like nothing at all unusual has happened. He's clean-shaven—the soft moustache and scraggly hairs from his chin are gone. Nobody says anything. The percolator on the counter jumps, and you can see splashes of coffee in the glass knob on top.

When Daddy comes into the kitchen he doesn't say anything, doesn't even look at Roy with surprise. It occurs to me that maybe they talked last night—but I would have heard it. Daddy lights a cigarette as he goes out the back door. "Better hurry up there, Son."

The one time I'd like to go with my father to a job, I don't.

All day long at the pool I'm thinking about it, wondering what is happening. The water is like broken glass, and the sunlight is too bright. When I go home, my head splits with the refracted light.

When they come home in the evening, there still isn't a word said between any of us. My head screams with the desire to know, but no one offers anything.

Roy makes supper—hamburgers on the stove and frozen french fries in the oven. Daddy stays in the shop until Roy calls him to come in.

After supper I am sitting on the front step, thinking about leaving, about packing up some things and just lighting out. I'm also thinking about walking into town and getting some ice cream at the High's.

The screen door creaks open behind me and then slaps shut. A lighter clicks behind me, and then I can smell cigarette smoke and naphtha. I don't know whether it's my father or Roy, and I don't look.

"Jack," Roy says. I don't say anything in response. I can hear him drag on his cigarette. It's dusk, and the evening is wild with cicadas. "I think you ought to know I'm leaving."

"Good. When?" I say. I'm surprised by how quick and hard it comes out.

"Couple of weeks."

I reach down and pick up a piece of gravel from the flower bed that's next to the porch. I hold it in my hand, feel the smooth shape of it, then throw it down.

"We went to Richmond, Diane and me. I don't know why we went. It was her idea, I think. I enlisted in the Air Force." He is a step or two behind me, and I don't turn.

"We got a room in a shitty hotel on Broad Street, and we walked around, had a couple of beers in a couple of bars." He drags on his cigarette when he talks, and it gives his words a round, puffy sound. "The thing I couldn't believe was how different the world was. How every street seemed like a whole different world. I just couldn't believe it. Diane had wanted to do things, visit people she knew. All I wanted to do was walk around. She got mad and left the first day. I stayed in the hotel, and the Armed Forces recruiting office was next door. I walked in the door one morning the first minute it was open and took the physical."

Now he's silent for a long time. I can't believe what he's telling me, and I get up off the porch where I'm sitting and start walking out into the grass.

I want to leave. I don't want to hear any more. I hate him for this, for turning everything upside down. I think of Daddy and Mrs. Stannard, and I know that it will end. I turn around a moment and look at him, then take a few more steps out toward the street. *Goddamn you* is what the words in my head say.

"All of my friends are going off to college. Diane doesn't want to see me anymore. There are a lot of things I could do, probably, but I thought I'd join the service."

Suddenly I'm turning back away from the street and heading toward him. All over my body the skin feels hot and wet, and I just want to explode. I want to hit him. I want to scream. In the dusk-light he looks just like Daddy, stony and hard.

I'm two steps away from him now, down from him. It figures he'd join the service. Just like Daddy. I press the knuckles of one hand against the other, and I'm thinking about hitting him, then I'm thinking about hitting one of the square wooden porch columns, but I don't.

He pitches his cigarette out into the yard, and it spins out like a comet and sparks trail off it.

# THE
# INVISIBLE SON

On the walkway, I stack the photographs. I'm taking them. If my father knew they still existed, he'd probably destroy them too.

I take everything and go to the end of the walkway, and slowly, cautiously, push down the ladder mechanism enough so I can see the hallway, down the stairway to the edge of the living room. For a long time I lie here, listening, trying to make sure he isn't home. There is no sound. The refrigerator purrs in the kitchen, the heat comes on, and the pipes in the floorboard radiators click. I wait a long time, dazed, then push the ladder down, slowly unfold it. I climb halfway down the ladder, then pick up the book and pictures, the gun. At the bottom of the ladder, I freeze again, listen. The house has a stale tobacco smell, and my legs, stiff already, want to go out from underneath me. Suddenly I wish I could have seen him, somehow seen his arms and head, the soft skin around his eyes, how he has aged in the time I have been gone, and done it all without his looking at me.

Jansens' yard and Croutys' yards are empty. It's still cloudy out and looks like rain. I open the kitchen door—look to see if there's a light on in the shop; there isn't—then slip out. Then I stop, turn around, go back inside, and leave one of the photographs on the kitchen table. I don't know why I do it—to be cruel, probably. It's a picture of the two of them together, on a stone bench somewhere. A garden—there are azaleas around them, daffodils at their feet. My father, looking eager and happy, has his arm around my mother's shoulder, and he stares at her face, while she has her hands clasped tightly together and stares at the camera with a fierceness in her eyes that is at odds with the setting.

Then I slip out the door and head for the woods.

# BLUE DRESS

He hefts the two five-gallon buckets of paint off the tailgate of the truck, and they're nearly solid weight, and it goes through his head that he should have backed the truck into the drive. The muscles in his forearms strain. Inside the house the telephone rings once, and it makes him start to hurry, but it does not ring again.

At the shop door, he sets the buckets down against the door, and the sudden relief of the weight makes his arms weightless. He unlocks the door and inside, puts the buckets beneath the shop bench. In a moment he's back outside again, heading for the kitchen door. It's been a long day, and after last night's nonsense—tossing and turning in his sleep, swearing he was hearing ghosts—he is exhausted.

He unlocks the kitchen door and pushes it open, and when the door is open, he turns toward the sink, but half a step toward it, wobbles and turns back. The air is thick and slows everything down. The table was clear this morning when he left, and so the photograph stands out against the table's emptiness.

Half of his face freezes—it's a weird sensation, gooseflesh up one cheek and into your scalp—and it goes through his mind that he's having a stroke, that this is what a stroke is like. But then the chill spreads to the rest of his face, his whole scalp and spine. He's not having a stroke. The chill won't go away but climbs down his arms.

He looks at the photograph, then at the ceiling, as if the picture might have fallen. He looks at the photograph again, and it makes him sit down in a chair, all the air and the volition gone out of him. Alison.

Washington, D.C. is where it was taken. Some park, a mansion with spectacular gardens. It comes back to him clearly, makes his heart suck with regret. Not regret about who he is or where he is, or even now, about her death, but regret because of how much time has passed, and how irrevocably, how quickly, and because in his mouth he can taste the day, the two of them getting in the car and just going, ending up in Washington, in Georgetown, and surprised that there was so much green, so much in bloom in the heart of the city.

He hasn't seen a picture of her in years—he didn't know any existed. He can't remember having seen one since the day she died. It hurts to look at her face. Until this moment he only remembered her generally—the shape of her face, the color of her eyes—but the specificity of the photograph jars him, as if she could just get up and walk at him.

He tries to stand up but can't. *There's blood on the walls of the bathroom—how the hell do you get blood off semigloss paint?* Suddenly his eyes are swollen, and tears start to flush out. *Fuck you, Alison.* Everything starts rushing at him, exploding. Alison. His body aches with the work he did today, but it might as well not exist. *Alison why?* He turns the photograph over and leaves it face down on the tabletop. His fingers burn: there is the scent of smoke in his nostrils.

*I'm going back on out to the shop now*, but there in front of him is the doorway to the living room. *Ghosts.* Roy's voice. And through the doorway is the patched place in the ceiling where the lamp used to be.

"I'm just gonna get on back to work."


Addie's up to his elbows in grout when the voice of his older son, Roy, comes from the front of the house. His words hit the still air shrill. And now Addie's pushing himself to his feet, the tile of the bathroom gleaming, the rag in his hands moving, wiping, dropping away. Mrs. Shearin, whose house is only two jagged blocks down the hill from his own, appears at the door, speaking, but he rises past her, sensing as he goes the soft of her shoulder beneath her dress, the living warmth of her breath. "Addie," she is saying, "I think you better get on home, I think Alison's gone and—" She continues, but he is past her now, stumbling in the impossibly long hallway. The air has gone thick, and in the interstices between the passing seconds it is possible to observe the indifferent, stable, material world around him—the Shearin family photographs along the hall, the wallpaper beneath them that he himself hung three winters ago. And then the screen door shudders on its hinges and flies back, slaps against the outer wall, and he is coming down the steps, the worn green grass flying up as he stumbles, runs on all fours, grout from his hands leaving white traces on the grass before he rights himself. His son is on the grass—nine, blond, impossibly beautiful, hair neatly combed from school—*why is he home?* Roy talks, but Addie doesn't listen, or listens only enough to know that she has finally done it, that he has finally failed.

The sunlight is hard and crashes on the sidewalk, on the blinding windshields of parked cars. It is a dimestore 3-D photograph, the air clear as glass, and within it, flat objects floating in front of other flat objects. The house, the trees, the crackling dry grass of the yard.

He runs, but there is no reason anymore to run—he knows this down to the gristle of his heart—but he cannot give up. He will never give up. *Alison goddamn it please.*

Inside, the house is clean, everything is perfectly in its place. And then Alison in the sunlight wearing a blue dress as formal as Sunday and absolutely motionless: her head cocked forward because of the cord that shoots from the thick of her hair at the back of her skull up to the light fixture above her, her hair down around and hiding her face. Beneath her one of the dining room chairs is overturned, and the gleaming polished legs shine beneath her shining high heels, one foot stuck in midstride slightly in front of the other. And as soon as he steps onto the carpet he is struggling with the thick air of the house like a man waist deep in water.

His other son, Jack, sits in the living room armchair, his legs beneath him, his arms pulled into his body, his small white-blond face emotionless and passive, and he starts to say something when Addie passes. "Daddy . . . ," he begins but silences himself. Addie glances at him, and there is a look of something like boredom to his face, a look of age or unknowable sorrow, and what he would like to do is pick up his son and hug him, but he doesn't. *What are you doing in here?* is the thought that tears through him, but there isn't time for questions.

He takes hold of his wife as if making an open field tackle. It is perhaps no more than a second since he came through the door. "Son," he says, lifting her, the word sticking at his teeth. "Go out to the shop and get me a pair of wire cutters." And even while he is saying it, as the boy turns and heads for the kitchen and kitchen door, he is thinking there still must be some way of reviving her—thinking of the time before, and the time before that. The pills and the bloody bathroom. But now the dead feel of her is seeping through his clothing—the hard feel of her legs and hips not like the muscular hardness of a young woman, the knee-weakening thigh-trembling hardness of a young woman but another sick and sorrowful hardness like a dog too long at the edge of the highway.

She's against him, against his chest and arms and turned face—the coarse fragrant wool notwithstanding, the hard feel of her gets down into him and makes his lungs and heart shudder. He lifts her and holds her up, kicks the chair, brings his foot down hard on one of the cross braces between the legs, and when he has it upright again, he's climbing it, thinking *her face in the kitchen this morning, her hands on the boys' jackets, their lunch bags in their hands—how could I have known?* And the boy is coming through the kitchen, rushing to hand him the yellow-handled dikes. He holds her, and, still lifting her, climbs the chair, reaches above her to clip the cord. Her face is next to his, and it revolts him, sickens him. She is moving, her hair moves, and he sees the silver dollars taped to her eyes. *How could you it's so goddamned selfish, so goddamned cruel?* And then she is loose and pure weight in his arms, and he struggles for a place to put her, struggles against the tears and the sucking horror at the back of his throat.

Jack is sitting again, staring. Roy is at the door.

Addie struggles her down to the couch, and when he is free of her, he rubs his hands together—the absence of weight makes his body rise. She is on the couch. He can smell her. The way she used to smell, but the smell of death too, heavy and pungent and low. It's on his hands, in the air. Maybe that's what's transfixed his son. His body is rising. Jack doesn't move, and in a way he is just a part of the scenery, only incidental to the last scene of his marriage.

He reaches out and touches the boy, says, "Go. Go over to Croutys', now," then repeats it when the boy doesn't move but looks at him in betrayal. "Go," he says, shouting, then picks up the boy, the contrast of his warm small shoulders giving him energy. He goes through the room carrying the boy. The door slams open; the hinges bounce. He puts the boy on the walk. There is Roy, standing on the grass now, his mouth bitten tight, his eyes hard. "Go over to Croutys', now." Mrs. Crouty is standing in the yard, an apron on, and they could be on the moon, the four of them, or the only survivors of some wild holocaust.

There is silence, and finally, with a kind of awe in their eyes, the boys back away, then run across the grass toward Mrs. Crouty. They hold one another as they run.

When he is alone with her the house is unbearably silent, and for a moment, in the storm eye of whatever emotion it is that's trying to blow through him, he paces, not wanting to look at her, but unable to keep his eyes from turning toward her, stiff on the couch, arms straight at her sides, hair in her face, feet still in midstride. He doesn't look at her eyes. He goes around the couch, into the dining room and back. He goes into the kitchen. Everything is sparkling, spotless. There is a note on the counter in her handwriting—she's left dinner for them with instructions for heating it. He looks at the note, and enraged, slams open the refrigerator and takes the casserole and heaves it out the back door. You selfish bitch. Everything—the years of it—would burst from him and tear the world to pieces.

It ought to come like some kind of relief now after everything, but there is no relief. There was only the life, and with the life gone, the only possibility now is sorrow: the world will whirl away without her, all perfect indifference. He sits down and for a long time sits in the silence, aware of her but not looking at her, aware that this is the last time she will be in the room, aware that soon she will be in the ground, having already begun an eternity of decay. He looks at his hands, rubs them together. They sting with the rawness of work. There is grout in his fingernails, dry on the back of his hands. *How could anyone want this?* But the question is just proof of how little he understands, how little he has always understood. The cruelty of it astounds him—as though she has orchestrated the whole thing as a repudiation of how wildly and foolishly he has loved her, how completely he has struggled to keep her afloat. It reels off in his head—the year in New York when she left him alone with the boys, the other attempts, the doctors and absences.

And then the ambulance comes and lights up the neighborhood. Mrs. Crouty must have called it. The telephone wires are already glittering with the news. He wishes he could avoid all of this, the true personification of his sorrow. He wishes he could just take her out in the back and bury her in the garden.

He begins to cry as they come up the walk, but then stops himself because he knows it's an act. The lights smear against the house; the siren attracts people in the neighborhood. He stands on the lawn, smoking, watching as they bear her away. Even though the scent of spring is in the air, even though you can see Church Hill from the yard and the spreading fields beyond it new with young green corn, it feels like fall because of the chill in the air, the way the sun is withering. He stands on the lawn, and the lawn has become as huge and indifferent as the rest of the world. He looks over at Croutys' house when he turns and sees his sons watching him, their tiny white-blond heads and pale skin braced at the window, and it seems like they should be with him when the men and women come and go, the women bringing food, the men standing at the edge of the yard in a straight line like oversized crows, smoking. There is lasagna, there are casseroles—tuna and noodles and macaroni—there are bowls of salad and vegetables. But when everyone finally disperses, he gets into the pickup and drives into town, to the Ranchero. He parks and walks across the square, the punching cool of the evening reminding him of a million things in his past, reminding him of when he first met Alison and how beautiful she was, and how it tied his lungs in knots when he first kissed her, first pushed aside her blouse in the hot pickup truck out on the dusty summer county road, and how the coming of spring and summer always made him remember that, the way her mouth was, the full, almost bruised-looking lips and the soft heartbreak of her shape.

Dave Handy is there, and big Jim Olsen behind the bar, and he gets a drink, orders roast beef and gravy and potatoes, and sits in the corner. As soon as he is seated, he gets up again and goes to the pay phone by the john and calls her parents. It must have been meant as much for them as for him, and he intends to sneer the news at them. The jukebox is loud. The scent of the bar is like nausea, like beer and urine, that sweet smell of fermentation or putrefaction that comes with the place, with the old fat rummies sitting around the tables, the jukebox glowing and throbbing Hank Williams. Someone answers but the bar is too loud for him to distinguish who it is. He starts to say it, to be cruel about it, but he can't say anything. Slowly he hangs up and makes his way back to his table.

When the food comes, the roast beef gleaming and textured like death itself, the gravy, canned gravy thick and starchy and almost the consistency of the potatoes, he eats it, then orders another plate, and another scotch. He eats and drinks until he can feel it in his sinuses, in his hands, then gets up. People look at him. And again the futility and foolishness of his life reels off in his head. He knows they'll be gossiping like the afternoon she broke down at the meat counter in the grocery store, yammering about the smell of blood and the sound of the animals screaming, and made Jim Halleran who was manager then call frantically—*Addie I know she's had her problems, but we just can't have this sort of thing, I mean, I've got a business to run*—and then how she left him to go to New York, the telephone wires always lighting with his troubles. He hates how people look at the boys as though they must be crazy too and Pore Old Addie the sad sonofabitch just trying to make ends meet, trying to make do for his family. He isn't even thirty yet and look what happens.

It sucks at him, and he knows he's got to stop feeling sorry for himself. He ought to get back over to Shearins' and get back to work.

When he's finished, when he's just this far away from throwing it all up but so angry throwing up is the last thing he could do, he goes back out into the cold night—it makes him shiver now in shirt sleeves—and starts the pickup and races like a fool back home.

In the truck on the way home he knows he's going to destroy her, and the rage blows him indoors. He bashes on every light switch. On, on, on. Methodical. The boys are still at Croutys' and he goes to the back of the house into the dark and kicks open the back door and begins to take her things out to the barrel where they burn the trash. The house burns bright as the moon. It starts to whirl in him, crazy and violent. It is a high pitch of anger, almost as complete as madness. *Goddamn you, Alison*, he keeps saying to himself. *Goddamn you to hell.* He gets the wheelbarrow out of the shed and smashes it through the back door, then piles her notebooks in it, her journals and her poems, piles her clothes and everything else she owned and carts them out to the back to the trash barrel and puts them on top yesterday's ashes, then douses them with kerosene and lights them. He has never been so angry. He imagines she can watch him now, granted by death a kind of omniscience, and he knows if she can see, she will regret.

Caught up in the whirl of his anger, unable to stop himself, he marches back and forth, hurriedly, knocking the wheelbarrow through the back door and parking it at the base of the stairs. Wary as if afraid someone will stop him, he brings every evidence of her out and puts it in the coil of flames, and while it burns, it keeps his mind like the flames, no emotion, just a wild, lively crackling. *I put up with too much. You regret it now.*

Back and forth, back and forth, the boys watching from Croutys' window, the whole sum of her material existence on the flame—her clothes, her letters, her pictures, her everything, on the fire. It stinks like hell—your whole fucking painstakingly and meticulously pre-served life comes down to this: a stinking mound of trash. He brings her desk, forces it down the stairs, and when it won't fit through the back door he gets an ax and smashes it to pieces on the step, drags the pieces of it to the barrel. If he were her, if he were crazy, he might just go and get his sons and put them on the fire too, because that's the way it feels. *Goddamn you, Alison. Goddamn you to hell.*

And then it gives way to tears. The anger breaks, and it floods him. He's in the living room now—the globe is still off the lamp and the cord still dangles from the ceiling, and his body is weak and he's choking with tears. He wouldn't cry except he can remember—the remember-ing hits him hard, invades him. Some interior mental thing wants to prove to him that it wasn't all futility, it wasn't all frustration. That it wasn't all him chasing her, trying to keep her afloat, trying but always failing to understand what made her work.

It's three o'clock in the morning when he has destroyed her, and he sits on the back step in the cold dark, the fire dying, the interior light spilling in geometric patterns on the grass, and he throws up on himself. It comes with as much surprise as anything today, the smoke thick and acrid in his sinuses. Vomit just bursts out of him, hot and bitter at the back of his throat. It steams on his knees and on the walk, and he wonders when the pain will leave him—leave him empty and old.

Twenty years later, her death still astonishes him with its clarity—she is dead, but the death gave birth to this memory and the memory lives brightly in him, as though the day still exists and will continue to exist until the end of time, and all he has to do is fall into the hell of sleep to reawaken it.

These days he lives half in his head, never dreaming except dreaming his mistakes, a kind of Sisyphus of dreams, pushing through each of his mistakes only to have it roll down and begin again. He'll awaken with the taste of smoke in his mouth, the taste of roast beef and vomit and scotch. It has been years, and he can still smell the smoke, still see her face, the silver dollars taped to her eyes.

# FIRST
# OF THE LAST

In the car I slide the rifle beneath the passenger seat and throw an old towel over the protruding case. I leave the photographs on the seat. The driver's seat is cold and hard, and it's just begun to drizzle. I'm shivering with the cold. I start up the car, turn on the heat. It all happens slowly, how you grow from one person to another, and you never even realize it until you turn around and can see the person you were, standing back in the distance, completely gone. I feel like a reptile just molted, turning and looking at the old skin, the new skin still raw and spectacular with sensation.

The heat comes on now, and the windshield wipers creak across the dirty windshield. I look at the pictures one more time before I put the car into gear and head off for home. As much as I might want it to, the face in the pictures doesn't connect at all. Not with who I am. She might as well be some great-grandmother I never met for all the direct influence she had on my life.

The gun shop is at the side of the highway, one of half a dozen over the last forty miles. I pull into the lot, windshield wipers going even though the rain has gone back to drizzle. There's a sign that says RIFLE RANGE, and I go past it, listening to the echo of rifle fire, into the shop. There's a fat man and a hard-looking skinny woman behind the counter. He's by the guns, and she's down the way, by the fishing gear. Jack Spratt and his wife in reverse.

There's a glass counter and beneath it is an astonishing array of pistols, ten yards of them. And next to the pistols, knives. Behind the counter there are racks of rifles of all shapes and sizes—assault rifles, shotguns, .30-.06s, Winchester .30-.30s, .22s. The racks extend fifteen or twenty yards beyond the fat man. All of them have locks on the triggers. The floor beneath me is concrete and swept clean. Below the racks, there are brightly colored boxes of ammunition, and I tell him what I want and ask a price. It amazes me how cheap bullets are.

Then I ask how much it costs to use the rifle range. He asks if I have a weapon or if I'd need one. I tell him I have one, and he gives me a price. "You got targets?" he says. I shake my head. "Got two different kinds— bull's-eye type and man shaped."

I pay for the ammunition, the spot at the rifle range, and some man-shaped targets.

Outside it's cloudy, but the drizzle has let up for the moment. I get the gun out of the car, walk around the building to where there's a man in a little hut. He explains what to do with the targets and shows me to one in a long line of little shelters. Half of them are occupied, most by serious shooters—guys with scopes on their rifles, heavy plastic ear-muffs. The gunfire is constant, regular.

I lay the rifle down on the rough wooden counter—it's carved with initials, splintered at the far edge—open one of the boxes of shells, and press them one by one into the side of the rifle. Then I hang the target on the wire and press the button.

The man wheels backward out across the bare field. The rifle fire is constant. Now and then you can see the dull impact of lead against the high mound of dirt at the far end of the range.

I cock the rifle and fire. It's been a long time since I've fired a gun, and I have forgotten the kick of the stock, the sound of the report. I have forgotten the quick sharp smell of burnt powder.

I can't see the impact—can't see if I hit the target or not. I fire again, and the rifle nudges me in the shoulder. I concentrate on keeping my hands steady, on not pulling the rifle to the side when I pull the trigger.

I aim for the face, the chest. I keep thinking about Chalky. Everything but the shooting is confused.

The cocking lever is cold against my knuckles when I push it out, then slap it back—the stock has warmed with the heat of my cheek— the spent shell jumps out and clatters on the concrete floor. When the rifle is empty I load it again and look around. The first time my father took me shooting with him and Roy, the recoil of the .30-.06 nearly knocked me over. Roy laughed. My father said to expect it; he said if you don't resist it but let it be part of the liquid motion of firing, it won't affect the shooting. He did a lot of hunting with his father when he was young. It doesn't take courage or heroism but a kind of willfulness to shoot a buck and gut it, dress it out. You have to ignore the similarities it has to you—or marvel at the beauty of its innards. By the time I was born, my father had given up hunting entirely. He still liked to shoot, but he got so that he even had to grit his teeth when he cut the head off a fish to kill it. I think about this now as I shoot. The drizzle and the overcast brings it, the percussive monotony of the rifle fire. I can see him sitting on some rocks on the edge of the Rappahannock in Fredricksburg, a croaker in one hand and a long slender fillet knife in the other, the fish making that clicking sound that gives it its name. I watch the trace of blood that comes when the knife cracks through the neck. In a moment, he made a perfect fillet to throw in the bucket with the others. He threw the head off away from the water's edge for the flies and birds, then swallowed hard when Roy brought him another fish to clean. I didn't see it then, the way he bit his teeth. I only see it now.

For a moment I stop shooting and stand listening to the gunshots around me as they blur into the compressed moisture of the day. Things drift in and out. How it is a man can struggle so hard to communicate with the world outside his family and fail within. How happily-ever-after turns to sorrow after the last page is turned. If I always wanted to leave so badly, what about Roy? Did Daddy chase him off too? There is a moment when you can reach out and touch a person when he is walking away, and then there is the eternity when that moment has passed. I used to dream that about Roy. I used to dream that he was right there and I could watch him, could reach out and touch him—and then I'd try and he'd be gone. The mind wants to reconcile these things: the remembering, and then the fact of being gone.

It makes me wonder what kind of stages you go through as a person, how you evolve. How he evolved. How I am evolving.

It makes me think of my mother's parents' house at the high edge of town and how difficult, how stultifying, how enervating it always was even for Roy and me, who were a part of them, to be there—and I wonder what it was in my father, himself son of a fix-it man, that could make him climb that foolish Rapunzel hill. It makes me laugh, finally, because it is some other version of my father, one of the fifty visions of him I have seen but never touched.

When I reel the paper man in I'm surprised how accurate my shooting has been. The barrel of the gun is hot.

# SLEEPING

He stands on the porch of her apartment building, beneath the awning, and just looks at her face for a moment, not sure at all what to do. It's dark and chilly, and they have been to a movie. He is still full of standing outside the theater in the darkness with his arms around her, half dreading, half hoping someone they know will pass them. He can still feel the dark of the theater, the sticky floor, and her hand in his lap, warm against his hand.

She ducks and looks in the window, up the stairs. "Hell," she whispers, "the hall light is burned out again." Then she turns and looks at him again, and her hands find the soft of his sides. "I'm glad you're here," she says. He could not be more vulnerable than he is now.

A car goes by on the street, and the hiss and the red taillights of it soak into the air as it sinks slowly away. In a minute or two, he can hear it shudder across the railroad tracks.

It's been a long time since he's been in a situation like this, and there are so many reasons to object to being here that if he doesn't leave in a moment, he's going to start listing them here in the darkness.

Suddenly the wild euphoria that's surrounded him the last several days since she appeared on his step has worn off, or rather has not so much worn off as begun to reorganize itself, to make itself permanent. Now he has begun to understand that if he does the thing he most thinks he ought to do—which is walk away—it will tear him apart.

She opens the door, and they go up the stairs in the darkness, Karen in front, Addie behind, listening to the sound of her footsteps, feeling in the air in front of him the weight of her, the shape and scent. She unlocks the door—it takes some fumbling in the dark—and then they are in her apartment, and because it is completely dark except for the bluish hollow of the living room windows, the fragrance of it hits him first. He can feel her go across the floor, and then the light is on and he is blinking.

"Would you like a drink?" she says, going for the kitchen without even looking back at him, taking it for granted that he will. "A gin and tonic?" she says.

"I think maybe I'd better," he says.

"Have a seat," she says. He starts to sit in the armchair, but then sits on the couch so that she can sit next to him.

He hears ice break from a tray and *dink* into a glass, hears liquid pouring and the ice popping beneath it.

There is a coffee table in front of the couch, with magazines laid out across it. They are not what he would have suspected her to read—not women's magazines like *Ladies Home Journal* or *Mademoiselle*. There's the *New Yorker* and *Harper's*, which make him think of Jack, and the *Nation*, which he has heard of but never read.

Then she appears behind him and hands him a drink, licks her fingers, and sits next to him on the couch.

"It's a nice place you have here," he says. He means it genuinely, but to his ears it comes out sounding hollow, as empty chat. "How long have you lived here?"

"Moved in right after I finished school. If I had to stay at my parents' house a day longer I'd have climbed right out of my head, my mother drove me so crazy. I went looking one day, and this was the first place I saw. I looked at a few others, then came back here three or four times before I finally just moved."

She's wearing jeans, and she has her legs pulled up beneath her, and for a moment she just sits in silence and stares straight ahead as if deep in thought. His drink is good if a little strong, and he drinks it slowly, letting it wash over him.

Though he has already known it, it occurs to him in baldness of fact that they are going to sleep together—it hits him in the shoulders and chest and makes him rock. He puts the drink on the coffee table and folds his arms together to hide the trembling in his fingers. "Do you think I could smoke?" he says. "Would it bother you much?"

*This is wrong.*

"It's all right," she says, and now she is facing him more, though he doesn't know how it happened. He has the cigarette out, but it's as big as a baseball bat and exaggerates the movement of his hands. She's smiling, watching him, the cigarette in his mouth now, and there's something about the knowledge in the smile that strikes him as older and wiser and more in control than he could ever be. He takes the cigarette out of his mouth and puts it on the table and reaches for her. Her smile goes to grin, and suddenly her mouth is on his, warm and softer than he can have remembered.

*This is wrong.*

She kisses him for a long time, and the absolute absorption of it is strange to him, it having been so long since lying with a woman was more than a question of animal satisfaction—since it was love.

*This is wrong.*

When he awakens, he is panicked, disoriented, woozy from the gin. Then when he sees her, he remembers, though he has not forgot. In the dark he can see himself with her in the living room, as though the whole scene has been filmed and is being shown back to him for shame. They are on the couch, and her blouse is open and her trousers are down, his hand is on the flat of her belly, the fingers brushing up against the coarse edge of her pubic hair. He is not surprised how it frightens him. *What right do you have?* a voice in his mind says. He can see himself with his arms around her as awed as an eighteen-year-old, the feel of her familiar yet utterly strange.

For a long time he sits in bed while she sleeps, trying to decide whether he should get up and leave. It is wrong to have slept with her, and now, morbidly, he can picture her walking around town pregnant with his child—the absolute shame and embarrassment for the both of them. And that is enough to make him climb out of the bed and pull on his shorts, his trousers. The change and keys in his pockets tinkle in the darkness. She rolls over, reaches for him, then sits up. He can see her in the darkness, and she is naked. Her breasts wag with her movement, and he wants to make himself look away for the burn of his shame, but his head will not turn.

"What are you doing?" she says.

"Getting dressed." He means to whisper, but it comes out a croak. "Why?"

"I'd better go. I'm very sorry about this."

"About what?" she says to him, blinking, as if trying to pull his image into focus.

"About this whole thing," he says.

She reaches for the bedside lamp and then both of them are squinting in the sudden brightness of the light. "Sit down," she says. He turns away. She starts to pull the covers around her, but then doesn't when she sees that's why he's turning. "What whole thing?" she says, still squinting, but traces of anger burning in around her mouth.

"Sleeping—you know."

"You make it sound as though you raped me. Or I raped you."

"I—that's not what I—it's," he says, stumbling, sleep still thick in his head.

"Don't you *dare* act this way," she says.

The words stop him cold, and he just stares at her. "I was afraid I might have got you pregnant." He doesn't mean it exactly, but it's the only way to put the sensation he has that he has ruined some part of her—that he has destroyed or abused something.

"Not a chance," she says, starting to smile. "Not a chance."

This stops him for a moment, and he just stares at her.

"Why are you looking at me like that? What? Did you think this was the first time I've ever done this?"

"No," he says, looking away, not sure how things have come to this, but now more confused and hurt than ever. Suddenly now he has greeted the possibility that she has, as she says, slept with others—but who, and why? Not Jack. The confusion and especially the hurt are as stupefying as everything else.

"What is it about men," she says, looking at him but not really talking to him, "that has them convinced that women are property to be owned? What is it?" Her eyes are wide now, and they make him want to answer her question. He tries to think but can't. If she would just cover herself. He knows it's true—that something in him, now that he has slept with her, wants to possess her, feels that since he has slept with her, she should all along have belonged to him, her past, everything. For a moment he is silent, and then he simply shakes his head in the manner of a child unable to answer a teacher's simple, reasonable question.

"Either you get back into this bed, Adolf Pleasance, or you go out the door and never come back again," she says.

He looks at her and then, knowing he is helpless to do anything else, unbuckles his belt, unfastens his trousers and lets them drop onto the floor, then gets back into bed with her, knowing as he does that something in his life has changed irrevocably.

She moves toward him, and he can feel her breath on his face. "What is it you think?" she says. "Are you ashamed?"

"You're just a child," he starts, by way of explanation, but he can't, and only shakes his head.

She puts her hands on his face, and he can feel the warmth of them soaking into his cheeks. "I am not a child," she says. "Not even close."

"No," he says, and he can feel the tears on his face and it makes him want to hide.

"Why are you such a beautiful man?" she says, but he can't listen to her for the noise in his mind.

"I love you," she says, and though he has heard the words everyday on television or on the radio, somehow the way they come from her mouth renders them completely new. It's the first time in nearly twenty years that a woman has said this to him, and it leaves him dazed.

Later, when he is not certain that she is still awake, he says quietly, "You see I have never been able to find a balance between what you might call sexual desire and sexual aggression." Outside he can hear the whine of trucks out on the highway in the distance. "One is proper and the other is morally wrong, and I have never seen the correct line between them."

She doesn't say anything, and he is silent for a long time, trying to figure out what it is he wants to say to her, what it is he wants himself to understand. "I have always thought that this—that sex—was a dangerous thing. Necessary of course, but never equal—" He lets himself trail off. He is surprised to hear himself talk this way—as though he has thought out what he is saying carefully over the years even though he hasn't. It just comes out this way.

"I'm glad you worry about it," she says. "Most men don't." Her voice sounds dreamy, sleepy. "Whether they like it or not, most men, for that matter, most people, view women as community property, and in a way, because they share their bodies with people—I mean lovers, children— you can see why people look at them that way. But what they give is *theirs* to give, not someone else's to take or to own." She rolls toward him, and he can feel the brush of her hair against him.

He listens intently, surprised by her voice. He wants to say to her that being with her is like shedding an old skin—that being with her leaves him completely new.

"Have you ever seen the way complete strangers come up to pregnant women and ask to touch their bellies—or sometimes don't even ask? Try, try to imagine what it would be like to breast-feed. To be responsible that way to another person. No man can understand it."

Despite what she says, it feels to him this minute as though he *has* understood, perhaps for the first time in his life. He *does* understand.

"What is equal desire?" he says. "I mean it should always be reciprocal. Always, but how do you—I mean, what makes it equal? What is the line—"

"The line is if she wants to sleep with you too."

"But even if she does, even if she does, when is it giving and when is it taking?" He means it earnestly, but the sound of his words is utterly inadequate. He isn't making himself clear.

She laughs. "What I hear you saying is that you're frightened that a woman might have sexual desire."

"No," he says. "That's not what—"

"It is. That's exactly what you're telling me. A woman's not supposed to be aggressive. A woman's not supposed to want to get banged the way a man is. There's something wrong with that. If she acts like that, she's a whore or a nymph or something." She rolls over and props herself up on her elbows and looks at him hard.

He wants a cigarette, but he presses the urge away.

Later, again, he awakens and though it is still dark, he sits up in bed, pulls his knees up close to his chest, and wraps his arms around them. She is asleep and doesn't seem disturbed at all by the movement his awakening imparts to the bed. He listens to her breathing, listens to the world outside. Maybe it is only that he is in a strange bed, in a strange house, that he cannot relax completely. Maybe it's only because it has been so long since he slept with a woman in bed next to him that the worry will not leave. Maybe time is the only thing that will make him comfortable.

When he wakes up in the morning—it is Saturday, and the sun is bright and he has no idea what time it could possibly be—she is against him, her head on his chest, her hair fanned out warm against him. He is stiff, but he remains utterly still so as not to disturb her and waits for her to wake up too, hoping almost that she will not, that this morning will continue for eternity.

Later in the day, after it is all over and he has gone out to take care of his own business—he is at the Texaco in his pickup—he finds himself unable to think of anything but her, and when Terry talks to him he's afraid the image of her in his head is so vivid that everyone else in the world can see. There's a vibration, a hum, that being with her has given him, and every movement makes his mind and body glow.

"Came by your house this morning to borrow your chain saw," Terry says, "but no one was home."

"Got up early," Addie says, brushing his burning palms together, then tugging a cigarette out of his pack. "What'cha cuttin'?" The match flares, and the smoke in his mouth tastes like sulphur.

"Tree came down a week ago during the storm—what are you grinning about?" Terry says, looking at him closely.

"Am I grinnin'?" Addie says, flicking ashes, leaning against the truck.

"You look like you swallowed the goddamned biggest canary in the whole world."

"Maybe I did."

# FAITH

# HARLAN

It's the middle of the afternoon, and just this moment, the elementary school on the hill behind Terry's filling station has let out for the day and the children pour through the doors, running, walking, pushing, carrying books and brightly colored pieces of paper. They give off a hooting, chattering sound like a flock of geese on their way north after winter.

Addie is standing just inside the first bay door of the filling station when the children come out. He's watching them, feeling the way the sound trills and expands in his own chest, when Jim Harlan's pickup swings across the Texaco parking lot, then, popping gravel, stops in front of the air pump at the edge of the lot. Addie's only half looking when the red Chevy short bed halts, the door opens, and the driver climbs out. Owen Harlan is what registers in the half of his mind that's paying attention—the same drunken red jowl skin, same gray stubble, same horn-rimmed glasses, same bowlegged hitch in his walk. Jimbo's father. He stops in the middle of the oil-stained pavement, hands cupped and head bent to light a cigarette. Owen—except Owen's been dead for fifteen years. The children's voices are dying now—dispersed on their routes home—and a sensation of being outside time wobbles Addie momentarily.

But it is Jimbo Harlan—he knows that much when he looks back. His gut is gone, and he looks about half the weight he was when Addie saw him last, three or four months ago. He looks meaner, older, the way Owen looked. Jim leaves a cloud of blue cigarette smoke in the air and starts toward the filling station office. Daryl drops a wrench, and Harlan turns at the clang and squints to see into the dark, cool, grease-smelling bay.

Addie turns to say something to Daryl, but Harlan's voice barks out, "How do, Add?"

"Goddamn. Well it is you." Of course it was—it's just a thing to say. Addie turns back toward the door and the sunshine.

Harlan's hand is still strong and calloused, but he's lost a hell of a lot of weight. "Yeah, it's me," he says, his voice hoarse from cigarettes and drinking.

"What'd you do, go on the Hollywood diet? Cut out beer on a permanent basis?"

Harlan laughs. "*Hell* no, not me. I just been losing weight. Ain't even been on a diet," he says, cigarette pinched tightly in the center of his mouth. "I eat like a bulldozer, but I just can't seem to keep it on." He looks down, pats his stomach, then pulls a pack of Pall Malls from his T-shirt pocket and offers one to Addie.

Addie shakes his head. "Been off those things for a while now," Addie says.

"No shit," Harlan says. He stands on one leg and shakes the other. "Goddamned leg's asleep again," he says, more to himself than anyone. "I *hate* that tingling."

Addie pulls the blue pack of Trident peppermint gum from his shirt pocket, unwraps a stick as if to prove the unbelievable.

Harlan coughs out a laugh as he puts his Pall Malls away.

When he comes in, Karen's sitting at the kitchen table, he says hello, but he's busy with an idea and he doesn't quite look at her, only notices that she's there. She still only lives in his house on a part-time basis, but in his mind there's a naturalness to her presence in his house that makes her shape, her sound right.

He comes out of the bathroom, hands folded together, rubbing but still damp, and saying, "The transmission is okay, so it's not going to be—" He walks into the kitchen, looks at her straight on, and it stops him dead like he's walked into a thick glass wall. For the years he's known her she has always had long, thick dark hair, the thickest hair he's ever seen. This morning her hair came down to the middle of her back. And now all of it is gone. It doesn't even reach to her shoulders.

"Oh, Jesus," he says and blinks, as though when he opens his eyes again maybe it will change. "Oh, Jesus, what did you do?" He stands in the middle of the floor, a man in the middle of a lake who's suddenly forgotten what little he knew about swimming. He remembers reading in a woman's magazine someone left in the john at Terry's Texaco of all places that people only cut their hair drastically when they feel the need to change their lives drastically. It makes him panicky, and he just looks at her, surprised by the vague notion of betrayal.

Maybe she's even more beautiful now, but it makes her look like an entirely different woman. Since the moment he first kissed her, he has been waiting for someone to turn on the light, waiting to wake up—she is, after all, twenty years younger than he is—and maybe this is the first sign. The day hangs above him like a wire, and the things he's said and thought about her hang from it, vulnerable.

"I've been thinking about it for a while," she says, smiling one of those inscrutable, I-swallowed-something smiles she wears when she knows she has to win him over. (Nothing wrong, everything's fine.) "I even went to Paulette at the beauty salon a couple of times to talk about it, and today I just did it." She raises her eyebrows, reaches up to touch it, but then just lets her hand drop again.

He breathes deeply, nervously. "No," he says, and it surprises him that he says this. Her face darkens a little. It makes him feel like he doesn't know her. "I hate it," he says.

"Addie—"

"I can't believe you did this without even saying anything to me."

"What are you talking about? It's *my* hair." And of course he knows that. He *knows* that.

"What was wrong with it? What was wrong with it the way it was?"

"It just wasn't very stylish. It wasn't very fashionable."

"Stylish," he says, and the word tastes metallic in his mouth. "Fashionable."

Later, Karen sits at the dinner table, one elbow on the table, the opposite hand pushing a piece of cauliflower through the residue of salad dressing in her salad bowl. She listens as Addie tells her about seeing

Harlan, thinking he was his father at first. She listens as he talks about loneliness—his own and Harlan's. When he's finished, she doesn't say anything. She eats the cauliflower, then gets up and takes the dinner dishes to the sink. She's behind him, and he doesn't turn to look at her.

"Honey," she starts. The almost-exasperated tone of voice makes him wary. For a moment there's silence. Water runs in the sink. A car sails past on the street in front of the house—kids, probably, going that fast. "You know you don't have to be the dog pound," she says finally. She's still mad at him about her hair, and that's coloring the way she says what she says.

He gets up from the table slowly, pushes his chair in, and backs away to lean on the part of the L-shaped counter perpendicular to where she is. "What's that supposed to mean?" he says, brisk, clipped. He can see her neck, a wisp of hair that underlies the body of her hair—something he's never really seen before.

She turns toward him and smiles, then sighs a little when he won't soften his look. "It only means—I mean." She looks back at the sink, then out the window in front of her. He watches her arms, the slim shape of her shoulders. Softly, musically, she says, "You're just like a kid, sometimes, bringing home strays."

It catches him off guard, and he doesn't know what to say. For a moment things in his head twist, quarrel. "What's that supposed to mean?" he says again, but this time the words have a completely different consistency.

She turns to him again, leans her left hip momentarily against the counter. There is a pair of yellow rubber gloves slung over the dish rack, and she picks them up slowly, one at a time, and slides them over her hands. "What can you do?"

He shrugs. He has no idea, now, where he had originally intended this conversation to go. "Nothing, I guess. People make their own beds."

"That's right," she says.

"But it doesn't—I mean I've been alone myself."

"What did he ever do for you his entire life?" she says. "He's lazy, dishonest. You loaned him that trailer, and when he gave it back to you, six or how many months later, it was packed with mud, the lights were broken, and both tires were flat. You told me so yourself. He never even offered to try to fix it or pay for the damages."

He has his arms folded in front of him, and he looks down, presses his lips together. He sighs. "I never asked." For a moment he watches Karen as she fills the sink with water, angrily squirts green Palmolive dish-

210

washing liquid in under the stream of water. He wishes he had a cigarette, but instead, gets a piece of Trident from the pack in his pocket, then pushes off the counter.

"I've got some cleaning up to do out in the shop," he says. It's not true, but he can always make work for himself and at the moment he wants to be alone. He goes past her, purposely brushing against the curve of her back, then out the screen door, across the patio, and opens the shop door.

When he looks back at the kitchen window before closing the shop door, she is not looking out, but down, at the work she's doing. The kitchen light is bright, and framed in the window she looks alone, independent, more womanly and less girlish than before. He has the irrational sense that she—and everything—is slipping away from him. The urge to go inside and apologize again for the way he acted wells up in him, but it seems weak and useless. In a moment, he closes the door behind him and turns on the shop vac. Tonight, work is his sanctuary again. It has always been his sanctuary, and tonight is no different.

What she doesn't understand about Harlan is that everything that ever happened to him could have happened to Addie, if the circumstances of their lives had been a little different. If he, Addie, had had a taste for beer. If Alison had been a lush instead of who she was.


It's January 1955, and there is always distance; the snow that snowed all last night and the night before only increases the distance.

Now, as Adolf Pleasance stands at the bottom of Turret Hill next to his father's pickup, its rusted yellow plow attached to the front, it is still snowing—that soft, light, whirling end-snow that spins weightlessly in the air like it will never stop coming down, like it is what the air has become. Even now, it's starting to be sunny, and the vast blanket undulate pastures of Turret Hill have a glow beneath the coming sun like a headache.

It's early in the morning, but with half a dozen cups of coffee and the trip to the hospital in Charlottesville behind him already, it could be midafternoon. The air has that hungry midafternoon feel.

Turret Hill, the Hadley Estate, is at the highest edge of Hadleysburg. It is for them, the Hadleys, that the town was named, and by them that most of the town was once owned. Turret Hill is the biggest estate between here and Leesburg—or at least Charlottesville—and it sits on the highest spot of land in the county except for Church Hill, which it faces to the east with something like secular defiance. The driveway at the end of which Addie is standing is perhaps a mile and a half long, perhaps longer, and continuously upward sloping, curving not for any kind of dispensation to the shape of the land but utterly for the aesthetic sensation of sloping turns and slides against the elegant bracket of horse fence. The fences—horse fence is the only name Addie knows for them—border the black tongue of drive with brilliant white sculpted grace. You see them at a distance and marvel at the white fences against the black drive and green pastures. But now the snow dulls the perfect white electricity of them—you can see the yellow in the paint, the imperfections against the pure white of the snow.

The truck off and clicking in the cold, his hat pulled down close over his ears, and his worn and split gloves shoved in the pockets of his denim jacket, Addie walks up the left side of the drive. He is going to ask about plowing it, certain even as he goes that the answer will be no, but doing it because something in him says that he has to, that it is something to be conquered—even if conquering it means walking up the hill, hearing the word "no," and then turning around again. Still, as he goes—the fluttering, worn skirt of coffee blowsing in his head, the empty-stomached adrenaline making his hands shake—he is trying to come up with a price that seems fair. He concentrates on it. But still there is distance, between him and everything.

He walks at the edge of the drive rather than at the middle of it so that if he is given the chance to do the plowing, he will know, from his footprints, where exactly the blacktop ends and the grass begins. If, after he knocks and asks, they agree, he will walk down the other side and plot that edge similarly.

There is distance, but you don't watch the distance. If you watched the distance it would always be too much; it would swallow you. Like the boat out of San Francisco to Hawaii and then the Philippines. If you watched the distance, if you'd known how unfathomable it would be, you would have jumped and drowned.

The snow is shin deep, and the open pastures let the wind come sliding down off the hill. Snow skates off the surface of itself—no edge, no limit. His nose is running, but he doesn't move his arm to try to wipe at it. His gloves are chamois, old, soft, but full of holes in the fingers. He doesn't look up as he walks, just down at the fence posts, feeling for the hard or soft of pavement or grass. The ground is frozen hard beneath the snow, and it's difficult to tell, because you can't hear the crunch of frozen grass.

In Charlottesville this morning, he was glad he had the pickup, glad he had thought enough to shovel sand into the back the day before, because the streets were all still knee deep in snow—even at the hospital parking lot, which you'd have thought they'd clear first. Half the streets he went down, his was the first vehicle to come around all night, and he listened beneath the sound of the truck to the sound of the tires against the snow. Transformation. Whir. The sknick of compacting snow. He watched the clapboard houses as they went by, watched the soft light of the early morning snow, and wished he were anywhere but where he was—inside some deep soft house somewhere, some soft bed, the snow saying, *Go back to sleep*. Except here he was, at the hospital, parking the truck, and going across the snowy drive into the emergency room door, because it was the closest, and because it was the only one he'd ever been through before.

Snow collects on the legs of his dungarees and freezes on the already damp fabric. There's no way to avoid it. He's halfway up the driveway, and walking is always harder in the snow. He's in full sight of the house now, and anyone looking could peer down out of any of the massive windows and see him, this ragged figure coming slowly, his truck parked in the distance like a cipher—respect, deference, mechanical difficulty.

"I never thought I'd be one to say I'm glad to be in the hospital," his father says, his already hoarse voice muffled from behind the oxygen mask, "but I sure as hell am glad I'm not out in that snow." Addie looks out the window involuntarily, and it makes him shiver. There's a roof below them, another building beyond, and the snow comes hard in swirls, piling up against the edges of the buildings, skating across the air like the atmosphere has become some kind of particulate mass that moves and moves and will not stop moving.

From in here, where it's stifling, the outside looks like a new ice age. His father coughs, and it has that wet sound to it, even inside the oxygen mask, like pieces of lung are falling off.

"They give you any idea how much longer you might be in here?" he says, knowing as he says it that it's a foolish question.

"They never tell you anything but when you ask they tell you a million things you don't understand."

Addie nods, not wanting to pursue it any further.

Silence endures. The oxygen mask hisses regularly, and the man who shares the room with his father shifts through a magazine. The silence feels foolish; he's come all this way, and they can't talk. But there is nothing to talk about but work. There never has been. The thing is that he is here. Korea is over, and even though his head is still full of things that don't belong here in Charlottesville or Hadleysburg, he is on solid ground, understanding, wishing that he could make others understand as easily. The snow outside the window is hypnotic, streaming. The flowers on the windowsill seem almost laughably incongruous, like so many things.

He says, because the snow reminds him: "I put the plow on the truck." He put the plow on the truck at five o'clock this morning, but it's only now, in the hospital, looking out the window at the swirling snow that the idea of going to Hadleys' to see if he can get himself hired to plow their drive has occurred to him. "I'm going to go up to the Hadleys' to see if I can plow their drive," he says.

His father laughs and then coughs—inside the oxygen mask there are flecks of red—his face burns red and hot for a moment, and Addie moves away from the bed, stifles the urge to grab his father and hold his chest in place with his own hands.

"Got a lot of flowers," Addie says after the coughing has subsided.

"Too many of the goddamned things," his father says. "There's only so much room in one of these goddamned little cubbyhole rooms—," he says but coughs again and can't get out anymore.

After a little while more, Addie promises to return tomorrow afternoon, when he gets work out of the way, and then he is just standing here, the linoleum floor beneath his feet—movement outside the door—waiting at the now between where he is and where he will be, and knowing as he waits a kind of dissolution of time—of present time.

He backs away, toward the door, and for the second time since he walked into the room catches a glimpse of the man who shares his father's room. He sits in a wooden armchair, in one of those hospital gowns, his feet propped on a stool and a pile of pillows. His skin is translucent, and his legs are swollen like if you touched them they'd burst. Addie smiles when the old man looks up. He has very thin white hair, and his scalp has patches the color of rust. The old man wears nothing beneath his hospital gowns—he wears two of them, actually, one tied in back and one tied in front, maybe for warmth—and his old crotch is visible to anyone who might walk by. The Philippines goes through his head again—two old men sitting at the edge of a rice paddy, barefoot, the rice paddy flooded and the two old men looking at him and his partner in their sharply pressed uniforms as if they had just landed from outer space. Except the Filipinos were used to soldiers— more used to soldiers than Addie would ever be used to being one.

He's shivering furiously when he gets up to the top of the driveway. There's a massive circle where he can imagine horsedrawn carriages pulling up and letting off tuxedoed and begowned ball-goers on some burning spring evening. But it's all too new for that. It has the colonial look—everything fashioned down to the last detail, except he's sure there was never a ball. He can see Church Hill and the spread of town, and the view surprises him—a wholly different town from the one you see from Church Hill.

Right now, walking up to the doors of the Hadley mansion, a memory slides loose—this is four years ago, in high school, and he is sitting in a car on a muddy lane outside a pair of house trailers. It's dark and he's drinking a beer, and Jim Harlan and the two others he came with are inside—it's a Negro's (Nigra is what he says, nigger is what they say) trailer, and they've come to buy moonshine. It's dark inside, dark outside, but when the door opens and the three of them come out, there's a spline of light and he catches a glimpse of the person holding the door, a woman. Yellow-eyed, wrapped in an old overcoat. Harlan holds two Mason jars, and the others laugh.

So what was it about old Addie Pleasance that he was so naive?

The front doors of the mansion are double, solid walnut. The wind eddies in the entranceway, and he knocks, his hands finally free of his pockets and sore with the cold. The knock seems barely audible. It would take light years for such a small knock to echo through this house.

The massive door opens with a sound like a gunshot—the cold and damp and its not having been opened all night. It's a man at the door, tall and slim and middle-aged and wearing something between a bathrobe, a smoking jacket, and a housecoat. The sound of the door opening has knocked Addie back, and he's on his heels.

"May I help you?" the man says, and Addie wonders if this is Hadley or someone who works for Hadley. The voice is patrician, not a Virginia accent like his own but something nearly English, musical and pleasant.

The sun has come out now behind him, and everything outside the house has the brilliant, blind light of burning phosphor. Addie pushes his glove back on—the knuckles still sting with the impact on the wood.

"I have a pickup and a plow, and I was wondering if you needed someone to plow your drive?" he says, looking down, not meeting the man's eyes for more than a moment—instead looking at the frozen legs of his dungarees, the torn pocket of his denim coat.

"All right," the man says, and the words make Addie's eyes go up to the man's face. It's soft and narrow, refined looking, nearly a woman's face. Or if he were a woman he'd be a pretty one.

He has been thinking about price and not thinking about price, and now he knows this is the place at which they've arrived. How much is his time worth? How much is the service worth? As far as gas goes, it will only cost him pennies, but it's the work. These people are rich, but rich people are that way for a reason.

"How much?" the man says; then, "Do you want to come in for a moment and warm up?"

Addie looks at him, then beyond him into the foyer of the house. The floor the man is standing on in his slippers is white marble with tendrils of smoky color running through it. There's a marble-topped piece of furniture Addie wouldn't know what to call against the wall, beneath a gilt mirror. He can see the edge of what might be a living room—more windows looking out on the other side of the house, and brilliant light reflected off the snow, and then the edge of a staircase. He looks at the man and knows that no matter how cold he is now, if he comes in he will be a thousand times colder when he walks back down the drive.

He looks at the staircase again—it's oval shaped, and he can just see the last down-sloping outward curve of it, and now there's a woman standing at the edge of it. Black haired and white skinned—he forces himself to look back at the man, sure that in his hunger and dreaming he has just imagined her.

"Thank you, no," Addie says, "if I thaw out now, I'll probably freeze to death." He laughs.

He's thinking about the woman, trying not to look. But he can see her clearly, though he's not looking at her—that must mean he's dreamt her. She's his age, maybe younger. She wears a long pleated blue-black skirt the color of her hair and a harshly pressed blouse as white as the snow. Severe.

"I was thinking twenty-seven dollars," Addie says. He was thinking thirty-five dollars, but it seems such a huge sum he can't make it pass his lips. He likes the arbitrariness of twenty-seven. There must be a reason for the odd figure.

Before the man has a chance to say a word Addie says, "I walked up your drive to plot out the edge, to make sure I wouldn't be tearing up any of your turf."

The man nods; he pulls his robe-housecoat closer around him. An eddy of wind brings snow across the marble foyer. There's a cloud and then sun again, and the sun is even more brilliant now. The girl is there—she just watches. Then from the side opposite the stair a black woman comes through from another room carrying folded linen. "I was wondering where all that cold air was coming from," she says.

"Seems fair enough," the man says.

"Mavis," another, harsher voice says, and now Addie feels adrift, ready to turn and walk away. The owner of the voice that called out "Mavis" comes into the back of the foyer. Not old, or no older than the man, but wizened and hardened—a blue dress, stockings, makeup, hair like she just walked out of a beauty salon. "What's going on here?" she says, pushing up next to the man.

"This young man's going to plow our drive," he says, and even though they've only said a word to one another there is a magnetic tension between their voices.

"What about Yardley?" the woman says. Addie can tell they are the parents of the girl who stands in the background, that they are the Hadleys, and in the rough configuration of the three of them—girl on the stairs, the soft-faced, nearly pretty man, and the hard little woman—his empty mind starts spinning out stories about them.

"Don't you dare pile snow against my fences," the woman says sharply. Addie wants to believe she's being humorous, except there's no hint at all of humor in her voice. "You pile snow against the fences, it'll not only knock over the posts but those it doesn't knock over it will rot by the time it melts."

"I know exactly what I'm doing, ma'am," he says, and he's surprised at the force of his voice, the way her tone makes the anger seep out of him.

"Well, I don't know that you do, and that's what worries me."

He stares at her a moment. The air, the whole situation is molting:

the morning is starved and is laden with too much. The layers want to peel. The man smiles a reassuring smile. The woman takes a step forward and makes it known she is closing the door. Addie lets his gaze turn to glare as the door closes.

He turns on his heel and starts down the other side of the drive. Twenty-seven dollars. It seems such a massive amount of money.

He's not shaking anymore by the time he gets to the truck—he can't tell whether it's the job, or whether some strange thing has taken hold of him from inside and given him his peculiar serenity.

The truck is cold and it starts sluggishly, but then comes to life, and in minutes the heat is on, thawing out the frozen legs of his dungarees. He starts up the hill. It shouldn't, but it amazes him how rapidly it goes after walking up the hill. At the top, everything spread out around him, he gets out and lowers the plow, then gets back inside the truck and starts plowing the swath he plotted for himself. The black asphalt gleams beneath the sun, and the streaks of snow melt when the black accumulates the sun's heat.

It's a perfect job—snow nowhere near the fences. The entire shift of it perfectly symmetrical. When he's finished, he leaves the truck running in the circle by the front door and climbs out, goes to the door.

It's the girl who answers. In a small town you think you know or have seen nearly everyone that exists. He stands looking at her, gawking even, because at the distance he had seen her before he had only a vague idea how attractive she was. Now she looks at him, wide-eyed—the foolish thing that comes to mind is that her eyes are the bright green of sunlight on emerald.

"All finished," he says, hoping she is ready to pay him.

"What's your name?" she says. It's a question that comes out flat and even, no suggestion of flirtation or even curiosity. He can't make out anything at all beneath the voice. Except the voice is rich and full.

"Pleasance," he says, surprised. "Adolf Pleasance. Most people call me Addie." His body has the sensation of floating sideways, swimming, and he rubs his hands together for poise.

"Adolf," she says.

"It's a family name," he says.

"Do you live around here?" she says.

"Sure. All my life," he says. The breeze works at the pleats of her skirt.

She gives a shrugging kind of smile, as if to acknowledge what she's missed by being who she is, living where she does. "Maybe we'll run into each other sometime," she says, and he looks at her, tries to push beneath the surface of it. He's so hungry, though, that everything is afloat, imprecise.

And then she is handing him money, smiling. "Thank you," she says.

"Thank you," he says. He looks at the money, and there are forty dollars.

"This is more—," he starts.

She shakes her head and closes the door.


It's nearly two weeks later, a Wednesday, that Jim Harlan calls Addie in the middle of the night.

He's pushed seeing Jim at the Texaco to the back of his mind. Too much else to worry about: Tim Woolford, the kid who works with him, has been in bed with strep throat, or "stripped throat" as Tim says. The same day Tim got laid up, Dale Sawyer called about a bathroom job. Toilet had been leaking for years, rotting out the floor beneath it so that the only thing holding it up was the cast iron pipe it was seated on. Dale got off the john one morning, stood up, and came right through the floor. Addie's been rebuilding the floor, which means he's had to take out everything, including the bathtub and the cabinets.

It's nearly two in the morning when the phone rings, and it's a long time struggling with wakefulness, comprehension. He's not sure that he's dreaming, not sure he's doing anything but drifting, floating. Karen answers the phone, and she pushes him. "Come on, honey, wake up. Come on. It's Jim Harlan."

"I got a little bit of a problem here," Harlan says.

"What is it, Jim?" he says, his voice cracking with sleep, his head thick like it's stuffed full of wool. There's nausea at the center of his gut as he pushes himself into a sitting position.

"I can't seem to move, old buddy. I—"

"What?" Addie can hear the TV going in the background.

"I can't seem to move." It's only now that he's awake enough to make out the scared tone of voice. "I been sittin' here watchin' television, and I tried to get up and my legs are asleep. They ain't even tingling. I can't feel a goddamned thing." He's silent for a moment, and Addie can hear canned laughter jumble through the line. "Addie, I didn't know who else to call."

"You want me to come over?" Addie says.

"I think maybe I ought to go to a doctor," Harlan says.

All the way across town to Maypole Lane, Addie can't shake the sense of unreality he has about everything. The roads and the house and the trees and the lights all have a silvery glaze of stupefaction, things refusing to be known, understood—as though all the nerves and systems have been overloaded with electricity.

When he gets near Harlan's trailer, he can see that the lights are on, and when he swings his own pickup into the bare yard, he can see that the door's open. He pushes out of the truck and hurries up the walk, but the ground beneath him is uneven, wobbling—the walk is longer than he remembers. He can hear the TV playing still, and he hurries up the old, soft wooden steps. He pushes the door open and calls softly, "Jimmy? Jimbo?"

The trailer smells bad, like vomit and ammonia and rot. Harlan's dead. Things are that cold. Addie's been in too many rooms where people have been dead, and these rooms have that feel to them. The wood knows it, the metal knows it. Curious to him is that the sensation leaves his chest wide-feeling and powerful. *It wasn't me.* He wishes Karen could be in his shoes right this second, so she could understand.

Then, below him, he hears Harlan's voice, pale and used up. "Right here, Add."

He pushes the door back and steps inside. The smell is almost overpowering. The trailer's a mess, as if it's been ransacked—clothing everywhere, old beer cans on the floor, grease-stained paper bags full of garbage against the wall next to an overflowing can. Harlan is against the wall too, next to the door, skinny and broken looking. His old gray head is hung down, and it looks as though he's been crying—but whether it's from exertion or emotion isn't clear. Addie crouches down in front of him.

"I'm glad you came, old buddy," Harlan says. "I didn't know what the hell else to do, but call you. I hate to admit it, but I think I pissed my pants," he says and turns his face away.

"Don't you worry about it," Addie says, sick at his stomach but doing his best not to show it. "What happened?"

"I was sittin' there, watching the TV, and I tried to get up to go get another pack of cigarettes, and I just couldn't move." His eyes are yellow and wet and old and womanish. He takes a deep breath. "It was like somebody pulled the goddamned plug on my legs." He can't quite get his breath. "Could you maybe get me a cigarette?" he says. "I tried, but I couldn't reach the goddamned carton."

"Sure," Addie says. He's dizzy when he pushes himself upright, and he has to work to hold himself steady as he wades through the living room to the kitchen. " 'Bove the sink, Add," Jim says softly. Addie finds the red carton of Pall Malls, takes out a pack, and brings it back to where Harlan is sitting. He opens it, shakes one loose, and hands it to Harlan. Harlan takes the cigarette, puts it in his mouth, and wipes the back of his hand across his nose before he lights it.

"What d'you want me to do?" Addie says. "You want me to call an ambulance?"

"If you could, I'd appreciate it if you'd just drive me on down to the hospital yourself. I can't stand the thought a no ambulance."

"Jim," he starts, but Harlan probably has the magnitude of things worked out for himself already. "You want to bring anything?"

"Just my cigarettes," he says.

In a minute, Addie swallows hard, then reaches down, puts one arm beneath Harlan's legs—his pants are wet—and the other one behind his shoulders, then lifts him up. He's light as a bird. "Damned nice of you to lose all that weight," Addie says.

"Maybe we could put on a dry pair of pants?" Harlan says.

Addie holds him, nods. Harlan cranes in the direction of the other room, and Addie carries him into the bedroom. More of a mess. "I can't believe how weak I feel," Jim says. The wet of his piss has soaked through Addie's shirt, and it surprises him that the thing that comes through his mind is his own father's voice, saying, "There isn't anything in this world, Son, that you're too good for."

He puts Jim down on the bed and helps him out of his pants. Jim uses his hands and wipes off his wet skin with a sheet on the bed. Addie stands a moment, dazed, trying to survey the room for a pair of pants, a pair of shorts. Harlan points him in the right direction.

In a minute, he's holding Jim, carrying him through the door and toward the truck, and sorrow swells up to his teeth.

"You got your keys?" he says.

"Yep."

In the truck, things are silent for a long time. The closed cab, the lights ahead of them, make the cab of the truck feel like some encapsulated eternity, the two of them together on their way into the beyond. The highway is only two lanes, and it takes concentration to stay awake, to stay on the right side of the road. The overhanging trees are gray in the dim light—now and then when they go around a curve, the headlights of the truck throw color into weeds and trees.

"You know what's happening to me right now?" Harlan says.

Addie says, "No, I sure don't," thinking Harlan is talking about whatever illness it is that has hold of him, about dying.

"It's funny, but I got this kind of movie show going on in my head." He reaches over and pushes the cigarette lighter in. "I got my life flashing before my eyes, just like they say happens when you're gonna die."

"What the hell makes you think you gonna die?" Addie says, his voice too alert, too eager to deny.

When the lighter pings out, Harlan takes hold of it and mashes it against the tip of his cigarette. "Just seems likely, is all." For a moment, the cab of the truck is full of the toasted smell the tobacco makes just before it catches light. "I was thinking about how good it feels to swim, sometimes. You know? Like a hot summer day and you've been workin', and you dive into the water. I remember this one particular time—must've been in the goddamned fifties or something—going out to Sandycove with Darlene. It was summer, long before we were married. Hadn't planned to go swimming, but we got out there, had a couple of bottles of beer. It was hot, you know." Harlan opens the window a little on his side, and Addie can feel the sharp edge of the night air as it whirls through the cab. "She took off her clothes. Every last bit of her clothing. There was no one else around, and that was the first time in my life I had ever seen a woman nekkid head to toe, if you want to know the honest-to-God truth of the matter. 'Come on,' she says, 'Let's go in the water.' I don't know why I thought of that now. I don't know why. You're goddamned right, a woman can change your life, Addie. You're goddamned right."

Addie cracks his own window, and the night air feels good. Cigarette smoke sucks over him and out the window. His jacket and shirt smell like Harlan's urine. He's having a similar sensation—that his life has become a tunnel, all the impatient moments, all the loneliness and sunlight have telescoped down into one tiny focus, bare scrapbook glimpses at the end of a life.

"You remember that Mrs. Crocus you were taking care of?" Harlan says hoarsely after a while, more distant now.

"Mrs. Krakus?" Addie says. That was her name, Krakus, but all the kids called her Crocus. Jack was in high school when she died—she had relatives in the West, and they kept saying they were going to come help, but no one ever did. Addie even had to make arrangements for her funeral. Addie had never figured out why they needed to call her Crocus instead of her name. It could have been the pinched, toothless look of her mouth. Still, she didn't look like the flower, and it irritated and baffled him that the kids could be so disrespectful.

"Yeah," Harlan says, voice modulated with the correction. "That's right."

"Sure."

"I was thinking about her too. I once did some masonry work for her, just before she got sick. She was nice."

"She was always nice to me."

"I just wanted to know if I'm like that, Addie. We go back a long way, and I know I ain't been the greatest human being on earth, but I don't want to be like that—a charity case or something. I mean I know what you did with her—Junior said how you and your boys took care of her."

"I don't know what you mean," Addie says, arms and face iced with anger suddenly. The old, lazy, manipulative Jim Harlan sliding out from beneath the rock of his distress.


It is nearly four o'clock when he gets to the hospital the next afternoon. The parking lots are all plowed now, and huge bergs of snow sit at odd angles at the edges of the lots.

"They give me morphine, Add," his father says when Addie gets to his room. He's sitting propped up in bed, the oxygen mask still on his face. His mouth is heavy with the drug.

"I did the Hadleys'," Addie says, grinning, trying to ignore the pale, translucent look of his father, trying to ignore everything around them.

"Your words," his father says through the hissing of the oxygen, "have a kind of funny sound," and Addie looks at him closely, trying to find an answer. "Dreamlike. Like you're dreaming, and I'm reading your dreams as they come out." He laughs. Addie can't help but think of the nurse in the hallway, the vivid dreamingness of her face, but he knows that's not what his father's talking about. It's the morphine.

A nurse comes into the room—Addie can hear the whoosh of her shoes against the floor, can tell without even looking that it's a nurse. The curtains that separate the two beds have runners on the ceiling, and there is the sound behind Addie of the other man's curtain being closed.

"It getting any warmer out there?" his father says.

"Sun's been out all day. Still in the twenties, so I don't know if anything's going to melt soon."

He looks at his father: head against the white pillow and the long wisp of hair at the top of his head curled off into the air; the oxygen mask; the intravenous tube hooked painfully to his arm. His helplessness galls him, galls him that there is nothing he can do.

He knows at the bottom of his heart that his father is going to die soon, that the whole thing is mapped out in front of them. He looks at his father hard, and without willing it panic shivers his bones and makes him step backward. The nurse at the other man's bed is directly behind him, behind the curtain, and when he reaches out to steady himself he bumps into her—his hand strokes her side. "Hey," she says softly.

"I'm sorry," he mutters. His father hasn't noticed. Dead soon. It's something that wants to have meaning—something his own mind strains toward. What it will mean. *I love you Daddy* is what he wants to say, and it hovers around in his mind for a while, not being said, not being said mainly because of its not being understood.

*We often don't have anything to say to each other, but we share a lot of things together—we share this similar body, yours not working and mine all right, strong.* He has never thought of himself this way before—so physically similar to someone, an echo of a kind of echo.

When he leaves his father's room he's only been there for fifteen minutes, but it feels like forever. It's awful how time does that, makes itself wasteful. He makes his way slowly down the hall, takes the stairs instead of the harsh, stainless steel elevators.

He goes outside for a moment and stands in the cold, surveying the parking lot, trying to decide what to do. He lights a cigarette, and the wind comes around. The tobacco tastes good—tastes like the first thing he's been able to get to the heart of all week. Cars move like slow fish in the parking lot. Old people walk toward the doors—slow, slow, everything slow. When people get to be a certain age they must spend forever at hospitals, is what he thinks.

Beyond the glass doors the emergency room is lit with scalding white fluorescent light. After the dark road out from Hadleysburg it seems too bright, too real. Addie parks his truck along the curb in front, then climbs out, comes around, opens the door, and lifts Jim out. He pushes the door closed with his shoulder, then comes up the walk, through the automatic, supermarket-style doors. The nurse behind the desk gets up and comes forward around the desk and meets him with a wheelchair. "Thanks, old buddy," Harlan says as Addie puts him down onto the seat of the wheelchair.

Businesslike, the nurse asks what's wrong, then pushes Harlan around by the desk and starts asking other questions—name, address, insurance—reducing the sum of his life to two pages of carbonless paper. For a moment, while this is going on, Addie stands where he is, his arms damp and smelling of Jim Harlan. He turns, looks outside to his truck, then says, "Jim, I'll be back. I'm gonna go park the pickup."

It's easier to breathe outside the emergency room. In the truck, alone, it amazes him that he's all the way out here, in Charlottesville. He thinks of calling Karen, but he doesn't want to wake her. He parks the truck and comes back into the emergency room, but there's no one in sight. It's now past four o'clock in the morning—the drive from Hadleysburg took better than forty-five minutes. He stands for a moment, trying to decide what to do. Far off, he can hear voices, the way you can sometimes overhear other peoples' conversations in the telephone line.

When the nurse returns, it startles him a little. "Do you know what's wrong with him?" Addie says. It feels such a foolish question.

"No," she says. He waits for her to say more, but she doesn't. It's only when she glances up at him again that he realizes he's been staring at her expectantly. "Are you a relative?"

"Just a—" Addie starts to say "a friend," but though he's known him most of his life, Harlan's not a friend. Not in the true sense of the word. "Just a neighbor." The sound of the word coats his throat.

"As a guess," the nurse says, softer now, friendlier, noting the look on his face, "I'd expect the doctors would want to keep him for a couple of days. For tests."

Unstuck by the circumstance, Addie rattles the keys and change in his pocket. His throat burns for a cigarette. He stands where he is, staring out the windows into the blackness of the outside world. His hand goes to his shirt pocket to look for his pack of Trident, but it's not there. His mind wants to think, but there is nothing but the glass, the mercury light of the pavement outside.

"Maybe I ought to go," he says. The nurse says nothing. There's no reason for him to stay. He's only here because he brought Jim. It's late, there's no reason at all to be here anymore. He says too loudly, "Tell Mr. Harlan if he needs anything, he should just call me."

The automatic doors swish open in front of him, and on the way back to the pickup truck a tremendous wave of guilt for leaving Harlan alone washes over him.

The drive home, into the dawn, is peaceful, beautiful. Somewhere, he imagines, two young people on some dirt road have just climbed up out of the depths of lovemaking and sit together, half dressed, in the back of a car, amazed by the beauty and brilliance of life.

Karen's getting ready for work and doesn't say anything to him when he comes in from his trip to the hospital except, "Addie, please, I'm in a hurry." Then, "Good-bye." She kisses him perfunctorily on the mouth and disappears.

He loads the truck with his tools and goes to the job, and during the morning calls Tim Woolford at home. He's still hoarse as a toad. At lunchtime, he gets in the pickup and drives to the bank where Karen works. He's surprised to find that she's already out to lunch. Sherry Evans says she just went up the street, to the diner. Addie smiles. Despite the warmth of the people at the bank, he always feels big, old, dirty, out of place—a lumberjack walking out of the woods into a tea party.

The pickup is parked in the lot, and he walks around to the front of the bank, toward the diner, then changes his mind. He has no idea what he's come to say to her, and in his mind he looks like a dog run off and come home two days later, its fur stuck with mud, its eyes shifting and guilty.

He puts the pickup in gear, and as it swings around the front of the building, he catches a glimpse of her going inside with Peter Renfry, one of her friends, a teller who takes night classes. He's smiling and has his hand on the small of her back as he holds the door for her. She's turning to smile back at something he's said, and as she does she sees Addie's truck, and the smile stops, transforms into an awkward mix of looks, like a photograph of someone midsentence. He doesn't slow down—waves. That picture stays in his head the rest of the day.

In the evening he puts his arms around her, runs his hands through her hair. "I'm beginning to like it," he says, needing to mean it more than meaning it.

"If I weren't around to keep you straight, you'd be such a fuddy-duddy." He looks for the loose, surfacy thing he expects in her voice, but it's not there and it makes him grateful.

"I keep thinking of life as always one single moment," he says, still holding her tightly, his mouth pressed into her hair. So often in his life the place he has come to in time and space has left him amazed—like a hand has just dropped you here on the threshold of whatever circumstance, while you rub your eyes like an infant, amazed as much as horrified. It was the way he felt when Alison died. Dumped into some unexpected morning. It was the way he felt sleeping with Karen for the first time. It was the way he'd felt when the two men from the government came to tell him that Roy had been killed in the military. The caves of the here and now sing with how well you behave, how worthy you are.

"The place you are now," he says, trying to explain it to her. "Like there's a window that surrounds you all the time. Now. You're alone in the window, and when I saw Jim Harlan on the floor of his trailer soaked with pee and all gone, I thought the same thing I always think—is this what it comes down to?" His voice trembles like drapes in the rain. He wants her to understand, but it begins to dawn on him that it is part of what he is talking about—aloneness—that cannot be understood.

"Addie," she says, pulling back from him and putting her soft hands on the coarse of his cheeks, "people have the lives they deserve, largely. That you do what you do is one of the things that made me go against everything that's considered normal and fall in love with you. What you have to understand is that you are not Jim Harlan." *So this is part of it.* She stares at him, and he has to avert his eyes from the deep brown clarity of her gaze. "You think you could have been, but you couldn't." A hand exerts pressure on one side of his face, brings his eyes back to her. "Take me with you next time," she says.

Karen is already asleep when he comes in off the front porch with his empty glass and walks through the hallway in the dark to the kitchen. It's past midnight, but he isn't tired—it feels a little like the old days when he was alone and sometimes wouldn't sleep for days (old, stuck in some endless state of falling toward winter). He can't get the image of Harlan out of his mind—slumped up against the door of the truck where Addie'd parked him, the seat belt holding him like a bag of laundry.

He puts his glass in the sink and stands in the kitchen alone for a long time, listening to the house, to the world outside.

Jack. His son's name comes to him, and for a moment the word just howls in him. Jack. John Hadley Pleasance. And the thing that comes like hunger is a desperate want for the physical proximity of his son.

And then in a moment, he's going up the stairs as quietly as he can, undressing in the bathroom and folding his clothes to carry into the bedroom, trying in every way he has learned over the years to hold back his tears.

The bed is pale with spilled light from the mercury vapor streetlight outside. Karen is snoring a little. Sometimes, on better nights when he comes to bed after her and she wakes, he jokes with her, "You wouldn't know where all that sawdust in the bed came from, would you?"

He settles down in bed next to her, glad to feel the warmth she's left on the sheets, glad for the sound of her presence.

When he wakes, it surprises him that he's been asleep, because he hadn't expected it so soon. But now he's wide awake. Karen's no longer snoring, and the light in the street has gone out somehow. He has no idea what time it is—no idea what day it is or, for that matter, what year. He thinks about going downstairs and making himself another drink, just to put him back to sleep. Once the notion gets into his head, he can't evade it. He sits up in bed and starts to climb out—softly, so as not to wake Karen—but he's off balance. The bed moves, the world moves. He's falling sideward, out of bed, trying to figure out what's happening. He nicks his head on the nightstand, then the carpeted floor hits him hard. "Karen," he says, but there's no response. And then he reaches down to touch his legs, and his hand sweeps over empty air. He tries to look, but his eyes won't work.

"Honey?" Karen says, garbled. "Honey, wake up." And then there is sunlight through the front window. Karen is in her nightgown, toothbrush in her mouth.


In the morning before going to the hospital, he goes to a diner in the middle of the city for breakfast. He has eggs and sausage. The floor of the diner is covered with dirty, melted snow, even though a man in a stained white apron comes through every few minutes and runs a mop across the linoleum.

There are students mostly, and he is envious of the easy way things seem for them—books piled on tables, tousled hair, wrinkled shirts and dungarees.

Finished with his food rapidly, he sips his coffee slowly. Gets another cup. There's a radio playing big band music in the kitchen, and a woman, one of the cooks or waitresses, maybe, sings along with it.

Maybe he'll move. Maybe when his father dies he'll sell the house and move some place like this. Go to school, maybe, on the GI Bill. Start up the business again in a place like this. There has to be money in apartments here. He stares at the cracked lip of his coffee cup, and it begins to dawn on him that things are possible. Maybe somehow he'd get married, have kids. A house.

He gets out his cigarettes, shakes one loose, then lights it, blows the paper match out with the first puff of cigarette smoke. The sulphury smoke hangs in the air in front of him a moment, and he is looking toward the front of the shop—where the door opens, and a kid in dungarees with shaggy hair kicks heavy-booted into the restaurant. As the kid goes toward the counter, Addie's eyes wander, then stop at the booth beneath the window where the diner's neon sign buzzes and snaps.

There, again, she is. The Hadley girl.

Alone at her booth, deep into a book, her black hair giving blue glints in the sunlight that reflects off the snow and through the window. This time he's certain it's her. He stares at her for a long time.

He doesn't have any idea how long he's been looking at her when she looks up—she's felt him watching her, and at first he dodges his glance away, but he can still feel her looking. A waitress comes by with two steaming plates of pancakes and sausage balanced on one forearm, and he can smell the meat, can smell the syrup in the thick glass beaker. In her other hand, she has a plate with two eggs, bacon, toast. And so now he looks back, curious, everything from the last forty-eight hours ringing in his head with meaning.

He smokes his cigarette slowly. There are times when a cigarette tastes good in a way that startles you, and now is one of those times. Suddenly every pore of his body has opened up, and he can feel the world around him and his own individuality within it. He's staring at her now, thinking of his father in the hospital bed, thinking of the snow curling up in front of the plow in the blinding sunlight. And she can see all this, it occurs to him. She has put down her book—it's a library book; it has one of those plastic protective covers, and the sunlight glares off it while the diner sign buzzes. Everything is molten and molting. She melts from here to Hadleysburg, not so much a woman as an incarnation of an idea that's been trying to form. Cigarette smoke exhales from him. A man's voice behind him says, "I just don't know about Thursday, Darla," and now she is getting up out of her booth seat, her book is tucked beneath her arm, and her cup of coffee, which he hadn't seen before, is in her hand, and she's coming toward him, eyes fixed on his eyes the way his eyes are fixed on hers.

She puts her coffee cup on the table first. The coffee is black, hardly drunk. She puts the book down now—*For the Union Dead* is the name of it, a narrow book, dignified by its slightness, by her absorption in it earlier. "Do you mind if I sit down?" she says.

"Not at all," he says, standing clumsily for politeness, his skin alive with a new kind of electricity. *Where have I been and where am I now?* "I thought you were a Hadleysburg boy?" she says, and she says it with a kind of patrician lilt to her voice like her father had. "I didn't expect to see you in Charlottesville."

"I am a Hadleysburg boy. I'm out here because my father's in the hospital."

"I'm sorry," she says, distant, perhaps disappointed. "I hope it's nothing serious."

"It is. Serious. He has pneumonia."

She turns away from the statement as though it is not something to be readily assimilated, not part of the conversation she has planned to have. "I'm sorry we were not or have not been properly introduced. I'm Alison Hadley."

She lifts a hand across the table to shake his. "Adolf Pleasance," he says, knowing he's said it before—knowing word for word, moment for moment what he said to her at the entranceway to her house.

"Adolf," she says. "You told me that before?"

He nods—in his mind it is a patrician nod, acknowledging her neglect.

"It's a family name, but mostly people call you Addie."

There is sunlight all around him. Her face is narrow but for her cheekbones, which are high and prominent. Her skin is pale with winter—perhaps is always pale—but has a kind of flawlessness he's not sure he's ever seen before.

"I thought maybe you were a student at the University," she says.
"No. You?"

She nods. "I thought maybe you were a GI Biller."

"I've thought about it," he says.

He wants there to be conversation between the two of them, but his mind presents him with nothing. The silence aches with the sound of the talk of others. The silence scares him.

When he looks at his watch, he's surprised by the time. "I'm sorry," he says. She still hasn't touched her coffee. "I have to go. I'm supposed to see my father."

"Of course," she says.

He stumbles as he gets up, his legs heavy from lack of use, heavy from lack of sleep. He pays the waitress, and now he stands in the middle of the floor, heavy, uncertain, and looks at Alison Hadley, looks at the rest of the diner—different from how it looked when he came in, steamier, shabbier, the walls dim with years of cooking, years of smoking students. "Good-bye," he says and makes his way toward the door. There is sunlight, and there is distance, and the door is upward, upward.

The outside cold hits him in the lungs at first. Then in the hands. The food in his stomach feels good, as though it will last. The coffee makes his head ring. When he starts the truck, he can see the Hadley girl at the table, behind the glaring glass. What he can't tell is whether she is looking at him.

The Dunnington County Jail is a new one, and from the outside, except for the chain-link fence topped with shiny concertina wire, except for the two guard towers and the old, medieval-looking jail in the background, it might not be a jail at all but a new apartment house. There are no bars on the windows—no bars at all visible from the outside.

He follows the drive around to where the sign says VISITORS PARKING and slides the pickup into an empty space. The sunlight is bright on the tarmac lot and makes him swallow hard at the emptiness of his stomach.

There are plenty of bars on the inside, and when he comes through, signs in, then goes down the hall toward the visiting area, the guard shuts the gate behind him. The clang resonates in the hallway for a long time and makes him wish he hadn't come.

The visitor's area itself is a long counter divided down the middle by thick Plexiglass, with seats evenly spaced, and partitions between each of the spaces. A guard wearing a baseball cap shows Addie where to sit down, and in a minute, Junior Harlan comes through another gate—Addie can't see it, can only hear it open and shut—and sits down. He shakes his head. "They tole me it was you, but I di'n't b'lieve it," he says. "You got a Winston for me?"

"Sorry," Addie says. "I stopped a while ago." Junior scowls. For a moment Addie has the impression that he will get up and walk away, but he doesn't. His eyes are hard as bullets. It occurs to Addie now that he's rarely seen Junior when he wasn't at least a little drunk or high on something. Maybe that's why his eyes look so hard. The sound of television filters into the room from somewhere.

He's bigger than Addie remembers. He's always been big. And it startles him how much he looks like his father—the way his father doesn't look now. He has a full, bushy beard that makes him look even bigger, and wears an old, yellowed sleeveless T-shirt. He folds his arms across his chest and leans back in the chair. He has the kind of muscles you'd only get if you had nothing else to do all day but do pushups. He has tattoos, too—crude, black, colorless.

"How's the family?" Junior says. "How's old Karen cupcake?"

Down the row, two men, one inside and one out, are talking passionately and quietly about something—he glances at them—and as he turns back toward Junior it hits him how your mind loses painful things, and through his mind comes the hot image of Jack outside a Hadleysburg bar smashing the windows and headlights out of Junior's pickup to get him to leave Karen alone. He does everything he can to put down the swell of hatred that comes up in him.

"The family's okay," he says. Then: "I came because I wanted to let you know I took your father to the hospital the other night. I thought you'd want to know. He isn't doin' too well."

"Liver fall out?"

"No. Somethin' called metastatic cancer of the spine. It's spread just about everywhere else, and they're givin' him about a month to live."

The younger Harlan looks away. When he looks back, he's grinning a bizarre grin that could mean anything. "Guess that means I'm gonna miss his funeral, 'cause I got four more months and sixteen days to go in here."

"I just thought you'd want to know."

"That it? You came all the way out here just for that?"

"That's it," Addie says.

"Well, tell him I said hi," Junior says, then bangs both massive fists against the counter—Addie can feel the concussion of them—and starts to push himself up to walk away, but stops, sits down again, and leans toward the Plexiglas. "What the fuck's in it for you?" Junior says. His eyes are narrowed, and the veins on the sides of his head, above his beard, bulge. Addie's glad the plastic is between them. "You came all the way out here just to tell me that? You get some kind of charge out of this?"

Why he didn't expect this kind of response, Addie couldn't say. "You don't care?" he says as tightly as he can.

"Why the fuck should I care?" Junior says.

"He's your father."

"Your son care about you? Old Jackie come back yet?" Addie frowns, and it gives Junior pleasure. "I can tell you one thing, my daddy sure as hell wouldn't be drivin' all the fuckin' way out to wherever to tell Jackie if you were dying, so I hope you're getting a whole lot of pleasure outta this."

"I was just trying to do a neighbor a favor," Addie says.

"Mind your own fuckin' business." Junior stares at him for a minute, then gets up and walks away.

At the hospital when he gets out of the pickup and comes walking toward the entrance, he knows the inevitable. He can feel it in the wind. Intense cold has set in after the snow, and the wind shrills, irrational, over the black field of the parking lot. It works into the fissures of his clothing, finds the soft of his neck.

Beneath the ice pack the river churns into the distance. Why is it so cold?

Inside, the heat of the hospital interior is so sudden it makes him faint. Up the stairs, the unsteady earth imparting to the stairs a rubberiness that will not release. The hallway is meant to be cheery, but the white walls are smeared and oppressive. His head is full of sheeting snow, the wild furl of the wind. His back is sweating, his hands inside his gloves are wet—partly it is the heat, partly the crawl of certainty.

Someone calls his name. "Mr. Pleasance?" And he whirls. A colorful poster; a hardwood bumper midway up the wall. It should take forever, this turn.

"Yes?"

"Could you come this way, please?"

What will not reconcile is standing next to his bed yesterday, the oxygen hissing from the wall. Being with him. Being. And now this, the breakneck speed of the river. The past nothing but the bones and dust of the bank.

The nurse is all white efficiency. His throat sucks with what he does not know. The scope of it. There is nothing at all that can prepare you.

The doctor is soft faced, young. Probably younger than Addie. Oh yes. Mr. Pleasance. I'm afraid the news is not very good.

Maybe I can sit down somewhere, he thinks, but the words don't come out. Now he mouths them. "Maybe I can sit down somewhere." Maybe I can sit.

I'm sorry. Please. The lights are bright. There's a ceramic coffee cup on a counter, someone's half-eaten breakfast. At the end of the hallway, absolutely pure white light comes through a dirty window. *I shouldn't have stopped for breakfast. I should not have talked to her.*

There are old people. Doctors and nurses. People talking in subdued voices, slippers going softly across the tiled floor. He sits down. Everything is drugged, melting. He shucks his coat and gloves. He wants to shuck everything down to his skin.

"Maybe this isn't such a good idea," he says and stands up, knocks over the wooden chair as he does so. The heavy wooden chair hits the floor with a crack, and people turn to look.

"I don't mean to be excessively, hmm, efficient, but what you need to do is make arrangements with a funeral home." What he remembers is his father's handshake. The rough of his fingers and palm. The strength of it just yesterday.

He nods. There's so much else to think about. It's January, and the ground is hard, and there's so much sunlight, so much else.

God what a mess," Karen says after he climbs through the window, then comes around and opens the door. She takes a step inside, toward him, then recoils. "Jesus, it stinks."

"I know," he says. "Old garbage. If you want to change your mind—"

"No, I said I'd help, and I'll help." It amazes him that she's here. The way Jack and Roy used to react to this kind of thing made him sure he'd never expose anyone to it again. Except they were kids. Maybe that was the mistake. "If it were ordinary circumstances—," he starts, then leaves off.

"We're such good Girl Scouts," she says. She laughs at the expression on his face. "Okay, Boy Scouts," she says. She takes a step toward him. She wears jeans and an old T-shirt beneath her jacket. She carries a bucket with a bottle of sudsing ammonia and a pair of rubber gloves in it. She looks very trim, a little worried—like maybe Junior might come home.

"Some housekeeper he was," she says thoughtfully, turning to look at the kitchen, at the narrow dining room. Was. There are garbage sacks everywhere, all in different states of disrepair. It looks like squirrels or rats might have come in. "That's our handiwork," Addie says and points at the kitchen counter. "Jack's and mine."

She gives a dry, white-lipped, humorless smile, and he knows if he did not before that it makes her uncomfortable to be here. "What's first, boss?" she says.

"I'll get the garbage out, and you can start with the kitchen. We can't reorganize everything for him, all we can do is make it a little more livable for when he comes home."

She puts on her gloves wordlessly and goes to the sink. He props open the door and starts hauling the garbage sacks out the door, down the walk, and into the back of the pickup. When she's up to her elbows in dishsuds, he sweeps up the old coffee grounds and bread crusts from the kitchen floor, then moves into the narrow living room. Into another garbage bag, he stuffs all Harlan's old laundry, which is everywhere, then takes it out to the truck and puts it in the front seat.

In the bedroom, where he didn't notice it the other night, there's a .45 pistol on the nightstand next to the bed, laid out like another man might lay out a book.

She's finished with the dishes now, and he suggests—to get her out of this atmosphere—that she take the clothes back to the house and wash them. She looks at him for a moment—gaugingly, another colorless smile—and then kisses him on the mouth with surprising softness. "All right," she says.

While she's gone, he sets to work vacuuming, mopping, scrubbing the bathroom. It's a small place, but even so it takes hard solid hours to get the place reasonably habitable. When she comes back, he's in the bathroom and has all of the windows in the trailer open. She's wearing a sweatshirt, an old jean skirt now, and her legs are red with the chill of the afternoon. He's kneeling on the floor, looking up, and she carries

Harlan's laundry in her own laundry basket. "Should I try to put this away?" she says.

He shrugs, dazzled by her legs. The afternoon suddenly smells clean and clear—the worst of the world can just be washed away. "I doubt Jim's going to be able to do it," he says at last.

She's in the bedroom when he comes in. She stands with neatly folded undershorts in her hands. The bedroom is at the very end of the trailer, and sunlight mottled by locust leaves streams through a window at the back. All you can see is woods.

"God," he says, and looking at her makes him feel as though he's been punched in the chest.

"I don't know why," she says, putting the pile of underthings on the bureau and turning toward him, "but I really want you to make love to me."

He's trembling. He's blind scared, and he doesn't understand it. "I feel the same way," he says, and in a minute his mouth is on her, biting, sucking, his hands are on her, tearing at her skirt, her sweatshirt. It is that love is irrational, that it is the only path out of aloneness, that makes him seize her in this filthy, ruined shell of another man's life.

The nurse takes the clothes Addie's brought for Harlan, then closes the door and leaves Addie standing in the hallway. In a few minutes, a man Addie guesses is an orderly slips past him, through the door, then wheels Jim Harlan out in a wheelchair. "Thanks for coming, Add," Jim says. He's wearing the little plastic bracelet they put on him when he came in, and it looks as though he's aged twenty years in the four days he's been here. Still, Addie's surprised at how relaxed he looks, how at ease. Maybe it's the drugs they gave him.

"No problem," Addie says. "No problem at all."

Addie walks beside the wheelchair as the orderly pushes it. He wants to speak, but being in the hospital makes him silent. Too many bad memories associated with hospitals.

They go slowly past open doors—curtains hang around beds, old people with translucent skin sit propped up on pillows watching television in the middle of the day.

Addie pulls the pickup around to the curb, leaves the engine running, then comes around and opens the door. He's ready to lift Harlan up into the truck, but the orderly insists on doing it. Addie watches, then nods thanks to the orderly. The young man puts the folded wheelchair in the back of the truck.

"That feels really good," Harlan says as he lights a cigarette.

"What does?" Addie says.

"That sunlight. I'm glad it's sunny. Jesus that feels good."

Out of the stifling, quiet, echoing church, the cold hits you in the knees, then in the lungs. It's blistering cold.

It surprises him how many people are here, surprised him the first moment he walked into the church. Nearly a hundred people. Even Owen and Jim and Darlene Harlan. When he gets up in front of them all to say the little piece he prepared for himself, his eyes are glassed over and he can't see anything properly. He laughs. Some people laugh with him. He imagines the woods outside, the spread of them in the snow, the fall of ice from the branches, the close and distant click of it. He remembers hunting with his father in the snow—snow turning to rain. His father bringing down a deer the two of them carried out of the woods once it was gutted. Coming out to the truck, the deer's coat matted and stuck with leaves from the wet and the blood. The musky deep-woods smell of it on him.

Then the church is quiet, and the early brilliant winter light makes streaks from the stained-glass windows along the wooden floor. Standing here, half panicked, he wants to say, *why don't we just turn off the lights, so we can all sit here and feel the presence of God.* Except it isn't the presence of God he feels. The bodies of the funeral-goers rustle in their Sunday clothes. The universe is vast and indifferent. If there's anything you learn in the world, it's that the universe is vast and indifferent.

"You never know your parents well" is what he is saying. "In some sense you know them more intimately than they can be known by others, but in another sense you can't know them. There is too much standing between you and them. It was no different with me and my father. I learned from him. I'm what is left of him. I miss him desperately." This is something he had not known yesterday. This is something that has occurred to him only now.

His voice cracks when he says it. It's like having part of you removed. Like you have never been alone in the dark before. *We should turn off these lights and just look at the sunlight through the stained glass.*

He stands with his hands in his pockets, next to his Aunt Vivian—not really his aunt, his father's oldest friend in town. And next to her, Charlie, her husband.

It's all already over for him. It ended at the hospital. Or maybe it ended before. Whenever it was, it ended long before arriving at the church this morning. His eyes tear in the cold, and the minister, with gloved hands, says some things over the coffin, and then he and the others are lifting it into the ground.

She's at the funeral, the Hadley girl, alone, on the empty trampled snow at the edge of the crowd. He doesn't know if she was in the church during the service—she has appeared here the way she has appeared in every other instance he has seen her.

It seems unreal, all of it. It couldn't possibly be real. At the end, people slide into their cars and some head for home. Some gather at the doors of the church. Most head for Vivian's house for food, conversation. For a long time he just stands out in the snow. The Hadley girl is there. Tombstones are everywhere. She has been waiting for him, or he has been waiting for her.

"I'm sorry," she says. "I didn't know it was this serious." She reaches out and touches his arm, and the naturalness of this human gesture, a woman in a black coat reaching out and touching a man on the arm, strikes him as breathtaking.

"It was nice of you to come," he says.

"What was he like?"

Wind blows. A car starts. "He was just a man. Smoked too much. Didn't like to go to the doctor when any fool could see that he should. He was good with his hands. Good cabinet maker." It makes him feel light-headed to say these things. It makes him feel like he's standing at the end of his father's road totting up his accomplishments with nothing to count.

"Why don't you come for coffee?" he is surprised to find himself saying. "At my Aunt Vivian's?"

She smiles. Her face is one of those narrow, vulnerable faces; it reminds him of a miscast porcelain doll—more beautiful than the ones properly cast, but somehow wrong. She has the beauty of her father, his softness of features, but the brittleness of her mother.

She leaves her car in the church parking lot and rides with him in his father's pickup. The pickup is cold, and he wishes he'd offered to let her drive.

"I've never ridden in one of these before," she says, and he takes it as confirmation that he should have let her drive, but he does not look at her face; her voice is light.

"Seems like the only thing I've ever ridden in," he says.

At Vivian's he parks in the street, and they walk together up the snow-packed walk.

They are at the place where the shoveled walk heads up to Vivian and Charlie's door from the road, and in turning, they stop. She looks at him, one of the three or four looks he's seen from her since he met her—open eyed, nearly blank. Expectant. He wants to lean over and kiss her, but the utter inappropriateness of it keeps him from it. And then what the look says hits him. Now more than before he wants to kiss her, but he doesn't. The step he takes feels like the first step into a new world.


Harlan says, "What the hell happened here?" when Addie pushes open the door and swings him inside the trailer. The air smells of Lysol.

"Didn't think you'd mind if I took back a few of your empties," Addie says.

"Smells like a goddamned hospital in here," Harlan says. Addie laughs as he puts him down in a chair in the kitchen, then swings open the refrigerator to show the two new six-packs of Budweiser. Jim smiles, and abruptly the smile snaps to a grimace; his face looks like he's been hit with electric current.

"You okay?"

"Addie," Harlan says, after a long silence, "I need your help." The grimace is gone now; his face is pale and waxy.

"What can I do?"

Harlan doesn't say anything but takes out his pack of cigarettes, fingers it for a moment before he shakes one loose. He flicks the wheel on a plastic butane lighter, then pulls deeply on the cigarette. "Maybe you'll have a can of beer with me."

"All right," Addie says, "but first let me go get that wheelchair." Harlan nods.

Outside the air is fresh and sharp.

Addie hoists the wheelchair from the truck and brings it back inside. For a moment he just stands looking—at Jim, at the shabby kitchen beneath the patina of clean. Then he turns and unfolds the wheelchair.

"Maybe tomorrow I'll come by and say hey," Addie says. Then, without looking at Harlan, he opens the refrigerator and pulls two cans of Budweiser from the plastic rings that hold them.

"Thanks," Harlan says when Addie hands him the opened can of beer. "I been dyin' for this." He tips the can up, drinks it the same hungry way he's been smoking his cigarette.

Harlan leans sideways in his chair. "I thank you for what you've done."

They are here. Earlier they were at the hospital. Addie is amazed by this.

Addie opens his own can of beer; it tastes bitter, unpleasant, but he makes himself drink it. He thinks of Karen with him two days ago, and though the thought of her with him makes him want to feel guilty, it doesn't.

"I just wanted to say thanks," Harlan says. "That's all. You didn't have to do any of this."

"Sure," Addie says. He leaves his can of beer on the counter and straightens up. For a moment Addie just stands where he is, looking at Harlan sitting in the cheap metal-and-vinyl chair. He looks away, picks up his beer again, and drinks from it.

"There's nothing—," Harlan says slowly, thoughtfully. "I mean I guess I'm a chickenshit for not facing up to this. But I'm a chickenshit from way back. You know what?"

Addie shakes his head.

"I never told nobody this, but I got kicked out of the Marines."

Addie laughs. It doesn't make any sense why right now it seems so funny. "Doesn't seem much like the time to be worrying about that," he says.

Harlan laughs too, through his nose. "No."

Addie blinks. Words won't come. There's a long pause.

"I was thinking while I lay in that hospital bed. It come to me that I had never done much thinkin'. I drunk a lot of beer, and I watched a lot of TV, and I never did much thinkin'. Maybe that's the difference between the two of us, Addie."

"Stop it."

Harlan pulls the refrigerator open and takes out another can of beer. "You want one?" he says. Addie shakes his head. The first one hit him in the skull like a ballpeen hammer.

"Tomorrow morning, the nurse is supposed to come. I think I can make it until then. First thing, though—I mean I'll just ask you one more thing. Put me into bed, turn on the TV."

Addie nods. He picks Jim up and puts him in the wheelchair, then pushes him through to the back of the trailer. It's a long trip. The sunlight from the other day is gone, now only shadows. The bed is smooth, made. "I can't believe what you all did here," Harlan says. "I don't have the words to thank you."

Addie picks him out of the wheelchair and puts him onto the bed. Then goes and turns on the black-and-white TV that sits on a stack of boxes. It takes forever to warm up, and when the picture comes on, Addie flicks the channels. Harlan tells him to stop on an old rerun of "Hawaii Five-O." Addie looks at the picture on the TV, wanting to be entranced by the glow of it the way you're supposed to be, but then turns back to Harlan. Involuntarily, his eyes slip to the .45 on the nightstand. Harlan sees the look, follows it. "Well," Addie says.

"Well," Harlan says.

"You gonna be all right?"

"Best thing for me is some time alone," Harlan says.

Addie looks at him a moment, nods, then turns, walks down the narrow hallway, the knurl of the worn brown carpet palpable through the soft of his shoes. He goes through the door and down the wooden steps, across the broken concrete walk, then climbs into the pickup. It's always been important to him that a man have humility in his life, that a man never, ever, get the idea he's better than someone else.

The engine rushes, and he pushes the accelerator. The sun bursts out from behind a cloud, and he's not on Maypole Lane anymore but on Graham Street and everything is lit brilliantly—all the houses look chiseled in some fine, soft stone, and the painted colors of the shutters and cars bloom and burst against the savage sky.

Instead of going home, he heads into town for the bank, desperate just to see Karen's face.

# THE SEEDS

The stars are out bright and hard in the cloudless sky, and the light is milky and soft. There's barely a breeze, but the air is cold and feels good when it bucks down your throat. It's close to midnight, and the pale light bathes the knee-high, dead weeds at the edge of the road, makes silver the barbed wire strung between hewn wooden poles. The gravel road twists past deserted, falling-down chicken coops that still stink of guano. I am running. There's a sign in front of a darkened house—BETTY'S BEAUTY SHOP—in hand-painted lettering. It hangs by S-hooks from an arm of white-painted galvanized piping by the mailbox.

Sometimes out here it feels like eternity. Sometimes out here it feels like the universe could be dead and in the slow process of freezing. You hit an open field, and the sky and stars are vast above you, and there is no sound but the weeds rustling in the breeze, or sounds so faint they might as well be imagined. Everything is vast, and you are nothing, and if you thought about it, it would devastate you for the loneliness of it. You let your breath and the sound of your feet fill your head, fill the world around you, because they're the only sounds that mean anything.

I'm running because it's late at night and I couldn't sleep, and grew so wild with it in the trailer that I decided to wear myself out so completely I couldn't stand up.

I'm running because I can't stop thinking about Sandy, and about Chalky, and because sometimes running helps to work things out.

A pickup comes rattling past and leaves a cloud of dust in the air—everything near the road is dusted with fine blue powder—and I try to hold my breath but keep running.

The gravel road dead-ends into a paved side road, two lane but narrow, the kind of road you drive the crown of unless you've come to a blind rise or there is another car coming. I spit the taste of gravel from my mouth, turn onto the paved road, and start to work my way back toward the lake. There is an open field on the left, white horse fences on the right, and a house on a knoll. In the car or on the bike, the road seems short, fast. Now it's slow. There's a dead snake flattened at the crown of the road—it's nothing but skin now.

I'm nearing the turnoff for the lake when a car flashes around the turn ahead of me. The headlights hit me straight on and hard, and I put my arm up to shield my eyes and start for the edge of the road, but the car veers onto the lake turnoff. It goes fast and quiet, and the lights go out as soon as it hits the turnoff. I have the idea that it's Chalky, but a million other things are going through my head. There was a farm where they raised angus in Hadleysburg not too far from our house, and way back in the woods off one of the pastures was a little shack. About five feet wide and maybe fifteen feet long, it had a ledge on one side that might have been a bed, and windows on the opposite side in a high, narrow row. Roy and I thought it was as remote and unknown to my father as you could get, and one day when we were supposed to be doing something else, we spent too long there, and suddenly there he came, walking through the brush, ducking to avoid a low-hanging limb. It stunned us; it was unreasonable that he should know everything. And yet it made sense. That was him.

The lights have ruined my night vision, and I wait at the edge of the road until the glare in my head subsides.

I go up as far as the turnoff, listen to the car as it rattles down the road and stops. The engine goes off. A door creaks open but doesn't slam. The sound of boots on gravel, then silence as they move onto the path. When my eyes are accustomed to the dark again, I cut through the weeds into the woods and work my way down to the lake. I'm wearing sweatpants and a T-shirt, and the sweat has gone cold on my arms and chest.

At the lake, I cut up toward my trailer. I know the path, I know the area, and I stay to where I know the leaves are thin and I can walk soundlessly.

I move up through the woods, silent as I can be, and I think I see the shape of someone in the darkness. I get up toward the edge of the trailer, and I can hear the scratch of boots on the porch. Leaves are everywhere, but it's damp and they don't crackle the way they would if it was dry. I walk around to the edge of the front and stand there. Chalky lifts the .45 and bangs the butt of it on the door, and the sound is loud through the air. He waits a moment. My breath is held tightly. He knocks again, and as he does so, he tries the handle. I left it locked—I always do. He pushes, then swears softly under his breath when it won't open. He goes to the edge of the porch and reaches over to the window, jiggles it. Then off down at the lake, a bell jingles softly. It's the kind of bell you put on the end of a fishing rod when you're catfishing. Once, twice, it jingles, then insistently. I turn around and look, but of course there's nothing but darkness. It could be half a mile away.

Chalky jumps down off the edge of the porch and comes around to the corner of the trailer. I back off into the darkness and trees. In a moment, he is where I was standing a moment ago. I can feel the heat of him in the air. He looks off down toward the lake. I wish it were cloudy. I do not breathe but watch, my eyes straining against the dark for the slightest indication he can see me. The bell jingles again and stops. He starts humming softly to himself, the way a scared kid will. I wonder if the dark and the isolation spook him, and for a moment I feel a strange kinship with him: the isolation, the sense of abandonment. Something in me wishes we were more alike. If he only turned his head, he would see me.

If I had a gun and the volition, I could drop him instantly. If I were fool enough, I could jump him. The idea goes through my head, and it's everything I can do to put down the charge of adrenaline. And yet at the same time, some too reasonable thing in me wants to talk to him, to find out if he really knows.

An owl calls off above us. For a long moment, he stands in the darkness, then he gets out a cigarette and lights it. The flare of his butane lighter floods the woods—it feels as though I am bathed in light. He must not be looking at me but at the light; it guarantees that he won't be able to see. I can taste the cigarette smoke in the air.

In a moment, he stumbles back up toward the road in the dark. When he's gone, I stand where I am for a long time and wonder what to do next.

The hardware store stinks of fertilizer—green-and-white bags of it are stacked by the doorway, next to a metal rack of rakes. It's Sunday, and a radio behind the counter quietly plays hymnal music that floats through the silent store. A man at the counter in a worn suede blazer is buying a seeder-spreader, and the green and white and red box sits on the counter.

I slide through the aisles, pick out a cheap jigsaw, a set of piano hinges, and some screws, and pay for them at the counter. I'm alone in the store with the man at the counter—there's a dirty window behind him that catches the last of the afternoon's sunlight, and next to it, a pegboard rack of drill and router bits. He reminds me of what Sandy told me about her father, and I think of my own father, and momentarily the thought makes me desolate inside.

Across the street, in shadow, is a man who looks from a distance like Chalky. No.

I still have the rifle under the passenger seat of the car—I keep it with me, in the car or in the trailer.

When I get back to the lake, I drive around the gravel roads that wander through the woods surrounding the lake. The trees are mostly bare and barren, and the houses and trailers look dirt poor and desolate. Back when they engineered this lake as a reservoir for Middleridge, it was supposed to be a resort, but there was never a near enough or wealthy enough clientele, and the people who did build houses for weekend or summer use ended up having to rent them for less than it cost to build and maintain them. Now, like everything, they have gone to seed.

There's a weedy hill at the far end of the lake that overlooks the earthen dam and the concrete spillway that juts out into the water. The gravel road tapers into weeds and I turn the car around, but before heading back down the hill to the trailer, I park the Chevy at the top of the hill and look down. I cut off the engine and roll down the window. The chill, motionless air drifts into the car.

I can hear the water falling down through the spillway—it's a nice sound, like a natural waterfall muffled by a tunnel. Below the dam, on the other side, I can see where the water trickles out and flows away through the bare trees. There's the rusting skeleton of an old Dodge in the woods, and it's impossible to tell how it could have got there.

I stare for a few minutes and then start the car again, put the car into reverse, and pull around, head back down through the woods to the trailer. It always seems that things jump forward, that things never change but change too rapidly. You get used to the loneliness, start thinking that you have come to the point where you will never be torn apart again by trust or love, and then it steals in on you again and like Prometheus, you get your heart plucked out again.

I park the car and take the tools and rifle down to the trailer. I leave the tools on the wooden steps, slip the rifle out of the case, and take a walk around the trailer. The rifle is warm in my hands from sitting beneath the seat in the direct path of the heat vent. It's loaded, the safety is on. The woods are quiet and cold. Through the trees I can see the lake. The leaves crush beneath my feet, and the sound carries clearly in the winter air.

I come back to the front, unlock the door and slip inside, the bag of tools in one hand, the rifle beneath the other arm. I'm hungry, but I don't bother to eat. I take everything out of the narrow hall closet and move it to one of the back bedrooms, measure out a square twenty-four inches by twenty-four inches, then drill holes through the floor at each of the corners. It doesn't surprise me that the floor is so thin.

I pick up the rifle and go outside again, then around to the back of the trailer and crawl beneath it where the closet is. What I'm looking for is to make sure that the hole I'm going to cut doesn't destroy any wires or pipes or support beams. The space is shallow—a little less than two feet—and the leaves are damp and cold. Beneath the trailer, the ground is loamy and soft with old rotted leaves, but dry. I find the fresh sawdust and run my fingers along the underside of the floor where I drilled the holes. It's midafternoon, and the light is dim. I find the holes with my fingertips, then run my hands around the underside of the floor. No obstructions.

In a minute, I slide out from beneath the trailer and walk slowly around the building, rifle in hand, leaves stuck to my shirt and in my hair. I look up toward the road, then back toward the lake and up the hill through the woods. Nothing but silence and emptiness.

Inside, I slip the blade into the jigsaw, snug up the locking screw, then plug it in and shove the blade into the holes I drilled. I cut along the lines. The humming movement of the blade vibrates through my arm and into my chest. The floor shudders; the shrill, rasping sound fills the trailer. Fine sawdust blooms on the floor around the blade and the guide plate, and I have to blow it off regularly to keep the penciled line visible.

When I get around the last side, the square sags then falls through and lands on the loam where I lay a few minutes ago. I reach down and pick it up, lean it against the closet wall. After the noise from the saw, the silence of the trailer is magnified. I get up off my hands and knees and walk to the window. Outside everything is getting dark. No cars out on the road.

I go back to the closet and climb down to test it out. It's a narrower fit than I thought it would be, but I can still climb through quickly. I test it—push my legs through, knees upright, then sort of heel-walk the rest of the way down. Then I try it knees down and backing under. Finally I try head first.

I unwrap the hinges from the puckered plastic and cardboard and fit them along the edge of the hole closest to the back wall, then drill holes. I screw them on and fold them back. I have to go up to the shed to get some scraps of wood for underside support, and I take the rifle with me. My stomach crows with hunger as I go through the woods, up the path. The work has kept my restlessness at bay, but now the evening crawls with the unnamed.

I stand by the road, and there is a wind. The sun is behind the mountains, and the wind is cold. Things fold and unfold, and I can't remember what I came up here for—now I am here.

I turn around and walk toward the shed. The door is bent where it was not bent before, and I lift the rifle up and point the barrel of it through the opening, then reach out and take hold of it. It sticks and screeches as it wrenches open. The screech echoes. Then, inside, a crash, and the motorcycle falls over, bangs into the wall, sends scraps of wood and other junk clattering against the flimsy tin wall. I stand back, door open, and look, then look up the road, at the car, at the trailer.

Someone's been here—it's funny how you can feel someone else's presence in the air, even long after they're gone, as though the shape of them has left an indistinct imprint that your own body can read. The gun comes from beneath my arm, and my hand finds the place on the stock where it is meant to fit perfectly, where my fingers slide into the trigger guard and cocking lever.

I edge back and poke into the shed. Painted sloppily in white paint and glowing on the inside of the door are the words "your dead meat pleasance." I reach out toward the door and touch the paint—it's cold and dry. I have no idea how long it's been here. I wonder when Chalky— if it even was Chalky—came by and painted this crap. "You ignorant fuck," I say to myself when I bend down to see if the bike's been vandalized, "it's 'you're,' *y-o-u* apostrophe *r-e*."

I right the bike. It seems fine, but it's hard to tell in the dark. Nothing else seems to be different from how I last left it.

For a moment, I stand hypnotized—not by the painting or the words but by the woods, the silence, the presence of the gun in my hand, the sequence of events over the last few days. A squirrel runs through the underbrush up the hill, and the crackle of dried leaves shakes me out of it. I reach into the shed, grab a couple of scraps of old one-by-two, then lock the shed up again and head back down the path toward the trailer.

I drop through the hole again onto the cold ground with a flashlight, then glue and nail the pieces of one-by-two at the edges of the hole on the underside. I climb back inside the trailer, and, kneeling inside the closet, the flashlight lying on the floor and the beam spraying against the wall, fit the piece I cut out back into the hole. I drill more holes and screw the hinges to the edge of the cut-out. Now I have a trap door.

I fiddle around with the door for a moment—the opening between the floor and the cut-out is too narrow to get my fingers into, so I find a piece of string and nail it to the inside edge of the opening—I'll know it's there, but someone else will have to look for it.

With the flashlight, I climb beneath the trailer once again, this time spread the leaves away so there's a clear space beneath the trailer that won't crackle with the sound of crushing leaves. I work for a long time in the dark, lying down in the damp earth, the butt of the flashlight in my mouth. I don't know what time it is when the car comes over the hill, but I'm near the front of the trailer, by the porch. I hear the tires on the gravel before I see the lights, and I freeze—glad to be where I am so I have a view of the hill—and wait to see if the car will stop at Swansons'. No. The car's going slowly, and it takes a minute before the headlights crest the hill. I don't wait any longer but wriggle backward toward the trap door, climb back inside the house, and cut off the light that's on, grab the rifle and the box of shells, then drop them through the floor, pull the closet door closed, then drop the rest of the way down under the trailer myself. The car stops in front, by the path. From my angle I can't make out what kind it is. I pull the door closed over me—cushion its falling with an upturned palm, then crawl toward where I was working a few minutes ago. I have the gun next to me, and the box of shells is somewhere behind me.

Now I lie up close to the edge of the trailer so I can see who's coming down the path. My eyes aren't completely used to the dark, so I wait, listen. The gun is extended out from me, my hand on the grip, on the safety.

It sounds like only one person. In a moment, I can see an outline. I lift up the gun, put the stock to my shoulder, and aim the way I did at the rifle range.

But it's a woman. Sandy. My heart chunks up hard at my throat, and I have to stop myself from calling out. I let the gun rest back on the loam.

Since I went to her house, I've been hoping this would happen.

She gets closer, and now I can see it's not Sandy but Sylvia.

She stops at the step and hesitates. I wonder if she can sense me in the utter quiet of the woods—hear my breathing or my heartbeat. She's only eighteen or twenty inches from me. In a moment, she takes a step up onto the stair, then knocks on the door. She steps all the way up. I can hear her breath, can hear her mutter something softly, but I can't understand it.

She knocks again. When there is still no answer, she calls out softly, "Jack? You in there? I just want to talk." She stands waiting a long time and then says, "Goddamn you," loud enough so her voice carries. It's not until she has gone back up the path, climbed into her car, and driven off, not until the night is completely silent again, that I push up through the floor and into the closet again.

Late, the night moonless and cloudy, I sit down with my back against the wall by the closet, the rifle and a plug-in lamp with a low-wattage bulb on one side of me, the photographs on the other. For a long time, I look at them, try to understand whatever it is that a photographic image can tell you, but it's like watching an airplane against the sun—the longer you look, the more it hurts, the more it begins to disappear. I wonder why my father wanted so desperately to destroy them—and why he was so concerned that we never see the side of him that destroyed them.

Was he ashamed of her? Was he ashamed of himself?

*My mother sits in the kitchen, and my father is out in the shop, working.*
*Since she came back from her short time living in New York, he stays close to*
*home, doesn't spend more than forty-five minutes away from the house.*

*"Do you hear it?" she says. Roy leaves the room. I shake my head.*

*"The glass."*

*"What glass?"*

*"The glass in the cabinets is singing," she says and then grits her teeth and*
*closes her eyes as tightly as she can. I do not know if she is playing. Sometimes she*
*plays. Other times things bother her so much that it is hard to understand.*

*When Daddy comes back in the house and says he's going to go install the*
*shelves he's been working on, the squint leaves her eyes.*

*"You going to be okay?" he says. She smiles at him. Pretty.*

*"Because they are cylindrical," she says when he is gone, "they vibrate. Can't*
*you hear them?"*

*I shake my head. She is joking.*

*She takes a glass from the cabinet and holds it in her hand. "Don't you see*
*it?" she says.*

*I shake my head.*

*She opens the back door and throws it onto the concrete steps. When it smashes,*
*she gets another from the cabinet and smashes it too. I laugh when she looks at me*
*because I don't know what else to do. It is a big thing she is doing—something*
*decisive, huge, dangerous. I laugh. Soon there is glass everywhere. Roy hears the*
*sound and comes into the kitchen and stares at her, then me. Instantly I am*
*ashamed of laughing. I look at him, then at her. She doesn't look at him. I don't*
*know what to do.*

I listen to the woods outside, listen to the darkness, and sometimes I
think I can hear crying, but it must just be the breeze in the eaves of the
trailer. Winter is coming, and I have no idea what I'm doing here. Like
the sense sometimes in Richmond I got that I would sink through the
pavement of the street outside my office. I can see Sandy a few nights
ago at the edge of the road and I can see her inside here, the bottle of
wine and wrapped in blankets, and I can't figure out where it went or
why I can't feel it anymore. It's not that time passes, but that it passes
with such permanence.

# DELIA'S

Monday morning at eight o'clock I am at Delia's—she comes to the door in her bathrobe and half giggles as she says, "My, my, my, you are true to your word. And no one can say I'm not true to mine," and backs away from the door, then closes it behind me.

"That is some pair of jeans," she says as she turns to lead me down the hall. She has a stout walk, stiff legged—a female Falstaff.

"I've had these since high school," I say. "They're my paintin' pants."

"God, what I wouldn't give to be able to wear my clothes from high school," she says. She giggles—it's a warm sound, a chubby staccato.

She's got the three buckets of paint, the roller kit, plastic drop cloths, and brushes laid out on the tiled floor. "Have you got a mop?" I say.

"Oh, yes," she flutters and opens a tall cabinet next to the sink. She gets out a sponge mop and a bucket, and then from beneath the sink, a bottle of sudsing ammonia.

The kitchen is clean—no dishes in the sink or on the counter. I put the bucket in the sink, pour ammonia into it, then run hot water. Delia stands behind me, watching, then says, voice elevated to rise above the sound of running water, "I'm just gonna be in the shower, in case you need anything. I got to get ready for work and all."

I glance back at her and nod. Sylvia's told her what's gone on between us—I can see it in her eyes, in the way she moves. I'm going to have to do something about Sylvia.

I turn back to what I'm doing.

I move the table and chairs out of the kitchen, move everything else that's loose, then get to work on the walls, scrubbing them with the sponge mop. The wall above the stove is the worst, and it comes clean slowly, the mop sticking, again and again needing to be dunked and rinsed. I'm surprised how fast it goes, surprised how lost in the work I get without even noticing it. One moment I'm scrubbing a wall and the next I'm in the trailer, last night, sitting stiffly against the wall, half asleep, dreaming of the past. The ammonia strips the grease, the accumulated dirt. One thing floats into another.

A clearer picture of my mother than I can ever remember imagining: she is standing in the kitchen at my father's house, Roy and me at the table next to one another. She is wearing a black-and-white suit, a black-and-white pillbox hat, an apron over her suit.

And then there is Delia. "My," she says, "I'm tempted to tell you not even to paint, those walls look so good."

It is like being awakened, and I look at her a moment without comprehending. The mop is in my hand.

"But since we have an agreement," she says, in her bathrobe at the edge of the kitchen, shrugging and giving the giggle she gave earlier. The bathrobe has no belt, and she only holds it closed with her hands in the pockets.

"I'm going to start painting any minute," I say. She stares at me and her eyes want to hold my eyes, but I break away, kneel down and with a screwdriver, open a paint can. It's an oyster shell white latex semi-gloss—and the scent of it is clean, and the clean is intoxicating. I put the flat stirrer into the paint, and instantly the wood is coated white and gleaming. She watches while I stir the paint, then rip the plastic wrap from around the roller set.

I look up at her. "I don't work too well while people are watching," I say.

She nods—there's more than a flicker of disappointment and insult on her face—and turns away from me. "It's all right," she says, "I got to get on to work anyway."

252 |

In a little while, fully dressed—I've started to paint the ceiling now—she comes back and says she's leaving, that she'll be back in the early afternoon. "Here's my work number, in case you need anything," she says and leaves a piece of paper on the table, "and the stereo's over here—since you're a man I'm gonna assume you'll know how to work it. You can help yourself to anything in the refrigerator if you get hungry. And I gotta tell you again, that pair of jeans is really something."

"Air-conditioned," I say, not looking at her. I look at my watch. It's already nearly eleven—the time has simply disappeared.

The roller snaps across the ceiling, and tiny white flecks of paint spatter out; I can feel it on my face and arms. The clean space expands. The latex fragrance of the paint makes my father materialize in the room. I can see us in a living room somewhere in Hadleysburg, hot moments of winter sunlight burning outdoors, my father neat and precise and plain as the ceiling we are painting. We don't speak, the two of us; we don't need to speak.

Or it's months later, and he leans against the pickup truck and doesn't say anything. We are in front of his house, my car sits beyond us, and it is nearly summer. He leans and smokes and looks off into the hazy vanishing point of distance that is the Blue Ridge, that is our relationship, and as I stand there, fingering my car keys, ready to climb into my car and sail off to Richmond, I keep thinking that it has happened to me before, this leaving him. The sense is strong, as though there is some familial memory that exists in this yard, on this street, simply because of our existence here, his dogged persistence in the face of everything.

"Son," he says. I have the suitcases in my arms. I am at the back of my car. And now he is not leaning on the pickup anymore but floating to me, floating so close that I can smell the sawdust, the tobacco, and then I am putting down the suitcases and my body is becoming light, and he is stopping, putting his arms around me, anchoring me to this earth, the only thing that is keeping me from floating clean off into the morning air. His body is rigid and hard, source of my life, source of my restlessness. He releases me and stands there, the morning surrounding him, and I turn, open the back of my car, take one of the suitcases, and hoist it in. He takes the other. "It's your mother you get the restlessness from," he says, and I wonder for the thousandth time in my growing up if he can read my mind. "I mean even if it's something learned or something you were born with." It seems as much a statement of fact as an admonishment. And then he is being pulled back across the void that separates us. He is being taken back.

And now I am in Middleridge again, climbing an old stepladder Delia borrowed from one of her neighbors, with a brush and the paint bucket to do the corners where the walls and ceilings meet, to do the places where the cabinets meet the walls. The corners are easy, fast—the thing that takes time is moving the ladder. You hold the brush as if it were a big flat pencil, dip the bristles halfway, then run the tip across the rim of the bucket to kill the drips. The brush makes a slapping sound as you work it back and forth, then smooth out the work.

Next to the cabinets it's a little different. You dip the brush the same way, but start out away from the edge of the cabinet, then pull it toward the dark wood, establishing a bead of paint that runs along the fine edge of the cabinetry and only approaches the wood. If you do it right, hold your hand steady, you can save yourself years of time masking, because masking doesn't always work very well.

*He leans over me, his tobacco breath at my ear, in my face, and holds my hand with his hand, his hand cupping around the brush to guide it. His grip isn't loose, but it isn't hard either—like a hunting dog's mouth around a bird. "You just push it along—the bristles act like a thousand tiny wicks, and your business is to guide them. Yeah, like that." He lets go a minute, and I'm sorry that his hand is gone, sorry for the loss of the surety of his grip. But my hand does what it is told; the paint gleams; the sorrow holds. "Watch your brother, he's got the hang of it."*

*"It's just the three of us, isn't it Daddy, like the three musketeers?" Roy says. I don't look at him because I don't want to see the look on his face.*

*"That's right, Son."*

*"You sound glad of it," I say to Roy when Daddy leaves the room. Now I'm looking at him. It's three years since it happened, but when we're working, he never lets go of it.*

*He doesn't say anything but keeps painting. I think of how it is in the mornings—every single morning—how glad I am to see the both of them. How glad I am that they are both still there. Or when we come home from school and he's sitting in the kitchen, smoking a cigarette, having finished his day's work, I can't tell how happy I am that he hasn't gone. I hate the constant feeling of distrust, the constant restless feeling that the earth is not a solid place, that it could move and shift without the slightest notice.*

*If I just had time to think it all out. If I could find some way to reconcile*

*everything, maybe I could understand. Sometimes it feels this close, understand-*
*ing, but then it slips away. Sometimes I wake up in the morning feeling like it's*
*only an arm's reach away.*

Now I'm filling a paint tray with the pale, oyster white paint, and the roller snaps up the walls, around the molding at the entrance to the dining room.

At lunchtime, I leave the roller and brushes in the empty roller pan, put the top lightly on the bucket of paint, and, leaving the door unlocked, walk down to Sylvia's.

The street is cold and gray—on a cross street in the distance I think I see Harry's pickup go past.

There's no answer at first, and I knock again. The wind blows through the holes in my jeans. I didn't wear my coat because I want this to be fast. I haven't eaten since early this morning, but I'm not hungry. I have a sandwich in my car; I have the Winchester under the seat. I didn't know I was going to do this when I got up this morning, but now it seems right.

I knock a third time, and she answers the door as I'm knocking. My fist is still in the air when the door swings back. "I din't expect you," she says, but there is no surprise. "You wanna come in?"

"No, that's okay. I've got to get back to work."

"You got paint in your hair."

"It's one of the hazards of the job."

She doesn't say anything for a moment and neither do I. I don't look at her but past her. I sort of expect her to say something about last night, about coming by my trailer, but she doesn't. A car goes by in the street, and involuntarily I turn to look.

"You nervous?" she says.

"Sylvia, I came over to say that I don't want to see you anymore."

"Just like that."

"Yeah," I say, adrenaline now infusing my hands, making my heart go. "Just like that."

"It don't matter that I still want to see you."

"It matters, but it doesn't change things."

"You sure you don't want to come in? I could get you some lunch. You eaten anything yet?"

"I have to get back to work."

"No, listen. Don't go. We could just talk about this. I have something—no. Just wait a minute." She moves away from the door and goes inside. I should just walk away, but I don't.

When she comes back she has a book in her hand. "Have you ever heard about this? *The Total Woman?*" The look on her face is pathetic, eager. There's a momentary sense I have of seeing her for the first time—I mean really seeing everything about her, age and loneliness and fear, the slowly wrinkling skin of her face, the gray at the roots of her hair. "See, it's this book about how a woman can only be whole when she lives for a man. It says that a woman was made for a man, like you take the biblical interpretation, a woman being made from a man's rib, then she's part of him, and until she recognizes that she's a part of him, and made to serve him, then she's nothing, half a person." She says this all fast, presses it out quickly before I have a chance to evaporate. I almost wish I could. The more she says, the more desperate sounding it gets. "We could try it. You and me."

"Sylvia," I start and regret fills my belly. Regret that I am so blind and foresaw nothing of this. Regret that I can't see the Jack Pleasance she thinks she sees. I want to say something more, but all that comes out is "No." Her eyes are red. In a moment, tears are on her cheeks.

"Fuck you," she says, and suddenly, convulsively, she slams the door. Air whooshes at me. I turn and start up the street, back toward Delia's.

Halfway there, I can hear the crack of the door opening again. "Jack," she shouts, but I don't turn around. The black asphalt of the street is smooth, and where it has cracked, the cracks have been filled in with tar. It keeps the winter out—keeps water from seeping in and freezing and ruining the road. The curbs are white, and the house numbers are painted on them in black on white-painted rectangles. There's a wind now, and it makes me shiver.

"Jack," comes my name again, now a scream. Now there is the sound of her high heels on the pavement behind me, the sound of her breathing hard with running.

"Jack, what can I do? What can we do?"

I shake my head. I have my hands in my pockets and my head down.

"I want to know what the shortcomings are. I want to know what I've done wrong."

"Sylvia, stop," I say. Houses go past in the wind as I turn to her.

White clapboard, black roofs, black windows. "Just please stop. There's nothing to do."

"It's that little redneck bitch, isn't it?"

I turn away from her and start back toward Delia's. *She's no more redneck than I am* are the words that come to my mouth but remain unspoken.

Now she screams, shrill and loud, "It's that little redneck bitch!"

I'm nearly finished with the job by the time Delia gets home in the late afternoon. Adrenaline and anger have speeded things up. Distracted, I paint with the expectation of a door opening, of a fist against the cold wood of the kitchen door. Every time the wind blows it makes the storm door creak and I turn, expecting to see Sylvia's face in the window, but there is nothing but the grass of the back lawn, the shudder of the wind.

Delia comes in the front door as I'm rolling out the last wall, standing on one of the plastic drop cloths, the roller snapping and licking. "My lord," she says, standing at the edge of the kitchen. "You are brilliant. You are magnificent." She says it as if in imitation of someone from television.

I laugh a little. "I didn't think it would go this fast," I say. "But when you estimate, you want to provide for contingencies."

She nods. "Of course." Then, after a moment of looking at my work, she says, "Listen, hon, I'm just gonna run and jump into something more comfortable."

I don't look at her but at the wall I'm painting. I can feel it when she moves away from me.

"I can't believe this is my kitchen," Delia says. "I like to walked into the wrong house." I don't look at her until I've finished with the wall I'm doing—the last wall. She's wearing a housecoat now—underneath she still has on the white blouse she wore to work.

The baseboards are all I have left. I put the roller in the sink and fill it with water, then sit down in the corner with the roller pan, still full of paint, and with one of the brushes start working my way along the molding of the baseboards.

She gives me a check when I'm finished. "Listen, you give me your telephone number, and I'll tell my friends about you. You do good work."

"I don't have a phone," I say.

"You don't? How the hell do you like that? I haven't met anybody since I was a little girl who didn't have a phone."

"You give me your phone number, and I'll call you," I say.

"Sure, sure," she says.

In the car I reach down and touch the rifle case beneath the old towel that covers it. I can feel the hardness of it. I go to her bank, cash the check, put the money in my pocket.

# THE EDGE OF IT

Herbie Kelleher is a fat man with more chin than neck, and gleaming silver braces on his teeth. He works only one or two nights every other week at his diner, sometimes less. Every time I see him he's gotten fatter, but his teeth will be straight.

"How is everything?" Herbie says, leaning over the counter and saying it not like the owner of a highway diner but as though he's the maître d' at a four-star restaurant checking up on his brilliant but unpredictable chef. I'm eating Salisbury steak with mashed potatoes and gravy and overcooked peas. I'm eating them fast because this is the first food I've had since breakfast and I don't really care what it tastes like.

"Fine," I say, but halfway through the short word I catch a glimpse of Sandy coming around the corner in her boots and sunglasses. It's dark, and the lights give the outside lot a glassy, spacey appearance. Suddenly my appetite is gone. "If I can get you anything else," Herbie says, "just holler."

"I'll take the check," I say.

He shrugs and turns away from me as the door is opening and Sandy is coming in. I don't look at her, just feel her in the undulant air. "I saw your car," she says. "I went by your house."

She's next to me now. I turn toward her on the swivel stool, reach out and touch her hip softly, look into her eyes. Her face is more discolored now, even though she wears makeup, but that's the way it is when bruises are healing. "You okay?" I say.

"Yeah. No. I don't know. Chalky went out with Dean and Buck, and I just had to get out even though he told me not to—maybe we could go to your place?" she says softly, secretively, as Herbie slides the check toward me.

"All right," I say.

Outside, after I've paid, she says, "I felt like I was going to explode. He was doing coke all weekend, watching me. I didn't used to be afraid of him. But I don't know, now."

"You going to follow me?"

She nods.

"I'm not gonna go directly to my house. We're gonna park somewhere else, then walk, keep the lights out."

"Okay," she says. Then, as she's going toward her car. "It's just nice it makes him, you know, limp."

Even though it's only been in the lot a few minutes, my car is cold, and I'm shivering by the time I turn on the heater fan.

I drive to a pasture near my trailer, climb out and open the gate, then drive over the rise and cut out the lights. She follows, parks next to me. I slide the rifle out from beneath the seat of the Chevy and lead her back up through the gate in the darkness, holding her hand.

"You too," she says about the gun.

I close the gate behind us.

"Look at the sky," she says, and I do. It's clear, and in the absence of the moon, the stars give the sky a milky glow.

I stand for a moment at the edge of the road, put my arms around her. "How much does he know?" I say.

"Nothing, really. He just suspects, is all. That's why he beat me up, trying to get me to tell him. I wouldn't. You haven't met stubborn until you met me. Guys at work have never liked him, and they were ready to go give him a taste of it himself, but I knew what'd happen, and I told them to lay off."

I smile at her, but I don't know if she can see it in the darkness. "Work?" I say, because I don't know where she works.

"At Garvey's Lot, out on Route 27. I do paperwork, billing, that kind of thing. Preparation for the accountant. And I dispatch the two tow trucks we have."

"Maybe you should have let them go after him."

She shakes her head. "It's not their concern, and they'd have no idea what they were up against."

"Do I?"

"I think maybe you know better than anybody," she says, "but I don't know why I think that."

"Neither do I."

"He knows it's you. He found the book. He stayed up all night tearing up my things, all my books. I went out and bought another one to replace yours. You're the only person I told this stuff to. I told them it was a little car accident where I got these bruises, though they didn't believe me."

"I'm sorry."

"Nothing for you to be sorry for."

"Here," I say, heading for the wall of trees. "There's a path. I want to stay off the road."

"You're more paranoid than I am."

"There's a difference between paranoid and cautious." She can't know it, but I regret saying it—I can hear the corrective tone of my father's voice in my own.

I go along the edge of the woods, holding her hand. There's a path, and when I find it, we plunge into the dark of the woods. I hold up the rifle in front of me for spiderwebs. She asks about it, and I tell her.

"I don't think spiders are out in the winter," she says.

"Neither do I, but did you ever have a web wrap around your face?"

"No."

"Talk about creepy feelings."

The trees are bare, and the milky starlight makes it easy to keep on the path. We end up near the lake, then work our way around toward the trailer. The laurel is thick and rustles as we go past. Everything is dark around the trailer. About twenty yards from the trailer I slip the Winchester out of the case, hand the case to her, and tell her to stay where she is. I walk all the way up to the road, the gun cold in my hands. I stand in the dark and silence and shiver at the aloneness of it. No sign or sound of anyone at all. Now and then a squirrel or bird rustles the dried leaves, but there is nothing else. Satisfied, I come back down, circle around the trailer once, then go back and get her. She's standing in the dark, shivering. Everything is raw, astonishingly real. The moonlight, the reach of the trees overhead, the soft loam of rotted and rotting leaves beneath us, the endless tangle of roots and branches, the warmth of her hand and the texture of her skin. I love her, but I don't love her. It's too early to love.

What I love is that it is now and I am alive.

Inside the trailer, I don't turn on the lights but get out some candles and light them, and with the shades drawn, we sit on the floor together. "What are you going to do?" she says.

"About what?"

"I don't know exactly. Anything, everything."

I look at her in the unsteady light and wonder if she's trying to get me to take control, and in my mind I go over the loose plan I've been trying to form if I can't convince her to leave him. I even picture it the way I've tried to picture it before—breaking into her house, smashing him up, and making it so she has no choice but to come. But I can't make any sense of the expression on her face. It's just too far out of my ken. Finally I don't say it. I say: "What about you?"

"I don't know either. I don't know if I'm going to go back. But I don't know where I'd go."

"You could come here."

"And this is the first place they'd look."

They.

We sit in silence—the only sound is our breathing, the now and then breath-pop of the candleflame when the air moves. Outside there is nothing but silence. The candle light flickers.

"I read the book," she says. "I'm not sure I understood it, but that character Dewey Dell, the one who's pregnant?"

I nod.

"I liked her. But I'm not sure I understand a lot of it. The dead woman talking. I mean I had a feeling like I did. Understand."

"You probably did."

"My father used to talk to the boy he shot. He tried a million times to apologize."

One of the candles is between us, and I slide it across the floor and move closer to her. I put my mouth on her mouth, and it surprises me the way it did the last time.

The warm air of the living room scrapes like laughter, turning my head out, turning, saying, *Come into this room. Come into this room and see.* And so I am rising out of the black pull of the darkness, myself or some earlier, forgotten version of myself. Rising all the way back to 1964 and a room, a morning, I have forgotten exists. These places are so easy to get to when you remember how. Down the hall, through the door. *Come into this room.* The door opens easily into bright light—*the kitchen*—the same kitchen in which my father sat patiently, smoking and waiting when I left him. But this is before. Years and years before.

At the table, my mother sits in light so bright it peels the scales from your eyes. She's five feet seven inches, twenty-seven years old, and weighs ninety pounds. Her skin is the color of the light, the color of the cream in the glass next to her plate. *Hello, Mother.* There is on the plate a single scoop of tuna fish, pink and pale as baby flesh. She stares at it, the bones in her face high and hard, her eyes slightly out of focus, her head on her neck as unwieldy as a sunflower.

A door has opened. He has a gun in his hand. The teeth are laughing, and they are Chalky. The food disappears. The room disappears. There is nothing but my mother, surrounded by bright light, her face getting narrower and narrower, no longer able to fight it, then just dissolving. The warm air is rushing, sucking, hard as laughter. Then there is white light again, and my father and I are walking across the yard. We are walking across the yard. My father's legs are huge next to me, and he has my hand in one of his huge, coarse hands. The brightness is the sun. The green lawn crackles beneath us. Now we are walking across the Croutys' yard, and there are gleaming holes covered with glass that we avoid as we walk. Inside them you can see sky. His voice is high up and far away. "Come on, Son," he says, because I am dragging. We are on the way to Mrs. Krakus's house. The hill goes down. Mrs. Krakus's house is in the distance, not far but somehow hung off and tilted, swimming on a soft lawn. The distance patched out by brightness, by peeling paint, the killing, luminous stone walk up through the loose grass. "Come on," my father's voice barks again. Roy materializes on the wooden porch. The wood is silvery and shines hard, and it's all too much to take in.

The wood, the house, the sound of rasping breath, and Mrs. Krakus's morphine dreams that howl up from inside the dreaming house. Yes, yes. Come on, Son. His arm yanking mine so that now the shoulder is sore. *Sorry about your wife, Addie,* Mrs. Krakus said, but it's in the past now. *Sorry about your mother, boy.*

Sorry is the thing that has my father here. Sorry is the thing that made him keep Mother alive when she wanted to die. Sorry is the thing that makes him do what he does. Something hard glides up, and it is a door. Opening, opening. The room is bathed in orange light, and the air smells like piss. You know the smell, even ladies have it. Mrs. Krakus, who used to make cookies and stand on her porch with a rasping broom, is now in her bed and the air stinks around her because she is rotting to death. Roy's face is white and in my mind I can see him across our bedroom, sitting up in bed, some other night not this one: It's not like Mom, his voice says but his mouth doesn't move. She's dying a different kind of death. But death is everywhere now. You can smell it in the room. You can smell it in our house. My father's secret winter partner. Sometimes you walk through a room and the cold of it hits you and you turn. Death. It whispers at you soft as snow. And now we are next to the bed and my father lets go of my hand and with his hands he says, "Hello, Martha," in the soft voice he uses with everyone but me and Roy. "Hello, Addie," she says, but her voice comes hard, like her teeth and gums are stuck together by gummy strands of elastic. "Are we ready?" he says, and she struggles with "Yes, but I'm sorry to say I had a little accident." She struggles for dignity as he helps her out of bed. "That's nothing to worry about," he says, soft. While he is gone with her to the bathroom, we—Roy and me—do our part of the job. We strip the stained, shitty, and yellowed sheets from the bed. The water runs in the bath. Cold air comes through the room. We close our eyes and hold our breath, and with a bucket and sponge Roy cleans the plastic mattress cover, and then we put new sheets on, hurrying, wanting to have it done fast so our father doesn't have to stand holding Mrs. Krakus forever. Then he is in the room and the yellow light is paler, and he puts her down on the bed—she's smaller than before, clean, small as a bird, and he puts her down onto the clean sheets and she starts to sink. Her face is gone, and she just sinks down through the bed. It swallows her and gives off a grinding sound as she goes. It grinds a long time.

Sandy awakens with the grinding, and I am close to her, behind her, my arms around her, still inside of her.

"Oh, shit," Sandy says. Neither of us expected to fall asleep. It's dawn. "Shit, he's going to be home. He's going to kill me."

I listen hard. The candles have burned down, and there is wax on the floor. I get up and go to the window. It's a garbage truck, rattling up the gravel road. "Stay here, then."

"Jack." She's up. The room shivers. Now I can see the bruises on her ribs, on her legs, that I couldn't see before. She sees me looking and gives me a hard look that makes this air between us suddenly very impersonal. She pulls on her underthings, then her jeans. "Do you have hot water?" she says, standing in front of me in her jeans, her hands behind her fastening her bra. "Do you have hot water here? Could I take a shower?"

I shrug. "Yeah, sure."

She stops fastening her bra and pulls it off with one hand. I can't stop myself from looking, then looking away. The bruises on her ribs are olive colored, turning from or to purple.

"Do you have a towel?"

"Yeah, sorry."

"I'll just go straight to work. I probably don't have time to make it home and then to work anyway."

I put my hand on the small of her back and slide around her, the sight and fragrance of her filling my head, and from the laundry basket in the closet where I keep clean laundry, pull out a towel for her. She puts it around her shoulders.

I go into the narrow bathroom with her and show her how to work the shower, then sit on the lid of the closed toilet and watch her take off the rest of her clothes. She looks me in the eyes when she pushes down her jeans—the white panties stick down her leg until she hooks her thumb into the waistband. When they're off, I get up and put my arms around her, and now she is crying. The room fills slowly with steam. The sound of the shower drowns out everything else except the sound of her crying, which is close to my ear. Her arms are around my neck, and she gives a little hop and locks her legs around my hips. I want to breathe her in, to consume her, but it is she who consumes me. I push off my trousers and take her into the shower. The cold of the plastic shower stall shivers against my feet. "If someone comes, we won't be able to hear it," she says. I'm trembling, fitting myself inside her. The steam is hard, pulses in pressured clouds through the tiny space.

"No one will come."

The spray of water is on her shoulders, in her hair—sprays into my mouth. I hold her as tightly as I can.

"God," she says and starts to cry again.

In the corner she sits and tugs her boots on. "I just can't believe this," she says, resigned now. She stands up and stamps on the floor to jar her boot the rest of the way on. "I can't believe it."

"Listen," I say, "if things get bad, just let me know."

"How the *fuck* am I supposed to do that when you don't have a fucking phone?"

"I'll come by."

"That'd be smart. Listen," she says, almost dancing with impatience, "take me to my car."

We go through the woods, toward the lake, then work along the shore. Her hair is still wet and steams vaguely in the chill of the morning. The lake glistens beneath the steam that curls off it in the early sunshine, but I can't pay attention to it: at the center of my chest, the fist of the present takes hold of my insides, clenches.

She says nothing as we walk, only now and again shivers. I want to know why she won't leave him. I want to ask if she still has any kind of loyalty other than fear for him. Maybe fear is enough. But I don't say anything. I walk ahead of her, the rifle in its case in my hand, my coat pocket full of shells.

We slip out of the woods and toward the cars. There is frost on the ragged brown grass, on the windshields. It's still early, and the light is soft, cold. Down the ragged pasture by a barbed wire fence, three cows stand together utterly still, the only sign of life from them the steam of their breath. Farther down, where a stream cuts through the valley, there is another cow laid out on the ground, probably dead.

Sandy unlocks her car and starts it up fast. The engine roars. On the road, I can hear a car rattle by where the blacktop turns to gravel. Now she's out of the car and scraping the windshield. She's so small she can barely reach to the middle of the massive windshield.

I open my car and slide the gun under the seat, then get in and start it up. I don't have a scraper so I turn up the defroster hard, turn on the wipers. The blowing air is cold, and I have to keep my foot on the accelerator to keep the engine going. In a moment, she climbs into her car and puts it into gear, then stops, gets out again and shouts at me, "Come on," because I have to open the gate for her.

I put the Chevy in gear and with the window open because I still can't see out the windshield, turn around and push the reluctant car up over the rise. I stop near the gate and open it. She has her car turned around, and she tears through the opened gate, back wheels spinning on the frozen turf, and roars off. My car chugs and stalls. I get back in, restart it, then pull it through the gate.

On the road I'm thinking about following her to her job, but instead I drive into Middleridge, to the 7-Eleven for coffee.

"Hey, Stoney" are the words that hit me in the 7-Eleven, as I'm stirring cream from one of those little plastic, paper-topped cups into my coffee. Dean's voice, some drunken night. *Stoney, man.* Everybody's Stoney. I turn, edgy enough even before the coffee. The dripping Bunn-o-matic coffeemakers go past. Racks of donuts and candy and tall cylinders of cups and cup lids. It all swims in the imprecise water of my vision until I focus on Dean, standing behind the coffee counter at the other end. Dean.

"What's the story, man?" I say to him. I don't even think about it before I say anything, and then I watch him, try to gauge things. "What happened to the guy? At the fillin' station?"

He shrugs, gives his sheepish smile. "He pulled through, but I don't know if that's so great." Hands in pockets. Even teeth gleaming. His eyes are bloodshot, though, and he looks wired. "You workin'?" he says.

"A little. When I can find something. What about you?"

"In a manner of speaking," he says. It's not his phrase, it's Buck's. He says it exactly the way Buck would say it: curling his lips together and saying the *n*s in "manner" out of the side of his mouth.

"Harry?"

"I kicked his ass," he says, the grin spreading. His voice has that low, hesitant stability that coke gives you even though what's happening inside is anything but hesitant or stable. "He tried to fire me, but I let the fucker have it."

"That was good. That was smart. What exactly was the point of that?"

"He deserved it, man." I rip off a triangular piece of coffee lid and press the lid down over the rim of the cup. "Superior motherfucker. Speakin' of asses gettin' kicked, Jack, Sandy—"

"Listen, pal, this is a family establishment, and I'd appreciate it if you'd keep the profanity to yourself." We both look toward the counter at the same time. The guy at the counter is by the big Plexiglas cube they keep the donuts in, and he's heard what Dean said. He's burly, sleepy eyed, wears a cigarette at one corner of his mouth like a growth.

Dean looks at him in disbelief, laughs. He thinks the guy is joking. "This is a fucking 7-Eleven, man, not a church."

"I'll have to ask you to leave, please," the counterman says sharply, the words enunciated in the almost prissy fashion bar bouncers sometimes use when they're about to throw you out.

It's the fragility of the coke state that makes him do it—or that's what I tell myself when Dean starts toward the counter, lifts his jacket, and pops the gun out of his belt. I close my eyes for a moment in disbelief, then look at the counterman. His expression hasn't changed. The gun's a .357—I only see it for a second, and then it is hidden by the donut case on the counter. His face is all anger now, something I've never seen in him before.

"Keep your hands where I can see them, motherfucker," he says. "I want you to know that you'd better watch out who you're ordering around, okay?" He gives his shuffling, sheepish-sounding laugh, but still he has the angry look on his face.

The counterman says nothing; his hands are flat on the drawer of the cash register.

"Now, slowly, I want you to open the register drawer."

The counterman doesn't move. He just stares at Dean, then lifts one hand, turns the key in the register, pulls it out, and tosses it across the room. It clatters against one of the glass-doored refrigerators and clicks on the floor. "Not a chance, pussy."

"That was a stupid fucking thing to do," Dean says, but he's a little confused now, the anger gone and frustration in its place because coke muddles your thinking even though you think you're the smartest guy in the world.

"Shoot me, pussy," he says. You can tell he was maybe a football player at VPI or UVA, and he's into this posturing shit—knows it much more intimately than Dean does. I can see Dean in the car that afternoon after Chalky shot the dog, and I'm hoping the counterman doesn't have a gun.

And then, as if suddenly remembering, Dean turns around and looks at me, then glances at the gun in his hand. The white teeth show again. He shoves the gun into his jacket pocket, then turns and hurries out the door. The counterman watches him go through the doors, catches his height in the multicolored scale taped to either side of the door. Five feet, ten inches. Buck's outside waiting in a car for him, and peels out of the parking lot.

I go up to the counter to pay for my coffee. "Just a minute," the guy says as he picks up the telephone.

"Darrell in?" he says. "Yeah. Darrell, listen, some little fuck punk just pulled a gun on me in here. Huh? Naw," he says, "there was another guy here when it happened, and the two of them were talking when the punk pulled the gun. Sure. Okay." He puts his hand over the receiver and shoots me a look. "You know that guy?"

"Only by sight. Used to live near me."

When he hangs up the phone, he slips from behind the counter and goes to where he threw the cash register key. "Sorry about that," he says when he returns. "Listen, sheriff wants you to hang around till he gets here."

"Can't do it, pal." I know the large coffee costs sixty cents, and so I drop seventy-five on the counter and head out the door. Last thing I want to do is see Darrell Planey—I'm going to be seeing him soon enough.

It's dark when I pull the Chevy into the edge of the lot at Garvey's. A couple of ghostly mercury vapor lights have gone on in the back where all the wrecks are lined up in the weeds, and you can see them, the dull shine of hoodless, wheelless rusting hulks, as they ascend the hill off into darkness beyond the brief, cinderblock building that is the office where Sandy works. The Torino is still parked up next to the building—it's only just a little after 5:30—and so I sit and wait. There's a small, square window with bars on it in the front, a venetian blind pulled, but the window still glows with soft, yellow light.

I flip the key back in the ignition switch and turn on the AM radio. In one of those radio signal flukes, right now I can get WNCP, the station I used to listen to in the car in Richmond. The voices sound far-away, but I recognize the voice of the guy who does the news, and it makes me sad—I can see myself in the car in the evening after work, driving up Hanover toward the International Safeway to get something for supper. It makes me sad not because I miss Richmond but because the only way I know to feel about the past is that it is lost, and the loss is permanent.

She comes out about 6:10, and it's a relief to see her—it feels as though I've gone too long without seeing her. She heads for the Torino, but then a car door slams and I turn. On the other side of the lot, a guy about Buck's size, but with shorter hair—or at least I think so in the dark—has just got out of a black Plymouth and heads toward her. She sees him, stops. Still watching, I lean down, inch the Winchester out from where it sits under the passenger seat. My hand's damp and cold, and I'm trying to remember what Buck looked like today when I saw him in the car, what kind of car it was, but the only image that will come is one of glare on a windshield, his jowly, makeshift face.

She stands where she is, and I slide the zipper down the length of the gun. He comes and stands next to her, over her. The gun slips out of the case when I pull at it—the barrel noses into the dirty carpet.

This is somebody I don't know, maybe somebody she works with. She doesn't seem to be scared of him. Though I can't hear them—I crack the window to no avail—they talk for a minute, then he leans down and with one arm quickly circling her shoulder, he kisses her. From the shape of it, from the dark quick of it, I want to believe that it's a kiss on the cheek, but it doesn't resolve in the hazy light. The idea goes through my head—fast, loose—that her relationship with me, if you could even call it a relationship, is nothing more than a gambit, a gambit she has working on someone else too.

He leaves her at her car and walks toward the cinderblock office. The sound of the Torino starting reaches me through the open window, and I snug it closed. I put the rifle back in the case and wait till she gets out on the road before I start my car and follow her.

She's out in front of me on the flat, narrow, empty highway. Beyond the headlights there is nothing but black. Her red taillights float in the distance, and I think of the inside of her car, the scent of her, and for a minute I get a whiff of her perfume, as real as if she were in the car with me. So real I have to turn around and look to see that the back seats are empty.

I lose her a moment. Suddenly I'm alone on the desolate highway, but then from a dip in the road her car rises up again, then disappears over another hill.

She goes straight home. I sort of expect her to drive around for a while, maybe even wait until he's asleep, but she doesn't. When she turns off on the gravel road I drive on for five minutes or so, then turn around and come back. I don't want to be coming up just as she's getting out of her car.

I go up the gravel road slowly. I've only been this way a few times before, and then only in the daylight. I want to park the car in the same stand of bushes I parked in the last time I was here, but now that it's dark, every stand of bushes looks the same.

I'm surprised at the infinite calm that has invaded my chest, my lungs. When I cut off the lights, then turn the car around and back it into the bushes down the road from her place, it's as though my heart stopped beating a long time ago. For a moment I sit and debate whether or not to keep the car running, or whether just to leave the keys in it, but I have no idea how long this is going to take, and I don't want to draw unnecessary attention to it, or run the wild chance that someone could steal it out from under me. Finally I cut it off but leave the keys on the floor.

The rifle is in my hand, and there is a television going somewhere, the distant sound of canned laughter and an announcer's voice. Then there's Chalky's voice, loud and shrill but muffled. The earth is worn; now and again ground into the frozen dirt there is a car part, a spark plug. Where there is grass it is long, brown. Chalky's voice skates. "You fucking well expect me to . . ." I'm at their house now. There are lights on, but I can't see either of them through the windows. "I don't wanna hear any more fuckin' lies," he says to her. His voice has a hysterical edge to it, and I want to get to her fast, before he breaks. "I don't wanna hear any more bullshit." The Torino clicks in the drive. I work my way around the rusted cars that sit in the yard, then over the dull gravel drive in front of the Torino and around the side of the house. "Where the fuck were you last night? Where? I told you not to go anywhere. The only thing that's going to keep me from beatin' the absolute livin' shit out of you is you tell me the goddamned truth." I go around past the porch to where the porch swing hangs next to the door. It dangles lopsided from one set of chains. "Chalky, I am telling you the truth. You just gotta listen to me." At the back of the house now, in the bare yard, I reach up to try the door. "I'm gonna get my fuckin' belt," he says.

The doorknob won't turn. There is a breeze, and winter brown leaves that stick still to their branches rotor in the moving air, making a constant clicking sound.

Now I can hear feet on the floor inside, coming toward the back door. My absent heart explodes in my chest and now adrenaline burns through everything, sets my arms and legs on fire with the boil of anticipation. "Goddammit," Chalky mutters. The light smashes on, and suddenly everything is brilliantly illuminated from two floodlights directly over my head. I blink against the light. The door comes open. Now he's on the porch and so close I can feel him. He's got his leather jacket pulled on, and weirdly, wears a pair of threadbare pajama bottoms beneath. He swears again and starts toward the end of the porch. I make sure the safety is off and cock the gun. It cracks the air between us, and he turns around. It's a graceful turn—head snapping quickly like a danseur spotting in the middle of a spin, the rest of his body following more slowly, amazed that he's been caught unaware like this.

Chalky looks at me with a surprise that's quickly overcome by wariness. "Well, well, well, what have we here?" he drawls slowly, black eyes chasing back and forth—my gun, the doorway, the dark beyond me. I take a step up onto the porch. The wood creaks beneath me, and in the infinite porousness of the world I can feel his weight on the porch, feel it as he takes a step toward me.

"You better be ready to use that thing, chickenshit," he says, "because I'm gonna grind your fuckin' ass into the dirt." When I give him the step forward, he thinks he can take more, until eventually he'll come up and take the gun from me. I look at him and my hands tighten on the stock of the gun, around the trigger mechanism, and it's nearly all I can do to keep myself from succumbing to the easy thing the hatred wants.

"Don't fucking think about it," I say.

I press the safety on and motion with the gun for him to move inside, and it's then that he lunges toward me. I can see the pattern of it in the air long before he's started, and I swing the gun hard and fast—it's a piece of action too quick for thought, controlled completely by adrenaline—hands tight on the blued steel, the butt of the gun out and sweeping upward. Chalky starts to recoil, grimaces. But he can't get out of the way. Behind me, inside the house, I can just hear Sandy's boots in the hallway. The brilliant light throws hot shadows, and I can see myself, the swinging gun, and Chalky in high relief against the peeling yellow-painted clapboard. I can feel the cold of the air on my bare hands, and I can see him trying to dodge the blow that's coming. The butt of the gun catches him square in the middle of the chest, and now I can hear the crack of impact, can hear the gust of air that comes from his throat, and feel the give of his plexus as he stumbles backward, eyes bugged open, hands out to break his fall. Chalky smacks his head against the side of the house, then his back, bounces and thuds onto his butt. Sandy's in the hallway and says my name in nothing but breath. I flip the gun down and come toward him, point it barrel first at his mouth. Glance into the house: Sandy in the hallway, stopped dead in her tracks, still in the same clothing she wore this morning, but one cheek bright red where he must have hit her. The yellow inside light shambles out against the brighter light. The hall carpet is old and dirty.

"Get up, motherfucker." I press the gun toward him. He sits gasping shallowly, one hand against his ribs.

"I still think you're too chickenshit to use it," he says. The words balloon.

"Oh?" I say, nearly blinded with anger toward him. "I don't think you ought to make any bets." For a moment I get a picture of what it would look like to shoot him—not like the neat purple holes you see in people's foreheads in the movies, but his skull like a busted jack-o-lantern. The thought makes me sick to my stomach, but it's the kind of thing you can't think about. When I ease off, he coughs again, presses his hand to his chest, and gasps.

"Get up." The world around us whistles at its own emptiness.

Sandy's in the doorway now. She looks at him. "Go inside and get your stuff together," I say to her. I'm glad for the distraction of her face.

"Jack," she says and looks at me. I glance at her again but then back at Chalky. Confusion warbles up into my chest, my throat—I've had the vague and probably self-important idea that I'm freeing her from his oppression, but it hits me that I really don't even know that she wants to be freed. And suddenly my voice ordering her sounds like my father, yet another oppression.

"It's time, Sandy," I say, trying to soften it.

Chalky pulls himself up. Grimaces. I can feel her start to turn—I don't look at anything but Chalky's eyes. "You gonna leave with this chickenshit?" he says. His mouth slashes the words, but I'd swear I detect the same thing I heard the night the three of them came to my trailer, something nearly pathetic—as though he's ready to burst into tears at the thought of losing her.

She hesitates, then turns and goes down the hall.

"Get my .45, Sandy, and shoot this motherfucker. You do that, and I'll never touch you again. I'll give you a divorce, whatever you want." His words are slurred, and he wipes his nose on the back of his hand. The serenity that overcame me in the car is gone now, and all I want is for this to be over.

Sandy comes down the stairs with a bag in her hand and comes into the hallway, then disappears again. He sees her and I can see the defeat in his eyes, but it isn't over yet, and I'm starting to think about it—the ramifications of everything.

"Get inside, Chalk," I say.

He raises his eyebrows as if to try to make me believe I'm making a mistake taking him into his own house—but it's a mistake I've already discounted.

I push him through the doorway—he breathes with a wheezing sound.

"So what's with the pajamas, Chalk?" I say.

He starts to turn to look at me, but the ribs stop him and he just groans. "Fuck yourself, Pleasance."

With the barrel of the gun, I nudge him into the living room. Sandy's just coming out of the kitchen and stops at the sight of him. The ancient console color TV is on, and the sound junks the air. On the table between the couch and television are a mirror and a plastic baggie with maybe a quarter ounce of coke in it. Next to the baggie is the hollow casing of a Bic stick pen, crusted with white. I push him toward the front of the room, away from her. "You get my gun, and you shoot him, and I'll never bother you again, I swear to—" he starts but stops when she pulls the .45 out of her bag.

"Sandy." I watch her.

I don't know why I didn't think of this. She holds the gun in both hands, fits her left hand into the grip of it, finger curling around the trigger. *She's left-handed.* The air aches. Her hands look so small against it. Now she looks at him.

"Sandy? We gotta get moving," I say softly. Now she lifts the gun up and aims it at him.

"So this is what it feels like," she says to him.

"Baby, you don't want—"

"Oh, shut up," she says. "You're such a coward," and she abruptly puts the gun back into her bag.

"Get his guns. Get all of them, ammunition too. Make sure not to touch any of them with your hands—use a bag or something."

He watches her. My hands are damp and cold against the Winchester.

She puts her bag on the floor, then goes into the kitchen. Chalky turns around and looks at me. "Want to do some blow?" he says. I should have known from the look of him that for the last twenty-four hours he's been sitting here getting high and watching television and waiting for her. His eyes have that narrow, wired look. I'm glad I came when I did. People get paranoid on coke; people get completely irrational. He looks gaunt, probably hasn't eaten for at least a day. That's why the pajamas.

"That's very generous of you," I say.

When she comes out again, she has a shopping bag. Chalky looks at me. I move the barrel of the gun up from his gut to his chest. She leaves the shopping bag in the corner, then goes off again. He turns and lunges toward the bag. I snap the safety and pull the trigger, and the gunshot smashes the room, slams off the close walls. It stops him cold. She jerks and stumbles. The cloud of smoke is instant and barks your nostrils. I've shot just over his shoulder, and a picture on the wall, glass smashed, dangles for a moment before dropping to the floor. Sandy turns and stares. Chalky looks hard at me.

"I think I've got everything," she says, shaking a little.

"You got any duct tape? Any heavy tape?" I say.

"Yeah," she says and gives a canny smile. Smoke hovers in the room. She disappears into the kitchen for a moment and comes back with a big roll of heavy silver duct tape. "This good?" she says. I love the grin on her face.

"Can you tape him?"

She nods, nervous.

"Chalky," I say, "have a seat," and push him toward the couch. He sits and stares at the gun, at me, then at Sandy, and you can see by the wariness and brevity of her movements that being this close to him is not something she relishes. "Put your hands together," I say, and I let him see that I've got the safety off again. Her hands are tiny compared to his. The tape loops around once, twice, a third time. Despite everything, she does it with an innate gentleness.

I start to tell her to do his feet, but I stop. "Sandy," I say. "I'll do his feet." She stands up and looks at me. "You know how to use this?"

She rolls her eyes.

I hand her the gun and take the tape, but keep an eye on Chalky. First I put a heavy strip around his chest, to hold his arms down. I go around him about five times and he's groaning with pain from where I hit him. To listen to him, to feel his breath on my neck, to be this close to his pain, makes me want to regret, and when I tear off the tape and start for his feet, I'm nearly overcome by it, by sadness. I look at Sandy. She is silent, staring at Chalky, the gun huge in her arms. He's silent too, and staring back at her, and for a moment I get a glimpse of the depth and heft of the thing that exists and existed between them; it makes the floor wobble beneath me. I grab his legs—the pajamas are thin, and his legs are bony—and tape his ankles together.

I start to put tape over his mouth, but I don't. "How many telephones do you have in the house?" I say to Sandy.

"One, that works."

"Take the cord."

She hands me the gun and runs upstairs, then comes back down again with the telephone cord and puts it in her bag. All this time, Chalky is silent, and if it weren't for Sandy and the red slap-bloom on her cheek, if I didn't know what he had done to her, I'd feel sorry for him—in a way I can't stop myself from feeling sorry for him.

"You ready?"

"Yeah," she says. In one hand she takes her overnight bag, and in the other she takes the shopping bag full of guns. There are four of them, a sawed-off shotgun, two revolvers, and the .45. I'm hoping one of them will be the gun they used to shoot the guy in the gas station.

Chalky starts to shout. *"You fucking miserable little whore, you dirty fucking slut."*

Outside, I take the distributor cap and rotor out of the Torino. *"You're fucking married to me. You're mine."* I start to ignore the GTO because it doesn't look like it's run in months, but just to be thorough, I take the distributor cap and rotor from it too.

We go through the bushes, Sandy head-first and plunging. I go more slowly, with my back turned, watching the house. The windows are bare, and the lights inside are bright and yellow. I'm trying to think if there was another way of doing this. If I have been so blinded in my thinking like the rest of them I have failed to see the easy, simple thing. But I don't see it. *"I'm'onna kill your ass. I will hunt you down and burn you fuckin' alive."* Out on the road, I point, and then start running toward the car. The exhilaration is starting to hit me, and I almost can't breathe, my lungs are so full. But it's a weird kind of exhilaration: here one moment but replaced by sorrow the next.

She sees the car, and goes toward it, pulls open the door, and throws her bag inside. I search my pockets for the keys, but I can't find them.

The bushes rustle, and lights of the house burn through the foliage. Suddenly Chalky's silent. I go through my pockets again, try to be methodical. I must have dropped them in the house, at the back porch. Sandy says, "Jack, what's the matter? Come *on*." I pat my pockets again. Turn, glance toward the house. I'm shaking now. I pull open the door. "Sandy," I say, leaning in, but I don't say any more, because the keys are where I left them on the floor of the car.

I hand her the Winchester and jump in, then slam the key in the ignition, my hands still shaking, as ready to laugh as I am to cry. The key goes in. The starter churns. I can see the gravel road in front of us, the bushes beside us, and I keep waiting for him to appear, dive against the car. But now it jumps to life, and I slam it into gear. The sudden burst of the headlights throws the gravel road into high relief. Gravel sprays out behind the car when I pop the clutch and take off. Sandy starts to laugh.

We get to the stop sign, and she says, "Oh shit, I can't believe this." I pull out onto the highway and shift up from first to second. The engine whines. I hit third, then fourth. She says again, and then repeats it, "I just can't fuckin' believe you did this."

"Put the rifle in the case," I say, and she does it. I glance over, and I can see the shake of her hands, the trembling throughout her. This is what adrenaline does: keeps you absolutely focussed when you need it, then in the backwash leaves you wrung out and sparkling everywhere.

When she has the gun in the case, she sits back, and both of us are silent. It amazes us both. You sometimes take a step, and it might as well be over a cliff, as much as you can go back to the way things were before. In a little while she takes hold of my arm, pulls herself across the transmission hump that separates the seats, and holds herself close to my arm. She stays that way until the next time I have to shift gears.

I head toward the interstate—too fast, my eyes jumping: rearview mirror, side windows, looking for headlights, afraid we'll get pulled over for speeding with all this weaponry in the car.

"Are you hungry?" I say. It occurs to me that I haven't eaten anything for hours, and all that has happened has left me wildly hungry.

"Yeah. Really hungry," she says hesitantly. "But we shouldn't stop yet."

"No. Maybe we'll stop in Charlottesville."

We take 27 toward Charlottesville. It rises and falls through the mountains, and we don't talk much. For me everything's high, all of the last few hours smash in my head.

At Charlottesville, we take the 29 Business route and meander through the town a little. My hands are shaking, and I can't make decisions. "What do you want to eat?" I say.

"Anything," she says. "Anything."

I jerk the car off the road at a rustic-looking place, pull the car around back, and park in darkness. When the car is off, we look at each other. The keys are in my hand. The red has gone from her face, and she looks beautiful, flushed with excitement. We are forty-five minutes or an hour away from the cliff, and the world feels patterned around us. The shape of your body determines the angle of descent.

It's a beef house, and we order beer and barbecue sandwiches, the house specialty. The tables and chairs are thick, rough-hewn wood, and the tabletops are coated in thick, transparent epoxy. She sits next to me, and we face the wall, and now and then her hands dart out to touch me.

The meat is braised and so tender it dissolves in your mouth. The sauce gets you half in the tang of your mouth, half in your nostrils. The potatoes are corkscrew french fries with rough homemade ketchup. I feel almost as though I am absorbing the food rather than eating it. She sees the look on my face and nods. Every pore of my body is hungry at this moment, and I say to her, "I wish we could stop here because I'm dying to touch you."

"I know. I keep thinking about that, but I also keep thinking someone will walk through the door—"

It makes me turn around; when I turn back, I say, "Yeah, me too."

From 29, we get on 64 and head east toward Richmond. The wide-open, well-lit superhighway makes me feel more at ease. "Where should we go?" she says.

I've been thinking about it but wanted to let her say it first. I've gone through all the possibilities—taking her to my old place in Richmond or to Gary's house. To her parents' house. Or just to drive and keep going. The final possibility is to take her to my father's, which I know I won't do. "I don't know," I say, "we could go anywhere."

"Paris, then."

"Right," I say. "Paris it is."

"What are you going to do, Jack?" she says.

"I want to get you somewhere safe, then I'm going to go back."

"What for?"

"To finish things."

She sighs, and I look over at her. She looks back, uncertain. I know why this has to be done—I know it like I know other things I can't find ways to explain. It's a rhythmic thing with its own musical logic—it's part of the pattern, and by nature the pattern has to be completed.

"Then you should probably take me to my parents' house. That'd be the safest place. Chalky doesn't know where they live, and he'd think I'd go to hell before I went there." She laughs hoarsely.

"Where is it?"

"Beyond Richmond. They used to live closer to Middleridge, but they moved a couple of years ago. I got the address, but I never been there."

I nod. After a few minutes, she says, "But I don't want to go there just yet. I don't want to go straight there. How long will it take to get to Richmond?"

"Couple of hours."

"Can we get a motel or something there? For tonight?" She looks weary, stares out the window. It feels safe now that we're out on the highway, away from Middleridge, because what we're doing is completely random. We're suspended between what we have done and what we will do. As long as we are driving, things will be safe.

"All right," I say.

It's a little after midnight when we get into Richmond, and I drive her around a little while—show her where I used to live, where I used to work. I need a little time to acclimate myself. My sense of time is completely bent, and there's still an element of unreality to what we've done.

The streets are mostly empty. Now and then someone on a bicycle. Now and then a couple walking home from a club. It hasn't been long since I left, but everything seems to have changed. It seems nearly a different city.

"I never been here before," she says. "I guess there's a lotta history here."

"One time we'll be tourists and see some of the history," I say.

I head toward the outskirts of town. Outside the city, there's a motel by the side of the road with the orange neon VACANCY sign out.

It's next to a McDonalds and a Steak & Egg Kitchen, which is still open. I pull the car up by the office.

I leave Sandy and go inside. The carpeting is soft. My vision sparkles, and parts of it have blacked out. In the darkness it was easy to ignore. The bright fluorescent lights of the lobby make it impossible.

The lobby has the familiar and comfortable cigarettes-and-air-conditioning smell of motels. I ask for a double. The man at the counter is nothing more than a boy—some eighteen-year-old doing his first night shift—and he watches me indolently as I fill out the form he gives me. The blind spots make it harder, but I've learned to work around them. I pay in cash, and the kid gives me a key and directions around the back of the building.

"I registered as Mr. and Mrs. Van Kalkenberg," I say in the car. "He'd never think to look under his own name." She laughs. I pull the car around to the back, park in the shadows thrown by the lights of the Steak & Egg Kitchen.

"You don't think he'd look for us here?" she says. She takes hold of my arm and stops me to say it.

"It's too random. No one would find us unless we wanted to be found." She tugs on my arm, pulls me toward her, reaches up, and kisses me.

We take everything except the Winchester inside. I make a second trip outside for it and come back inside only when I'm convinced there's no one around to see.

She's on the bed and has the TV on. There's a remote control. "I felt kind of alone," she says, "so I turned on the TV." She doesn't look at the television, but at me, at the shadows the television throws against the walls and blinds. "You sometimes think of how vast it is, the world, the country, but most of the time you don't. Most of the time it's your street and your walls. Some of the time you wonder how you got where you are."

"Funny thing about motels is you could almost be anywhere in the country once you're inside the room."

"I like the smell. It makes me think of . . . I don't know. I mean it makes me think of being free." Some things she says she says like an old redneck housewife, too far gone to change anything. But other things come out like a young kid, still full of hope and naïveté about the world.

"Are you tired?" she says.

"Yes," I say.

She comes toward me. Stops. Looks at me. "You're a funny man, Jack Pleasance," she says. Now she comes toward me again.

"Why's that?" I don't remember being called a man by anyone but the children when I was mowing lawns.

She stops, looks at me again. "I wish I knew. A barrel a' contradictions."

Now she comes the rest of the way across the carpet to me and starts to unbutton my shirt. "Things can happen." She looks up into my eyes, and the whiteness of her eyes, the clarity of her skin make me nearly want to cry. I don't know why. Because she is real, solid.

"Things *can* happen," I say, and I feel very old when I say it. Another button comes open. "You know that Hemingway shot himself."

"I know. I read it in the library." Another button comes undone, and now she tugs the shirttail out of my trousers.

I have my hands on her shoulders. She strokes the shirt back from my belly, her fingers now and then working into the waistband of my trousers. In a little while she says, "I don't want you to have the wrong idea about me." Hesitation. "About us. Right now I need you, but I might not always need you." I have finished unfastening her jeans and pushing down the zipper. "I don't know that now. I don't."

"I know. I don't either. But it's not the time to talk about it." I move away from her, to the bed, throw back the bed clothing. The air is cool against my skin, and although I know we are out of reach, I have the overwhelming desire to go to the window and look outside.

"You know I did love him once. I don't remember why anymore except in bits and pieces. He wasn't always like he is now, at least I don't think he was. We used to have fun, but it was kid fun, you know. Sometimes I think you become a whole 'nother person when you hit puberty—" she says peeooberty, pronouncing the *u* long, like my father "—and then when you become an adult, you sort of go back to who you were before and wonder why the hell you did what you did."

I don't know what time it is—the night ranges, and time has lost its crispness—but I am on top of her, inside her, moving. I have been moving for hours. I am not asleep, but neither am I awake. The highway is in front of me. Her face is beneath me. When I close my eyes, I almost have to stop moving, because the urge to sleep is so strong.

*Headlights splash out in front of the car, and Karen reaches across the seat and holds onto me so tightly I can't downshift* Sandy's hands leave my skin raw, her touch is silk and milk *and have simply to depress the clutch and let the momentum of the car carry us as I swing it off the road and into the driveway of the kennel where she works part-time, and which she is taking care of while her bosses are out of town. Dogs bark—it's a wave of sound* doors slam at the Steak & Egg, headlights shift across the windows *that rises with the arrival of the car. She looks at me, then opens the door.*

Sandy brushes the hair back out of my face and holds my face in her hands. Her lips brush my eyelids, my cheeks. I move inside her, a kind of motioned stasis, a kind of temporary lostness I have always wanted from women but which has always been too temporary. *What is it you want to lose? says Jean. Everything. I want it to be all future and no past.*

*Karen gets out of the car. It's my birthday. Is it my birthday? It's summer, and the Hadleysburg night is loud with insects. She wears a red-and-white sundress with thin spaghetti straps that tie at the shoulders. She leads me softly up the gravel walk. Dogs bark off in the distance in the runs behind the house. Shrill yaps and deep baying. She leads me up the walk, unlocks the door, then, when we are inside, locks it again behind us, then chains the door. The house smells like dogs, like flea dip. Her things are in the living room: she is sleeping on the couch.*

Sandy's breath is warm against my face. Her hands are on my back now, stroking downward. The circling motion of her hands pulls these worlds out of me. There is the sound of rain, but there is no rain. There is the relentless highway sweep of headlights that makes the dull light in the room. Sandy breathes, and I move in and out, in and out, while she slips her butt from side to side. The bed turns to water. We are turning to water.

*"Just a minute," Karen says, putting a finger to my lips like she must have seen someone do in the movies, then turns away and goes to the kitchen. When she comes back, she's carrying a cupcake with a single candle in the center of it. "Make a wish," she says, next to me again.* All sex. The world is alive in its own pores. Every movement of air is a woman's hand. *Jean stands next to me at a party at Gary's; I watch Judy Rogers twitch her butt while she dances, and it makes me think Desire Desire. It is all desire.*

*I blow the candle out, take the cupcake from her, and put it on the coffee table. "Did you make a wish?" she says, her hands coming back to me, and I nod, then slowly untie the strap on one shoulder: the fabric falls, the skin swells, is taut with gravity; then the other. The skin of her shoulders gleams in the lamplight. For a moment, the dress holds where it is, then falls away. Her panties are white, and the skin is pale pale white where her bikini top has blocked the sun.*

Sandy pushes at me. Says something in my ear in another language—the language of heat, the language of soft.

*Karen holds me, and we go down. "Happy birthday," she says.*

It is spilling. It isn't my birthday.

# THE DISPOSITION
## OF LOVE

The morning is spectacularly bright, a thing utterly indifferent but seeming full of promise. The air is stiff and cold.

The car sits where we left it, the windshield frosted over. She sits inside and keeps the engine and defrost going while I go into the lobby again and check out.

We pull the car over into the back of the McDonald's parking lot, next to a little corral where a kid in a McDonald's uniform is closing the gate with an empty garbage can in one hand.

Inside, standing at the gleaming chrome counter, I'm so hungry I'm nearly shaking. I get coffee, an Egg McMuffin, and hash browns. There's something about the food—the salt of the processed cheese and meat and egg, the carbohydrates of the chewy English muffin—that corresponds precisely to some ten-million-year-old animal need programmed deep in my soul. It's exactly the right thing to eat at exactly the right time.

She has scrambled eggs and sausage, and eats haltingly—first tearing into it, then stopping, looking around, and tearing into it again.

"How are you?" I say. It's nearly the first thing I've said to her during the stunned morning. My body is raw with sex. It's later than I wanted it to be—nearly 10:30. I keep thinking of the relative peace of this space, the look of people in the normal arc of their lives, and then thinking of Chalky back at his house. I can feel the jerk of the Winchester as I fire it in the living room, the picture smashing, it wanting to fall but the shreds of it holding to the fractured wall. I can still feel the sensation in my hands and arms of Chalky's chest giving way beneath the hurl of the rifle butt, and I chase it from my mind.

"Nervous," she says. The food she eats is on a yellow plastic foam container, and she uses her plastic knife and fork in tandem to cut through the sausage and into the plastic.

"About what?"

"About everything. About seeing my parents. It's like when you've lit a firecracker and wait for it to explode." She sets down her knife and fork, and lifts her hands, presses them together, gulps a breath of air.

I nod. For a moment there is silence. "When was the last time you saw them?"

"About three years ago. It was the last time I talked to them, too, you know." Her laugh is nervous, shuffly. Her hand turns and brings a napkin across her mouth. "I still talk to my brothers, and I get news, you know, but I haven't talked to them, you know, directly." It makes her tremble.

"If you don't want to go there," I say, "I have friends around town here you might be able to stay with."

"No. I have to go. I want to go." After a few moments of silence, she says, "I didn't tell you that. About how things were the last time I saw my parents."

"If you don't want to—"

"No, I do. I just. . . . We didn't part company on the happiest of terms. I don't think they'll turn me away or anything, but I don't know that they'll be overjoyed to see me. Being with you they'll probably think it's the same old thing happening again." She looks at me straight in the eyes, and I want to turn away but I can't. "And maybe it is, but I don't think so. I think it's the end of the cycle."

"God, I hope so."

She gives me an odd look. She can't know I'm talking as much about myself as her.

She goes to the ladies' room, and I sit at the table. The sun is higher now, the light harder and warmer. I finish my coffee. Outside, there's a pay phone, and suddenly I have it in my head to call my father. I don't know why, but I do. People go back and forth with trays of food. A woman goes to the trash can and thrusts her tray through the hinged door of the trash can. The glass panes of the walls gleam with ammonia and vinegar. I stand up and start for the phone. My pocket is full of change, and in a moment, I am outside, the cold biting. The hand piece of the telephone is cold against my head. The coins stumble in. I stamp for warmth.

An operator comes on and asks for more money, which I insert.

The phone rings once, twice. It sounds faraway, *feels* faraway, even though it's only a hundred, a hundred and fifty miles. I wonder what his voice will sound like, but I know when I hear it, I'll regret it. It'll feel like no time has passed, nothing at all has changed between us. Finally there's a click, and a woman's voice says, "Hello."

The confusion makes me turn, look for the car. "Oh, I'm sorry. I was calling—I must have the wrong number." Something starts to register but won't fall into place. "I was looking for Addie Pleasance."

"He's here. Let me get him."

"Who's this?"

"Karen. Who's this?"

The word takes time, silence to sink in. Karen. *Karen.* I should have recognized the voice. Of course. *Karen.* "No," I say, "I have the wrong number" and hastily hang up.

Sandy comes through the door and shivers with the cold. "Who you callin'?" she says.

"Since we're going to your parents', I thought I'd call my dad." I laugh what sounds to me a caddish, cavalier laugh. There has to be a rational, sensible explanation.

"Did you get him?"

I shake my head. "No answer."

The car warms up quickly, and for a long time she is silent except to give me directions. It feels as though we're heading into my past rather than hers. I think about those nights the three of us—Karen Anderson, my father, and me—had dinner together at the Ranchero. Sitting between the two of them, I felt completely unconnected to both of them, tied together with them only by a basic fact of geography. It never occurred to me then that they were tied together by a million things that had nothing to do with me—their ease in that world, their easiness with who they were.

I was always thinking of somewhere else, of shedding the skin that was that life.

She opens the little blue address book and says, "Yep, this is it. This has to be it." Her address book makes my heart bend: she was in a drugstore in Middleridge—or so I imagine—buying Tampax or toilet paper when she went through the school supplies aisle and saw it.

I park the car in front of the house, and we get out slowly. I wait for her and she waits for me, and we walk next to one another up the concrete-and-slate walk. It's a brick house, a tract house from the twenties or thirties—one story and modest. There are shutters on the iron frame crank windows, newer storm windows. A couple of lawn ornaments on the winter dry grass. There's a weathered-looking aluminum storm door with a *D* monogrammed in the center of it, sixties style. The monogram of some long-gone resident. Somewhere a dog barks. She gets close to the door. I'm a little behind her now, alight with anticipation. There's a television going somewhere—maybe two televisions. She pulls back the storm door. It creaks, but in the quiet of this suburban midday it echoes like a shriek. Her knuckles bite at the plain, red-painted wood of the door.

Silence. A muffled voice. TV. The storm door sinks closed. The pneumatic arm on it hisses softly. In a moment, the door swings open, and there's a little old man with a bloated face in the dim of the house. Somewhere deep in the cheekbones and nose of the face is buried a resemblance to Sandy. Despite the bloated face, his frame is skinny, and his trousers hang on him, secured only by the belt. There's shock on both of their faces—his at the apparition that has materialized at his door. Her shock is more complicated: how much he has aged, how much he has departed from the picture she has carried in her mind. I look at the street, gray now under the clouding sky. "Daddy," I hear her say from the middle distance.

"Sandy," he says, his voice coming wet and phlegmy from the middle of his chest. He coughs as I turn back, and the cough clears away his surprise and the choke in his voice, and now his voice booms as well as it is able. "Come in, come in," and with one hand he pushes the storm door open while the other sweeps at us to draw us into the house.

"Who is it, dear?" comes a woman's voice from some other part of the house.

"You're never going to believe it," he says, voice like Christmas.

The first thing that always hits you about houses is how the smell of them is different from your own. The smell of theirs is like polite meals and still air and slowly decaying flesh. The garbage goes out every night on time, but you can't evade decay. I catch the gin on Sandy's father's breath. The hallway is too tight to miss it.

Her mother comes into the narrow hallway from another room and stops in the spill of light from the door frame. She nearly stumbles. Unencumbered by a past with them, I must know more about them than Sandy does. "Hi, Ma," Sandy says tightly. I know she's expecting the worst. I watch her mother's expression of hurt and sadness exchange itself with one of joy and confusion. Then slowly the honesty of those initial expressions is lost beneath a veneer of the now. She's going to give Sandy what Sandy deserves. From the side, awkwardly, as though to make up for it, Sandy's father rushes at her and hugs her. It all strikes me as sad and pathetic.

"Ah wish y'all'd called," Sandy's mother says, now merely polite, her southern accent deeper than Sandy's.

"It's so good to see you, dear." Her father's voice sounds aristocratic, patrician—a kind of effortless politesse.

"This house is just a wreck. Thahngs 'a' been so busy at chu'ch, Ah haven't had tahme to do a thahng."

"Oh, don't worry—," I start but Sandy cuts me off.

"Ma, I've left Chalky. This is my friend Jack. He brought me here."

"Well," she says.

"Jack, this is my mom and dad, Mr. and Mrs. Weaver." Her maiden name surprises me. I've never even thought to ask.

"Pleased to meet you, Son," her father says and puts out a hand for me to shake, "Call me Bud."

"Glad to meet you, Bud." His hand is dry and strong, and he squeezes hard to show that even an old man can have a grip.

Her mother nods.

"Is anybody hungry? How long y'all been drivin'?" Sandy's father says. One television—his, I guess—plays a game show off somewhere to the right. Another, hers, plays a talk show from the other direction.

"We had breakfast in Richmond but not a thing since," I say, hoping that the task of food will make all the eyes separate, get us out of this small hallway.

"Ma, could you point me in the direction of the little girls' room?"

"Oh, honey," her father says, "come this way" and leads her past me, away toward the sound of his television.

Suddenly Sandy's mother and I are alone in the hallway. "You gonna run off with her now?" The apron she wears is as much a part of the uniform of her life as the cautious permanent in her hair.

"I think I just did," I say. I think it and say it at the same time. As soon as it's out, I'm afraid it sounds defensive, angry. Then, softer, not looking at her but at the cheap worn carpet on the floor, "It's not really like that at all."

"Well," she says, and her lips press hard together and her eyes fix me, surprised, I think. Maybe because she has discounted her daughter as irretrievable. It takes her a long time to look me over. I hear the sound of water running in the walls. The sound of Mr. Weaver's TV stops, and the balance of noise against silence is thrown off.

"I'm sorry," I say. "It's been a long night, and I'm a little tired." I get a flash vision of myself this morning at the McDonalds, the sunlight stunning the chrome of the phone, Karen's voice on the line.

"You like to wash up, Son?" she says finally. "There's another wash-room in the back and down the hall. If you like, I'll get you a towel."

"That's more than kind of you," I say, and say it wearily to try to drain any possibility of sarcasm from it. She was a beautiful woman once, like her daughter is a beautiful woman now. And as she points the way, then follows me around the corner and down the hall, something hits me about female beauty, about the temporary and shifting nature of it, how it is so completely unlike male beauty. The women I always liked best weren't the younger ones, but the ones who had lines at the edges of their eyes, streaks of gray in their hair, the ones at the edge of their clock time, at the edge of middle age. There is something painfully beautiful about them—you see a woman in the grocery and maybe she has a child with her—her face makes you turn, bends your heart.

We go past a bedroom where the bed is unmade and there is clothing on the floor, and she pulls the door shut to try to keep it from view, and we go by another one, the one next to the bathroom. The bed is neatly made, and there is a sad-eyed, WASPish-looking portrait of Jesus on the wall. A sculpture on the night table of hands folded together in prayer. A Bible with a cloth bookmark strung through the pages. She opens a closet in the hall—I can hear Sandy and her father talking now—and gets a towel for me. It's pale green and soft with years of use. I look at her when she hands me the towel. For a moment, the two of us are connected by the towel—she hears Sandy and her father too—and then she drops her end. Maybe it's just weariness, the weight of the last twenty-four hours, but when she turns and heads back down the hall away from me, I am hit with a tremendous wave of affection for her. Absolute endurance, absolute bravery. It frightens me, the strength of it, and I can't help the tears that come to my eyes. I go into the bathroom and close the door, and for a minute, tears just stream down my face. I can't help myself, and I have no idea what's going on.

I bury my face in the towel. I wash my face, and I'm still crying. I have to sit down on the edge of the bathtub and wait it out. I can't help but wonder if this is what my parents' relationship would have been like had my mother lived. Like my mother's parents' relationship, calcified by years of contempt. Like the relationships of so many of the older married couples I grew up around—couples who even in public lost their ability to appear friendly toward one another, who no longer bother to hold down the contempt they've grown into. There are no happy endings, it all winds down to despair and dissolution. Happily-ever-after is a nonsense concocted by the old to comfort the gullible and still-hopeful young.

"These tomatoes here, they came out of your mother's garden last summer. Yes ma'am, this was about the best year we've had, garden-wise," Sandy's father says to try to press the silence out of the kitchen. They're stewed tomatoes, canned, with saltines broken on top and soggy. Her television, which sits on the counter near the sink, is off now, and the silence is cold as death. The clock in the top of the stove has an electric hum, and it's easy to see why they keep the televisions going.

"They're very good," I say and wipe my mouth.

"I don't know why he always says it's my garden when he's the one who does all the planting and weeding. Everything." She says it to me, to Sandy, to the walls, to anyone but him.

"Sandy tells me you know a little about hardware," he says. The kitchen table is one that looks like it came out of the Sears catalog. Particleboard and formica. The chair I'm sitting in has started to come apart at the joints and wobbles.

"I know a little. My father's a fix-it man, and I grew up working with him."

Sandy's father nods. "My boys used to work with me in the old days.

It's good for a kid to work. Me, I've been working as long as I can remember. Teaches you, gets you out in the world. Nobody could ever call our kids spoiled."

"Except you don't work now." There is no veil on her derision.

"Well I'm *retired*," he shoots back.

Sandy hasn't eaten. She sits across from me at the oblong table. I look at her and then out the kitchen window behind her at the gray December afternoon, and it occurs to me that Christmas is just three weeks away. It's an amazing discovery. It was winter when I left Richmond, and now it's winter again. I don't know where the time has gone. In June I will be twenty-seven.

"Ma," Sandy says, "as you can maybe guess, Chalky and I didn't part on the best of terms, and I was hoping—I mean if it's not any trouble or anything, if I wouldn't be putting you out—maybe I could stay here for a couple of days." She glances at me. "Jack's going back today, but if—" and she just trails off.

"That'd be wonderful," Mr. Weaver says.

Mrs. Weaver fires him a glance—she, after all, is the one who has been asked the question—and then looks at Sandy. "I don't see why not," she says.

# INTO THE NOW

Sandy stands next to the car with her hands in the back pockets of her jeans and her feet cocked to the sides. Right now she reminds me of Karen Anderson, but I don't know why. "Call me," she says. My skin feels too tight. She gave me the number to her parents' house a few minutes ago, and it is in my wallet, tucked in between my driver's license and an old school photograph of my brother.

"I will," I say and then reach out to touch her arm. She's not wearing a jacket, and I can feel how cold she is. I have a picture of her in my head last night in the motel room, and the picture feels precarious, where I am standing now. I could lose it the way I have lost too many things in my life. The car is full of weaponry, and it's beginning to get dark.

She starts to lean toward me, and I say, "Don't kiss me."

She stops, shivers, pulls her hands from her pockets, and folds them beneath her breasts. "Am I going to see you again?"

"God, I hope so."

"I don't know, Jack."

"Don't know what?"

"Right this minute I'm full. I've never been full in my life, and you're responsible."

"I don't know what you mean."

"It just means that you might be someone I could love down the line. I've never loved anyone as a full person. I don't know. Maybe I can be somebody you could love too."

I watch the leaves in the small yards blow across the grass and catch in the waist-high, partial chain link fences that separate the yards. I watch the flesh of her arms turn pink and rough with gooseflesh. I look at the turn of her hair in the frigid, lazy wind, and I think I am already in love. It's hard to know. It's something deep in the blackest pit of my mind, and it's hard to know. I can feel the wet in my eyes again, but now I can blame it on the wind. "I'll call you," I say and turn away from her. For the first time in my life it feels like I am walking into a future instead of just continuing on in some endless present. "I want to see you again."

The car door is opening; the keys are in my hand; my body is crouching, lifting itself into the driver's seat, and pulling the door closed. The car starts effortlessly, and she stands next to it, shivering, crying. Now she comes around to the other side of the car and makes me unlock the door. She gets inside, out of the wind. I love the feel of her in the car, the way it fills my head. She grabs my hair, and we are both crying. Her lips mash against mine, and now her mouth is open and everything is warm and liquid. Now she is pulling away from me, the door is opening, and she, still crying, says, "Be careful," slams the door, and runs for the front door of the house.

I depress the clutch and push the Chevy into first gear. The house recedes; second gear and the first corner is turned. Third gear and the house is out of sight.

I don't have to, but I drive through Richmond. I head toward the Fan and drive over to Hanover Street, to my old house, and park up the street. It's evening now, and there are leaves blowing in the mercury-lit street. The room that used to be my living room is brightly lit, and with the car running, I watch it for a while. I don't know why.

A million things dream in my head—I can almost see myself coming home late from work last year, the useless briefcase in my hand nothing more than an oversized lunch box. *Jean is already home and in the bath when I get home. She invites me to join her as I'm hanging up my overcoat and untying my tie in the hall, but instead I go to the kitchen and look to see what's in the refrigerator.*

*I'm in the bedroom changing clothes when she comes out of the tub, towel around her. "Let's do it," she says jokingly and thrusts her hips toward me.*

*"Aren't you hungry?" I say as I pull on my jeans and fasten the button.*

*"I'm hungry for your bod," she says.*

The shadows cast by the lights and the trees move in the wind, and now and then, despite the cold, there are people on the sidewalks. I remember the outdoor cafes in summer. I remember sitting on the grass at Bird Park in the summertime. I remember fucking Jean the first months I knew her until my body was sore with it—I remember fucking her in every place in every conceivable configuration of our bodies in a wild desperation to get close to her. I knew every crack and crease of her body, every mole and plain and mound, and yet I had no idea—

A woman at the corner stops, touches the man she's with, and points at my car. Overcoats, scarves. After a moment of hesitation, she starts toward me. The sight of her stuns me out of my dazed dreaming, and I flick on the lights, smack the car into reverse, and when I'm clear of the car in front of me, smack the shift up to first and hurry out into the street. She stands there, and I make the mistake of looking directly at her as she mouths my name. "Jack," she says, utterly inaudible to me, her mouth drawn wide to accommodate the word.

It's after midnight when I get into Middleridge, and the first place I go is the sheriff's station, a cinderblock pillbox with a four-story aerial jutting up from the center of it. I check the parking lot—Darrell's cruiser isn't in the lot, and then I grab the bag of Chalky's guns and, leaving the Chevy running, hurry inside.

The only person in the station is a woman deputy—a skinny woman I've never seen before. She has a very narrow waist and round hips and wears her gun belt turned so that her pistol is at her back. It's a funny way to wear a gunbelt, and I look at her for a moment when she stands up. If she wore it at her side, the barrel'd stick straight out with the curve of her hip.

She's behind a tall counter at a Motorola FM two-way radio—I can see it when I get up close. She barely pays attention to me. I heft the bag of guns up onto the counter—all she can see when she looks at me head-on is the handle of the sawed off. It makes her jump and puts a momentary look of stunned hesitation on her face. "These belong to Chalky Van Kalkenberg and may be the weapons used in the gas station holdups. Tell Darrell—" I say as I'm turning and hurrying out the door, "—Darrell will know." The woman shouts at me to stop, but I'm through the glass door and outside the cinderblock building.

I'm pulling out of the lot and onto the highway when she comes through the glass doors and shouts.

I park in the field where Sandy and I parked last night—no, the night before. I take the Winchester and make my way through the woods toward the trailer. It's cold and overcast, and it feels like snow—there's that pale night light you get with snow, and the woods have a glow to them. The Winchester is warm from being in the car so long, and the warmth of it radiates through my gloveless hands. The woods are utterly silent, and even the slightest sound I make carries in the darkness. There's a cushion of mist over the lake. I come up through the laurel, the green leaves hard as plastic in the cold. It feels like it gets colder by the minute as I go, though it's probably just having been in the car so long.

I don't know what I expect when I get to the trailer—that it will have been burned down or vandalized—but it seems the same as I left it, which is, in its way, more alarming than if it were destroyed. Slowly, I make my way around it and check the windows. None of them have been broken, none forced open. I check the door and then go up the path through the woods and check the shed. I don't open the door, just peer inside. Nothing seems different. The silence and sameness push up my apprehension—every hair is raised on my neck, every pore breathes expectantly.

Now back down to the trailer, crawl underneath, and for a while just lay in the loam and listen. The loam is damp but not frozen—it doesn't seem capable of freezing. I wait ten minutes, half an hour, listen for some sign that someone might be inside.

There is nothing but absolute silence, so I go back out, down by the lake, and back to the car.

Headlights out, adrenaline driving my nerves at high alert, I pull it around to the front where I usually park—I want Chalky to know I'm here—then leave it and hurry back to the trailer, slip around the back and underneath again. And again I wait and listen for a long time before I move beneath the hole in the closet floor and push on the trapdoor. Then push again. It should just lift open, but it won't give, and the resistance makes all the wires light. Hands trembling, I wait, try to think how I left it, if there is something that could have fallen on it to make it stay closed. Nothing. My memory is blank.

I wait, take a deep breath, and shove hard—now it comes easily, like the resistance was never there at all. After the jump, I lift it slowly, and once it's up, I don't move, wait for the barrel of a gun to come poking through. I wait. There is nothing. Slowly, I put my head through. The closet door is closed. I lean the Winchester against one corner of the opening, then pull myself up through the hole, then grab the gun and ease open the closet door.

The house feels damp, smells like burning candles and vaguely, perfume. The gun cocked, I start in the bedroom behind the kitchen and work my way through the trailer, looking for evidence that someone is here, that someone has been here. It's entirely as Sandy and I left it. By the candles and blankets, there's an earring—a single pearl on a gold stem—on the floor. It must be Sandy's. I'm such an idiot I never notice things like earrings.

The blower for the heater comes on and startles me, but I'm glad the heat is going and can feel immediately the increase in warmth.

I could melt almost, melt into hours and hours of dead sleep. I lean against the wall where I leaned before and wait, the Winchester leaned against the wall next to me.

There is the sound of tires on gravel outside in the distance. I put down the book I was drowsing over and get up, go to the window in the front of the trailer. The headlights needle up over the hill, then dip down-ward, and I lift the rifle, unconsciously flick the safety back and forth. Softly the headlights float along the road; gravel spits, dangerous as a rattlesnake. But the car passes, slides around the curve and up the rise; the red of the taillights resonates in the darkness.

The sound of tires on gravel comes again and knocks me out of a drowse. I leap up, stumble, press my face to the window in time to see the headlights stab over the hill and descend. I take the gun, the box of shells, and go for the closet, step down through the opening, draw the door closed behind me, and heel-walk my way down until I can drop down and pull the gun down next to me. Flat on my back, the crack-shot of tires on gravel stopping next to my car, I pull the trapdoor closed, roll over and belly-crawl up next to the place the porch stairs descend.

The lights go out, and the slamming of a car door echoes back across the lake. I wait. In the pale light of the overcast night I can see one form working down through the trees. It's a woman, unsteady in high heels. Sylvia. She wears a puffy white fur jacket that'd make her a spectacular target. She comes up the steps, and I can see her ankles and her shoes. She raps hard on the door. When there's no answer, she raps again. "Open the door you dirty sonofabitch. I know goddamned well you're in there, and I'm not going anywhere until you have the decency to talk to me."

I pull the Winchester close, shift a little so I can see the hill.

"I'm not leaving. I don't care if I freeze to death. I've been here every goddamned night, and I fucking well know you're here."

How can I be such an idiot about people? How could I have not seen this coming?

"All right, then," she says, sits down on the porch. I can see the backs of her legs, her wobbly heels. She lights a cigarette and drops the match in the leaves. "All right then I'm just gonna sit here until you decide to talk to me or I freeze to death, whichever comes first." She stamps, and when she flicks ashes the air is so suddenly silent I can hear them fall into the loam and leaves. "You just don't know," she rambles, "you just don't know the kind of hurt you've put me through. Nobody's ever made me feel like such a woman. Nobody. I can't let that go. I can't."

Slowly, saddened and embarrassed by her rambling, I slip backward toward the trapdoor and climb up into the closet.

I come to the front door and open it slightly. She whirls around and tries to stand but falls on the unsteady footing of her spike heels. I lift the Winchester and point it directly at her. "Get out of here and get out now," I say and cock the rifle for effect.

She looks at me blankly. There is nothing, nothing at all behind her gaze. When I first saw her on her lawn that hot afternoon, I saw nothing but leg and cleavage. I didn't look beyond it. I'm not sure if I knew then *how* to look beyond it. Now all I see is emptiness. "You have no idea what you're getting yourself into."

Indignant, she says, "I certainly did *not* know what I was getting myself into."

"Sylvia, go, now." But she just stands there, stubborn and foolish.

"I'm not going anywhere."

"Just what is it you hope to accomplish?" I ask her, but there's the sound of tires on gravel and a pair of headlights needle up over the hill and down again, and this time I know the deadline has passed. I reach out and grab her arm and yank her through the door, then slam it, turn off the lights, and drag her to the back bedroom.

Slowly, listening to the sound of the car as it grinds to a halt by Sylvia's car, I say, "Lie down on the floor, behind these boxes, and don't get up for any reason at all. There is probably going to be some shooting, so don't do anything at all. Don't say a word."

"Jack," she says and starts to turn, and I have to throw her down on the floor.

"*Stay there*," I spit through my teeth, then turn, shut the door, and go into the closet and drop down again. I nick my head against the edge of the opening, but get the closet door and the trapdoor closed before the car doors slam and the voices start. Chalky and Buck. A third door.

I crawl around to where I was before and watch. It's just beginning to snow, and the forest is lighter than ever. One of them limps, and that's Chalky. The other one's Buck, and they come down through the woods in single file. I can hear their feet in the leaves. When they get close enough, I can see the one in the rear is Dean.

"We oughta burn the motherfucker out," Buck says. They're close enough now that I can't see their faces, only their legs, torsos. They stand a few feet apart from one another, and Chalky moves around.

"I'm gonna shoot the motherfucker myself," Chalky says. "Remember that."

"Listen, man, the fucker shoots at me, I'm gonna shoot him, man."

Then Chalky shouts, "Come on out, Jackie boy." The sound carries. "Sandy, you come out now, and we won't shoot you. I know things have been fucked up, but I don't want to shoot you."

Still there is silence. For the moment, Sylvia stays silent. "Maybe they ain't here?" Dean says, his voice soft and hesitant. I can tell he doesn't really want to be here—but then he *is* here.

"This is stupid, standin' here like a bunch of fuckin' whores," Buck says and fires through the thin walls of the trailer. Whatever kind of weapon he has is automatic, or semiautomatic. I can see the muzzleflash of the gun against the woods—the light bounces off the trailer and fires into the trees like light from a flashbulb. Above me, I can feel the splintering, the smash of the slugs in the walls. Now I can hear Sylvia whimpering. It makes the floor shiver above me.

"Let's go inside and take the motherfucker," Buck says.

I crawl close to the edge of the trailer in the dirt—right up beneath the wooden porch. I try to think of what to do. The forest is glassy with the slowly falling snow, and the ground is cold beneath me. I think of Sandy in the motel room, I think of the warmth of it, and I can't believe I am where I am and that last night is in the past.

Chalky takes a step up on the porch, silent. Another step, and he tries the door. It's unlocked. Now Buck moves over, sniffles, takes a step onto the porch. "You think he's trying to trap us?" Chalky says. Even their whispered voices have the brittle sound of coke to them.

"Maybe he's not even in there," Dean says, nervous. He's behind them, on the path. "His car's there, but that don't mean he's here." I can see Dean's legs now—he shifts back and forth on his feet, from side to side. I hadn't thought Dean would be part of this.

Now I can hear Buck's weight on the floorboards above me, and I listen as he goes into the trailer. Chalky is behind him. "What a fuckin' pit," one of them whispers at the door.

Now Dean comes up to the porch, steps up on it. "I don't think he's here," he says, shifting his gun from hand to hand, then taking another step up. In a moment, there's a flurry of voices from inside and then a squeal from Sylvia. I wait, listen. Now Dean goes inside. Sylvia screams short and hard, and the voices, too muffled to make out, come again, fast. Now I can hear them dragging her through the trailer, room to room, probably using her as a shield.

I know I have to make a decision, but I'm stuck.

In a moment, they've gone through the whole trailer and not found me, and now I can hear them coming toward the door. "He was here," I can hear Sylvia say, her voice loud enough and high enough pitched so that it comes through the floor clearly. "He was here, and he put me in that room, and then he disappeared."

They kick the front door open, and I can hear her high-heeled shoes on the wooden porch first. They push her out into the darkness, down off the porch and on the path, all three of them behind her. I slide over, away from the porch, the gun stretched out in front of me to get a better view of them. They're a few feet up the path when Chalky calls, "I know you're here, Jack, and I'm gonna start shooting pieces off the bitch if you don't show yourself."

Dean says, "Man, she knows who I am. This is one of the ladies whose lawns we mowed."

"Don't you worry about it," Buck says.

They move up the path. Dean starts to drift away from the two of them. Quietly, I cock the Winchester. The sound of it carries; the air is too clear. Buck turns. "You hear that?" he says.

"I heard it, I heard it."

"Where'd it come from?"

"I got no idea where it come from." Their voices are hard whispers, but they carry as easily in the cold air as the snowlight. Buck has his gun up, and he's next to Sylvia, slightly behind her. Dean's near him, a few steps to the outside of him, and Chalky's on the other side. I move over a little more, try to get a clear shot at Buck. The angle is bad. If the gun pulls to the right, I'd miss entirely. If it pulls to the left, I could catch Sylvia.

"I'm tired of waiting," Buck says. "Where should I shoot her?" He laughs, and I can see him poke her with the gun. She's crying, stumbling, and then there's a window and I have Buck's chest and neck cradled in the sights of the rifle and I squeeze the trigger. Like so many other things, it's a nearly thoughtless act, something that happens smoothly, cause and effect. The sound of the gun smashes off the ground and up against the floor of the trailer, and it takes a moment but Buck just drops. There's the sound of Sylvia sobbing, then a weird croaking sound that must be Buck, and in a moment Dean and Chalky are on the ground.

"Where'd it come from?" one of them whispers.

"The trailer," the other one says.

Sylvia stands like a drunk, sobbing, wobbling, and starts to move away from his crumpled form but stumbles in her high heels. I cock the gun again and aim toward Chalky, but the porch keeps me from getting a clear shot, and I push myself more to the right, to get a better shot. The scent of powder is heavy in my head, and Chalky reaches up and fires at Sylvia. He has to raise himself up to shoot, and I squeeze the trigger again as he does. Sylvia dives forward and screams, and Chalky grunts and rolls. I don't know if I hit him, but now they know where I am and they start shooting—both of them. The wood of the porch splinters. I belly-crawl to the end of the trailer, dragging the gun and squinting against the impact of the slugs against the trailer and porch. I can hear some of them whistle under the porch and tear through the leaves behind the trailer as they fly toward the lake.

Near the trailer hitch, I crawl out from under the trailer, lift the rifle. Sylvia is crying, and Chalky is standing—so I must have missed. Dean stays on the ground. I'm in the trees—press up against a narrow white oak that won't cover all of me, press the rifle to the tree to steady it. I get Chalky in the sights again and squeeze the trigger—but there's nothing. In the flurry of everything, I've forgotten to cock it. Hurriedly, I cock the rifle, and now Chalky is firing. Slugs slap into the boughs of the trees, and you can feel the impact of them when they tear into the meat of the wood, send splinters and bark flying.

It's like being kicked hard in the side—someone standing in front of you and kicking as hard as he can, knocking you backward and pushing the air out of you, but there's no one there—and it's only a moment later that the burning comes, the brass taste in your mouth and the instant thought that you are going to have to vomit. Now the burning traveling through your whole gut and the wet sensation and everything focussing toward the burning, focussing away from your hands. You have to force the focus back again. Cock the gun. Aim. Fire. You can feel the tree shudder in front of you as the other slugs hit it. Cock, aim, fire. There are now lights in the distance, the watery sound of a car, but it could be just the echo of the gunfire, an echo of the fire that crawls up the side of your body and spreads out into your ribs as if they are veins and the blood in them burns. Cock the gun, aim, fire.

The shape of the man is a target on a wire, and he won't fall because he's suspended by that wire, and in a moment, when you've finished the ammunition, you can press a button and he will skate through the air toward you, holes in his silhouette, except the dark makes it hard to see.

Headlights nose out in the darkness. Two solid searchlights paired hard together and inevitable. Cock, aim, fire, but someone has tripped the wire and the target has fallen. How much time has passed?

Now with the beautiful cutting of the headlights in the darkness there are more lights. The moons of Saturn have fallen. White moons. Eternally blue moons. The bright wash of a searchlight. The blue and red moonbeams above them all. The moonlight has fled. The leaves carry lights beneath them, and they are calling out. Cold. Come down to the cold. And there are bright fibers of light in the bare winter branches of the trees. More lights bouncing in the darkness. The rasping cereal morning croak of a radio, and you have to dream of sitting at a breakfast table somewhere in the past, my father ignoring me, talking to my brother, the cereal saying from the lights of the bowl, *One Adam Twelve. There's an ambulance on the way. We're going to need more than one.*

# MRS. WILSON

My father's pickup is entirely too huge, but the blood is smashing in my head, in my ears, "Go. Go get the truck," he says, and the keys smash out in the air. When I reach out for them they aren't there but come spinning through my hands, and the sharp, silvery jingle of them comes slamming into my cheek. My cheek burns.

"Go, boy, *go.*"

Mrs. Wilson is in her bed coughing blood and chunks of phlegm like bloody birdshit, "*Go* goddamn it," and we have only walked here like we do every afternoon, to see to it that she has a decent supper. "Get the truck."

The edge of the road is gravelly and disintegrating, and it slides beneath my feet, too long until it finally dissolves into weeds, dandelions, crabgrass.

I climb into the truck and try to adjust the seat but it won't work. I fumble and can't find the lever. *Jack*, his voice booms across the empty neighborhood afternoon. *Jack.* The key gets into the ignition, and it's good that I've watched him, good that I've wanted to learn how to drive for so long that I've memorized the float of the shift in neutral, the foot on the accelerator, the foot on the clutch. *Jack.* And the truck roars, and you can smell the rich of the exhaust. I put it into gear. The hood is vast, and I can barely see over it. The truck moves out of the drive convulsively, the kick of the clutch making it leap and stall. Gasoline strong and hard in the air. *Goddamn it, Jack* comes the howl of his voice as it echoes up the street. I stomp the accelerator, and the hammer of his want hangs over my head. The pickup lurches up the street, and I go past the Wilsons' gravel driveway, try to back the truck up the drive, but it chunks to a stall half in the street and half in the drive.

"Jack," my father says, the sharp bark edge of his voice hard through the door before I get inside Mrs. Wilson's house. Mr. Cullen from next door comes ambling up the lawn behind me, but the lawn trembles and won't move fast enough beneath me.

"*Jack.* Come on, goddamn it," his voice more than sharp now, something else. Close to hysteria. "Jack," he screams, and I come through the door, the keys to his pickup in my hand. He is over Mrs. Wilson on her bed, his head on her chest. "Goddamn you," he says, but he's not paying attention to me. Mrs. Wilson doesn't cough, doesn't move. "Goddamn you," he says again as he kneels next to the bed and puts his finger in her mouth, then cocks her head back. With one hand on her chin and one over her nose, he puts his own mouth to her bloody mouth and breathes so hard into her you can see her chest rise with the aspiration.

Mr. Cullen is in the doorway now. *It's not my fault.* "Addie."

Daddy blows hard on her mouth and her chest rises again, but she won't breathe on her own. You can see the anger in his face—blood on his mouth, on his hands. Veins on his face.

"She's dead, Addie," Mr. Cullen says, but Daddy doesn't see Mr. Cullen, only me.

"Shut up," he says. "Help me." And he takes hold of her upper body and starts to pull her off the bed, "Take her legs," he says to me.

"No," I say.

"She's gone, Add," Mr. Cullen says and takes a step forward.

"Goddamn you, I said take her legs."

"Daddy, she's dead," and then at my words he drops her and strides toward me. I want to move, but I can't move. He is my father. He reaches out and takes me by the hair and jerks me toward him—I'm eleven, and Roy's not here, but still he's bigger than me. The pain slaps through my head, my face; Mr. Cullen's voice says "Stop, Addie," but the stop just floats in the air because the air flies past me and the bed rises, pillows like yellow clouds, and Mrs. Wilson's bloody face hovers up hard *he wants me to be him* and smashes into my face. I press my eyes closed and hold my mouth tightly shut and do not breathe, but the blood is there. *I will not be like you. I am like her. I will never be like you.* He presses and holds me as if to grind me into her and says, "God*damn* you, you do what I tell you," and he says it again, and finally there is the lurch of Mr. Cullen against him as he takes hold of my father's arms and pulls him away. I am drifting now, my face wet with tears, with blood and vomit. I am drifting, and he will never catch me again.

I stare at him. He struggles with Mr. Cullen for a moment, tries to wrench his arms free, but Mr. Cullen is bigger. I want to vomit. I can feel the exact pressure of his fingers still on my neck, and his fingers burn and burn.

"Stop it, Addie. You've done all you can. Leave it alone." Mr. Cullen's face is pale and scared, and his voice is pale, and finally my father not so much softens as collapses.

The hatred is soft in my chest, looking for form.

I wash in the bathroom, and my father sits crying silently in the kitchen. I walk by the kitchen once, twice. I want him to stop me, say he's crying for what he did to me and not for Mrs. Wilson. *Goddamn you* is what whistles in my head—*why do you give this much to a dead woman and nothing at all to me? We all knew she would die, and I'm still alive.* Is it monumentally selfish to want for me what he gives to everyone else?

"Stop feeling sorry for yourself," Roy whispers on the porch when he comes home from football practice.

I hate him too, and the intensity nearly overwhelms me. He should be on my side, but he never is. Like he thinks he's Mother now or something. But Mother would have been on my side. "He loves the dead," I say. "He must." The words spin wetly through my lips.

Roy is holding his football helmet beneath his arm, and as he turns toward me he lets it drop then catches it by the face guard. He stares at me and then turns away.

I wash again to get even the memory of the blood off my face. I walk by the kitchen again. *I want from you,* my heart screams, *how come you can hear all the want in the world but mine?* I walk by again, but still he doesn't say anything, and the hatred begins to harden.

In a while, it begins to howl. At night, in dreams, Mrs. Wilson's face flies into mine.

# PASSING

I wake up on a cloud, not awake or asleep. I know the shadows have chased close and left me here. Somewhere nearby a telephone rings and someone's soft voice says, "Recovery?" and I close my eyes against the medium darkness and the voice drones softly into itself. Huge white birds alight next to the bed. Crows. White crows. I move my head, and I am awake. Now there's a window and a curtain between the bed and the window. I move my head and there is another bed, and the movement echoes through my bed. Thin worn white sheets and a single pale, white-skinned, and translucent-looking foot. Another foot slides beside it.

Outside, beyond the window, it looks like spring, that hot kind of sunlight, aching with space and distance.

Now there is a nurse at the edge of the bed. Slender and silent, the deep chocolate brown of her face is spectacular against the white of her uniform. "You awake?" she says softly.

I nod, or I think I'm nodding. "I'm awake, how 'bout you?" I say, and the weakness of my voice startles me.

She laughs. "I'm plenty wake. You just hush, now, honey," she says.

Or I think she says it. The words arrive at the edge of the cushion that holds me, light as chiffon.

Beyond me a sound slurps at the air, at me.

"What day is it?" I say.

"Pearl Harbor Day," she says, and the combination of words feels weird in my air. December 7? It's been only a day. It seems remarkable how time can be so indeterminate, so completely subjective.

"Isn't that the truth," she says as she turns and wheels the blood pressure machine next to the bed. I hadn't known I was talking. She takes my arm in her hands and wraps the upper part in the wide black cuff strap that extends from the machine.

The slurping beyond me doesn't stop but keeps on steady and constant.

She squeezes a black bulb in her hand repeatedly, and the cuff tightens on my arm. I let my head fall to the side, and I can see the word Baumanometer on the side of the machine. When she's finished with the blood pressure, she takes my temperature with a digital thermometer with a disposable tip she pops into the trash when she finishes.

When she's through with me, she crosses beyond the curtain and does the same to the person on the other side. I can only see his feet, and the place on the wall where a bottle gurgles with mucousy-looking blood.

Her voice is soft and has its own hum. I lift up my sheet, the thin cotton blanket over it. The room is hot. I wear a hospital gown, and there is a hard scab and the spines of sutures sticking up through it. Everything is calm now. There is a tube that goes into a wad of tape on my arm. I close my eyes and try to will Sandy into my mind, but all I get is her mother's face, her changing expression in the hallway.

The pain echoes in the bed. Early morning and I have neither eaten nor drunk since I came here, and now my mouth is solid with the burn of thirst. Water is all I can think of. I move myself up a little, and the pain rips at my side. The cloud of morphine is gone, and I am on my own. The pain whistles loud and bright.

In the hallway there are voices, soft shoes. My neighbor snores in his bed. A telephone rings. The pores of the world are open wide.

Street shoes on tile, clack, clack, and three doctors march into the room and stop at the end of my bed. One of them picks up the metal clipboard that hangs on the end of the bed. "How you feeling?" the oldest of them says.

"Terrific," I say. Then, "Thirsty."

One of the younger ones scratches the side of his head, squints, and says, "That'd be the morphine."

He says it to me, but it's the older doctor who nods. "We don't want you to drink just yet."

The other young doctor, this one with black tortoiseshell glasses, takes my covers and pulls them back, then lifts my gown. The first young one draws the curtain around the bed. The old one reaches down and puts his fingers on my belly. Pain smashes through me from the inside. I jerk back, and it gusts even more. White and blue cellophane blow in my head.

"Sorry," he says. "Why don't you get him something?" he says to both of the younger doctors. One of them, the one without glasses, turns and leaves the room. They ask questions, but it's hard to talk because of the pain, hard even to register the questions.

When the other doctor comes back, he has a syringe and comes close to the bed. He taps the side of the syringe, pops the cap off the needle, and squirts a hair of liquid, then he pushes the tip of the needle into the wad of tape and tubing where the intravenous tube ends. There's a burning in my arm and then a softness that relaxes my muscles, pushes me down. It comes stronger and stronger, pushes me down into the soft folds of the bed.

When I wake up again, the sucking has stopped. It feels like midafternoon, but I don't have any idea. The curtain between the beds is pulled back, and the man in the other bed is sitting up and seems to sense it when I look at him. "Hello, neighbor," he says softly. He's an old man and wears pajamas instead of the hospital gown I wear. In the back of his left hand is a wad of adhesive tape like the one that surrounds the place where the intravenous line goes into my arm.

They must have me on a milder painkiller, because while I only get the most distant signals from my gut, I am more clear-headed than before. "Hello," I say. "How do you put the bed up like that?"

"Levers on the side," he says. His hand swings down low on the side of the bed and points to a little panel with two levers on it between the two sets of bars that keep you from falling out of the bed. "This one's for the head," he says, pointing to the one nearest his hand. "Just pull it this way." He has an accent—French, maybe.

I reach down and pull the lever. Slowly the head of the bed grinds upward.

"Your name is Jack?" he says. "I'm David." Maybe his accent is not French at all, but German.

"How did you know?" I say.

"It seems you are something of a celebrity." His consonants have a sibilance that isn't American—but it's not German either.

In a little while, I say, "Does this telephone work?"

"Might give it a try," he says. "They bill you for everything, so the telephone likely is not any different."

I lift the hand piece, and there's a dial tone. The only person I want to call is Sandy, but I can't remember her number, and I have no idea what happened to my clothing. I start to call information, but someone comes in. I put down the phone gingerly, turn, and there's old Darrell Planey in full uniform, hat in hand. He seems huge now that I'm on my back.

"Nice to see you're awake," he says.

"I figured you'd probably drop by sooner or later."

"Ain't you glad to see me?"

"Sure, Darrell, I'm pleased as hell." Half a dozen questions circle around in my mind, wanting to be asked, but I don't say anything yet. There's something about his being here that makes me lonely, I don't know why.

"I wanted to thank you for that collection of artillery," he says. "Still, I can't help but think you ought to've let the law take its course."

"Couldn't help myself."

"You gonna put me out of a job, old buddy."

I reach down to the lever to put the bed up a little higher, but I get the wrong one, and my feet start to elevate. When I get the right one, I'm twisted the wrong way and pain lances through my belly and makes me gasp.

"You okay?"

I take a long, cautious breath. When it doesn't hurt I say, "Yeah, I'm fine."

There's a chair against the wall, and he pulls it up to the side of the bed and sits down. He has to rearrange his holster. His boots gleam. He puts his hat flat on his lap. It's the first time I've been physically close to him without being angry since we were kids, and I can see he's uncomfortable being in the hospital. His hair is thinning, and he has a rash from shaving too often. We sit and look at each other for a long time, but he doesn't say anything, just sits there, looks at me, looks around the room. The television plays behind me, soft but insistent.

Finally I can't stand the silence any longer. "You have any idea what they did with my clothes and stuff when they brought me in?"

"Most of your stuff's in the closet over here," Darrell says, and his voice has the dry, unused sound to it of someone who's been asleep for a long time. I watch his eyes until I can't see them anymore as he turns and points to the locker set into the wall. "Your jacket and shirt were pretty messed up. They put those in a plastic bag. If it were me, I'd want to save them."

I nod.

"When they let you out, you could have a friend get you some things from home." He smiles.

I smile back at him. His words repeat themselves in the air. A friend.

The shimmering wordglass of the television shatters in laughter. I look up at the TV, and a beautiful blonde woman hugs another, younger woman who might be her daughter—the sides of their faces press together. I look back at Darrell. I can see the lines in his face, the vague impression his hat rim has made in the skin that covers his skull. I can see the whiskers on the skin of his cheeks, and every fine dark follicle of hair that sweeps back from his sideburns. The saliva in my mouth turns sour and sends a wave of nausea through me. A friend. I can't keep the burning sensation out of my eyes.

Darrell sees the expression on my face and says haltingly, "If you want, I could go by for you and pick up a few things."

"Thanks, that's okay." I try to pull myself up to regain my poise—I have a vision of myself like one of my father's old invalids, slumped down in the bed, incontinent, completely helpless. The thought disgusts me. But as soon as I move, it feels like the stitches are being torn out of my side. I can't keep the hoot in my mouth.

"You're gonna have to stop wiggling around like that or you're gonna tear yourself up," Darrell says, that old scolding, ain't-you-a-dumbfuck, I-told-you-so voice.

And then the blackness hits me—pure, overwhelming anger slamming so hard into my face I don't see anything but him, can't think of anything but doing whatever I possibly can to hurt him. "Why don't you just get the fuck out of here, man? You come here to say I told you so? Fine, then fucking say it and get out of here. I—," I start, but I can't continue. As suddenly as the anger came it has fled and here I am, as pathetic as Sandy's dad.

He looks at me with the same disbelief he did that night he nailed me with his nightstick. His jaw is set, but he doesn't get up and walk out. Maybe because I'm about to bawl like a stupid baby. "Darrell," I say. "I'm sorry."

"Let's not talk about it," he says. "You been through a lot."

"I want to talk about it. I've been an asshole."

He purses his mouth and pushes his lips to the side, bites at the inside of his lips, but doesn't say anything.

I wipe my free arm across my eyes. "I want to talk about it, but that's all I got to say." A weak laugh shuffles across the words.

"Can't say I disagree."

He has his hat in his hands and his elbows on his knees, and he turns the hat over and over, then takes the brim of it, pairs his right thumb and forefinger and pulls the edge of it along the fingertips. He doesn't look at me. A nurse comes in and takes my temperature, my blood pressure, makes soft, birdlike chat, and still he doesn't say anything, just stares down at his hat—now and again looks up and out the window, where it has begun to get dark.

"Darrell, what happened to Dean?"

The nurse is gone.

The question walks on the ice that surrounds my heart, but the ice won't support its weight.

He sniffs the way you do when you're getting a cold, then makes a quick glance up at my roommate's television. "He passed on last night." He's not looking at me when he says it, and he says it fast.

"He didn't want to be there."

"He was there, and armed." I wince a little, look toward the window. He lays his hat flat on his knees.

"What's it like outside?"

"Warm as hell. Has been ever since it stopped snowin'. You'd think it was April. My wife's worried her daffodils and tulips are gonna come up and then all get frozen out." He speaks slowly, sadly, deliberately, then stops, folds his hands together, and stares at the rough conjunction of them.

"Sylvia?"

"The Nickerson woman's okay," he says tightly, giving a wag of his head. "Broken arm. She's upstairs on seven." He looks back at me from the television set. "She thinks you shot her. Couldn't convince her otherwise." He shrugs.

"I'm glad you couldn't."

"Old McClanahan and Van Kalkenberg—," he shakes his head and a grin starts to blossom on his mouth, "man, when I pulled up I could hear intensive rifle fire, and I had no idea what was going on. It was snowin', and I came tearing down through the woods on foot, my service revolver drawn." This lights him up, makes him enthusiastic. "Your buddy Dean and the Nickerson woman were groaning. Really, that Nickerson woman was babbling about you. She's somethin'. I found McClanahan first. You dropped that old boy like you was a world-class marksman. Right in the forehead," he plants a forefinger just above the spot where his nose and eyebrows meet. "I figured you musta had a deer rifle with a scope or something—where the hell'd you get that old Winchester?"

"It's my father's."

"Man," he says and shakes his head in something approximating workmanlike appreciation. Then, businesslike, "He know you have it?"

"Not in so many words."

He stops and turns back to the television. Maybe he doesn't know that I have no idea what happened. "And Chalky—," I start.

"Hell, yes. I'm sorry. Man oh man," he says, grinning, giving the sheepish laugh I haven't seen since we were kids playing football, "he looked like that low-fat Swiss cheese they advertise on television. I mean *ventilated*. You musta hit him ten or eleven times. I saved the newspaper for you. Biggest thing that's happened around Middleridge since that woman shot her girlfriend over gas ration coupons in 1944." He laughs.

I swallow and look at the ceiling. I remember shooting Buck. I remember the snow starting and the three of them coming down through the woods, and just remembering makes my heels push hard against the foot of the bed, makes my heart pick up, and sends a jolt of pain through my belly.

I remember with hard, nearly photographic precision firing the rifle and watching Buck drop, Sylvia wobbling, and then the rocking, narrow space between the earth and the dark floor of the trailer as I belly-crawled to the end of it and pulled myself out from beneath it. Then there are smaller memories—the hard kick in the gut, the taste of powder in my mouth. The cold of the ground calling at me, and then bright lights and people surrounding me, the whole of it feeling funereal—I had been released from my physical form and floated away from it, took this all in at a distance. I want to say something. What I want to say is about how it's too easy to point the rifle and have the man you point it at drop. It's too easy. But I can't find the words for it.

"Am I gonna be—you know?"

"Self-defense, far as I can see. Personally, I don't see any need to pursue it further."

He stands up, raises his eyebrows and nods in salutation, flips his hat between his fingers, then says, "So long, Jack. Stop by the station, and I'll give you your dad's rifle."

"Is the area code 703 in Richmond?"

"Naw," Darrell says, turning and then turning back again in bemused surprise "804. I thought you used to live there."

"I did. I can't think very well at the moment. The drugs."

"Got to stay off those drugs."

The ceiling is suspended acoustic tile, old and dirty with age. The kind of ceiling I have hung with my father in basements and studies and family rooms.

Long after the nurses have brought and taken away my neighbor's supper, long after visiting hours are over and the bustling sound of the hallways has ebbed, I stare up at the patternless design, the grid of metal strips. From out in the hallway comes the subdued sound of televisions, of nurses talking. Some old man moans: "They're killing me, please, get me out of here, they're killing me. Nurse, nurse," repeating himself endlessly, softly, like a human tape loop. "You there. Please. I don't want to die. Help me, *help* me." After a few hours, his voice loses its human quality. Together all of it is what madness must sound like: endless rooms, endless voices, none of the channels corresponding to one another. All is chaos, ordered only by the geographic proximity of its elements.

I have killed three men, and I don't remember it—or remember killing only one of them. I can dream their faces up out of blackness more easily than I can dream my mother's face. I can see their eyes and smell their breath and hear their voices. And the only person in town I considered a friend was one of them. I try not to think about him, but I can't help it. None of it can be reconciled.

312 |

When my mother died, my idea of death—which had scared me to my soul when I first found it applied to me—turned hard, scaly, like a dried lizard, and became something entirely different. One of my professors in school used to say that at birth all we have to look forward to in life is death, and it's a wonder that we all don't just do ourselves in and get it over with. I used to think about that and about my mother, but what I would sometimes forget was what he said after that: what we have to decide is why most of us opt to live out our lives and find value in what is inevitably bleak.

I have no idea what time it is, but I desperately want to talk to someone. The only one I can think of is Sandy, but now the thought of talking to her is almost like the thought of talking to my father.

Midway through the first ring there is a chunk on the line and Sandy's voice, breathy, breathless. "Hello?"

"I hope you don't mind me calling this late, but I needed to talk to someone."

"I don't mind. I hope *you* don't mind. I been waiting by the phone ever since you left. Hope that doesn't make me sound like some dumb schoolgirl." Giddy but cautious. Nothing has changed since I left.

God. What hangs between us is fragile as crystal, and I can feel the pressure against it growing. Sooner or later, slower or faster, everything shatters.

Then: "What'd you do, get a phone?"

"No."

"You sound funny. Where are you?"

"Hospital. I figured you knew. It was all in the papers here."

"Oh shit, no." Hot. Anxious. "Are—are you okay?"

"All things considered, I'm a lot better than anyone else concerned."

There's silence—through the line, faintly, in one of those cross-connections you get, I can hear a voice I would swear was my father's.

"I've got a bullet wound in my lower left abdomen, thanks to Chalky. They resected my bowel, and I'll be here for a while more."

When she speaks again, her voice is more somber. "What happened, Jack?" meaning, I guess, what happened to Chalky.

"Maybe there was another way out of this. I don't know. Maybe there was."

"Jack—"

"Maybe there was another way, but if there was I couldn't think of it.

Sometimes you just burrow down into the hole of your thinking, and you can't see what else there might be."

"What happened?"

"Chalky and Buck and Dean came after me at the trailer. I knew they would. At least I knew Chalky and Buck would. I don't know why they had to bring Dean. I don't know why he came. I don't know why they thought I wouldn't expect them. They were just so fucking dumb about the whole thing."

"That's my Chalky, stupid as a cow."

I don't say anything. I don't know what to say next. I want this all to be over with. I want what I had with her in the car the other afternoon when I left her. I want not to have killed anyone.

"Where are they now."

The phone is hot against my head. The room is hopelessly stuffy. My back sweats against the mattress. "All three. All three—they're all dead, Sandy."

For a moment there's silence, and I search in the line for the voice of my father but it isn't there.

"Jesus jumpin' Christ," she says finally. I can feel the sudden loss of velocity in her words. I can hear her breathing, and then I can hear her sniffle. After a moment, hard as nails: "What I don't understand is why no one called me, you know? I'm his wife, and no one called me."

"Maybe they called the house."

"So that makes me a widow. Hunh. You know, I'm fucking glad he's dead." She laughs a brittle cackle. "I am glad. I mean, I'd probably have shot him myself if I'd had the guts."

I'm mired so deeply in everything here, I've forgotten her situation. "How's everything there?"

"Oh, shit, Jack. It's been kind of weird. I guess it's okay." The cadence of her words is peculiar, then she just stops. "Shit. Shit shit shit shit. He's dead. I feel like Mary Poppins. I mean not Mary Poppins but Dorothy—Dorothy from *The Wizard of Oz*. What the hell was Dorothy's last name."

"Sandy—"

"No, it's—. No."

There is a long silence, and I am afraid I have lost her. I want to speak, but there is nothing I can say. I see Dean without closing my eyes. I see her without closing my eyes, but I also see David in the bed next to me, old and dying of cancer, limbs nearly translucent.

"I went away from here," she says, her voice sounding more steady. "I mean I left my parents years ago, and you know, you carry a thing in your head—the way a person is will just stick. I looked at them one way. Now I come back, and *I'm* a different person. That's the thing I can't believe—that *I'm* a different person."

Somehow Sandy has a knack for giving voice to my own thoughts. I want to say something in agreement, but I can't speak.

"Some ways they still treat me like a fifteen-year-old, or they make me feel that way. But now I can say no to them—or now I don't need to. Jesus I can't believe Chalky's dead."

"I can't believe it either."

"You did it?"

"I wish I hadn't."

"I don't know what to feel—like I want to feel some tremendous weight has been—you know. But it's just so wicked to be glad someone's dead."

"I don't know."

"I guess this means I'm free now. You know I used to love him. I really did. Now I don't understand why, but I used to get swept up in him and dizzy. But it stopped a long time ago. I don't know why he couldn't just let go. Love can be such a hard and disgusting thing, sometimes." When she stops talking I can't say anything. The pillow wants me to sink down, stop thinking.

"What are you going to do?" I say after the silence has begun to hurt.

"What do you mean?"

What I mean is are you going to come see me, do you love me, will you make love with me, but I can't say it because this is a bridge I have crossed only once in my life and it was burned behind me. What I say is: "You coming back to Middleridge? To your job and stuff?"

She sighs. "Jack, I haven't really thought—you know. Sure. Yeah. I guess I will. My life is there. You know the house is mine. I mean we bought it, took out a mortgage, and I'm the one who did everything because I'm the only one who had credit. Maybe I'll fix it up."

"I could help."

"You know it's funny, I mean I just thought of it, and I haven't thought of it in years. When I first met him, he loved carnivals. I know it sounds stupid. He had a job with one once for a few weeks, but he loved that stuff—he'd go and throw the baseballs at the milk cans, get his fortune told. Try to win me stuff. And then it just stopped. He could be funny, too, in a childish kind of way. Toilet talk, my mother would call it. I don't remember the last time he went to a carnival or was funny. He just turned hard."

"You outgrew him."

"I don't want—when are visiting hours?"

"Eleven to eight."

After a while she says, "If we ever fell in love and had kids, we couldn't do it, because they'd ask us how we met and we'd have to say, Daddy met Mommy when Daddy used to buy drugs from Mommy's husband. Daddy and Mommy were the only two who made sense out of things and survived." She laughs, and then she starts to cry, and finally, she says, "So long, Jack," and it has the hard feel of finality to it.

Dean is alive after all and sits on the front fender of his Starfire. He's got his legs crossed beneath him Indian style, and he has a cigarette going. The narrow of his face is colored with the late evening sunlight, which makes him look more tanned than in daylight. We're talking about girls, about some girl he met last night at Charades. He says something else, and there is silence for a long time. Things happen in the sky— there are shapes that wander in the darkness, there is music the stars dream that you can only barely hear. Dean has a worried look on his face. *Oh yeah* is what I think. Right. He's worried what's going to happen to him.

"What?" he says, one eyebrow going up, his eyes lighting. "You were looking at me like you were going to say something."

"When you were in the service, did you know a guy named Roy Pleasance?"

"Sure. Why?—" but he cuts himself short in the middle of the word. "Oh shit," he says. "I never put the two together. What a fuckin' dumbhead I am. Pleasance. Pleasance." He uncurls his legs from beneath him and starts to swing them down off the fender of the Pontiac, but when he does, there's light beneath the car. I'm on the grass, and I can feel it softening. "Oh shit," he says and folds his legs back beneath him.

"It's just lights, man."

"Tell me when they're gone, man, tell me when they're gone. I don't want to go."

# INDISCRETION

He's upstairs in the bedroom putting away laundry when the telephone rings. He picks it up at the same time Karen does—immediately he can hear the sound of a street, of cars going by on pavement, a car door slamming, and can also hear that it's long distance—but she says hello before he has a chance to. He stays on the line to see if the call's for him, then says nothing when the caller asks for him.

The caller is surprised at a woman's voice but asks for Addie Pleasance—like that—anyway. The caller's a man, and the electric thing that wires through him says *Jack*, and when he says "Who's this?" nausea sinks through him. "I must have the wrong number," the caller says, and then the line is dead. He presses the button in the receiver cradle as quietly as he can, then hangs up. Maybe Karen won't have heard him get on the line.

It's chilly out, but the bare branches of the trees against the window make the day seem infinitely colder, infinitely less hospitable. It's early yet, but the sunlight already seems gray with evening.

He doesn't go downstairs immediately but stays where he is, the perfumey-smelling laundry set out on the bed, the dresser drawers open.

When he goes downstairs later, she is on the couch reading a book, and she says nothing about the phone call. He has no idea whether she says nothing because she thinks he already knows, or because she thinks he doesn't know. But the time to ask "Who was it?" passes, and the moment hardens into history.

Tonight she goes back to her apartment to sleep, and even though she does so several nights a week, he wonders if tonight she did it because of the sound of Jack's voice over the telephone.

Alone in bed, he sleeps restlessly, the whole world in his eyes, in his mind. Jack could have been on a street in Pittsburgh or San Francisco or China, for all he knows, and he dreams of the three of them—him and Jack and Roy—driving in the pickup. The boys are young, and neither of them wear clothing. Jack is maybe seven or eight. Their bodies are wiry, and they sleep, Roy against the door, Jack against Roy.

They drive for a long time—the road seems endless. It begins to worry him that they don't stop, that he can't stop, and that the boys don't wake up.

Finally the worry overtakes him, and he lets go of the wheel and reaches out to touch them. They're hard as death, and they're covered and hardened with sleep—not just crusted in the eyes but all over. Stiff as death. Then suddenly Jack's mouth drops open and there's the fiery grin of white skull teeth, and at the same time, the pickup veers off the road, but there is nothing beyond the road and they sail off into a horrible endless descent—he wants to wake the boys, but what will he wake them to?

# FAMILY

Sandy sits on the bed while I shove my things into the bag she brought. Her father waits outside in his car. My gut is tender, but now it's the kind of tender where you're constantly testing it, going farther against the pain everyday. The last thing I do is lift out the transparent plastic bag where they put the jacket and shirt I was wearing the night I was shot. The blood has set and turned brown. I start to hurry it into the bag, but she stops me with one hand on my hand, and then her hand goes to the plastic. It's that thin kind of soft plastic they use at the dry cleaners. Her hand goes over the crusted wool and finds the hole. It's amazingly small. I start to say that an inch over and it would have got my kidney, but I don't. It's not important.

The outside air is crisp and brilliant, and the feel of it makes me think of playing football in the blowing leaves. Christmas is a week away. I can feel the texture of cold pigskin in my hands—spit on leather, dogshit on the grass.

Her father's car is an old Plymouth Fury III. It's a city-block long and must have cost him fifty dollars in gasoline to drive her out here. We all three sit in the front seat, and still there's room.

He takes us first to the trailer where we drop Sandy off with my car keys, then wait for her while she starts the Chevy, warms it up, then leads us back to her house. The two of them have been working on the house for the last few days, clearing things out, cleaning things up, but still I am leery of staying there.

Bud and I sit in silence in the car, two tiny men at distant ends of a long bench seat. He is sober, and it does not suit him. The sunlight is scalding bright, and I am raw and overly sensitive to everything in this new, outside world. Bud drives with his hands at the top of the steering wheel, hunched close to it, glasses on and eyes focussed intensely on the road, on the business of driving. He plays the radio, has it tuned to a station that plays songs from the forties and fifties, with the repeating slogan "The music of your life." To me it sounds like the music in the supermarkets when I was a very little child and rode in the folding seat of the grocery cart.

Out of the blue, he says, "I shot a man once," and though I have known it nearly since I've known Sandy, I have forgotten. It comes back again, shaped differently.

"Sandy told me."

"I didn't know him from Adam, though."

"Death is a funny thing."

"I always wonder what they'll say to me on Judgement Day."

I give a perfunctory smile and then turn to stare out the window. The winter is spectacularly beautiful the way it settles into the countryside. Death is a funny thing. But is winter death? The fields are brown and the woods are bare, and everything, even in brilliant sunshine, has only one shade—a million variations on the single shade of brown-gray. And still there is life everywhere. Maybe it is life that is the funny thing.

The Chevy jerks off the gravel road and into the driveway. We pull off the gravel road behind her and pull alongside. The old couch sits at the side of the road, bags and bags of garbage piled on top of it, waiting for the trashmen to come cart away that last chapter of her life. She has been hard at work. The Torino sits where it sat, the hood still open.

We go through the door and the smell of Pinesol hits me. Everything is bright and cold and clean. She has begun to take her old life and transform it. But the cleanness of the house points up the flaws in it. The old plaster wants for paint, but it sags and the walls are cracked and buckled in places. It needs so much work, but it's good to have work in front of you: it's the cleansing thing.

Inside, Bud has a drink with lunch. It's early afternoon, and you can watch the alcohol travel his veins. His relief is instantaneous and grateful.

Later, we go out in the Chevy, Sandy driving, Bud in the back. I'm amazed at how weak I am from my weeks of inactivity. I am amazed that all the things I once took completely for granted have to be worked through painfully and slowly. Walking, standing up from a sitting position, going to the bathroom.

She pulls off the road in a little field where a man sits in a folding chair in front of a kerosene heater. On the ground, leaning on a stake, is a piece of three-eighths-inch plywood on which is painted X-MAS TREES in black paint. Behind the man, there is a wooden rack, and against it lean dozens of recently cut young fir trees. The fragrance of them is everywhere. Some are bundled in plastic twine, some are upright and standing canted on the uneven ground in red-and-green tree holders.

The man follows us as we go along the row of trees. He needs a shave. When two more cars pull off the road, he turns. One is a station wagon, and children pile out and run toward the trees. Sandy holds my arm as we walk. My legs tremble, and I sweat inside my coat. The children— there are three of them—run between the trees; their voices warble with excitement. Bud talks to them; they are too young to see the gin in his eyes, in his jowls.

On the way home, pine scent and cold blowing through the open hatchback of the Chevy, Sandy stops at a drugstore, runs in and buys a bottle of tonic water, a box of multicolored glass tree ornaments, and a string of colored lights.

While she makes supper, Bud and I put up the tree in the bare and clean-swept living room. He has a gin and tonic going, and it pulls a picture of my father up inside my head, but I chase away the thought.

By the time we finish supper, Bud has consumed nearly half the bottle of gin. We bring the kitchen chairs into the living room and plug in the Christmas lights. Sandy kisses me, and Bud sits in a wooden chair and cries. No one is a perfect parent, though every child expects it. For the first time I catch a glimmer of what my father must have wanted for Roy and me, and how plunging headfirst into his love for us and for my mother, he was torn apart a million times. I watch Bud cry. Sandy leaves the room. Perhaps a parent's bravery is allowing yourself to be torn apart by love. Allowing it again and again.

In the morning, hung over but hung in the sharp focus of Sandy's cinnamon coffee, Bud drives back home and leaves the two of us alone.

It is Saturday, and in the late of the morning, she drives us to the bank and then to Benjamin Franklin where we Christmas-shop for each other. I slip out and walk down the concrete concourse of the shopping center and into the overcrowded bookshop that is there. I buy her *Moby-Dick* and *Anna Karenin.* She is coming out of the Ben Franklin as I approach, and she says, "I was wondering where you got off to." It's a warmish day, and she looks unbearably ripe in her gray sweater and turtleneck.

Midnight Christmas Eve, and she is in bed. I stand in my underwear in the nearly empty living room and try to figure out how I came to this point in my life, but there is no explaining it. It is only in retrospect that the randomness of events seems to take form. The incision and stitches at the side of my belly itch, and I know the scab would come loose and hang in the sutures if I tried it, but I don't. I put her gifts beneath the tree and turn out the lights.

Upstairs, in the new bed she bought to replace the bed she discarded, she sits up cross-legged in a T-shirt that doesn't quite reach the waistband of her panties. The flesh of her breast shifts slightly as she moves and runs her hands through her hair. "I'm thinking of getting a new haircut," she says.

"Do," I say.

"What would I look like with short hair?"

"Beautiful."

She holds her hair up and behind her head. "How's your gut?"

"Better." I get closer to the bed, aroused just by the look of her. The air is cool against my legs and arms.

"You've gained back some of the weight."

I pull my T-shirt over my head. The brown railroad track of scabbed scar climbs out of the elastic of my shorts.

"I don't want you to get too comfortable here. I mean I think I don't want to get too used to you being here."

"No," I say. "I'm going back to the trailer as soon as we get the Torino running." You have to be hard as nails about these things—that's what each of us is saying inside. I want to be hard as nails with her, but I can only pretend on the outside. Inside it will not work.

I push off my pants and stand in front of her, completely undressed.

It feels like something I've never done before—stand before a woman absolutely nude. Something is falling away from me. My penis is extended and hangs in the air. The cut on my belly throbs distantly, vaguely. I want to say I love you, but I don't. I do love her.

"Are you starting a new career as a flasher?" she says.

I tremble. She sees the look in my eyes. She pulls her T-shirt over her head and says, "Don't say it. Just come here and don't say it." I fall into the bath of her arms and breathe her like I have never breathed.

Christmas day is a Wednesday; it's warm and drizzles, and we walk together through the field behind her house. She wears the same gray sweater she wore a few days ago, and glassy beads of water stand up on the fibers of the sweater. We don't talk but push through the weeds, down to the woods and the pond. In the woods I pull off my sweatshirt for her to lie on, and I mount her in the damp and rustling leaves.

In the afternoon we build a fire in the fireplace and on the rug in front of the fireplace, she mounts me. The fire makes her skin blaze. I am stronger now.

Friday morning I drop her at work and pick up a new distributor and rotor from her shop. I go back to her house and get the car started, then jack it up and take the wheels off the back of the car and drive them into town to a Goodyear dealership to have new tires mounted on them.

By the time I have the new tires on the car, I am exhausted and have to nap before evening comes and I go to pick her up.

New Year's Day she follows me back to the trailer in the Torino. It feels strange to drive—the doctor has said not to because of the surgery and the danger of flying into the steering wheel in an accident, but there is nothing else to do and I don't tell Sandy.

What little remains in the refrigerator is spoiled, and we throw it out. With caulking compound, we fill in the bullet holes in the walls, and then she leaves me alone.

It's a whole new year, and the silence of it is stunning. After the controlled madness of the hospital, after the days of her proximal warmth and constant breath, the trailer seems thin, unsupportable.

I wander through it in the dimming late afternoon light, the bare rooms and boxes, the hard floor where I slept on nothing but blankets and pillows. I try to bring the last several months into relief, but it doesn't come. There's nothing there at all—or there's nothing here, in this trailer.

At night in the rush of shadows my sleep is restless. I dream of Chalky. Dean is a fugitive in the witness protection program, and he comes to us, to Sandy and me, in tears in some dark room where he cannot turn on the lights. Chalky is always near the darkness. Buck's malleable face metamorphoses—he is made of wood, of leather and appears everywhere. I wake up in the morning sore, alone, with nothing to do but walk in the woods or read. I look at the pile I have made of my mother's pictures.

In the afternoon, I go into town and ask about having a phone put in.

The stitches in my belly come out. The winter plunges toward spring. Half of my evenings I spend with her, but always she rolls me out of bed as it nears midnight and makes me go home. Hard as nails. I get stronger and am able to take on more work. I take a page from my father's strategy book and hook up with a hardware store, give them five percent for the jobs they float in my direction.

The evenings we spend working on her house. The upstairs bedroom first, the upstairs bathroom next. She picks up the knack for this kind of work quickly. She's practical, focussed. I look at myself in the mirror, covered with plaster dust, wearing an old sweatshirt and a baseball cap, and I have become my father. I say things, and what comes out is his voice, his transmitted knowledge.

It's late in the evening, and we are working in the living room. I am cutting through the old plaster and lathing with my new Japanese circular saw, scoring it so she can come along after me with a hammer and smash the pieces, and with the claw of the hammer, yank the chunks of old wall off the studs. White and gray dust streams out from the back of the saw, fine as smoke. Both of us wear face masks and safety goggles.

When I cut the saw off, my ears sing with the shriek of it, the silence echoes with it. She slams the hammer against the wall once more and then turns to me. She is covered with dust from the walls. The dust settles slowly, and I pull off the mask and goggles. She laughs. "You have tan lines from the dust." Dust is in her hair, in her ears, and she pulls off her goggles and mask too. Dust falls to the floor.

"You do too." I stand across the room from her, the saw still in one hand, the elastic straps of the goggles and mask in the other hand. My

arms are numb from work, and it's a beautiful feeling. There are no blinds on the dusty windows, and the night is black beyond the hard interior light.

"Fuck me," she says. I turn the word over in my head, and the way she says it gives it a thick, delicious sound. Fuck. It takes nearly the whole mouth to say it, and the whole body to do it.

"Then we're finished for the night, boss?"

"We're finished for the night."

Upstairs, in the shower, I stand close to her, gobble a mouthful of water from the spraying shower head and softly blow a stream of it in her ear to get the dust out. I hold her, one hand on the small of her back, one hand on her belly. Then slowly I turn her and do the other ear. The shower steams split glass and neon, her breasts wag and my penis hangs in the damp air. She does the same to me, and I have to crouch down to accept the stream of water.

And now I'm standing with my hands on her shoulders—her arms are hard from the work. The water hits my shoulder, hits her front. "I love you," I say, and she just looks at me for a long time and then pushes toward me and clings to me so tightly we will explode. When she releases me, she puts her hands hard on my cheeks and pulls me down, kisses me with the same desperation I felt the first time she kissed me.

In bed I melt into her, and she lets me stay the night through. I am plunging into the future.

# GOING

It is nearly dark by the time the bus comes into Christiansburg. I've only been on for forty-five minutes, but already it feels like I've been on the bus for hours. My side aches vaguely with the early summer damp where the stitches were.

I have to change buses here, and I get off, go inside the station. The station is noisy with talk and the grind of diesel engines. Somewhere a toilet has overflowed, and the edge of the inside air is barked with the scent. I buy a sandwich from a machine against a wall, then take it outside again into the warm evening and just stand on the curb for a moment, looking at everything, wondering what home will look like. I know Christiansburg from the past, and it never struck me the way it does now—as shabby, Appalachian, stuck in some year early in the century when it last saw a boom. Sometimes traveling, when you're leaving the thing that's come before and not yet at the thing to come, there's a wonderful feeling you get of being cut loose, adrift, as though suddenly things are possible and you really hold your own future in your hands; this is why I took the bus and left the car.

.  .  .

It's dark by the time the new bus picks us up and rolls into the country. The land is hilly, and if you stare close at the window and let your eyes get used to the dark, you can see the hills, the fields between, the farmhouses. It is just a few days before my twenty-seventh birthday.

It used to be when you came into Hadleysburg from the north side, the main road was a narrow two-lane road that wound up and down through the green hills of pastures that edged the town. It used to be that you had to go past my grandparents' house, which was for all practical purposes the only mansion anywhere nearby, and it loomed above the road from behind the safe cushion of two or so hundred yards of neatly manicured lawn.

But now there is a highway bypass, black and new and unsullied, like many of the larger towns used to have, and when the bus slips off the highway in the spring early morning dark, we have already passed their sad hulking house.

The bus station—a gas station where the old glass bay doors were fixed shut and the old lifts were taken out and cemented over—is closed because of the hour, and I stand for a few minutes in the dark with my knapsack while the bus grinds back out toward the highway. Even when I came home from college, I did not see Hadleysburg like this, as just a place, interchangeable with any of the other little towns between here and Washington, between here and Richmond.

Once it was home, and nearly every part of it made sense to me. Now I am a ghost, an outsider.

The bus station is at the edge of the old part of town, and I shoulder my knapsack and walk down the road toward my father's house. It's about two o'clock in the morning, and it astounds me how quiet everything is. The darkness has an astounding quality too, the completeness of it. The sky is clear, and now, as my eyes grow accustomed to the dark, the night is pale with stars.

I go up the hill at South Street, past the narrow row of shops and houses where mornings before high school I used to deliver papers, and used to know nearly every person in nearly every house along the street. For a moment it's almost as if I could close my eyes and then open them again, and my knapsack could be a sack of newspapers wound with rubberbands, ready to toss onto front porches.

At the top of the hill, South Street plateaus out into the town square, the center of town. I toy with the idea of going straight to my father's house, but it's too early yet. I don't want to knock and wake him in the middle of the night. I go across the pavement, across the empty angle parking spaces, across the concrete walk, and into the square. Flowers are in bloom—tulips, geraniums, crocuses. I haven't smelled the deep, breathing green world like this in a million years, and it is intoxicating. There is honeysuckle in the air, the damp scent of summer. The grass of the square is thick and wet in the darkness, and suddenly I am very sleepy.

I go past the worn soil of the playground at the town center—the swings and slide and climbing bars are silhouettes against paler silhouettes. There's an area of picnic tables in the center of the square where sometimes I used to eat lunch in the days when I worked at the photo counter at Dunkel's Drug during the summers when I was in college, or in the evenings during the year I worked for my father. The old all-wooden tables my father helped make are gone, and in their place are new wood and metal ones. I take off my knapsack and toss it onto one of the tables, then climb up myself. There are lights all around the square, smearing in the damp air—the movie theater, the Ranchero, Dunkel's, the Lamont Women's Clothier. There's a new Pizza Hut, a new 7-Eleven. You can hear the highway in the distance, now and then the sound of a car moving along one of the back roads, hissing like water in a skillet.

I lie down on the table, pull my knapsack beneath my head for a pillow. I zip up my jacket and shove my hands deep into my pockets. I doze a little bit, on and off, but it's mixed with flying glass, pictures of my father like Sandy's father, old and wizened, alone in his house and rattling like corn dried in its husks. There are shadows and ghosts everywhere in the house, my father is just the most substantial of them.

The air is thundering, the table is shaking. I wake up, turn. The sun is just coming up, and the mountains in the east are in bright, over-whelming relief. There's a garbage truck roaring up State Street on the east side of the square. I swing my legs around and sit up. There's color in everything now. The trees are full, the air is warm. All around the square the buildings are painted brightly, and in my grogginess it all seems a little unreal, something yet the property of dreams. I try to shake my head awake. The clock on the savings and loan says it's just after 5:30. Leaving a place freezes it solid in your mind, unsubject to change. And then when you return, the place has grown, changed, and you are left to reconcile the frozen image with the reality.

I go up State Street toward my father's house. It's still too early, but now in the light I'll be able to see it, and that's what I want to do. I don't know what to expect, and as I get closer to the hill where it is, I start to wonder if this was a good idea.

When you're coming up my father's hill, you can see Church Hill, where my mother and brother are buried, in the distance on the left. You can see the occasional twist of a street beneath the canopy of trees. It's not that high—the grade is slow and graceful—but the distance and the way the town is laid out give the impression of height. Church Hill stands up above everything, and sometimes it feels as though you could step across the intervening space and be there in an instant. If you could look the other way, which is blocked by trees and houses, you could see my grandparents' house.

Someone is cooking bacon somewhere. The air is quiet, and there's just the slightest chill. I look up again, and there it is. The yard is green and looks well kept. The driveway that used to be two bare dirt ruts has been paved, and my father's pickup sits collecting dew. There's another car parked in front, an old red Maverick, that must belong to someone across the street.

I had the idea that the house would look old, maybe a little battered. I don't know why exactly—my father has always been a neat and precise man. But it looks new, freshly painted. Not only is there a paved driveway, there is a new flagstone and concrete walk that arcs from the drive to the porch.

The lights are out, and you can see the screens in the opened windows. The house would be warm inside. There are a couple of folding chairs on the porch, a little wooden table he probably made. Birds cry in the trees, and the air is full of the sound. I stand at the edge of the road in the gravel, ahead of the red car, and stare at the house.

It makes me think of Middleridge yesterday, of the bus ride—I have begun to come to some kind of understanding of how I got here. It's not just simple geography. You are walking, you turn a corner and walk through a pane of glass that shatters on contact, then stand where you are and try to figure out how you got to this place where you bleed.

I come across the dew-wet lawn, lifting my feet carefully to try to keep my shoes dry, then come up the walk to the porch. It isn't six o'clock yet. I put my knapsack onto the wooden porch and sit on the step.

For a while, sitting on the step, my head swarms with the past: The sky is blue, and my brother and I are walking. We've got fishing rods, and we're going down some country lane, and gravel and dirt kicks beneath our feet. He's seventeen or eighteen, and we've been fighting in the car. I keep wanting to tell him something, but my mouth won't work right. The sky is blue, and there are voices. The sky is blue. "How far do you want to go?" "I don't know. Mile and a half, two." "Where do you want—?"

Or some other time, years earlier:

*It's fall, and Roy is playing football with the team. Mrs. Wilson died last summer, and now the air is crisp with forgetting. We go to the high school together with Daddy in the pickup, my brother in his cleats, me in the middle, his helmet on my lap. It's only afternoon, and already the sun is starting to set. "You wanna ride on the bus with the team?" my brother says. He doesn't look at me but out the windshield. He punches his thigh pad, just to try it out.*

*"All right, sure," I say. I don't let on how suddenly it puts pictures in my head of descending down the bus stairs with the team, kids and girls around the bus, asphalt black beneath us and other buses around.*

*We get to the school and there are cars, other players in uniform with their parents. Roy gets out, his cleats click like deer on ice, and in a minute, Daddy says, "Go ahead," but when I get outside, Roy's nowhere in sight. There are others: Jim Follert, Rye Wallace. One of them chucks me on the shoulder, but I ignore them and work my way toward the bus. The cheerleaders are at their own bus, jumping with the chill, their legs white and their skirts short—when they jump you can see their underwear.*

*One of the bus windows clacks down, and Roy sticks his head out. Frowning, he says, "You understand, don't you?" He doesn't say my name but looks at me. "It's all right, isn't it, buddy?"*

*" 'S'okay," I say. I can't mind, but I hate him. He puts up the window and sits down again. I want to cry. God, I want to cry. But it doesn't work anymore.*

*I turn away, and I want to run because of how foolish I was to trust him, but I don't. I keep myself steady, float through the others, and ignore all of it. The pickup smells like peppermint and tobacco. My father says something, but I don't pay attention. I roll down the window a little to let out the cigarette smoke, then stare straight ahead of me into the glassy sunshine. There are mirages out ahead, on the dips in the straight, flat blacktop, and I think of skidding on ice. I think of my mother.*

I try to remember how I felt when I heard my brother was dead. I try to remember what I felt like when I heard. But memory gets tied up in complicated things. Did I hate him for dying while I was still angry with him? If I hated him, I loved him too.


He's awake with the sun through the windows, and for a little while he just lies in bed, sleepy but knowing he will not be able to go back to sleep. The house is cool, and the sheets are soft, and Karen's breathing is deep and rhythmic. After the rain they've been having all spring, the sunlight seems open and full of possibility. He lies in bed a little while, his mind relaxed, and lets things run. After a while, he slips quietly out of bed, but before he can slip downstairs, her breathing gets shallow, and she says, "Add?"

Her hair is in her face, and he comes back to the bed and lies in the middle of it, next to her. She mumbles, but if there are words, he can't make them out. He puts his arms around her and pulls himself close. She hums and wriggles closer. He kisses the soft of her cheek and is amazed.

In a little while, she is up, and he puts on his running clothes and watches while she pulls the tight exercise bra over her head and then snaps it into place. She makes eyes at him, and then they go downstairs and stretch in the living room. She stretches longer than he does, and he paces around a little, anxious to go, to start sweating so he will not have to think about smoking. "Ready?" he says when she is standing and zipping her jacket.

"Yeah," she says, and he goes toward the front door.

It sucks in the air when he pulls the wooden door open and starts to push out the screen door. But there's a thump and a rustling like when you open the back door at night and raccoons flee the garbage into the darkness, and there, sudden and bleary-eyed, struggling to his feet, is Jack.

*Here.*

Here he is, tired looking, dazed, standing on the stone step below the porch, a hopeful look on his face, something miraculous about him. Strong and young and *alive*, after all. Not like Roy or Alison. He's slimmer and harder—perhaps that is age—than he looked when he left. And the thing that hits him is regret that there wasn't any way to say something about Karen.

Standing here looking, he's forgotten completely that Karen is behind him. "Jack," he says, as if to make the thing real by affirming it with language. Karen pushes around him, and suddenly Jack has the expression of a deer frozen by headlights. And now a hole has been torn in the morning. Jack stammers out an explanation, and he, Addie, can feel his embarrassment growing.

The morning sky is blue, and there is a jumble of lawn and street and trees, and the breath is whistling out of me. Then I am off the porch and standing, turning. For a moment nothing will come into focus, and then everything is tight and the front door is open. My father is stopped in his tracks as he comes through the front door—stopped at the sight of me. He's wearing a T-shirt, a blue windbreaker that's open in the front. He's wearing gym shorts and white socks and blue Saucony running shoes. His legs look strong and young—he looks strong and young, nothing like I imagined. He stares at me, his mouth slightly open, halfway through a word he has begun to form, the handle of the screen door in his hand, his other hand just touching the door frame. His face goes through three or four expressions quickly—completely at a loss to digest what is happening. I am frozen where I am, and both of us stand this way until there is movement behind him, and then he comes forward and Karen Anderson *Karen?* ducks around him. *So it's true.* She stops too. She's also in gym shorts and windbreaker, and when she sees me, she stops too. Her face has the puffy look of someone who has just awakened. She has her hair shorter than I've ever seen it, and she's wearing one of my father's baseball-style work caps. I just stare at them in something like shock. The air is full of waves, and they won't sink in. I can feel myself getting angry, and I do everything I can to keep it at bay. *Why?* a voice in the air in front of me says.

Even though I know it, my mind searches for some other explanation. She slept here. *No.* The phone call.

Whatever I expected him to look like, this is certainly not it. Drunk and crumbling is what I expected. My absence has made him stronger.

He says, "Jack," slowly, musically, and then his hands search for pockets to slide into, away from trouble, but his gym shorts have no pockets, and neither does his windbreaker. I can see past him into the house, and it looks unfamiliar—even from when I was here a few short months ago to take the gun—a new couch, in a different place. New carpeting. His hands plant on his hips, then rise, come together to fold at his chest.

Karen says, "Jack, hello" and releases the screen door. "What a surprise."

She is surprised. *She* is surprised. "We'd wondered if we were ever going to hear from you again."

The door sinks closed slowly behind them, and for a moment, the hiss of it is the only sound in the universe.

Then the birds and the world start up again.

"Hi," I start, and then hang a minute, things still trying to fall into place. "Sorry I didn't call or anything, but it was sort of a spur of the moment thing, coming to visit. I should have called." I turn away from them a moment, look out across the lawn.

"Hey, no problem," my father says. It comes out loud and atonal, someone else's words. Karen nudges him. He laughs sheepishly, boyishly, and his hands come out again. He comes forward. He stops in front of me and reaches out to put his arms around me. I'm down a little from him, one foot still on the walk and one on the step. I drop my knapsack and put my arms around him, but the timing's all off and it's awkward as hell.

In a moment, he lets me go. "It's good to see you," he says and pats me on the shoulder. His eyes are milky behind his glasses, and translucent whiskers stand out on his chin and cheeks.

"It's good to see you too," I say, my eyes and ears burning. I back away and pick up my knapsack. I don't want to hug Karen.

"So," I start, and look back and forth between them, "let me get this straight." I focus on Karen. Things are confused and peculiar, and it feels like I've risen up a couple inches off the ground. I don't look at my feet. Karen's got a round, pretty, moon-shaped face, and her thick, dark hair curls inward at the neck. She looks older, profoundly different. The air between the three of us is clear, but chunks of light float randomly in it. "You've got my father running?" When I hear my voice, I know I've said it too loudly, too cheerily.

My father's laugh sounds like relief, like he expected me to say something else. "Believe it or not——," he says, but she cuts in——

"He's stopped smoking."

Her face beams. In a moment, when the two of them have gone, I will think about the expression on her face and know that I've stumbled in between two people who are in the throes of early love. Right now, all I can do is smile and nod.

"I'm up to two miles a day," he says.

"Well, don't let me keep you."

"No, this calls for a celebration."

"You go for your run. I'll make a cup of coffee or something, and we'll celebrate when you get back."

"Well," my father says, "all right."

I start to yawn but try to suppress it. My eyes fill with moisture from the yawn.

"Bye, Jack," she says. The sound of her voice wants to break things loose in my head, but I keep my eyes focussed on them.

The two of them come down off the step past me onto the walk. I can see Karen's shape through her gym shorts and windbreaker. Her legs are strong and sleek. They break into a trot and head off down the street the way I came. Together, they turn around and wave before they disappear.

As they are running, he is not sure how to feel. He can hear himself say *This calls for a celebration*, and he knows the cavalier falsity of the words was clear to Jack. He looks at Karen, ready to say something, but does not. She looks straight ahead—is perhaps avoiding looking at him. The road is flat and gray beneath them and empty of traffic, and the cool air has a sweet taste to it. The trees and houses at the sides of the road blur with movement, and now suddenly it feels as though the ground has moved a little—that what he would have said was true this morning now seems not so sure. *Why?* he wants to know, and the word jumps up hard and won't stop asking.

It's only now that he realizes how much he was afraid of Jack's knowing. He had gone over it again and again, how he might say it to him—sometimes working during the day he'd find himself having an imagined conversation with his son, explaining, sensibly, rationally.

The whole thing with Karen has been like a dream, and he's been terrified all along that one day he'd wake up and find that it wasn't true. And that's the way it felt this morning—like Jack's presence has blown a hole through it.

*In the dark, Karen's skin looks blue. It's summer, and I watch the flashing of her bare arms in the light that comes from the streetlight half a block away. "Ssshh," she says. The keys tinkle. Inside the front door, she takes my hand and leads me along a hallway and then up a set of stairs. The air is still. The scent of*

*wood and dust is high in the air. At the top of the stairs, I can hear but can't see*
*a key going into a lock. It's the apartment of a friend of hers who has gone away*
*for the weekend and left Karen in charge of her cats.*

*The door comes open, and I can feel a warm, furry body slide against my leg.*
*She closes the door behind us, and I put my arms around her. Her blouse has no*
*sleeves and isn't long enough to tuck into the back of her shorts. I slide my hands*
*down her back and lift the shirt. The bare skin of her is so smooth it makes my*
*head hurt.*

In a minute I go through the screen door into the house. Things are
different, newer.

I go into the kitchen and start coffee, leave my knapsack on a kitchen
chair. The kitchen is different, brighter. A new dishwasher, new pots
and pans, new dishes. I look at the phone and think about calling Sandy,
but I have no idea how I would tell her—my father's with my old
girlfriend. With.

While coffee's brewing, I go upstairs to where my old room was. It's
at the back of the house, and it's bright with early morning sunshine.
It's been cleaned out and sparkles with newness. New carpeting, new
bed, new drapes. Not the way it was months ago when I came for the
rifle. I slip across the hall to my father's room. Both sides of the bed have
been slept on, and this fact—the sheets and blanket pushed toward the
center of the bed into a single mound, an alarm clock on either side, and
her clothing folded neatly over the back of the bedside chair—somehow
hits me harder than seeing the two of them together.

I haven't thought about it for a long time—perhaps avoided thinking of it—but it comes again that I can't remember my father having a
single real date in all the years that passed between the time my mother
died and I left. The low, morning sunlight reaches across the hallway
from my old room into my father's room. There's a black-and-white
picture on his old dresser of the three of us, Daddy, Roy, and me, a long
time ago. There's also a much newer, color picture of Karen.

It never occurred to me in the old days to think that my father would
do anything but live for Roy and me. That's all he'd ever done. If we had
ever seen him as a sexual creature, we stopped. He lived for other
people, for us, for the old people whose families were too busy to take
care of them. People would say to us, "Ain't many'd do what your daddy
does." And they were right.

There were parts of our father's character that he almost never let us
see. I used to think then that it was a way of saying that our mother's

death was something not to be taken lightly, something we were all to blame for, and that we all had to atone for. I wonder now as I stand in the empty hallway and look at his bedroom that if by closing off certain facets of his personality to us, he was denying them to himself.

I go back downstairs again and pour a cup of coffee, but I don't drink it. I just stare out the back window at the garden. After a moment or two, I pick up my cup of coffee and go sit on the back step. There is sunshine on the step. The backyard is neatly mown, and the early garden is entirely weedless. Beyond the lawn there is a fence that's overgrown with ivy, and then there are woods and the land begins to fall off again. If you stand at the fence in the winter you can see the backs of the houses on the street below, the house where I used to live.

*Stop it, Karen whispers and pushes away from me. She goes into the kitchen, and when she turns on the light I can see her there, her shorts and her blouse, the shape of her. Her hair reaches down to the middle of her back and has the look of plenty. Sometimes she pulls it around and leaves it mounded on her shoulder. It has the look of fertility—a woman carrying a sheaf of wheat on her shoulder. A gray cat rubs against her leg, and she reaches down and scoops him up, then holds him at her chest. He squints his eyes and pushes his nose close to her.*

*I go up behind her and put my hand on the small of her back. There's another cat sitting coiled in a chair at the kitchen table. "Come on, Jack, stop, I have to get these guys fed," she says, and I say to her that we should stay, that we should just stay the night.*

*I'm leaving soon, moving to Richmond, and even though we both know it, somehow it doesn't feel real to me.*

*With my thumb and forefinger, I take hold of the bottom front of her blouse and lift it. The cat is on the floor, and she has her hands on her hips now, and her head is cocked to the side with a forbearing look. The blouse comes up until the fabric binds in the back. I can see the bottom of her ribs. "Are you satisfied?" she says. I tell her no, not nearly. "You had better be," she says, and there's a finality to her tone that doesn't exist in her words.*

I'm on the back step, in the direct sunlight, when they come back. The coffee has begun to make the sunlight glassy and hard, and I can feel the distance now, the weariness.

I can hear them when they come into the house—the soft, comfortable, echoing sound of their voices. In the kitchen, my father comes to the back door and says, "Are you hungry?"

"Yeah," I say, quietly, turning, "yeah, I am."

His face is red and wet with perspiration. "Give us a minute to shower, and we'll all go out to breakfast."

"Go out?" I say.

"Yeah, they got a real good early bird breakfast deal at the new Big Boy," he says and claps his hands together cheerily. "You get there before ten o'clock on weekends, and the breakfasts are almost half price. Karen and I go nearly every weekend."

I stand up and look at him through the screen. He's taken off his windbreaker, and he wipes his hands on his T-shirt. He doesn't look at me but says, "You sure you're hungry, now?" teasingly.

"Yeah," I say. I'm glad the screen door is between us. Maybe he can't see the bewilderment on my face.

"Hey, if you want to freshen up, take a shower or anything—feel free to use the downstairs bathroom. There're clean towels in there." He's turning when he says it, and in a moment, he's heading up the stairs. Does that mean they're going to be showering together? "Pretty soon, you and me can run together," he says before he disappears.

I go back inside, and I can hear water running upstairs. I get my knapsack and go down the hall to the bathroom. I get undressed and get in the shower. In a minute I'm standing beneath the hard, hot spray of water.

"You still running?" Karen says when we're in the pickup. We're all squeezed together and she's in the middle. He's got a smaller one now than he used to have, and she has to watch her knees when he shifts gears. Her hair is still wet from the shower, as is mine.

"Oh, yeah," I say. I've got the window rolled down, and I don't look at either of them but at town as it slides past. "I was out of shape for a while, but slowly I'm getting back into it."

"Good," she says.

I nod. Unconsciously my hand wanders to the scar on my side. The wind blows in my face. "Doesn't look like much has changed," I say after a few minutes of silence.

At the Big Boy the waitress brings a thermos of coffee, and my father pours some for Karen—"Son?" he says to me.

"No thanks. I'll start climbing the walls if I have any more."

He nods, fills his own cup. The menu is a foot and a half tall. The pages are plastic covered, and it's bound in imitation leather like some important document. There are idealized pictures of omelets and pancakes, of steaks and eggs with cups of coffee. My father asks Karen what she's going to have, and she says she doesn't know, "What are you going to have?"

There's something about Karen that is completely different from how it was when I used to know her. When the waitress comes back, everyone orders eggs. I sit back against the soft, orange plastic cushion of the booth and close my eyes for a moment. I wish I could go to sleep.

"Is the diner still in town?" I say and force my eyes open.

"Naw. Closed a few months ago. It's a Pizza Hut now."

"Oh, yeah, I saw that. I couldn't remember what had been there. It was the diner."

"Yeah," Karen says.

I look at her. I want to look at her for a long time—sort out the things that are going through my mind, but she sees me looking and probably misunderstands.

"Got anybody working for you these days?" I ask my father.

"Kid named Terry. Just finished with high school. Another kid named David sometimes. He's still in school, but he's got more of a natural bent toward wood and such than Terry. Terry's most interested in drinking and girls." This dismays him, and for the first time he looks the way he used to—smileless, always worried that the world around him and me in particular is going to hell.

"You still working at the law firm?" Karen says as the waitress is putting plates of eggs and sausage and hash browns in front of us.

"I left a long time ago," I say, one hand in my lap, the other holding my fork. I've been hesitant to say anything about my new work, and so I don't say anything.

"What are you doing now?"

"Not much, just some free-lancing stuff."

"What does that mean?" she says. It comes out with more irony than she intends. She has her fork in the air, and there is hashbrown on it, shiny with egg yolk.

"You don't need to press him, maybe he doesn't want to talk about it." My father says it lightly, sweetly, and I'm surprised by the way she looks at him, like he's just knocked her down.

"It wasn't an inquisition," she starts.

"It's nothing," I say. "I've been doing some woodworking stuff— shelves and a little remodeling."

My father puts down his fork, takes off his glasses, and rubs his eyes. I don't know if he's reacting to me or to Karen.

"When I left Richmond, I bummed around a little bit, had some money saved. People found out I knew how to do things, and started asking me to do stuff—painting, you know."

My father puts his glasses back on and starts in on his food. Karen looks at me, then starts in on her food. A hugely fat man in shorts with remarkably white legs wades slowly past us and sits at a booth next to the far window. I watch him for a moment but turn to my food when he looks our way. I wish I weren't so tired.

When we get home, Karen changes and goes in to work. "Sorry, but I have a million things to get done before Monday morning." My father is on the porch when she leaves, and she kisses him fast on the side of the mouth before she heads for her car. He watches her as she goes down the front sidewalk and gets into her car. I watch her too—the shape of her, the stab of her heels into the walk—and I watch him, his jeans and button-down short-sleeved shirt, his glasses and baseball cap. I turn away before he can come in and see that I've been watching.

When he does come in, I'm in the kitchen, dazed by the sunlight and where I am. "I think I'm going to take a nap, Dad, if you don't mind."

"Go ahead," he says. "There's clean sheets in both your room and Roy's room." Then he just stands there a moment looking at me, his hands in his pockets. "It really is good to see you, Jack." His eyes are clear and unblinking, and everything about him seems solid, sensible.

"I'm—it's good to see you, too." I turn, then look back again, "I'll take Roy's room, if that's okay." I'd rather have Roy's old room since it's downstairs and not right across from his.

"It's fine."

"Okay," I say and for a moment stand where I am before shrugging and turning away.

When he comes off the porch, Jack is in the kitchen, and there is a moment in the kitchen when Jack hasn't seen him yet, when he hasn't looked up, but instead looks out through the back window, and the look on Jack's face—or rather the *look* of Jack's face—hits him with a great flood of memory, not only of Jack but of the others too.

Though he hasn't exactly forgotten what Jack looks like in the time he was gone, there is a certain kind of surprise to seeing him again—whatever might have faded in his mind about his son's appearance, his mannerisms, is now bright and vivid.

And then Jack turns and stands up and says that he is tired, wants to take a nap, but Addie can't say anything, not at first. He's been thinking about Roy, and about how you can find yourself in a place in time, and though you know exactly how you've got there, it seems utterly a mystery how you could have come so far and so long.

"I'm glad you're here," Addie says.

"Me too," Jack says, but there is the echo of unreality to all of it.


You have to hold my hand when we cross the street," Addie says. Jack is two and a half, three maybe. They're in the middle of a block on State Street, and Jack shakes his hand loose from Addie's and runs out ahead.

"No, no, no," he says, his pants made huge by the diaper, his legs wobbly, stubborn.

"Come back here, Son," Addie says firmly, sternly. He hasn't the patience to deal with this at the moment. The boy turns and looks at him—he's still walking as he does, and turning makes him veer sideways. The expression on Jack's face is one that puzzles his father. Not defiance, not hate or stubbornness, but pure *something*: will, self. *It's what I should have named him, Will.*

In a few quick steps he has caught the boy from behind, and he grabs him beneath the arms, hoists him up. Jack struggles, but Addie has him firmly, then tosses him up so that he rotates half a turn. The tossing, the midairness of his condition, makes the boy freeze—he is dependent upon his father to catch him. Addie sees this in the moment before the boy falls into his hands again, strains his arms.

"What is it with you?" he says. "Why can't you be cooperative?" Jack's face is blotched with the red of exertion, and there's a scaling of dried mucus on his upper lip, a bulb of glistening mucus on his nose. Addie can smell the child-smell of him—baby perspiration, the diaper smell of a child—and while he wants to be angry with his son, with the frustrations that have accumulated in the day, he is not angry. Right

now the spectacular thing would be a straight, sensible, incisive answer to his questions.

But of course it's the thing you never get. Standing over both of his sons in their cribs after their births, he has talked to them, told them about the universe, about everything he thinks important. With the idea that maybe these things will make a difference some time—arise out of their subconscious lives to guide them.

"Down," Jack says. "Now." Pure something. Self, will.

She calls early in the afternoon when I'm sitting in the kitchen. The hollow ringing of the telephone surprises me because she's gone and my father's gone and I'm alone in the house. My body has softened with sleep, with weariness. The kitchen floor is hard beneath my feet.

"I thought maybe you'd like to go to the movies tonight. Just you and me." Her voice sounds different over the phone, and for a moment it feels like I should know who I'm talking to.

"What about—"

"Don't worry about your father. It was his idea that we get together, you know, and well, you know."

"Sure, okay," I say. "I was going to go out to visit some people, but I can put that off."

"Good," she says, but the sound of her voice says that she expected me to turn her down. "There's a show at 6:30. I'll come—I guess I'll pick you up around six or so."

I tell her that's fine, and when I hang up the phone, I go outside and wander around the neighborhood.

She's not dressed in her work clothes when she comes to pick me up, but in jeans and a white blouse and a blue blazer. So they're not living together exclusively. She has her own place.

She carries her purse in her hand in the tight, formal manner of a woman on her way to her first black-tie dinner. She goes into the house, then out the back door to the shop to see my father. Her car is old but maniacally clean. The black seat squeaks when I get inside and sit down. The interior smells of Windex and vinyl restorer. It occurs to me now that she was always the neatest person I knew—whenever I went to her house, her bedroom always looked like a museum, like no one slept there or studied there or relaxed there. Just like my father when it came to his work. "There's a new triplex movie theater out on the strip, but I still prefer the one in town," she says when she gets into the car. I'm still a little foggy from sleeping during the day, and everything she says feels formal, peculiar.

I nod.

She doesn't say anything more. I'm glad the ride is a short one. I just look out the window at the streets as they go past.

It's early, and we qualify for the discount price. She's businesslike when she buys tickets—"No, I asked you, I'll pay"—like this is not an event for pleasure but something obligatory.

She gets popcorn and a Coke, and we share them. She sits with her knees up on the back of the chair in front of her. Because it's early we're nearly the only ones in the theater.

It's Christmas break, early January. I've finished college and am working for my father. Karen's out of school for the break and isn't working tomorrow. When we come out of the movie theater, there is snow on the ground. "Look," she says as we are coming out, still in the angled, carpeted lobby before the glass doors. There are people here and there on the street, and the snow is coming heavily; it's like coming out of the darkness to a whole different world.

"Do you want to go home?" I ask.

"No," she says and takes my hand. "We could walk or maybe go for a drive."

We go through the theater doors, and the snow has taken the sound from the air. A few steps down the square, we could be a mile away from the theater. She's wearing a knit cap, and her hair falls down her shoulders, across the back of her ski jacket. She has a skirt on, and black stockings, and snow sticks to them now and again, and stands out brilliantly. There is snow in my hair already, snow all over my shoulders. The lights around the square have cones of white around them.

We walk down the block, Karen close to me. "God it's pretty," she says. I don't say anything. Suddenly I'm nervous with her. She stops and turns to me. "Maybe we should go back to the car. I'm getting cold."

I nod and turn. My car's all the way across the square.

I open the door for her. Snow sticks to the windows even when I brush it off. I go around the car, kick the snow off my shoes as best I can, but there are already new flakes on the seat and floor when I climb in. Snow is thick on the windshield. "We should just sit here and let it pile up on top of us," I say.

"I don't know if they were even calling for it. Who knows how long it will last." She doesn't exactly look at me, but straight ahead.

I reach over and kiss her cheek. It's pale and soft, and she turns a little, kisses me back, on the mouth. "You look so pretty." My face is still close to hers when I say it.

"So do you," she says. "You look pretty."

"You're not supposed to say that. I'm a guy. You're not supposed to say that."

"Even if it's true?"

"It's not true," I say and move back from her, point at my face. "This is not a pretty picture."

She laughs a little. The snow makes it warm in the car, and I lean toward her again. Her jacket is open, and I push my hands inside it. She's wearing a sweater, and it's soft beneath my hands—the good, dense breast softness. Sometimes in winter she doesn't wear a bra but wears a camisole and two or three other layers. I tug at the sweater, lift it up. My face is close to hers. The skin is soft.

She sighs, and her hands are no longer touching me. I want nothing more than to touch her, but I take my hands away, because the sigh gives me a mental picture of me in a car on the bald side of an empty planet, my hands inside the shirt of a woman who is staring straight up into the air with the rolled-back eyes of detached forbearance.

"I'm sorry," I say.

"You're just so undependable, Jack. I mean not you, but it. This. If we were both in the same place—if you were still in school and we were together. But I don't know if even then."


It's dark when we get out of the theater, and the evening is warm. "Do you want to go get a drink or something?" she says.

"I guess. Sure. What did you have in mind?"

She shrugs. "The Ranchero or something, you know. A beer or something." She has her hands in the pockets of her blazer, and she swings her head to point across the square.

"Okay."

We go across the grassy square, and I tell her about getting into town this morning and sleeping on a bench. It seems like longer ago than just the morning.

"Why didn't you just come up to the house and knock?" she says. It almost sounds like her sense of humor is coming back.

"I didn't want to freak anybody out or get shot or something. My dad and I don't talk that much—you know how much we talk—and as far as I knew he might have moved across town." As soon as I've said it, I wonder if "my dad" had a proprietary sound to it.

"Doesn't sound very comfortable," she says. Her head is angled forward, and she looks at the ground as she walks.

"I've probably slept in worse places."

She gets a gin and tonic and takes a long pull from it before she sets it back down on the cocktail napkin. The Ranchero's been remodeled again, and now it seems as common and indistinct as the Big Boy where we had breakfast.

I get a bottle of Pilsner Urquell and admire the tight fizz of it sparkling in my mouth. I don't know what to say. I haven't known what to say from the moment she stepped around from behind my father.

Behind the bar is a tall, square-jawed guy I feel like I ought to know but don't. The place is nearly empty.

Karen takes the plastic stirrer out of her glass and bends it between her fingers, evidently wanting to see how much it can flex without snapping. "Jack," she starts, flicks her eyes up at me, then back to the stirrer, "when I saw you this morning standing on the porch of Addie's house, I almost flipped."

"I don't know if I want to hear any explanations."

"Stop it. I'm certainly not going to make excuses or try somehow to circum—"

"No, I just—" I like her indignation.

"I think back before you left I was already starting to fall, you know, fall for your father." She pushes the last words out as if afraid if she doesn't hurry them they'll linger and fail.

"Karen."

"I used to look at him and think—I mean it was all my doing, most of it. I was the one who went after—I mean if someone is to blame for going after someone else, then I'm the one who went after him. I used to look at him and think that, well, what I had going on inside me was just some kind of thing, you know, like a kid getting a crush on a teacher or something." She lifts her glass into the air and squeezes it a moment before drinking from it. The light looks marvelous in the transparent liquid, the refractant ice. She looks everywhere but at me. "And I even went to the library to get books that would help me try to understand the kind of thing I was feeling. I'd sort of run into him now and again, and it would have this charge to it. I mean my seeing him. It would just you know bang or something, and there would be extra light. And then one night I nearly killed him." She sees my reaction and speeds up. "I was out driving. I kept trying to figure this thing out, because it had gone on for a while and nothing had happened. I wanted something to happen. I ached for something to happen. I'd go and drive by the house, sometimes stop in, say hello. Your father was always so respectful and kept such a distance, and I felt like a harlot or something, like a lunatic, really, and so I used to drive a lot. Go out into the country, and it felt good just to drive and hear the motor and see the road—it felt like you could think, which is what I was trying to do. Except most of the time what I was doing was dreaming about him, you know. I mean I know about everything, I know what kind of a man he always was . . . Anyway I was driving back into town, and your father was out driving too. I guess I was going too fast or wasn't paying very close attention, I mean it was like I was asleep and suddenly I woke up, and there was this pickup and it just went skidding and flying." Then she stops.

"I—," I start, but I stop, without looking at her I lift the glass ashtray and put it down again. When I left Hadleysburg, I was so involved with what I was doing that toward the end I hardly thought about her. When I was living in Richmond and then in Middleridge—I almost completely forgot about her until I phoned that morning from the McDonalds. And then with everything else, I had to forget about her again. Now suddenly I am remembering everything—the failure of my relationship with her, my own complete incapacity to go beyond a certain point in any kind of affection. There was no logic to it, only a useless, savage kind of selfishness. My old selfishness, what I have thought I've begun to give up with Sandy.

"And then I forced it. The night I almost killed him I got drunk, and I kept thinking about him standing in the ditch with his truck, how it was my fault, and how easily I could have killed him. I mean I guess you know this kind of stuff—that is you know how tentative life can be. I saw it then." She drinks from her glass. "And I knew I was either going to have to act on it or keep it to myself, and I knew I would burst if I kept it to myself."

She looks down into her glass—the bluishness of the tonic water. I want to put up my hands and tell her to stop.

"I'm sorry you had to find out this way. I kept after your father to tell you, but we didn't have any idea where the hell you were. Your opinion makes a great deal of difference to your father, and I think he has been terrified that you wouldn't approve, and that without your approval he couldn't approve himself."

This surprises me. I have always had the child's idea that nothing I ever said or thought made a difference to my father. The way she says "your father" has a vivid, stepmother sound to it, and it makes me uncomfortable. I wish I could be alone to try to digest some of this mountain of surprise.

"You called one day, didn't you, and I answered the phone."

"Yeah. I was between places. I was between lives, really, or almost."

"You say that so gravely. What have you been doing? I mean that crap at breakfast about free-lancing doesn't really wash. You look so different, so much older." She reaches out across the table and flips the hair at my temple. "And you're starting to get some gray."

Now her hand is gone. My own hand comes up in front of my face, and my finger rubs at the hollow space next to my eye on the bridge of my nose. "Have you ever been to Middleridge?"

She shakes her head. "Virginia?"

"Yeah. I've been living there since I left Richmond. Don't ask me why. Really. I just needed to sort things out." Right now all of it seems to me overwhelmingly absurd, and I cannot explain it and do not try.

There's silence for a while, and she doesn't chase after me. I finish my beer and think about getting a new one.

"It's just so funny," she says after a while. "If one of my friends had a man who was in his early fifties interested in her, or she was interested in him, I think I'd probably tell her it was an awful idea, that she was a fool." She reaches across the table and taps a finger against the back of my hand so that I will look at her. "But the thing is I am in love." It hurts to look at her so directly. "I have never felt the same way about another man."

I am too, and it is the hardest thing I have ever done.

. . .

The drive back home is smooth and silent, and when I think about the movie, it amazes me that it was tonight and not some night weeks ago.

We sit in the kitchen for a while, the three of us, and make small talk—about work, about tools. I agree to go with my father on a job on Monday. Tomorrow I'm going to go around and visit some of the people I used to hang around with in the old days. My father says nothing at all about my birthday being this week, and I wonder if he's forgotten. It seems to me bizarre that I can remember all my birthdays with the clarity and precision of a photograph album.

I call Sandy in the early evening, and when she answers the phone I am nervous as a schoolboy calling to ask for a date for the first time. "How ya doin', kid?" I say.

"I been wonderin' when you'd call."

"Wonder no longer."

"How is it?"

"I don't know where to begin—and I can't really do it now. I may have to wait until I get back."

"When's that gonna be?"

"You miss me?"

"*You* miss me?"

"God, I can't tell you how much."

"Well, I don't miss you," she says.

"I was just saying I did to make you feel good."

"You wanna make me feel good, you're gonna have to come here and do it in person."

"I will. Maybe a week. No longer."

I get in bed early, partly because I sense that the two of them want to be alone, and partly because I'm increasingly uncomfortable with them. I get undressed, tug a couple of magazines out of my knapsack, then lie in bed and read. I can hear them talking in the kitchen, can hear the soft radiation of their voices through the walls. I can't understand what they're saying, but it reminds me of the old old days, when my mother was still alive, when she and my father would sit in the kitchen late, talk, have a drink. Later on, when she had gone, Roy tried to replace her for my father. He would make me go to bed, then sit and talk to him, try to pull him out of the shelter he built around himself.

It surprises me how it feels to hear them talking, how natural and comfortable it seems. And then I think about lying in bed with Sandy and talking with her, and suddenly it hits me like it's never hit me. It nearly makes me want to cry, the world can be such a beautiful and painful place.

I don't know when it is—some time out of real time, some deep time— that I hear the shower start up. Between my brother's old room and the kitchen, there is the downstairs bathroom where I showered earlier, and now the shower is on. I can hear the regular pattern of water against the tiled wall and then, in a moment, the small sound of a woman softly singing.

Karen?

In a minute I'm out of bed, naked, and in the hallway. The house is light as daylight, but the light has a blue cast. The bathroom door is open a slice, and a spline of yellow light lays across the carpet. I push the door open and come in. The air is damp against my skin, and the singing is louder. I get closer to the curtain, then push it aside. Karen turns and smiles, and I am watching the water go over the curves of her, the way the light and the water make her skin gleam. I reach out, and she is soft. She is still singing when I pull her next to me. Sandy.

# FLIGHT

It's night, the window's open, the stairs are creaking, and my brother is breathing the deep-breath breathing he does when he's asleep. I can hear him all the way through the house. But the stairs are creaking, and every time I close my eyes the stairs creak more, and I can see my mother in her blue skirt, the scuffed bottoms of her shoes, the high points of her heels, and so I have to open my eyes again and look at the ceiling, look at the clowns on the drapes and try to ignore the sounds in the house. The clowns move, and the light seeps through them. They sway, and in the darkness maybe the clowns are breathing. *Move*, a voice in the back of my mind says, and I can see the fine pattern of the cloth. *Move*, the voice says, *pee*, and now the place in my crotch where the heat comes burns so badly that I have to get out of bed. The sounds say *Pee, Pee*, and I have to listen.

In the bathroom the sound of water in the bowl drowns out everything, and then the sound of flushing, and the green-gray sound of water rushing in the pipes, and when I turn out the lights again everything is a hundred times blacker than before and the black flattens, moves like the breeze. I can see my father, the day of it, the day of the thing my mother did, I can see him two months ago, fury and gray distress, flying around the house, talking fast fast fast, pushing us outside after the people had gone, taking us, coarse hands at the back of our necks, the rocky blue-green lawn stumbling beneath us, to Mrs. Crouty's. Now I can feel the texture of Mrs. Crouty's dress against the back of my neck, the back of my arms—and my father, with the wheelbarrow full of paper and clothes and things slamming through the back door, the back door exploding on its hinges. He dumps them in the barrel we use to burn the trash, piles them in, and sprays barbecue lighter on them—now the flame is jumping, and the sound of the flame saying *Why? Why?* and in the background Mr. Crouty. It's all weightless. All of it.

And then it's two nights later, and we are sitting on the living room couch, Roy and me, dressed up to go to some kind of church service they are having for her. But my father is not going to go. Our hair is combed with Vitalis. We are wearing ties, and my father is not going to go. He is in the kitchen, going back and forth, trying to make us supper before having to send us off, and I watch him. All afternoon we have begged him to go, or begged him not to send us alone. *"Someone's got to represent the family,"* he said in the same voice she used when she handed us our lunch bags.

"Are you going to be here when we get back?" I say, but the words don't come out.

I go back out into the hallway because there are noises and everything is lighter because my eyes are used to it. I go downstairs to my brother's room—I have to go through the living room and there is no one hanging—and I look at him in bed, his mouth open and his eyes with the smooth nearly seamless shutness of deep deep sleep, his breath going *Secret, Secret,* long slow and smooth, and then the stairs pass away beneath me and the carpet leads back upstairs to my father's room.

The door is ajar and I slip through the crack, and inside the dark is blacker than elsewhere, and there's the smell of Old Spice and old cigarettes—*his smell*—and I go up to the corner of the bed—*it's blind*—and I have beneath my hand the coarse but soft cotton bedspread with its circular patterns, and he is not there.

It punches me backward, and I gasp—panic, panic, exhilaration. There is no gravity, and the taste of salt is in my mouth, and the thing I've known was going to happen has happened and I am starting to float, the bead-knurled bedspread in my hand, the room full of air. She is climbing, she is climbing out of the bed and pushing back the sheets as she does, and I am floating. The window's open and the breeze is taking me, and she's on the bed, raveling on stockings—the stockings unrolling after the pressure of her toes and fingers. I shout out to her but she won't float, and the windows are open, and I'm holding onto the bedspread, and the hammer bleeds in my father's hand.

Her things are gone. The dresser is empty. Her pictures are gone. If you try hard, you can still smell the smoke.

"Jack," my father says, and his voice is as huge and distant as the moon. His huge hands pluck me out of the air, and his face peers into my face. "What is it, Son?" he says, and I turn and I turn and I turn, and his legs are in front of me soft and strong and hairy and hated. *What did you do to her?*

I don't realize I'm crying at first until his hands come down and lock beneath my arms and lift. The world shrinks. "You're crying" is what he says.

"I thought you were gone," I say, but at the same time meaning something entirely different.

# JOB

Monday morning I'm leaning against the tailgate of my father's pickup, which is backed around beside the house. I'm drinking black coffee and listening to the wild disarray of the morning insects. He's remodeling a kitchen across town, and he has made all of the cabinets and the countertop, and now has to fit them all in. He brings out the tools first. I watch. It's 7:30, and the sun is up, and the air is cool and damp. He puts the toolbox into the back of the truck, then brings out a skilsaw, a drill, and a jigsaw. "You want to put down that tailgate and give me a hand?" he says when the other tools are in the truck. I nod, wrench the squealing tailgate down, then follow him back into the shop.

"I've been thinking about tearing out one wall and putting up a half-garage door in the shop," he says. "Make it a lot easier to get big things in and out." He would of course have no way of knowing about my dream last night, but it is bright and foolish in my head. I come home and have a wet dream—*there's* something to tell the grandkids.

The cabinets are up on sawhorses. They're plywood with a wood-grained formica laminate. The shop smells like paint and contact cement. He's done a beautiful job with them, and I say so.

"I'm kind of pleased with them" is all he says before he takes one end and waits for me to take the other. We go toward the door.

"We'll take the cabinets first," he says when we have this section in the truck, "get them up, then take out the old countertop, and bring it back here and use it for a template to cut the sink out of the new one. That way we'll only have to do some trimming there." I nod.

The pickup is cold and the seats are stiff with morning when we get in. I laugh a little, because the ashtray, which in the old days would have been stuffed full of Winston butts, now is full of sugarless peppermint gum wrappers. We're silent for the drive across town.

He's already taken the old cabinets out, and they sit on the curb in garbage cans, flattened, waiting to be hauled away. He swings into the driveway of the Camerons' house, then turns the truck around, backs it up their drive.

Even though it's a simple job, it takes until early afternoon to hang the new cabinets, disconnect the plumbing, and rip out the old counter-top. We put the sink portion in the truck, then go back home for lunch. We don't talk much while we're working, but then we never have. I like working with him for the first time in my life, and I admire how logical he is, how his experience makes things fall into place. But at the same time, I wonder what it is that makes me like working with him now that wouldn't allow it before.

Working has begun to make things a little softer, looser between us. Maybe it's because of Karen, but it seems to resist the old patterns. We're friends now, co-workers. Maybe I tolerate better what I used to be unable to tolerate.

He stands in the kitchen with his back to me and makes sandwiches for the two of us. I'm sitting at the kitchen table, wildly hungry, and he has a plastic-wrapped loaf of wheat bread next to him, four slices laid out on the cutting board. He spreads them with mayonnaise, then opens one paper-wrapped package of Swiss cheese and one of ham, and peels the slices back, lays them on the bread.

He talks about the job. "Nice to work with somebody who knows what he's doing as well as you do," he says.

I get up. "I've got to wash my hands," I say and disappear into the bathroom for a moment. When I come back, he's got the sandwiches on plates, on the table with a bowl of fruit, and is pouring us both glasses of milk. We sit down together to eat, and for the first time since I came into town, I'm truly glad I came. There's more silence between us, but there's always been silence between us. You don't always have to talk.

I eat the sandwich, the banana, an apple, and drink a couple glasses of milk. When he's finished, he says he has to rip a new cleat—a piece of wood that will run along the wall, underneath the back of the countertop. "When you're ready, we'll cut the sink out."

I nod. He starts to roll up the sleeves to his flannel shirt. I get up as he goes out the back door. I tell him I'll be with him as soon as I go to the bathroom.


Behind him the back screen door sinks closed on its pneumatic arm. Sunlight sprawls across the backyard, and he thinks to himself that he'll have to get out and get some more work done in the garden. There's a breeze now, and he pushes up his sleeves and the air is soft on his arms. Then he is in the shop. There's more room now that the cabinets are gone. He moves the sawhorses, stacks them back beyond the radial arm saw. Along the back wall there's a rack he has built to carry scrap wood, and he goes to it, rifles it, and comes up with the longest piece of one-by-six he can find. It's about six and a half feet long, which is just about right. He checks the warpage of it, then leans it against the saw table.

He sets up the radial arm saw to rip the piece of wood in half—takes a couple of measurements, then draws the blade carriage out, swings it around, measures, and locks it in place. He pops the switch once to make the blade move, then, with the up/down crank at the top of the upright bar from which the radial arm swings, lowers the blade carriage so the tines of the blade sing when they dip down into the saw table. He presses his fingers to the side of the saw blade to stop it, then, with a whisk broom, sweeps the old sawdust off the table surface so that the piece of wood will move evenly and smoothly through.

He flicks the switch again, and as he goes to the end of the table, he pushes up his sleeves again and listens as the blade starts to move, starts to speed up.

He's thinking about Jack when he lifts the tail end of the one-by-six and starts to push it through the saw. He's glad that the two of them are working together again, even if it's only for a short time. In his head he can see the almost telepathic way they communicate—Jack hands him a hammer or a chisel, almost before the idea that he should be using it has congealed in his mind—and it pleases him, makes him think that maybe there is something between them he has never really fathomed.

The board is halfway through. The two ends of it veer apart and tremble with the movement, the vibration of the saw. The vibration makes his sleeve jiggle down his arm. When he gets close to the end— he's holding the wood against the table to keep it from flopping upward—he takes a look around for the old piece of broom handle he uses to push a ripped board the last few inches through the saw, but it's nowhere in sight. *There it is*, across the room, on the floor. He thinks about trying to grab it, even starts to bend over and go for it, then thinks the better of it—it'd be more foolish, probably, than just pushing the wood through with his fingers.

So he moves toward the front of the saw and keeps his thumb hard on the last couple of inches of board, slides around a little more, and takes the focus of his eyes off the blade for a moment and starts to reach around with the other hand to catch the wood as it comes through.

It is now that it happens. He's thinking about Jack, kneeling next to him in the Camerons' house, unsweating the old plumbing, pulling the sink out of the old counter.


I'm in the bathroom when I hear the saw go on. I've forgotten what it sounds like from a distance—the hum of it, the blank space, and then the deeper sound as the blade dips down into the piece of wood. There's a quality to it—for as long as I can remember, that sound was a part of my life.

I finish up in the bathroom and go back into the kitchen. The saw's a little bit louder because the kitchen is closer to the shop. I take the lunch plates off the table and put them in the sink, run water in them. When I shut off the water the saw sounds funny. I can't tell if it's off or on. It sends a wire of worry through me. No. I shouldn't worry. I start to get another glass of milk, but then there's the howl. Like a dog hit by a car. High pitched and abject—then lower. *"Jack."* For a moment I'm convinced I've imagined it—the combination of worry and apprehension from being here. But then it comes again, and I slap the glass I'm holding down on the counter and slam through the thick air of the kitchen, past the table, past the pushed-out chair where my father sat a few minutes ago, struggle a moment with the storm door latch, then burst out, down the steps and across the concrete walk between the kitchen and the shop. The concrete is brilliant white in the sun, and the shadow of the roof's edge is sharp, angled. The door of the shop is ajar and I knock it open, and for a moment I get a wide, nearly panoramic view of his shop. There's something about seeing it this way—having not set foot in it for two years and now doing so under the rush of adrenaline—that brings it all into sharp definition. Everything is angular, everything is precise and perfectly fitted with my father's obsession for the perfect physical mesh between things. The neat shelves of tools and hardware, the jars of nails and screws and nuts and bolts— neat as a hardware store but all finely dusted with a powder of sawdust. And then the saw, next to it a masonite and knotty pine box full of tossed wood scraps, and beyond it, the shop-vac with its knurled snaking tube hooked up to suck away spraying sawdust from the back of the saw. And there's my father, at the center of it, blood everywhere, the bare twin fluorescent tubes overhead giving everything a mercury color, making his blood look purple, making his blanched face look sick and yellowish.

I don't even feel my feet against the floor. I'm next to him, and he's talking softly, saying what to do, but I can't really listen because the blood in my ears is strong, and the skin of his arm is torn. One hand on the saw table, I press close to him, reach up and turn the crank at the top of the radial arm. He groans, staggers, but holds himself up.

His arm is torn badly, and you can see the way he looks at it, he's sure it must belong to someone else, like he himself couldn't possibly have made a mistake like this. It makes me almost sick to look at it—I can feel the pain in my own arms, the food I have just eaten climbing at the back of my throat. He says the word "tourniquet," and I am looking around, trying to find something, a rag, a rope, clean enough to put against him. But I can't. In a moment I'm yanking my shirt off my shoulders and tearing a strip from it. "Come on, Daddy, hold on," I say, and I'm shaking as I pull back the sodden cloth from the place the saw bit into his arm. The skin is splayed, ragged, and blood pulse-oozes from it. There is a loose chunk of meat here and there. I wrap the strip of cloth around his arm, just below the elbow, then wrap it again and twist it tight. He mutters and grits his teeth. "Are you just showing off for me, Daddy?" I say, meaning it to be funny, but he doesn't seem to hear me. I rip my shirt again, take more of it, and this time wrap it right around the wound. I've got blood on my chest, and it smears.

"I'm going to call an ambulance," I say to him. "I'm going to take you outside and then run inside to call you an ambulance." I can't tell whether he's paying attention. He's mumbling, has sort of a smile on his face.

I put his good arm over my shoulder with the idea of walking him through the opened shop door, but he feels loose, disjointed, so I put one arm around the back of him, then with the other arm scoop the legs out from under him. He's heavy as hell, hard and dense. I swing him through the door, and we are in sunlight now. I squint, and his eyes are dilated. He's still got on the CAT baseball cap he was wearing earlier, and I'm sure he's in shock. I put him next to the house, in the dry grass, face in the shade, legs in the sun. It takes two steps to get indoors; the door slams and bounces. When I get off the phone, I hurry back outside with a blanket and put it over him—it's what they always taught us in school first aid to do when someone is in shock.


The blade grabs the loose, unbuttoned cuff of his shirt and catches it up against the end of the board, then yanks his arm hard up into the blade. It all happens fast—maybe half a second between the time he feels the yank at his sleeve and the hard *stomp* clamp of the blade as it nails his forearm to the saw table, and the time in which he hears the *chunk* of the saw binding in the loose folds of his shirt and shifts his gaze from the flopping ends of the boards to the place where the blade has stopped and pinned his arm to the saw table. The saw whines and strains. The fabric of the shirt creaks with the tension. In the split second following the first one, he can see the configuration of what's happened. Can see it from far above, and it puts the metal flavor of regret in his mouth. There's no pain yet, just a split second of general awareness that he's in real trouble, that the next few decisions he makes are going to have repercussions probably through the rest of his life.

He howls just as the pain hits, and it slams against his arm like the whole thing's been dipped in pure fire. There's blood on the table now, and he reaches up, his eyes full of tears, full of the red sound of his pain, and slaps the red switch that shuts the saw off. The saw stops and he tries to lean forward over his arm to reach the up/down crank at the end of the radial arm, but he can't reach it. The movement sends another gust of flame through his arm. Only seconds have passed but he's bleeding furiously, and now there is blood flat out on the table, filling the flat, narrow dish shapes where the curve of the saw blade has dipped into the table. It's dripping off the edge into the sawdust. And for the first time in his life, it hits him that there is the distinct possibility he will die. Karen's at work. Who knows if Jack heard him? He shouts again, and he thinks he can hear noises off in the house, but other things are being noisy too. Things are coming. Ideas, pictures, sounds—things that haven't come in years. He can feel himself getting weak, but he tries not to think of the veins in his forearms. He's walking along a stream out in the country—he can smell the soil, he can smell the freshwater smell of the stream. He's about fifteen and got an over-under .410-gauge shotgun cradled in his arms, and he's hoping to get a turkey, except he doesn't really care. It's enough to be in the woods, to be walking. He hasn't been in the Navy yet, hasn't been to the Philippines and changed his life. But now, just thinking of it, he is there, at Subic, the fucking ships in the fucking water and the whores in the town, and it's all funny, it's just so funny that his life would want to rush before his eyes, just like they say. And then the door flaps on its hinges and sunlight boils into the room, and the sound calls him back from Asia. Addie. Daddy.

"Jesus Christ, what have you done to yourself?"

Then Jack's warm arms are around him, holding him. God, he's strong. The saw jerks a little and then raises up with Jack's cranking. He feels like going to sleep, and he shakes his head, says, "Jack, you gotta put a tourniquet on me."

"You're going to be okay, Daddy," he says, searching around the shop for something to tear, then rips off his own shirt and pulls it apart. Addie can see the squareness of his shoulders, the squareness of his chest. And then the scar rising ragged out of his trousers up his belly—where'd you get that scar? The sound of ripping cloth fills the air around him. Jack winces when he takes his arm and wraps the cloth tight around it to pinch off the flow of blood, then wraps the remainder of it around the place where the skin is ripped and the blood shows pink and wild. "I'm going to call an ambulance," he says. The sound of his voice is very close, very warm.

"We gotta get back to work," Addie says, drifting a little, the pain intense, making it difficult to balance himself, his thoughts.

Jack hoots. "Come on," he says, and Addie can tell that he's debating with himself whether to take the pickup or call the ambulance. Prescience, telepathy—it just comes to him. Jack's arms are around him, and now they lift him like he was a bird, a child, a small insignificant thing. In a moment he's outside, dizzy. Feels like throwing up. Can't

tell where his feet are, where his head is. Karen. Where the hell is Karen? *"The first time I ever saw her naked,"* he is saying to himself—and he has no idea whether he is saying it aloud—*"I was amazed by her. I don't see how as a man you could ever fail to be astounded by the sight of a young woman who has just undressed for the first time in front of you. How you could fail to find again that your life was changing. I guess there are a lot of kinds of people, people who are immune to things. We were in her apartment and it was dark, and we had started on the couch and then we were in her bedroom. I will remember this for the rest of my life. Her hair was thick, and her nipples were ham colored, and I tried to think of my life and where I had started and where I had come to, I tried to think of your mother—Jack? Jack?"*

*"No matter how egalitarian"* (Karen's word) *"you try to be with your children—your first child, well—you always remember the first moment you pick him up, and he is covered with soft blankets, and you can see the red pucker of his face—your face in his face—and you find yourself in this spot, this place in the world, and though you know exactly how you came to be here—you know the practical facts of it—you are still amazed that you are where you are and feel as though you have been thrown there."* Jack is next to him, his hand on Addie's shoulder, the earth indented slightly where he is kneeling. Addie is talking, but it may all be inside. *"I wanted to tell you,"* he says. *"I didn't want you to find out this way."*

The whoop is closer now and then though he cannot see it can feel the enormous white presence of the ambulance. The bandage is soaked through, and the tourniquet is wet too. *"I loved Roy. I didn't not love you. I still love you."* The men rush, and their faces are smooth and white, and Jack is next to him, talking, the stern shape of his words dark, sharp.

The grass of the yard where he is lying is dry and stiff, and in a moment he is being lifted. He can see the clouds, can see the blue of the sky. Jack really did call an ambulance. *I don't know that I ever rid in one before.*

The ambulance shocks me when it comes, how it rises, almost floats up the slow incline of the street, the square box back of it white and alive with lights. It comes like it's coming out of the back of my mind. I'm standing at the edge of the front yard when it sails up the street, the midday sunlight smashing against it, and for a moment, the panic of it sticks in my throat, hits me like a recurring nightmare carried into daylight.

I turn, look at Croutys' house. My skin is cold—shivered cold. It feels like there's someone next to me. I turn back toward the street, turn again. The white houses ride by in the water-thick atmosphere. I can feel the radiated warmth of another person's skin. *Roy* something deep in my head says.

"Back here," I say when the doors swing open and the two white-suited people jump out. I turn without really looking at them, without checking to see that they're following, and head around the pickup, to the back of the house where my father is lying. It's a man and a woman, both middle-aged. Somehow I expected them to be younger. I tell them what happened, suggest that maybe his arm is broken.

"You put the blanket on him?" the man says. He's taller than I am, has an oval-shaped face with very neat hair. His white suit—like a pair of coveralls—makes him look like an astronaut. There's no inflection in his voice, and I wonder if I've done something wrong.

"Yeah," I say.

He nods and doesn't say anything.

"Jack," my father says, his voice soft and distant, "we'd better get back to work. You just let me get myself straightened out here, and we'll get that job—"

"Bullet wound?" the man says to me, and it's only after a moment that I understand he's talking to me.

The woman is round faced. She puts a perfect-looking hand on his shoulder and urges him to lie down, to be quiet and relax. "We'll get you fixed up in no time, Mr. Pleasance," she says. I don't know how she knows his name.

I follow them to the hospital in the pickup after I've put on a new shirt. It's outside of town, nearly a half-hour drive toward Charlottesville. If you were dying, it'd be no closer than Mars. The roads are different, and I feel a little like I'm stumbling in space—surrounded by the big shape of the pickup. The hospital is big and white and new and plunked down in the middle of a mowed-down acre of forest.

I park off near the hot edge of woods, then hurry across the black pavement with its brilliant white new stripes, cross an island of concrete and unmown grass, then go into the emergency room, to the desk where a nurse is sitting.

"My father just came in in an ambulance," I said. "Cut his arm with a table saw."

"He's being seen to at this moment," she says. "I'd like to get some information from you so we can check him in."

"Can I see him?"

"I need some information from you."

"I don't know anything—I can give you his name and address, but I don't know about his medical insurance. I've been gone. I just came back this weekend, day before yesterday. I don't know much."

"We have to start somewhere."

"Karen's at lunch right now, can I have her get back to you?"

"It's kind of important—is she still in the office?"

"Who's calling?"

"This is Jack Pleasance, is she—"

"Jack, it's Denise Robertson. Remember? From eleventh grade?"

"Listen, Denise, I'm at the hospital, and I really need to talk to her if she's in."

"Yeah, she's in the lunchroom. Just a second." Denise Robertson. There's the rhythmic click-hum of HOLD, and I lean heavily against the pay phone and wait. There is the blood of my father on my chest and arms, and in my head a too brilliant image of him impaled on the saw table, then lain out and blanketed on the dry summer's grass. I know when I tell her she will hold me responsible, and I wish I could plan what I would say, but nothing will come. Already I am beginning to hold myself responsible for the foolish act of the most conscientious man I have ever known.

Beyond the pay phone there are floor-to-ceiling windows, and you can see the parking lot, the highway, the gleaming sunlight on multi-colored cars. Another ambulance swings into the place, lights out, then disappears around the building.

"Hi Jack, what's up?" Denise must not have told her where I am.

"Karen, I'm at the hospital." I don't wait out the silence. "Dad kind of chewed up his arm in the saw at home, and I guess they're sort of sewing him up or something right now."

There's a moment of silence, and I can hear conversation in the background at the savings and loan where she works. The silence has a hard sound to it. "Is he okay, Jack? What'd he do?"

"It's probably nothing," I say, knowing she can probably hear the sound of lying in my voice. "He sort—I guess he was ripping a piece of wood and got his sleeve caught."

"Jesus Christ, Jack, how could you let him?"

"Karen, I wasn't in the shop, I was in the house." I hate the defensive sound of my voice—hate it that she would accuse me this way.

"Did he cut it off?"

"No. I don't think he even broke the bone."

She doesn't say anything but hangs up. It takes all the self-control I've got to put the receiver back gently in its cradle. What I'd like to do is put my fist right through the phone.

# FILIAL DUTY

My father clouds out on Darvon or morphine—I know the look of it in his face. He is sitting up in the hospital bed where they will keep him for twenty-four hours of observation. I look at him and want to tell him what happened, about my own hospital stay, but it's not the time to do it.

His arm is wrapped to the shoulder, and he has a translucent, wan, unsteady look to him. He has aged ten years since the morning and wears a half grin that seems more an expression left on his face and forgotten by some long gone idea. A nurse bends over him for a moment, fixing the blanket on him, then lifting the bedside fences that will keep him from rolling off the adjustable bed. In a moment, she sweeps in front of me to the other side and fixes that one in place.

The other side of the room is occupied by a young man on an intravenous tube, but he has his curtain pulled around and reads in silence.

It's nearly dark now, and while Karen has been with him for the last couple of hours, I have been downstairs, making phone calls, letting people know that he has nearly cut his arm off. I wanted to do it—

wanted people to hear my voice, but still it was uncomfortable now and then. From the hospital room window, which is on the fourth floor, you can see a bare green field, woods, and then Route 29. The land is uneven, and on the highway you can see the silvery trace of headlights as they wind up and down through the maze of trees and growing darkness.

Karen is sitting in the chair at the foot of the bed, legs together, hair mussed from continually running her hand through it. She looks older too. When I look at her, she looks back at me, holds me in her gaze for a moment. The look is enigmatic. She blames me for this—for being here, for distracting him. She looks away, frowns. She's wearing a burgundy-colored dress with black crescent-shaped markings on it. She has her hands rested on the small flat space the dress makes between her knees. I can't help but look at her and wonder what is going on in her mind right now.

My father says, "It's so good to see you two together again." It comes out of nowhere and floats in the even, bright light of the room. Because of the morphine he is not here in this space in time, but in some other place. "You know it . . . ," he starts.

"Addie," Karen says firmly.

He looks up, lifts himself a little. His eyes look stunned, near tears. He's just penetrated his mistake and stares straight at Karen for some sign that he should not feel betrayed.

"I'm going to go on back home," I say, more to Karen than to him. "Things are a mess in the shop, and I can't even remember if I locked the doors."

Karen nods, weary, perturbed, but says nothing and doesn't look at me.

"Take care of yourself, Dad," I say, and then I slip out of the room. The last image of his waxy, falsely smiling face floats in my head as I go down the hall to find the elevator.

The blood is dried on the table, spotted on the floor, and I get a bucket of cold water, a bucket of hot water, and a bottle of ammonia and bring them into the shop. The overhead fluorescent lights flood the whole area with brilliant, humming light. I start with the tabletop and scrub at the blood with the cold water—I read somewhere you're supposed to use cold water to keep the blood from staining, but maybe that's just with washing clothes. He has a dusty radio above his workbench, and I turn it on, change the station to a classical station, then go back to scrubbing.

I have no idea how long it takes. It's the first time I've been in my father's shop alone for an extended period of time. When I was younger I simply would have refused. Now I am envious of this, and with the radio going, the door closed, the evening outside completely dark, I can nearly see how it is that he's survived all these years, how he's turned this place where there is no intrusion from the outside world into his own sanctuary, his own salvation. I remember times when I was growing up, when we'd sit in the house and think that he'd died in the shop, the only evidence of his not having done so was the occasional shir of one of his tools—the saw, the drill press, the lathe—and later he'd emerge with a dazed, almost drugged look. I always thought it was his aloofness, his lack of desire to deal with Roy and me, the rest of the world. Now I'm convinced he'd found a way to forget about everything else.

The blood makes me cringe because of the sadness of it. He would never do such a careless thing on his own.

When I get most of the blood up and the whole place smells of ammonia, I stop to do the sink hole in the countertop, as we had intended to do earlier. I measure the hole against the old countertop, mark it up, drill a pilot hole for the jigsaw blade to go in, then cut it along the line. The blade is sharp—sharper than the cheap one I bought months ago in Middleridge—and the cutting is like magic. When it's finished, I get out his shop-vac and go over the place. I turn off the vacuum now and then and listen for Karen's car or Karen in the house, but I hear nothing but the soft playing of the radio—which doesn't mean that she hasn't returned. I know she'll return; it seems as much her house now as his.

I vacuum up all the sawdust I can find. I go through the whole place top to bottom—dust off the old paint and polyurethane cans, the glass jars and old coffee cans full of nails and nuts and bolts. I dust off the shelves, I vacuum in the corners. I can't seem to stop myself, and I can't seem to bring myself to go back inside.

It is never dark, and even the parts of himself that he can feel have a distance to them. Everything is at remove. It's not that the pain isn't there, it's just that it is so far off and takes so long to arrive, it becomes easy to break down into the constituents of its meaning. You can feel the pulse of it, the distant movement, how it comes like an electronic signal, but muffled by time.

Now and then there are people in the room. They walk the way dreams walk, gliding, floating. Some of the gliders dream their own dreams—dreams that spin out into form. "Hello, Addie," goes one dream. And there is the dream of his living son. "Hey, Dad, you look pretty good compared to earlier."

He stands with Karen, who has a darker look on her face than Jack's, and Addie knows that he is adrift in time. It's difficult to tell where things are, where things go. *Where'd you get that scar?*

There is Jack and Karen walking in sunlight, near the house, and then there is Karen in his house, talking over a steaming cup of coffee, some early winter morning when it is barely light outdoors. He's happy to have them here, both of them, and he dreams that the three of them are together at the Ranchero again—or perhaps they already are. It floats in and out of the present, all of it unattainable. And then he can feel the heat of Karen's face. Loneliness. Separation. He's alone again. The young man who shares the room snores softly.

It's nearly midnight when I come back into the house. I come through the kitchen door, surprised at myself for having spent so long out of the reach of time, surprised when I step up the concrete step and pull open the door that I can feel him in my bones, in my vision.

The light is on in the living room when I come through the kitchen door, and Karen is sitting on the couch, in a white bathrobe, and the folds of it are pushed down between her knees. Her knees and calves look sleek, but I try not to look at them.

"How—how long are they going to keep him?" I know the answer, but conversation has to begin somewhere.

She doesn't look at me, doesn't appear even to have heard me. Then she turns, looks up, dark-eyed, drawn, "Tonight, maybe tomorrow night, just to make sure he's not in too bad shape."

"He's not. He's pretty resilient."

She frowns. I'm afraid she'll say, "How do *you* know?" but she doesn't. She just looks at her knees.

I want to tell her what happened, I want to explain that I wasn't in the shop when it happened, that I had nothing to do with it, but I don't know why I'm so anxious to be exonerated. I keep my mouth shut. She

doesn't seem to want to talk anymore, so I turn away, start back toward the kitchen.

"I think I'm going to make a drink," I say. I don't turn to look at her. "Do you want one?"

"I don't—no," she says.

I get a glass from the cabinet, get the bottle of Jim Beam they have beneath the sink where the rest of the liquor is, and pour the whiskey with ice. I put the bottle back, then sit up on the kitchen counter at the place where the two sides of the counter meet at a right angle. I can feel the bready aroma of the liquor all through my head when I sip from the glass. I can only just see the edge of Karen from where I am, and I don't say anything. I don't know what I would say. But it seems crazy, like a crazy still life—me on the counter, her in the living room, both of us silent, my father in the hospital. In my head I can still see brightly the image of him, his shirt bound in the saw blade, the blade stopped in his arm.

I don't know how much time has passed when I get off the counter—the tiled floor passes beneath me, the pattern swimming, and then it turns to carpet. The drink sloshes in my hand—the ice has softened and rounded. I sit down next to her on the couch. She doesn't look at me.

She sits for a few more moments in silence—long enough for me to finish my drink, slowly. The air feels tense, like something needs out, but it isn't going to happen.

"Good night, Jack," she says. I watch her get up and move away from me, watch her go slowly up the stairs until she is out of sight. A door closes. Then there is silence, emptiness. Now that she has disappeared it seems like she might as well have vanished into the eternity of space. It's like everything. The empty room has a sound like the world when it snows—the sound of close desolation.

I sit here for a long time, unable to move. I could go after her—I can picture myself going up the stairs, opening the door of their room. But why? My hands are on the coarse, pale fabric of the couch, halfway into the motion of pushing myself up, but frozen. The house feels alive, the shadows of past events frozen in the fibrous streaming matter of this physical space. The sounds of voices, my father's, mine, my brother's, my mother's. They rustle, flutter, whir, just out of the reach of understanding. There are other shadows too, just the texture of the voices. I'm just two or three feet from the spot where my mother kicked over the wooden chair, where I wandered in with my brother and found her—

that day is here, among the others, though I can't picture it. It whispers the language of the drowned.

For nearly twenty years my father lived with all of these ghosts, and for three-quarters of that time I lived with him and never knew what his life meant. I can see myself on the street in Middleridge, and later, on the bus, stone-tired, I can see myself in the town square in the darkness, and it amazes me that I am here, now, alone, and that moments ago, Karen Anderson was sitting here with me. It seems like such a leap, and astounding that in life such leaps can be made.

Everything in this room, everything in this town, has my father's imprint on it. It was supposed to be my grandparents' town, but my father's work is everywhere, so much more integrally a part of it than anything they ever did, and that fact impresses me. In that house they and their money are as dead as my mother is.

I can see my father sitting alone here, can see myself walking past him, not looking, completely unaware of who he was, or what he was. And then I can see him the other morning when he came through the door and saw me on the step—saw me for the first time in so long, blinking, wild with sleep and nerves. The look on his face was halfway between delight and horror. Something he'd been waiting for for a long time—and something he'd been dreading for just as long—had happened to him suddenly, and his face couldn't decide between the two.

In a little while, I get up to go to bed. In the bathroom, I catch a glimpse of myself in the mirror—one of those glimpses you get when you don't expect to see yourself, haven't prepared yourself for your reflection.

You spend all your life trying to escape your father's shadow, thinking nearly the only way to escape being just like him is to kill him, or to kill his image in your head, then one day when you're convinced you've gotten away from him, that you've actually become yourself and escaped it all, you look in the mirror and find his face gazing back at you.

The road is empty, and I'm walking. The air is bright and the grit of the street crackles beneath my feet. There are woods on either side of the road, and now and again there is the rustling of movement. Tulip trees hang over the road, the orange flowers hanging down. A squirrel, gray as smoke. And then on the road ahead of me is Dean, walking, wandering. Pale, anxious. "Hey, man," he says, "I'm goin' to work with your father," and he walks toward me, laughing slowly in the bottom of his mouth as he approaches. But then I see the flames in his mouth, the flames in his hands—the transparent place at the middle of his chest where the flames flicker.

"Where you gonna work?" is what I can manage to say.

"Where do you think?" he says, and the teeth are white and laughing.

It's maybe one or two in the morning, and I'm sweating in the evening cool of the house. Everything is absolutely silent. I go back into the kitchen and make myself another drink. When I break the ice cubes out of the tray, I try to do it quietly, but the silence of the house magnifies the sound, makes it loud as gunshots.

I stay in the kitchen to drink the drink—the first one hasn't worn off yet, and I'm beginning to feel slightly drunk. I lean against the counter and try to think. The air feels dry, and my skin feels desiccated.

"How long are you planning to stay, Jack?" a female voice says, and it makes my heart jump up hard against the wall of my ribs. I hadn't noticed Karen in the living room.

"You startled me," I say.

"Sorry."

"I—originally I was only planning to stay a day or two." I sip from the drink, come toward where she is. I realize I'm only in my underwear but come forward anyway. The ice tinks in the glass. "I don't guess I'll stay much longer. I thought I'd finish Dad's job for him."

"Did you talk to him?"

"Not about that. He was a little too out of it."

She's wearing a nightgown, and she sits a little forward on the sofa, with her hands on her cheeks and her elbows on her knees. I have the idea she was crying, but I don't know where I got it. "Are you planning to visit your grandparents?"

I laugh involuntarily. "It never even crossed my mind." I get a flash image of my mother's parents. Despite the mandatory visits, I never knew them, and after my mother died, it never seemed they wanted to be known. "No."

Again there is silence. I finish my drink, and now it feels like I'm floating. "You know, tomorrow is my birthday," I start. I'm surprised that it is my lips that are moving, my voice speaking. "I'm twenty-seven—I'll be twenty-seven—the same age my mother was when she died."

"Do you think about her a lot?"

"No. I mean sometimes I wonder about her. Which parts of myself are from her, which are from my father."

"Yeah."

I drift down into a chair across from her. "Is it important, twenty-seven?"

I wait a long time before saying anything. I know what I want to say, but the words won't come. Finally I say: "I used to wonder when I was little about my mother's, you know, taking—you know, her passing. I mean I used to wonder if I was going to do the same thing—if there was some kind of chain of necessity. I kept wondering if I'll get past this year. I used to wonder that. I don't anymore. I used to think of her, think that I loved my life, and if I couldn't do anything else in my life I'd make sure I lived into old, old age."

"Jack, I wish I—" A weak smile that comes and then dissolves.

"For so long I have felt absolutely—I don't know. I'm surprised that I'm here, and that I'm here now. It feels like the right thing to do, the right place to be—here, now, with the two of you. For now."

"For what it's worth, I'm glad you came. I'm glad you're speaking with your father again."

"I'm not sure that I ever intended not to. I don't know now what I intended."

"I have—," Karen says. "You know I had a weird kind of revelation not too long ago. Addie and I went out to Ohio to visit some of my relatives I hadn't seen since I was a little kid. My mother's sister Ruth and her family." She presses her knees together with her hands, and her thumbs extend into the air. They are fine, lovely fingers. Now he is Addie and not Your Father. "They hadn't—I mean my mother and my aunt, because of the distance—hadn't seen each other for twenty years, and I only remembered her vaguely. We went out because we were going to share things. You know. It was so funny, Jack," she says and stares wide-eyed at me. "It was so funny. I mean you take individualism for granted. The way we think, I mean. You take it that people are independent of one another and unique, but my Aunt Ruth could have—it just took my breath away, how much she was like my mother." She puts her head back, shakes her hair. "Things she said, the way she moved, so many things were uncanny. Were completely uncanny and had nothing at all to do with hanging around with my mother—it was all some mysterious process of relation. And the idea I had, the revelation if you'll forgive the expression, was that no matter how much you think of yourself as an individual, you're never more than really half of anything. I had never really thought of it before."

"I had a similar idea once—conception. The sperm and the egg each have half the genetic information, and yet when they come together as a whole, the whole can only provide half the information. And I thought, is this what love is about, why it is so necessary?"

The both of us are in darkness, but I can see her, and suddenly I'm hit with a tremendous wave of love for her. "Yes," she says. Then: "Oh, Jack." And then:

"It's like you and your father. I never saw it before because all I saw was you. And I saw him, and now I see you both. I find it all astounding. I wish I had known Roy. But it's, I don't know. It's uncanny, and it's peculiar, and I have this profound notion that none of us is anything more ever than half. Just half. And maybe that's what this is all about. Living I mean. Or loving, why we're always so hungry for it. It's becoming more than half."

"You're probably right. I never thought of it before. You're probably right."

"I'm sorry about things, Jack. I'm sorry you had to find out about Addie and me the way you did. We both sort of were afraid of you. I mean I think we both tried to figure out what it would be like if you came home and didn't know what had happened. I'm sorry if you feel as though we deceived you. We didn't try to."

"No. Don't worry about it." There are a million things I haven't said, wouldn't say—my pathetic wet dream about her, my still tortuous and conflicted emotions about everything—and it astounds me how much in human relationships may be true but isn't worthy of the breath to make it said, and should remain unsaid.

She stands up and comes around the couch, then leans back against the jutting wall at the end of the hallway, by the entrance to the kitchen. "You said something before about a girlfriend?"

"Yeah. Her name is Sandy." I laugh. "A typical Jack Pleasance story. Things are fine now, but we had a—well, sort of difficult situation."

She smiles wanly. "How?"

I wait a moment, try to focus my eyes on Karen. I stand up. Her nightgown is satin, and blue, I think. It's hard to tell in the darkness. I lift up my T-shirt, and for a moment I think she thinks I'm going to do something disgusting. "Can you see this?" I say.

"What?" she says, still on guard.

"The scar." I run my finger down the knurl of it.

"Jesus Christ," she says.

I let the shirt fall back down, then drift backward to where I was sitting before—the chair is still warm.

"What happened?"

"Oh, you know, a southern gothic kind of a mess."

"Did you—"

"Her husband was a gun nut, and a nut besides. He shot me."

"Oh, God, Jack."

"It's okay," I say, too much bluff in my voice, "I shot him back, and he got the worse of it. He was a hitter, and I took her away, hid her from him. I guess I humiliated him, taking her away, but I didn't think about it that way. I thought of her, not him."

"You haven't changed, have you?"

"I've changed a lot."

"I'm sorry," she says. "You have. I can see that. I'm just a little—you know—things are so crazy."

In the darkness I can see that she's crying. I don't know why. "Are you guys—are you guys going to get married?"

"Yeah," she says and laughs a little bit.

"Gonna have kids?"

"Yeah," she says.

"I think it's fantastic," I say. It is fantastic.

"You won't mind if I'm your stepmother?"

"I'd love it."

# THE WORK

In the kitchen in the morning, the phone rings. It's a little after 6:30. It's my father.

"How are you?" I say. For some reason I expected it to be him, and hearing his voice has a weird, elating effect on me. "I was going to call you."

"They don't let you get any sleep in here," he says. "My arm hurts like hell, and they keep waking me up to take my temperature and ask me how I'm doing and take blood out of me. How I am is tired. How the hell are you supposed to get any rest when they wake you up every five minutes?"

"Listen, Dad, I'm going to go back over to the Camerons' today and try to clean up some. I talked to Mrs. Cameron yesterday from the hospital and she was very understanding, but their kitchen is torn apart."

"If you want some help, call David, my helper. Karen will find the number."

"When are they going to let you go?"

"I think they're going to keep me until tomorrow. Are you still going to be around?" He says the last part with some hesitation in his voice.

"Yeah," I say, "if you want."

"I do. I do." There is a moment of pure silence. If I didn't know my father, I'd swear he'd hung up.

"Is Karen around?" he says softly.

"I'll get her," I say.

"Jack," he says, "it's nice to have you around."

I put the cleats he cut into the back of the pickup, then get Karen to help me lift the countertop into the back of the pickup. It's still early, and the air has the damp chill of morning. "Happy Birthday," she says.

"Thanks, Mom," I say. She laughs as she backs out of the shop with her end of the countertop. She's still wearing her shorts and windbreaker from her morning run, and before I climb into the pickup, she smiles and tags me on the shoulder with her fist. I leave her there and drive across town to the Camerons' house.

Mrs. Cameron, a trim little woman with the slowly softening skin of middle-age, lets me in, and I go straight to the kitchen and start to work. We left the tools yesterday, so everything is where it needs to be. I rip out the old cleats, measure the new ones, trim them, then put them up along the walls.

It feels good to work, good to be healthy and alive.

I get finished late, pack up the tools, and head home. There's a note on the refrigerator from Karen. She's at the hospital with my father. I should come out, and we'll go out for something to eat.

I will, and tomorrow I'll go back to Sandy's house, back to the life I have made for myself.